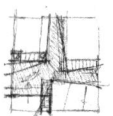

Secret Paths Editions presents

Stories People Tell

Alan McCluskey

First published in February 2018
Secret Paths Editions, Mureta 2, CH-2072 Saint-Blaise
Copyright © Alan McCluskey
Cover illustration by Alan McCluskey

ISBN 978-2-940553-09-9

2   Alan McCluskey

Other books by the author

The Reaches - The Storyteller's Quest Book One
The Keeper's Daughter - The Storyteller's Quest Book Two
The Starless Square - The Storyteller's Quest Book Three

Boy & Girl
In Search of Lost Girls

"We raise our fists in salute, not in threat but as a sign of solidarity. In those fingers held tight we embrace everyone however different they may be. Gay. Trans. Straight. Black. Brown. Yellow. White. All colours of the rainbow.
All are welcome in our London."
Annie Wight, London Whatever

1.

Annie looked up, startled. Nothing ever happened in the East End. She should know. It was her home. Yet, there she was, standing alone under the awnings of the Docklands Light Railway station only a stone's throw from her school, intent on returning home after a class outing, except that the only path not blocked by crash barriers led across the park and the football pitch through a raucous crowd sporting badges, waving blue banners, screaming, "Kard, Kard, Kard."

Sure. She'd noticed the posters plastered on the walls around her community school and on the deserted houses and warehouses awaiting renovation. Bright splashes of blue amid darkened bricks and vacant windows, but their gaudy colour did nothing to allay the ever-present battle between decline and gentrification.

She might be studying sociology alongside English Lit at A level, but she was not much interested in politics. All that bluster and the many broken promises got on her nerves. It seemed so pointless and fake. Why didn't they get on and do something?

She glanced over her shoulder admiring the ethereal architecture of the station with its stainless steel curves. Well, they did get some things right. Opening the railway had been a real boon. But there were no shops around the school. In the scramble to build high-value accommodation, shopping had been neglected or relegated to shopping centres. There were many more estate agents in the area than shops. What about the old or those who were handicapped or school children like her? If she wanted a snack, she had to bring it with her or walk miles for one.

Peering over the heads of the swirling masses, the main building of her school rose above the newer buildings that had spawned at its feet like a weary matron from another age scornful of the noisy crowd. Annie enjoyed attending school even if it had its limitations. That very morning, during their outing, she'd complained to Ms Denovic, their sociology teacher, how few computers there were for sixth formers, only to be promised that more were on their way. Not that Annie would benefit from them. This was her last year.

A brass band struck up nearby, blaring trumpets and trombones, even a saxophone, and the incessant battering of drums. The noise was so loud and strident it rattled every bone in her body. It conjured up images of war and devastation. During break, she'd heard them parading the streets, but she'd paid no attention. It was frankly not her taste in music.

On the walk to school that morning, she ran into several groups of rough-looking youths sporting large blue badges loitering down narrow streets, a fag in one hand, a can of beer in the other. Thank heavens they hadn't been in the underpass. They ogled her with a mixture of desire and disdain. Terrified, she had been so busy keeping out of their way, she'd had no time to wonder why they were there.

Of course, she'd heard of Kard. Who hadn't? You couldn't open a newspaper without his face leering out at you. The man had a regular spot on all the talked-of TV chat programmes. He reminded her of a stuffed pig. A thick-set, blundering oaf who constantly cracked jokes, most of which were in bad taste, often at the expense of women. Some of her friends thought he was a laugh. A few found him handsome. One even claimed to have met him. Her mother called the man a buffoon and was clearly amused. Her father said if he was a buffoon, he was a dangerous one. Ms Denovic said Kard hailed the end of history. Didn't she mean the end of the world?

Braving the crowd was out of the question. She chose to skirt the pitch, threading her way down the narrow passage between the high barriers designed to stop balls careering into people's backyards and the fences and hedgerows that bordered two sides of the park. She was going to be late and she had hours of homework to do. She should have known Denovic would give them a massive essay to write over the weekend. The decline of democracy. What a joke! The subject would have taken a lifetime to explore and she had just two days. That was school for you.

The press of the mob stamping and screaming only feet away was scary. Hopefully, the barriers would hold good. Kard's supporters were more brutish than human. Where had they come from? Her neighbourhood might have been home to a kaleidoscope of races, as was her school, but most of the people were open and friendly, not like this uncouth mob.

Reaching one corner of the pitch, she turned and prepared to squeeze behind a giant blue bus with 'Keep London Straight' scrawled across it in bold letters. Goodness only knew how it had got there. Driven across the pitch most likely. What a cheek!

A roar went up from the crowd. Apparently, Kard had climbed onto the stage. "Hello," he shouted. A rich baritone, not at all the high-pitched squeal you'd expect from a pig. "Be with you in a tick," he said, his amplified voice slithering through the audience like a caress. "Important business to settle." The crowd took up the war cry "Kard, Kard, Kard" getting wilder with every repetition. It was like a nightmarish pop concert.

A thick-set bodyguard in an ill-cut suit stepped out in front of her as she went to squeeze behind the bus. "Excuse me," she said. He didn't move. "Excuse me," she repeated, trying to ease past but there was no way around. "Let me by," she said, trying to push him. He wouldn't budge. So much for freedom of movement. She'd have to mention it in her essay. "I've got homework to do," she complained. He lifted his watch to his mouth and grunted at it as if issuing orders.

A slender woman dressed in a pinstripe suit and high heels appeared at his side. She stared at Annie, licking her lips in a way that gave Annie the uncomfortable feeling she was about to be someone's meal. "Nice," the woman murmured. The bodyguard stepped aside and the woman, gripping Annie firmly by the arm, led her to a small door in the side of the bus. She tried to tug free, but the woman was insistent and her hold unbreakable. "You won't regret it," she said as she pulled open the door with her free hand and shoved Annie inside.

Two carpeted steps led up to a plush lounge with a number of armchairs and a settee. A large bottle of whiskey stood on a low table along with several half-empty glasses, a gold lighter and a box of cigars. The lights were dimmed and the windows tinted making Annie half blind after the bright sunlight outside. Despite the gloom, she could make out a man sprawled at one end of the settee. She knew that piggy face. It filled her with dread.

"Found this one lurking at the back of the bus," the woman said casually, as if nabbing stray girls was a regular pursuit. Kard dismissed her with a lazy wave. Annie heard retreating footsteps and the click of a door. She was about to explain when Kard spoke.

"You know who I am?" He drew deeply on his cigar and puffed a large cloud of smoke in her direction. She coughed. Beneath the smell of cigars was another more unpleasant odour.

"I like your uniform," he said, his eyes riveted on the slender gap between the bottom of her pleated skirt and the top of her long socks. His insistence made her feel exposed. She wished she'd opted for trousers that morning. "The local community school?" he asked, glancing at the school crest on her blazer.

"Not very talkative," he said looking across the room at a camera pointed straight at her. "Few people get a chance to talk to Nolan Kard." He pronounced his name as if he were handing her a precious gift.

Pompous fool. She couldn't help it, she snorted, immediately trying to conceal her scorn with a cough and a hand over her mouth. Speaking her mind had got her into trouble several times at school. Only that morning a few critical words to a school inspector had earned her a summons to the Head's office.

Luckily Kard didn't seem to notice, no doubt still revelling in the sound of his own name. Close up, he looked even more like a bloated pig. Repulsive. And he smelt bad. Who would ever want to talk to him? Who would ever vote for him? She certainly wouldn't if she'd been old enough.

"Sit down," he said, patting the settee next to him. "Many important people want to see me. So I am glad I was free for your visit."

What visit? She'd been forced to meet him. If she'd had a choice, she'd be at home now. Blasted man. She stayed stubbornly where she stood, glancing around for exits.

"Don't be shy," he said, his voice sinking to almost a whisper, and he got to his feet. What a giant. He must have been at least six-foot-six.

She took a step back, beginning to feel afraid as he loomed closer. Her next step had her bag, which was still slung over her back, press against the wall.

"There's no need to be afraid," he murmured. Stepping closer, he laid a proprietary hand on her shoulder. The touch of his podgy fingers made her shudder. This was not right. It was the very scene the woman doctor had described at school in her talk about harassment and abuse. Face to face with an abuser, the talk seemed desperately short on practical advice.

His fingers glided along her collarbone as he leaned ever closer. Panic and revulsion surged in her and she froze. What could she do against such a massive brute? When he pursed his lips for a kiss, fury tore through her. How dare he? She refused to be his victim. Ducking to escape his lips, she angled her shoulder and shoved outwards and upwards with all her might. Her shoulder sank into his paunch, catching him off guard. He huffed, releasing his grip. She scrambled under his outstretched arms, jumped down the stairs and tried the door. It was unlocked. Hearing Kard in pursuit, she swung it open with all her force and darted out.

There was a sickening grunt from behind the door and it slammed shut, narrowly missing her but clipping her bag. The blow sent her spinning. For a moment she was all feet and legs, then she flung out her arms to steady herself. Kard fared less well. He screamed when the door smashed into his face. A groan at her feet had her looking down. The bodyguard lay clutching his bloodied nose.

On the other side of the bus, the crowd had worked itself into a frenzy screaming Kard's name. All hell would break loose the moment they saw his mangled face. The carnage would be on every TV and she would be blamed. Annie swallowed hard. Was she in big trouble! She ran.

2.

Annie dumped her bag in the only free space on the tiny kitchen table and sank onto a stool. What had she done? How could she be so pig-headed and impetuous? Kard would have the whole world on her back. Why hadn't she just gritted her teeth and put up with it? She shook her head. The thought of him kissing her was so revolting she couldn't bear it.

She stared at her hands. They were shaking. Her knees felt like they'd been replaced by Aunt Nelly's best jelly. The thought of the silly TV commercial didn't even make her smile. She cradled her head in her hands. Had that really happened? Yes! She could still feel his fingers on her shoulder, as if his touch had branded her for life.

With her eyes closed, she kept seeing Kard's face as he leaned closer. And the smell of him! She wished they had a shower and not a bath. She'd willingly have flushed him away, but there wouldn't be enough hot water for a bath. There rarely was. She shuddered. Maybe she should call the police and report him. She glanced at the phone sitting next to the rickety stack of her mother's cookbooks. None of your new touchscreen nonsense. Her mother preferred an old-fashioned finger-dialling phone. The mention of it had her school friends sniggering, so she was careful not to invite people home.

The empty house was oppressive. Her brother, Ted, told his parents he had rugby practice but she knew he was secretly dating a girl from Tesco or was it Sainsbury's. Her parents arrived late on Fridays, separately though, having almost nothing to do with each other outside the house. And precious little inside.

Apart from the insistent hum of traffic from the flyover beyond the backyard and the occasional screech of tyres on the slip road, the house was silent. Getting to her feet, she cupped her hands under the tap. The water was cold and smelt vaguely of chlorine. She swilled it around her mouth and spat it into the sink. It wasn't enough. She poured water into the kettle to make some tea, then flipped on the radio, another antique, a pink plastic transistor model, and turned the dial to a local music station.

It crackled then the music stopped. "We interrupt our broadcast," a newscaster said, "to bring breaking news." Annie was about to change to another music station when the voice continued, "Earlier this afternoon, Nolan Kard's rally in the East End was interrupted. Thugs broke into the Lord Mayor's campaign bus and beat him up and one of his bodyguards." Annie gasped. What a pack of lies. How dare he? "They also knocked out the surveillance cameras and made off with several bottles of whiskey and a box of cigars."

She'd heard the politician was not a believer in truth, but this went way beyond political falsehoods. Of course he wouldn't want anyone to see the surveillance footage. They'd lock him up.

She imagined him savouring every second of the recording in private. She turned on the tap and ran her hands under the water, the thought had left her feeling sullied. Not that she'd done or said anything wrong. Apart from smashing the Lord Mayor's precious nose and refusing to submit to him.

Her fear, which had largely subsided, surged anew. He might be so sick as to track her. He knew her school. He had pictures of her from the video. He might even try to corner her again. For a moment she looked desperately for a place to hide, then the kettle whistled and she remembered where she was. Was she safe there?

She rummaged through the cupboard in search of PG Tips and made a pot of tea, plonking granny's cosy on top of it when she was done. Granny's cosy was a legend. She said she knitted it during the long nights when Grandad was away at the war, but, behind her back and openly since Granny died, Annie's Mum swore she bought it at a jumble sale like many of her knickknacks and that Grandad had never been to the war because of some illness her mother refused to talk about. Annie leaned against the counter and took a deep breath. She was tempted to turn on the telly, but she didn't want to have to look at the man's face.

She stretched her arm into the back of the cupboard in

search of Mum's stash of biscuits. She hid them because of Ted. He was always starving when he got home from school, especially when he'd stopped off on the way to snog with his girlfriend. Of course, he knew where the biscuits were, but since he had a paper-round he bought his own. None of which Mum was aware of. Annie was hoping for Chocolate Fingers but there were only a few Rich Tea. She took one and closed the tin. Filling a mug with milk and tea, she headed up to her room in the attic.

She hung her blazer on its hanger from a nail in the rafters, slipped out of her skirt and folded it on her dresser. She undid the tie and unbuttoned her blouse which she hung over the blazer. Standing in her bra, pants and socks, she stared at herself in the tiny mirror inside her wardrobe. What could any man see in her? She was neither tall nor short. Ayana, her best friend, told her she was model-size which was probably Ayana's way of saying she was too skinny and looked odd. She was a late developer she told herself. Her breasts were barely formed and her hips had not filled out like all the other girls in her class. Ayana, in comparison, with her unblemished chocolate-brown skin, her deep brown eyes and her long pitch-black hair, was all curves and didn't hesitate to flout it, although, thank heavens, she didn't flirt with the boys.

Annie pulled at her hair. It was getting too long. Now there was an idea. No one would recognise her if she wore it short. She'd never dared have it cropped for fear she'd be mistaken for a boy. When she'd shared her concern with Ayana, her friend had disagreed. Boys could be pretty too, she'd said enigmatically.

She ran her fingers through her hair, glancing disapprovingly at herself in the mirror. Stop being silly. Nothing happened. That Kard bloke has moved on to another part of town, other girls. Sure, a voice in her head answered. Nothing happened, but that nothing made the news on the radio and probably the telly too.

The phone rang downstairs, strident in the silence. She struggled into her dressing gown and hurried down, knotting the belt round her waist as she did. It was Ayana.

"Have you heard the news?" her best friend asked, out of

breath, such was her excitement. Probably some revelation about a new romance or an unexpected breakup. "A detective is snooping around school. Apparently, some bigwig has been attacked."

Annie felt an icy hand grab her by the nape. She grasped the kitchen table for fear of falling and sat down. "How do you know?"

"I'm at volley practice."

As if that helped. Ayana wasn't very good at explaining. "So the police are there?"

"I don't think she's from the police. More like the secret service, an undercover agent or a spy." Ayana was gifted with more than average imagination. She was the one who had the physics teacher eloping with a fellow schoolgirl when in fact he'd been off with a bad bout of flu. If only she hadn't been so lousy in English, she'd have a chance as a story-writer.

"Did she interrogate you?"

"Sure." Ayana sounded excited, more like she'd been interviewed for the telly. "She seemed to think someone from school was involved."

Annie's fear spiked again. God damn it! This was real. She wasn't just imagining it. This wasn't another of Ayana's tall stories. When her friend finally got off the phone, having related her whole conversation with the woman spy, Annie vaulted up the stairs, pulled on tracksuit bottoms, a t-shirt and a hoodie then rummaged in her wardrobe for her savings. Haircut here we come.

3.

God was it cold! A biting wind had got up since Annie left the hairdresser's. She pulled the hoodie tight over her head, wishing she'd thought to bring a scarf. She glanced around, worried someone might spot her. Being inconspicuous had always come so easy, but now she wanted to remain unnoticed she felt like everyone was watching.

She shook her head. This was ludicrous. It had been less than two hours since Kard cornered her. Yet there she was, her hair newly cropped, hugging the walls, jumping at every shadow. This story was too big to contain. She needed to confide in someone before she went raving mad. But there was only one person she trusted.

She'd have to find a phone. She groaned. So few public phones were left. All her friends had cell phones, but not her. Her mother was against. Of course she was. Anyway, what use would a cell phone be to her? The cost would be beyond her means. The first public phone she found was broken, the second had no handset but the third worked. She dialled Ayana.

"You got time for a drink?" she asked. "But not around here."

"Sure," Ayana replied, sounding surprised. They always met somewhere near home. "But why not…?"

Annie cut her off, "At Marcie's." She heard Ayana suck in a sharp breath, but her friend agreed making no comment.

Normally Annie wouldn't be seen dead anywhere near Marcie's. The joint had a bad reputation. Girls at school whispered that it was the sort of place girls went to pick up other girls. Of course, they had been quick to add that none of them had ever been there. Annie was unsure if the stories were true, but if they were, it might deter would-be spies and Kard's henchmen from following her there. Then she remembered Ayana's spy was a woman. Too late. She had no more change to phone back and fix another rendezvous.

Marcie's skulked in the shadows at the end of a short alley boarded by disused shops. The only light in the growing dusk came from a red neon on the wall depicting a pair of lips pursed for a kiss under which was written Marcie's in flowing script. She headed for the light, shooting a look at every darkened doorway, half-expecting a rabid girl to jump out and grab her.

To reach the entrance she had to skirt an upturned bin. Cats had feasted on fish bones which lay strewn across her path. A fishy smell was thick in the air. Seeing the door resolutely shut, she was tempted to turn and run. She tried to peek in the only window, but the curtains were tightly drawn. Don't be silly, she chided and, steeling herself, she turned the handle and pushed open the door open. What if she bumped into someone from school? The rumours that would spark. She almost shrivelled up at the thought.

The interior was bathed in red light and surprisingly small, almost cosy, like a den, with round tables seating two or three. To her relief, she could see no one, but, judging from the clink of cups, somebody was there. She squeezed past the door and pushed it shut. Behind the bar-like counter was a slender boy wiping mugs. "What can I do for you, Sweetie?" he asked in a voice that was neither boy nor girl. So much for this being a place reserved for girls.

Annie blushed. Then realising why she blushed, she blushed even more. The boy continued to wipe mugs as he sized her up. When she didn't answer, he smiled saying, "Like the hair."

"A hot chocolate," she stammered, rummaging in her pocket for her purse.

"This one's on the house," he said, setting milk to heat with proficient gestures. "To celebrate your first visit."

She wanted to tell him he'd got it all wrong. That she wasn't like that. "I'm not …"

"I know," he said as if confiding in an old friend. "It's alright."

She retreated, balancing her free chocolate as she wove between the empty tables to a tiny alcove at the back. She leaned back in her seat so the boy couldn't see her, pulled out a mirror from her purse and examined her hair. The alarmed face looking back at her was almost boyish. At any other time she might have relished the change, it was daring and it did suit her, much to her surprise. Ayana had been right, boys could be pretty. But this change was not chosen. It had been forced on her.

Looking around, she could see that a part of the room, which had been hidden from view, extended to form a small auditorium with a stage and an upright piano.

The sound of the door opening had her head whipping back to see who it was as she pulled her hoodie tight around her face. Ayana. She let out a sharp breath of relief. The girl strode to the counter, not in the slightest intimidated by her surroundings, and greeted the boy as Kevin. Annie was shocked. To think she'd known Ayana all those years and not once had she mentioned she visited Marcie's. Kevin and Ayana were deep in conversation when the boy nodded in Annie's direction. Ayana turned and, spotting her friend, smiled and waved. Annie waved back, feeling self-conscious.

"Kevin was raving about your hair," Ayana said grinning as she slipped into the alcove next to Annie. "Let's have a look." Without waiting for permission, she pushed back the hoodie and stared at her friend with an appreciative look that verged on hungry. It left Annie troubled. She was reminded of the look Kard's grey-suited woman had given her. She wiped a hand over her face as if that would scatter unwelcome memories.

"Wow," Ayana said, gingerly stretching out a hand to run her fingers through the pixie cut. "Magic," she whispered as if speaking to herself. At her touch, waves akin to electricity rippled down Annie's spine only to wash back up in a fountain of emotions. Instinctively, she drew back. The place must be getting to her. Or maybe it was the nightmare with Kard. She burst into tears.

Ayana slid her chair next to Annie's and, wrapping her arms around her friend, cradled her, rocking her backwards and forwards. The warmth of her friend's embrace had her feeling even more uncomfortable. Ayana was a regular at Marcie's. What if she had misconstrued Annie's invitation to meet there? She tensed and pulled free of the girl's hug.

"What's up?" Ayana asked.

"I was molested," she whispered.

Her friend looked shocked. "By whom? Where? When? Have you told the police?"

Annie shook her head. Typical Ayana. A flood of questions. Now that she had a chance to speak, she was tongue-tied, unsure what to say. It would probably sound far-fetched. Absurd even. Had she overreacted? She shook her head again, in denial this time.

"Tell me," Ayana encouraged.

4.

"Poor thing. That's terrible," Ayana said, her lips twisted in disgust. "Why don't you call the police?" She glanced around then lowered her voice. "If it were me, they probably wouldn't listen. Black girls and women have got a bad reputation." She screwed up her face as if to say, 'Goodness knows why'. "But you..." She paused, her expression serious, her fists clenched. "It's sexual harassment."

Annie snorted at the expression. Sexual? For Kard it might have been sexual, although that was not at all sure. More like a power game. For her, it was just plain harassment. As for calling the police, Kard was already spinning a very different story. "Have you heard the news?" she asked.

Ayana shook her head, angling a thumb at her tracksuit. "I came straight from volley practice."

"Kard's telling everyone he was attacked by a band of thugs."

"Core blimey! What a cheek. That would explain the spy snooping around school."

"I doubt she was looking for thugs. They know full well what happened. She was trying to find me."

Ayana looked dubitative. Justifiably so. It was hard to believe Kard would go to such lengths. But then again he was known for doing crazy things, although Annie hadn't heard he had a reputation for pestering young girls.

"You ladies want anything more to drink." Kevin's voice at Annie's shoulder made her jump. She would have knocked over her cup had the boy not caught it. Their hands briefly brushed as

Annie hurried to recuperate her drink.

"We're fine," Ayana said giving him a broad smile.

Annie watched him saunter back to the counter, absently rubbing her skin where their hands had touched. "I thought this place was reserved for girls," she whispered.

Ayana chuckled. "Kevin is a girl. She just enjoys making believe she's a boy."

Annie spun round to get a better look. Kevin must have sensed her attention as she glanced up and blew her a kiss. Annie felt her face burn and ducked, quickly taking a sip of her chocolate. Was it her imagination or did the cup smell of the girl?

Ayana chuckled again. "Don't worry about her. She does that to every newcomer."

Annie chanced another glance. Kevin was still smiling at her. Such insistence was surely more than a passing game to embarrass newcomers.

"So why did you choose to meet here?" Ayana asked, touching Annie's hand to get her attention.

Annie wrenched her eyes from Kevin. "I'd heard it was for girls only, so I thought I could avoid that spy. When I remembered he was a she, it was too late."

"Oh," Ayana said, making an exaggerated show of disappointment. "There was me hoping you'd invited me here to declare your love for me."

Annie shot a glance at Kevin, then looked at Ayana aghast. The girl's grin was impish. "I wouldn't have said no," she continued, hanging her head to one side, pouting. Annie punched her lightly on the shoulder at which Ayana grabbed her fist and kissed her knuckles, Annie's pale skin contrasting with the deep chocolate of her friend.

Play, she thought, trying to reassure herself, just play. But as she looked up and saw Ayana's deep brown eyes full of barely concealed longing, she wasn't so sure. "Listen, Ayana. Now is not the time." She raised a placating hand. "Things are really complicated. This Kard business is likely to blow up in my face. One more challenge and I'm going to sink." She paused and sucked in a shuddery breath. "I need someone I can count on, someone who can save me from drowning. Can you be that person?"

Ayana took Annie's hand again and, uncurling her fingers, kissed the tips of each one. "I will be your lifeline, your lifeguard."

Ayana's words rang more like a declaration of love than a pledge to help. Could the girl be toying with her again? The light pressure of her friend's lips on her fingertips left her feeling more than troubled. If this was not a game, she needed to know. "Are you sure?"

"Yes."

"Thanks." Annie gently pulled her hand free, her fingertips slightly moist. She resisted the urge to wipe them on her tracksuit.

A couple of girls entered laughing and chatting noisily. Annie looked up to see the two hip-against-hip, their eyes bright with excitement. They greeted Kevin with kisses and called to Ayana who nodded back.

"You seem to know a lot of girls here," Annie observed. Given the reputation of Marcie's at school, Annie wondered if Ayana would deny her involvement.

"I used to come here often. I had a friend ..." Ayana's eyes glazed over and Annie wondered if she was going to cry, but instead she pressed her knuckles to her temples.

"What happened?" Annie asked, touched by her friend's sadness.

Ayana pursed her lips and shook her head.

"Please," Annie said, tentatively taking hold of Ayana's hand. It was warm. Her hands were always warm. "Let me be your lifeline."

Ayana looked up at her, surprised, and squeezed her fingers. "Her parents found out. They are Ethiopian, like mine, and staunch orthodox Christians. Thank heavens my parents are more liberal-minded. Most Ethiopians believe being gay is evil and homosexuality is illegal whether between men or women. They blamed me. I was a bad influence. So they carted her away.

To 'straighten her out'." Tears brimmed over and began flowing down her cheeks.

"I'm so sorry," Annie said. She had never lost anybody she loved. There had been no one to lose, but she could imagine. It must be terrible, like being ripped apart.

"Did you ever live in Ethiopia?" Annie asked. It was a subject they had never talked about, as if were taboo like Marcie's.

"No. My parents fled to England before I was born. My father was a top engineer. He had contacts here and was able to find a good job."

The couple at the counter were joking rowdily with Kevin and one of the girls burst out laughing.

"Let's get out of here," Annie said, knocking over her chair as she got to her feet in her impatience to escape. The girls' lighthearted joviality chafed her sombre mood. They seemed so flippant. But then how could they know the situation was grave?

Outside, Ayana paused as she pulled Marcie's door closed behind them. Still holding hands with Annie, she lent close to whisper, "Thanks."

From across the alley, a distinctive click had Annie pulling guiltily away, her hands falling to her sides. In the shadows, a man, phone in hand, was photographing them.

Ayana sprang across the alley and barrelled into the man. His hands flew uselessly in the air, swearing being his only line of defence. He staggered backwards catching his foot on the curb and tumbled. His spectacles and phone flew up in the air. Ayana scooped up the phone, leaving the man to scramble on all fours in search of his glasses.

Only when Ayana caught her hand and tugged her away, did Annie realise she stood frozen. "Run," Ayana shouted. Pausing at the entrance to the alley, Annie glanced back. Despite the growing gloom, she could make out the man still on his hands and knees.

Ayana chuckled. "Don't worry about him. I accidentally stepped on his glasses. They were that thick sort that only very shortsighted people wear."

Annie stared at Ayana, astounded. Wherever had she learnt to be so resilient? Certainly not at school and surely not at Guides.

"Follow me," Ayana said. "I know a place where no one will bother us."

Annie's heart was still thumping after their narrow escape. She might be preoccupied at being stalked by a photographer, but she wasn't sure she wanted to be holed up alone in an out-of-the-way place with Ayana.

The 'safe' place was in the attic of a disused warehouse. There were many such relics in the East End. The area had been on the decline ever since London's docklands had been scuppered by the growing container industry. Although that was well before Annie's time, the scars were still visible only a short walk from her home.

The two girls climbed a steep wooden stair that complained at every step and emerged onto a platform which must once have been a storage area. The faded names of destinations still hung on papers pinned to the walls but the wares were long gone. Annie was surprised no one had daubed the walls with graffiti or smashed the windows. No doubt the local yobs would find it sooner or later.

"Here," Ayana said fishing a key from her pocket and unlocking a door at the far end of the platform. Annie followed her inside. She was about to ask how Ayana had come by the key, but the question slipped her mind at the sight of the flat. She had expected a dusty, deserted place with broken furniture and cobwebs everywhere. But what she saw was full of colour and light. It was clean and cosy, pretty even. It felt lived in. So much so, Annie glanced around to make sure they were alone.

She wandered from room to room while Ayana pulled out the phone and began scrolling through the photos. There was a kitchen with washed dishes waiting on the draining board, the bathroom was also clean and smelt of shampoo and soap. Towels hung from a railing over the bath. In the one bedroom she found a double bed with two pillows on which a giant teddy bear lay reclined. On the night table was a single framed photo. She picked it up and looked closer. She recognised Ayana. She didn't know the other girl who had an arm slung around Ayana's waist and was smiling at the camera.

"Good Lord!" Ayana exclaimed from the other room. "Look at this." Annie put down the photo and went to join her. Ayana sat hunched over the phone eyeing the photos. Gasping every now and then. All the photos were of Annie. At the hairdresser's. Before and after. So much for her pixie cut being a disguise. On her way to Marcie's. Her hesitating under the red-lips neon. And then what looked like her kissing Ayana outside Marcie's.

"I know it's not the right thing to say," Ayana said, "but I wish I had copies."

The suggestion made Annie furious. So you can hang them above your bed and drool over them, she wanted to blurt out. But instead she said, "What am I going to do?"

5.

"I was with Ayana, Mum," Annie said for the third time, trying to keep the growing irritation from her voice. In less than a year she'd be eighteen and her mother would have nothing to say about when she came home or whom she met. Although, knowing her mother, she'd have to leave home to ensure her independence. So going to university was important.

"I don't care where you were, young lady," her mother replied, dumping a packet of cereal on the table. Being addressed so formally was a serious danger sign. "We eat supper at seven. Together." Her mum shoved bowls and spoons haphazardly onto the table. "I won't have you sneaking in at all hours of the night."

"It was ten o'clock." Annie wished she hadn't been so late, but she'd completely forgotten the time. They'd been discussing Kard. Not that their deliberations had done her any good. She still had no idea how to react. As for the phone, Ayana insisted it might serve as evidence. Annie was unconvinced. She'd rather have deleted the photos. In the end, Ayana hid the phone in her loft, leaving the photos intact.

One thing was certain. Annie wouldn't go to the police. She didn't trust them. For all she knew, Kard had them in his pocket. Only the other day, she'd watched a TV programme about police laxity. Several high-ranking officers were accused of turning a blind eye when rich men mistreated young girls.

"Are you listening to me?" her mother shouted, slamming a carton of milk on the table sending the liquid splattering across the breakfast things.

Annie looked up, alarmed, and quickly rescued the bread before it became soggy. Her mother often got annoyed whether it be with her children or her husband, but Annie had never seen her so uncontrollably angry.

"Whatever happened to your hair?" her mum asked, turning back to the pantry in search of margarine and marmalade, "You look like a boy. It's disgusting. I bet it was that Ayana. That girl's not normal, if you ask me. Those coloured people are all the same."

Letting herself get baited, Annie was about to point out that almost everyone in her school was 'coloured' and that nobody had forced her to cut her hair. What's more, it was none of her mother's business. A loud knock rang out at the front door causing Annie to start. Her thoughts flew to Kard. Surely not.

"Go answer that," her mother snapped. She hated answering the door in curlers. "I'm busy."

Annie reluctantly got to her feet, unable to conjure up a viable excuse.

It was the postman. He had a small parcel. Express delivery. She signed for it then realised it was addressed to her. Whoever would send her a parcel? A feeling of dread crept into her stomach. She glanced at the sender information. It was blank.

"Who was it?" her mother called out.

"Just the postman." Maybe she could ditch the packet and pretend the postman had made a mistake, but her mother came up behind her and grabbed the packet from her hands. "Oh! It's for you." She gave Annie a sour look as she handed the box back and waited for her to open it. "It's nothing," Annie said. "I'll open it later."

"Nothing? You don't get a packet every day. Open it."

Annie groaned and began tugging at the brown sticky-paper pulled tight around the packet. There was no message inside, just a brand new phone. The latest technology no doubt. She rummaged through the packing in search of a hint who'd sent it. There wasn't even a user's manual.

"What's this?" her mother asked, snatching the phone from

her and turning it over, a look of disgust on her face. "Your father will be furious. You know we don't agree with such things."

Annie shrugged. If it were up to her father, she knew he would say nothing. And anyway, she had enough other worries. Why the hell would Kard send her a phone? She was sure it was him.

"Where did you get the money to buy this?" She held the phone at a distance as if it might contaminate her.

"I didn't buy it," Annie said, feeling trapped. However could she explain that a nutcase politician had sent it to her to make her life a nightmare?

"Surely no one would send you a thing like this. It must cost a fortune."

At that moment the new phone rang. Annie's mum almost dropped it in her hurry to get rid of the device. Annie took it and wished she could throw it out the window, had there been a window in the corridor. Her mother stared at her in disbelief. "Aren't you going to answer?"

No, Annie wanted to say. I'd rather hit myself over the head with a hockey bat. She searched for a way to turn the thing off but must have pressed the answer button.

"Hallo," a familiar male voice said. If she could hear it at that distance, her mother could too. She hurriedly pressed it tight to her ear hoping to muffle the voice. "Do you like my present?" Kard asked.

In the circumstances she dared not reply, although she would have loved to swear. The sound of him sparked the same mixture of anger and helplessness she'd felt in his bus. He was going to get her. Sooner or later. And there was no way she could avoid it. There was a click and the line went dead. Her mother looked at her questioningly.

"Wrong number... I suppose."

The smell of burning toast had them rushing back to the kitchen. Annie used the distraction to ditch the packaging behind a disused flower pot in the hall and slip the phone into her trouser pocket, praying her mother wouldn't notice and, above all, that Kard wouldn't call again.

She set about scraping the burn from the toast, blackening the sink as she did, while her mother put more slices in the antiquated machine. It was at that moment her father breezed in. Dressed for work in his overalls and a cloth cap, he nodded greetings to Annie, gave his wife a peck on the cheek and sat down to serve himself cereal, oblivious to the tension in the room.

Once his bowl was full, he spread the morning paper over the many objects on the table. A giant picture of Kard filled the front page, his nose swollen a vivid red. "I hope they catch the blighters," her father said munching his cereal. If only he knew. "A mob went on a rampage through town, smashing anything they could lay their hands on. That's why we have to go to work today. To straighten things out."

"Annie got…" her mother began.

"Oh! Good Lord," her father said, hurriedly getting to his feet. "Is that the time? I must fly. See you this evening."

Grabbing a jacket, he was gone, with his wife staring down the narrow corridor at the front door as it closed behind him. The remains of her sentence still hung on her lips. Annie breathed a sigh of relief and sidled towards the door, the guilty bulge of the phone heavy in her trouser pocket. Her mother spun round, clearly determined to have it out with Annie if she couldn't berate her husband. "Don't think you're off the hook, Miss."

6.

Annie kept her head down, letting her hoodie mask her face. The post office was always crowded on Saturday mornings, mostly busy housewives in saris or abayas struggling to rein in screaming kids and not-so-busy pensioners chatting to the clerk behind the counter oblivious to the waiting lines. Today was no exception. She generally avoided going at weekends, but she had run out of pocket money. The haircut had been expensive. Not that she had much on her post savings account either. Annie had lived all her life in the shadow of limited resources, although she'd only recently become aware of it.

It took ages to shuffle to the counter, with every single person in her line being a special case. When her turn came, she asked for five pounds, not sure if there'd be enough. The woman behind the counter glanced up at her sharply. She looked like she'd had her fill of snotty customers. The scowl had become a permanent feature. Every time Annie saw her, the woman was in a bad mood.

"I'll take less if there's not enough," Annie said, feeling embarrassed, especially as the woman behind her was on her tiptoes peering over her shoulder.

The cashier gave her an odd look. "You can have as much as you like dearie."

Sarcasm. Annie felt her hackles rise. She didn't need some pesky post lackey poking fun at her. "Five will be enough," she said, her tone cold and distant.

The woman indicated she should slot in her card and enter

the PIN and then handed her a receipt. A doubt crossed Annie's mind or was it suspicion. "What's the balance?" she asked. The woman handed her a second slip. Annie stared absently at the paper. More than three hundred pounds! She'd never had anything like that sum. "There must be a mistake," she muttered, pointing to the figure.

The woman behind the counter glanced at her screen and shook her head. "There's no mistake." She sounded peeved that anybody should suggest it. "Someone deposited £300 in your account this morning."

Annie wanted to know who had paid in so much money, but the woman behind her was getting restless. She stood so close, Annie could feel her moist breath down her neck. It smelt of pickled herrings and onions. "Hurry up. We haven't got all day," the woman said. Annie glanced back and was about to make a rude remark when she spotted the badge on the woman's lapel. A tiny effigy of Kard above a slogan, Keep London Straight. Panic-stricken, Annie pulled her card from the reader, grabbed her money and receipt and fled.

Dashing out of the post office, she flew headlong into a boy, knocking him to ground. "I'm so sorry," she said, her head twisting this way and that in search of pursuit. She tended a hand to help the boy up and it was only then she recognised him. "Kevin," she blurted out. "What are you doing here?"

"I don't live at Marcie's, you know," Kevin replied, rubbing the hip she'd fallen on.

"Are you alright?" Annie asked, moving to brush the dust from the girl's leg with her free hand, only to stop herself at the last moment. What was she up to? She felt completely stupid and her cheeks were on fire.

"You look delicious when you blush," Kevin said. "Has anyone ever told you?"

"Quit playing with me Kevin," she snapped. "It's not the moment." It was then she realised she was still holding Kevin's hand. It had seemed so natural she hadn't noticed. She promptly dropped it. Seeing the look of hurt on the girl's face, she added,

"Sorry. Life's a bit difficult."

"Wanna talk about it?" Kevin asked, her expression serious for once. "I'll treat you to a drink."

That Kevin should suggest paying reminded Annie of the three hundred pounds. She clenched her fists, furious at Kard. Who else would have done such a thing? If only that door had hit him harder. She looked at Kevin who was waiting patiently for a reply. She would have preferred to confide in Ayana, but her friend worked on Saturday mornings. She hardly knew Kevin, yet she felt she could trust the girl and it would give her a chance to get to know her a little. "OK. But only if we cannot be spied on."

"I have the very place," Kevin replied, leaning closer and speaking in a conspiratorial whisper.

What was it with these girls that they all had secret hiding places? As they headed away, she stole a quick glance at Kevin who was still dressed as a boy. Annie found nothing shocking in that. Although her mother would have baulked at the trousers and the short hair, but they really suited her. It occurred to Annie that Kevin might be taking her back to her place in the hope of seducing her. She shook her head. The thoughts she had! As it turned out, the haven Kevin had in mind was Marcie's. The cafe was closed, Kevin explained, and they were unlikely to be disturbed for several hours.

The cafe was shrouded in shadows and remained so as Kevin turned on only a single light over the counter. While she prepared them mugs of hot chocolate, Annie perched on a stool across the counter watching the way the girl moved. She didn't sway her hips like most girls in her class, but her movements were more fluid and graceful than any boy she knew.

"So what's the problem?" Kevin asked, handing Annie a steaming mug. She rounded the counter cradling her own mug and hooked a stool with her foot, pulling it close to Annie's. "Un-requited love? Jilted? Parents?"

"Nothing of all that. Well, the parents are a pain but...." And she gave Kevin a potted version of the story.

"Wow! That contradicts all I'd heard. He's supposed to be more interested in boys," Kevin said. Then puffing out her chest and running a hand through her hair, she added, "But even girls can look like boys."

Annie couldn't help laughing, although she stopped immediately, afraid Kevin might misunderstand and be offended. "If that's the case, I need to look more like a girl."

"I'm sure that can be arranged, although I quite like you as you are," Kevin said, grinning then she shook her head. "I doubt it'll help. If he sees a boy in you, no matter what clothes you wear, he'll still see a boy."

Annie had the impression she was teetering on the edge of a world where all the rules were topsy-turvy. Who would have suspected such a world overlapped her own? She glanced at Kevin with her clipped hair and her boy's clothes. It was a world where people could be different. Annie felt a surge of dizziness as if she was about to fall headlong into it. Another step and she might never get back. She gripped the counter to steady herself.

"Are you alright?" Kevin asked. "You've gone awfully pale."

Annie shook her head. "I feel like an unwilling explorer who just tumbled on a new world in her back garden."

Kevin chuckled. "Love the image. You should be a poet."

"At school..." Annie began.

"Forget school. It's mostly crap. A place for mark-freaks and sausage-machine thinking."

Annie laughed. "Sausage-machine?"

"Yeah. They squeeze knowledge into thin, narrow minds."

Annie chuckled. "You too have a way with words."

A loud hammering at the front door tore then from their laughter. "Open up!" a voice boomed. "Police!"

7.

Annie stared panic-struck at the front door. The hammering increased. What a nightmare. Surely he hadn't let the police loose on her. She glanced at Kevin, unsure what to do.

The girl whipped a phone from her pocket and punched in a number. "The police are raiding Marcie's." There was a pause while she strained to hear over the hammering. "No. Only Annie and me." She hung up.

"The police will try to question us. Refuse to talk without your lawyer."

"But I don't have a lawyer."

"You do now," Kevin said grinning. "One of the best."

They wouldn't find the slightest clue. She'd done nothing wrong. Well, almost nothing. Annie felt the weight of the phone in her pocket. She pulled it out. "I need to ditch this."

Kevin took it from her, stuffed it in a pink plastic bag and tossed it down a chute to the basement. "OK?"

Kevin unlocked the door and hastily stepped aside. A scrum of policemen closely followed by a group of policewomen rushed inside, truncheons at the ready. Kevin was thrown to the ground and held there with a policeman's boot pressed in the middle of her back.

Annie cringed away, terrified she'd get the same treatment, but instead she was forced to raise her hands in the air while a policewoman frisked her. Had they treated Kevin so roughly thinking she was a boy, or did they have instructions to give Annie preferential treatment? Anything was possible with that bloke.

A policeman dragged Kevin roughly to her feet. When she tried to fend him off, the man punched her in the chest.

"That's a girl you're manhandling, you oaf!" Annie shouted, unable to contain her fury. Keeping silent was going to be hard.

The policeman shot Annie a filthy look and let go of Kevin as if she had a contagious disease. She crumbled to the floor in a heap. Annie tentatively lowered her hands and, when the police-woman said nothing, hurried to help Kevin up, slinging an arm around the girl's waist to support her sagging form.

She and Kevin were forced to sit at one of the tables with their hands on their heads. It reminded her of some sort of ar-chaic school detention. Except that it was a tense young police-woman watching over them, not a prefect or a teacher.

"Your colleague has probably broken Kevin's ribs. She's in pain and can't hold her hands on her head." The young police-woman nodded and both girls lowered their arms. In the mean-time, the police searched the cafe. Annie knew nothing of police searches but, judging from the haphazard, uninterested way they rummaged through shelves and in cupboards, they were unlikely to find anything incriminating.

One of the policewomen who had climbed down into the cellar, a blue plastic bag in her gloved hand, reappeared a time lat-er clasping a pink bag. "Is this yours?" she asked Annie. Why had the woman singled her out. It was as if she knew the contents were hers. But how? Annie stretched out to retrieve the bag when a voice rang out from the door. "Don't touch that."

All heads turned to see an elegant woman in a grey suit, standing in the doorway tall and imposing, an attaché case under her arm. Annie could have sworn she heard the policewoman with the plastic bag groan.

"You will no doubt want to have that checked for finger-prints before my client touches it," the elegant woman said.

The policewoman scowled and walked out of the cafe with-out another word, taking the bag with her.

"I would like to talk to my clients," the elegant woman said to no one in particular. "In private."

It turned out the lawyer's name was Megan Wainsdorf. She haggled with the police till they granted her five minutes before carting the girls off to the station. Megan had them sit in an alcove that was farthest from the door. She opened her attaché case and withdrew a tube of ointment which she handed to Annie. "Rub it on her bruised ribs," she ordered.

Annie had no idea of first-aid and was troubled at the idea of touching Kevin's chest, but it was the least she could do. After all, she'd brought this bother on Kevin. She cautiously hiked up Kevin's t-shirt causing the girl to wince. To Annie's surprise, Kevin wore no bra but her chest was bound tight with a bandage. Had she already been in a fight? "To conceal my blasted breasts," Kevin muttered. Annie shook her head in disbelief. The constraints the girl had to suffer to be like a boy.

The bruise, which was already red and turning a darker shade was just below the bandage. Annie unscrewed the tube and applied ointment, tracing hesitant circles with her finger tips over the girl's skin. There was no unusual bump. Maybe the ribs were not broken. "Just place your hand on it," Kevin said, "and don't move." Annie did as she was told. Kevin's skin was firm and warm. She had never touched anyone like that before. She could feel the girl's chest moving with each breath and beyond it she felt her heart beat fast.

"You'd better stop. The police could return early," Megan said. "God knows what they might imagine. So, let's get to business." She opened her case and pulled out what looked like headphones without wires and handed a pair to each girl and put on a pair herself. When Annie opened her mouth to ask what they were for, Megan raised a finger to her lips to silence her. Then she extracted a tiny phone from her case, placed it on the table and pressed a button on its side. A shrill almost imperceptible whistle filled the room.

"Now we can talk without them listening in," Megan began. "Have either of you any idea why the police are here, apart from the usual harassment of gay people?"

Kevin shook her head, then looked meaningfully at Annie.

Annie wondered if she should say anything. Her story was so far-fetched. The lawyer would surely laugh at her. But she could find no other explanation. And Kevin might well tell if she didn't. "I think I do," Annie said. She told Megan briefly about her encounter with Kard, about the telephone and then the money at the post office.

"Hmmm," Megan mused. "Kard is going to be a problem."

"You don't need to tell me," Annie muttered.

"So what's in the pink bag?" Megan asked.

"The telephone," Annie said.

"And whatever the police added," Kevin put in.

Annie looked at her startled. Surely it was only in films that the police framed innocent people.

"The policewoman carried a blue plastic bag down into the cellar and came back up with the pink one. My guess is she transferred something incriminating to the pink bag."

"I have no doubt they are working for Kard, indirectly at least, but we could never prove it," Megan said. "Where ever there's power to be had, you'll find Kard lurking in the wings if not prancing front stage."

Annie had hoped the woman might call Kard out about his misdeeds and lies, but even such a strong personality as Megan baulked at challenging Kard. "So what are we going to do?" she asked.

"Get you off with the lightest sentence possible."

Annie was furious. "But I haven't done anything. What about him groping young girls?"

"I know," Megan said, placing a hand on Annie's arm. "It's revolting. But there is very little we can do. He may seem a joke on television, but he's dangerous. He takes the Lord Mayor's post as a licence to do whatever he likes. Yet his outrageous behaviour has wide popular support. He's not an oligarch. He's a super-oligarch. All I can do is protect the victims as best I can."

"Time," a policeman shouted from the door.

8.

The walk back from the police station was shot through with dark looks and killing silences. Had her father been there, he might have eased the torture. He couldn't abide tension, his strategy being to crack jokes. But her father was caught up at work. Only her mother had been available to sign the papers.

"Whatever were you doing in that dreadful place?" her mother asked, hanging her coat on the stand in the hall. "It's a nest of bloody perverts." She spat out the words, her mouth twisted in disgust.

Annie thought of Kevin, of her tightly bound breasts, her bruised skin, her chest rising and falling as she breathed and she couldn't help sighing. Kevin might suffer to be a boy, but she was no pervert.

"That's the very sort of place they groom young girls like you. I read it in the paper. First they give presents..." Her mother's hands flew to her mouth. "Oh my God! Don't tell me that's where the phone came from." She wrung her hands, planted as she was in the middle of the hall. "The next thing we know you'll be getting large sums of money."

Annie turned aside to conceal her embarrassment. Thank heavens her mother wasn't paying attention. It was as if she were talking to the girl she imagined her daughter to be. Not her real daughter. Her mother's rant did have one advantage. It threw a perplexing light on Kard. It was almost as if he were trying to make it look as if she were being groomed.

The phone rang. Her mum started and ran to the kitchen. Annie breathed a sigh of relief. She hung up her coat and was about to escape upstairs when her mother thundered, "No you don't."

Annie followed her mother into the kitchen feeling divested of any will of her own. She sat down at the kitchen table and stared unseeingly at her mother. Her mind kept coming back to the feel of Kevin's skin. It was so warm and soft. Annie had a crazy desire to press her lips against it.

Her mother squealed, the phone still glued to her ear. "No. Really. I couldn't possibly. Not in front of so many people." From cold and white and condemning, her face had shifted to flushed and enthusiastic. Then abruptly she hung up.

"I'm going out. There's bread in the bread bin and paste in the fridge."

"What about Dad?"

"He'll be coming with me if he knows what's good for him."

Yesterday's bread and paste. What a feast! She'd had nothing to eat all day. They didn't serve up three course meals at the police station.

"You are to stay in the house. No phoning those friends of yours." Her mother said the word 'friends' as if the word had a bad taste to it. She didn't wait for Annie to react, but skipped out into the hall and pulled on her coat, whistling softly to herself as she did. The sight was alarming. Her mother never acted so girlishly.

Pausing on the doorstep, her mother looked back over her shoulder and said with a smirk, "Nolan Kard has invited me to speak at his rally." Then the door slammed shut.

A second door creaked open in Annie's mind and a load of creepy monsters wriggled out. What the hell was he up to? She rummaged in her pocket for the paper with Megan's number on it.

"Hi Megan. I've got a problem."

"The police again?"

"Nope." Annie groaned. "A different one. Kard has invited my mum to speak at his rally."

In a couple of sentences Megan spelt out what she knew of the rally.

"God. Against Marcie's! Mum didn't tell me that."

Megan went on to outline how Kard singled out a target then unleashed his supporters on the powerless victim.

Annie had visions of a screaming hoard tearing Marcie's apart. Anyone who had ever set foot in the place would get roasted and she would be atop the pyre. Her resolve went up in smoke, leaving her feeling downright helpless. "What am I to do?"

"I can't see an easy answer," Megan admitted. "But in the meantime, I can offer you a couple of hours' respite. Let me and Kevin come and fetch you."

Annie could hear Kevin in the background urging her to accept. She was torn between her mother's injunction and her own desire to escape. Going could hardly make things worse. "OK," she finally agreed. She heard Kevin squealing in delight only to be chided by Megan.

Following Megan's instructions she pulled on old clothes and went out to wait for the car. Number four was the first house of a long row of brick terraced houses built for dock workers in another age. It had once been painted white, making it stand out from all the others, till smog had decided otherwise. One step took Annie from the front door to the gate, through a front garden just big enough for a plastic dustbin.

She was leaning against the gate, when a strange lurching sensation seized her stomach as if it were being wrenched sideways out of her body then stuffed back in upside down. With one hand pressed firmly against her belly and the other griping the gate to steady herself, she drew in a shuddery breath.

A sleek blue car swished into the narrow street and halted in front of her house, blocking the road. The vehicle reeked of wealth and ostentation. Not at all the kind of car she imagined Kevin arriving in. The tinted windows made it impossible to see inside till one rolled down and Kard peered out, unsmiling. "Get in," he ordered. To her chagrin and alarm Kevin was seated on the far side of Kard. Was she his prisoner? Then she spotted Kevin's hand nonchalantly squeezing the man's knee.

Annie turned to run, only to hurtle into the folded arms of Kard's bodyguard. He herded her towards the car and shoved her inside. She tumbled against Kard but quickly righted herself, shifting as far away as possible.

Glancing at him, she was surprised to see his nose was unhurt. Come to think of it, the bodyguard's nose had been intact too. Had they got some miracle cure for broken noses? It must cost a fortune. What's more, she could have sworn Kard was greying. Now his hair was evenly black. Had he had it dyed? She hated to admit it, but it made him look younger.

Having gone to such pains to get her into his car, Kard then ignored her. He and Kevin launched into a long, slobbering embrace that was all hands and tongues. The slurps turned Annie's stomach. She tried staring out the window, but couldn't escape their laboured breathing and the growing groans. She tried stuffing her fingers in her ears. To no avail.

It was as if they were putting on an act to spite her. The noises were so exaggerated it could have been a scene from a poorly made sex-ed film about what not to do. The comparison made it no less revolting.

How could Kevin stoop so low? And with Kard of all people. To think she'd dreamt of kissing the girl's soft skin. Infuriated, she turned and hammered Kard's back with clenched fists. He paid her no heed. She clawed at his shoulder trying to stop him. She was about to punch him on the head when the door flew open and the bodyguard reached in and yanked her out.

The car slid silently away, abandoning her on the pavement, tears gushing down her cheeks. She got shakily to her feet, gasping for breath, when her stomach wrenched sideways as before and she sank to her knees wracked with sobs.

The sound of a car drawing up had her scuttling into their tiny garden, sure Kard had come for more. When would this end? She heard a car door open and hurried footsteps coming her way.

"Oh my God! What happened to you?" Kevin asked, reaching out to take her in her arms. Annie moaned and crawled behind the dustbin.

9.

Annie opened her eyes to find Kevin's boyish face inches from hers, the very lips that had kissed Kard so close. She turned her head aside and retched over the dustbin.

"Poor thing," Kevin said, wiping vomit and spittle from Annie's lips with a paper hanky. With an arm slung about Annie's waist, Kevin helped her to her feet and took a step towards the car. Annie panicked. Kard would be waiting. Not again. The slurping of that disgusting kiss. The desperation The hopelessness. She tensed as her stomach heaved. Bile rose in her throat and she was wracked by a fit of violent coughing.

Kevin wrapped her arms around Annie and in that hug she felt the girl's warm breath on her shoulder. She was torn between pummelling Kevin with clenched fists or winding her arms around her and pulling her in a desperate embrace. In the end she just let herself be led to the car like a lost child.

During the short trip, she was relieved Kevin did not ply her with questions. Nor did Megan who was driving. She couldn't stand the thought of reliving the scene. Instead, Kevin held her hand and, after a while, Annie laid her head on the girl's shoulder, stared unseeingly out the windscreen and dozed.

When the car came to a halt, she awoke with a start, unsure whether she was dreaming or not. They were parked inside a hangar in the midst of a gigantic flea market devoid of visitors, bar themselves. Rickety shelves housed row upon row of the magazines. Books stood in endless piles some of which had slithered to the floor. Old-fashioned dresses and lace slips spilled out of tea chests. There was even a score of military uniforms, hung from hangers on a clothes line. Toys of all shapes and sizes scuttled across the floor after each other. Coat stands topped with the wildest turn-of-the-century millinery collection vied with hatstands sporting all manner of wigs amongst a sea of disused wash basins and cracked chamber pots.

Kevin helped her out and laced arms with her, supporting most of her weight. Annie stared uncomprehendingly at the giant jumble sale expecting a hoard of screaming housewives to burst in at any moment and, in their rush to get bargains, knock her off her feet.

"The owner is a friend," Megan said as she wove her way between the hodgepodge. "He has a passion for all that is useless or valueless." She chuckled. "He insists such things have a special beauty." She led them to an office in one corner of the hanger. Nothing fancy. A desk, a few dusty stools and an old-fashioned filing cabinet with its metal drawers hanging open and empty. The windows had been boarded up, the only light coming through the open door from the hanger.

"You can never be too careful," Megan said. "Some people plant spies in the most preposterous places." Indicating the stools for them to sit, she sat too.

Annie slumped onto a stool and stared at her shoes. She sniffed her fingers. The smell of vomit clung to everything. She didn't look up when Megan spoke. "So what happened?" No. Please don't, she pleaded mentally. A groan was her only answer.

"We need to know," Megan said, her tone softening, "if we are to help."

"I have no idea," Annie blurted out. "It was a nightmare. No. Not a nightmare. I was fully awake. But like a dream. Things were not right." She thought of Kard's nose. His hair. And the bodyguard. But she was stalling. She glanced at Kevin perched on the stool next to hers, poised to catch her should she fall.

"I was waiting for you. A car pulled up. Not yours. His. I was forced inside. He was there..." She faltered and tears brimmed in her eyes. Kevin reached out to take her hand but Annie brushed her away. "You were there." It was almost a snarl. She nodded to Kevin. "With him. Next to him. And you …" She clenched her fists and spat the words out. "You kissed. It was revolting." Her hand flew to her mouth for fear she'd gag.

"I never did," Kevin objected, springing to her feet. "Rather dead than that."

"Sit down, Kevin. It's alright," Megan said, sounding more like a tolerant mother than a lawyer. "We know you didn't."

Annie stared wide-eyed at Megan. "Am I going mad?"

"I very much doubt it. Although I suspect someone is trying to make you think you are."

"But how did he make Annie believe I was there?" Kevin asked. "That's not possible."

"I haven't the slightest idea. We just have to assume he can. Alongside all the other dubious and illegal things he gets away with."

Annie slouched even lower on her seat. "Is there no way I can fend him off?"

"We could assassinate him," Kevin said grinning in her enthusiasm. Annie gave Kevin a weak smile. The idea was appealing, but it would never work. The blighter would have some sneaky counter plan. A decoy. A double. A bulletproof vest.

"Kevin!" Megan exclaimed. "We'll do no such thing. We won't even consider it."

"But we can't just let him get away with it," Annie said, taking Kevin's defence, hoping to stave off a feeling of futility. That Kard could make people appear where they were not and force them to do whatever he wanted, was unbearable. "He has so much power."

"However evil he is, however powerful he is, whatever terrible things he does, I won't have us acting outside the law. If we follow him into criminality, he will have won and there'll be no saving us."

"But that's hopeless," Annie complained. "We might as well just give up and let him get on with it."

Megan shook her head. "That's exactly what he wants. Why

do you think he sent the phone? Not so you could have fun ringing your friends. And the money? It wasn't a down payment on
a holiday. He wants you to feel hopeless and friendless, a victim
of his power. Why else would he make you think Kevin betrayed
you? And he probably won't stop there. Be warned. Enslaving
people is what he revels in. Knowing what he is trying to do is
your best line of defence.

She glanced at her watch. "You should be getting back. We
don't want your parents returning to find you gone. Better that
they know nothing of our meeting."

In the car, Annie and Kevin sat in silence for a while. "I wish
I could take some of the load off your shoulders," Kevin said,
her look earnest.

Annie shook her head. "Thanks. But I have to do this myself."

"No, you don't," Megan said from behind the wheel, her
tone firm but not reprimanding. "You can't do this alone. We will
always be at your side even if you can't see us. Remember that
when the going gets tough."

Annie shuddered. It was the sort of bond Kard would delight in breaking.

Kevin took Annie's hand. To her surprise, in doing so Kevin
slipped a small metallic object into her palm. Looking up at the
girl, she saw her shake her head almost imperceptibly. She ban-
ished the question she was about to ask and slid the object into
her pocket.

10.

Annie sat at the kitchen table, her head in her hands, staring at the blank TV. She felt lonely and out of place in her own home. Reaching in her pocket, she pulled out the object Kevin had given her. She raised it to her nose to see if it smelt of Kevin. Faintly. She examined it closely. It was a miniature phone with a tiny clip on the back.

She was trying to figure out how it worked when she heard the garden gate open. The last thing she needed was her mother finding the phone. Another one. She would go wild and confiscate it. Annie clipped it onto the inside of the elastic of her underpants and set about clearing away the remains of her meagre meal.

She expected her mother to make some comment about the vomit on the dustbin. Annie had meant to clean it up, but she couldn't face the task. Judging from her chatter, her mother was so excited she didn't even notice. She continued talking animatedly as she opened the front door. Kard this. Kard that. Annie expected her mum to greet her or make some comment about her being there, but instead she frowned and pushed past, switching on the telly.

"They promised it would be on the main news," her mother reminded her father who nodded to Annie as he came in. The news was just beginning and Kard's demonstration had the first slot. There were several shots of the crowd. So many people. Then Kard was on stage presenting her parents. The camera cut to an interview of her mother. Yes. Her daughter had been caught up in such a racket. They felt betrayed. She'd received presents from rich men behind their backs...

Shocked, Annie stared at her mother. Where ever did she get such nonsense? Now everyone thought Annie was a budding whore. Her teachers. Her friends at school. The boys. The people down her street. Everyone. Her mother had said it. She must know.

The news slot ended with a magnanimous Kard. "I will do all I can to help. These poor people have been sorely misled by their daughter who was aided and abetted by a band of perverts. Such twisted goings-on should not be allowed. I am sponsoring a campaign to pass a bill that makes such meeting places illegal."

Her mother turned the sound down, and brushing her hair from her eyes, said, "I thought I came over rather well, although they only used a tiny bit of what I said. They cut the part about keeping a tight hold on young girls, especially at that age. I liked that."

"They can't use everything," her father said and gave Annie a wink.

"Stop pandering to her," her mother snapped. "She's a disgrace to the family. You always did have a weakness for her. See where that has got us. You men are all alike. A bit of skirt and you go weak at the knees. That Kard bloke is something else. I bet he doesn't go weak at the knees."

No. He dribbles, Annie thought.

Her mother ranted on. "Thank heavens her brother is not here. Imagine how humiliated he would feel."

What would her brother do? Laugh probably. Or pester her for details. But he would feel humiliated, sooner or later. That was what this was all about. Rub people's noses in the dirt. She felt fury mounting.

"So how is your rich friend?" Annie asked. "Did he give you any nice presents?"

Her mother was across the kitchen in one bound and gave Annie's such a slap it knocked her from the stool. Sprawled on the floor at her mother's feet, Annie clutched her jaw, involuntary tears springing to her eyes. For all their arguments, never had her mother hit her.

To her surprise, her father pushed his wife out of the way and helped Annie to her feet. "Enough is enough," he said, crossing his arms as he moved to fend off any new blow. "I won't have you hitting our children. That disgusting man has gone to your head."

Annie wanted to cheer. At last someone who stood up to Kard or rather, her mother.

"You men are all the same," her mother said rounding on him. "You disgust me."

"Let's not change the subject," her father said. "Annie is right. Kard did offer us presents. I refused the job, but you accepted the lawyer."

"What lawyer?" Annie asked, alarmed.

"Mr Kard generously offered to loan us his lawyer to defend you at the trial." Her father sounded bitter.

Annie's heart sank. As she feared, Kard was trying to shut out Megan.

"He's one of the best," her mother said. "Not like that perverted bitch who claimed she was your lawyer. She's in league with all those whores you frequent."

"You're completely mad," Annie flung at her mother. "The only pervert who is dishing out presents is Kard. He sent that phone. He cornered me and tried to fumble at my breasts. Who do you think broke his nose? Now do you understand why I have no use for his lawyer."

Her father spun round to look at her, shock and admiration warring on his face.

"What a pack of lies," her mother said, shaking with rage. "Mr Kard would never. He's good. How dare you defile him?"

Annie would have received a second slap had her father not been standing between them. "You'd better go to your room," he said, a tremble in his voice. "Your mother and I have things to discuss."

After a stop in the bathroom to examine the damage to her

face, she smoothed in some cream then went and sat on the edge of her bed. Downstairs her mother was shouting. She could hear little of her father. He'd always been such a quiet man who only made a noise when he laughed. That he should stand up to her mother in such a spectacular way changed everything. She just hoped Kard wouldn't punish him for refusing the job. Her heart sank. Of course he would.

A strong vibration next to her groin had her jumping off the bed, alarmed. Then she remembered the phone. With some difficulty she unclipped it from her pants and examined it wondering how you stopped the damn thing vibrating. She pressed the button that had appeared on the little screen.

"Annie is that you?" she heard Ayana ask.

11.

"Ayana?" she whispered, not knowing if she should put the phone to her mouth or her ear. Silly really. There was no risk of her parents hearing. Her mother was still raging below, but Annie couldn't shake off the fear of using a cell phone. In her parents' home it just wasn't done.

"You alright?" Ayana asked.

"As right as rain," Annie replied, pitting sarcasm against shock and hurt.

"Kevin gave me this number. She told me what happened." Ayana paused as if waiting for Annie to say something, but she remained silent. "Can you get out?"

"I doubt it." The battle blazed on below. "Mother called me a whore." She hadn't wanted to say, but the thought wouldn't let itself be contained. She blurted it out, almost choking on the last word.

"I know. I heard. I saw." Ayana had never sounded so upset. "She doesn't deserve a daughter like you."

Annie snorted. "I'm sure she's convinced of the contrary."

"Is there no way you can sneak out!"

Annie crossed to the window that looked out over the back yard. The kitchen was a later addition, a one-storey extension with a flat roof just below her window. As a kid, she'd often climbed down. "I daren't. Mother'll go ballistic."

"She went ballistic ages ago, if you ask me. Go on. We could meet at the hideaway."

"Okay. In half an hour. If I'm not there by then, say a prayer for me."

She cocked an ear. The two were still hammering away. If anything the tone had risen, her father's voice getting the upper hand more often. She locked her door and pushed her little desk against it. An useless precaution that would not keep an angry mother out, but it seemed the right thing to do. She clipped the phone back in her underpants, shivering as the metal brushed her skin, and donned a hoodie that concealed part of her bruised face. Opening the window, she straddled the frame and climbed out.

Annie stood suspended at the door to the warehouse. Lit only by a distant lamp, the derelict and deserted buildings were frankly sinister. She glanced around, ensuring she hadn't been followed, and was about to open the door when her stomach lurched so violently she thought she was going to throw up. In the wake of the nausea, a wave of anxiety swept through her. Something was wrong. Terribly wrong.

She pulled open the door, hurried inside, and took the rickety stairs to the attic two at a time, her breath coming hard as she did. The door to Ayana's hideaway stood open, light flooding onto the platform. She peered inside, unwilling to cross the threshold. The kitchen was a shambles. The table had been upturned and chairs lay on their sides, legs smashed, backs broken. Shards of shattered crockery littered the floor .

Seized by a terrible dread, she moved cautiously inside and headed a step at a time for the bedroom. At first she couldn't understand. The photo of Ayana and her girlfriend was gone. The two pillows had been ripped apart, leaving feathers floating over a double bed which lay otherwise untouched. But where was Ayana? A groan from the far side of the bed had her advancing in slow motion to investigate. There lay Ayana, her face twisted in pain. As Annie leaned closer, Ayana's eyes flew open and stared at her.

"Why?" Ayana asked, her expression riddled with accusations, her voice little more than a whisper. Receiving no answer, her eyes fluttered shut and her head sagged. Annie recognised the moment. Had this been a film, violins would have played. In the absence of music, she burst into sobs, clinging to Ayana's hands. Even in death her skin was warm and silky smooth. Could she be mistaken? Had the girl survived? There were no signs of a wound.

Annie fumbled at her friend's wrist in search of a pulse, but could find none. In her desperation she rolled Ayana on her side, wanting to check her back. Her scream shattered the silence. There, protruding from a rent in the back of the girl's blouse was a knife, blood oozing around the blade.

As if that might undo the damage, she tugged at the knife which came away with unforgivable ease, pearls of blood dripping down her arm. She sank back against the bed staring at the red stain, the knife still gripped in her hand. In the distance, police sirens sped to the scene.

"I'll take that, Miss," a policeman said.

Annie had forgotten she was still holding the knife. Taking the handle between gloved fingers, he slid the murder weapon into a plastic bag and sealed it. A policewoman heaved Annie to her feet and handcuffed her wrists, leaving her to stare at her hands uncomprehending.

Was that Ayana lying there? Why didn't she get up? When the police woman guided her to the door, Annie glanced back hoping Ayana would follow. Instead two ambulance men pushed past, a stretcher lugged between them, and lifted Ayana's unresponsive body none too gently onto it. The policewoman hurried Annie down the stairs only to halt like a paltry guard of honour at the entrance while Ayana was trundled past to the waiting ambulance.

The light on the ambulance resumed its flashing at the same time the siren began to wail and the vehicle sped off. The policeman carrying the bloody knife at arms' length joined them and, without sharing the slightest word, he and the policewoman crossed the short distance to their vehicle and climbed in, leaving Annie alone at the door, handcuffed and abandoned.

"Hey!" she hurled, furious. "What about me?" But the couple slammed their doors and drove off without a single look back, their deathly silence lost in the fading roar of the car. Annie stared down the lamp-lit street, then turned to take in the shadows of the warehouse. Was there no one to come to her rescue?

She cringed at the idea of returning anywhere near Ayana's hideaway. But night had fallen and she shivered as an unforgiving wind rose and cut through her flimsy clothes. Stretching out manacled hands to open the door, a familiar wrenching in her gut warned her something had happened. Was the nightmare over?

Her hands were free, but the bloody image of Ayana remained etched in her mind. She had no idea how long she stood terrified in front of the closed door. When Ayana peered out, the whites of her eyes gleaming in the lamplight, Annie was so startled she trembled.

"I thought you'd arrive about now," the girl began, grinning at the sight of her friend. "But I wasn't sure you'd find your way so I tried phoning. I got no answer." The girl broke off, a worried look on her face. She must have noticed Annie was trembling violently. Taking Annie's hands, she exclaimed. "What's wrong? You're freezing. Come inside." She ushered Annie across the empty warehouse and helped her up the stairs.

When they reached the platform and the door to Ayana's place, Annie broke free and cringed away, moaning. Several times Ayana tried to persuade her to cross the threshold, but each time she baulked.

"Wait," Ayana said, raising a placating hand. "Stay there. I'll be back." She hurried away, returning with a chair and a blanket. She sat Annie in the chair and wrapped the blanket around her. "I'll get you something hot to drink," she said. "Would you like that?"

Annie nodded and closed her eyes.

12.

Annie sipped tiny mouthfuls of hot chocolate, her hands clasped around the mug. Ayana, also wrapped in a blanket, sat across from her, an upturned box serving as an improvised table between them. The trembling had abated, but Annie still had involuntary shudders now and then, mostly when the bloody image of Ayana's body resurfaced.

She was relieved Ayana didn't quiz her. She couldn't bring herself to talk about it. Ayana chattered about an alternative venue found to replace Marcie's now that it had been officially closed on order of London's Lord Mayor. In the face of hostility from Kard's followers brandishing the banner 'Keep Britain Straight', she delighted in the ever-growing solidarity between gay and trans people. "We've set up a Girls' Emergence Network," Ayana went on. "Just in case there's any trouble."

"Trouble?" Thoughts of knives and blood had her alarmed again.

"Several bands of thugs claiming to support Kard have sworn to rid London of what they call the 'crooked crowd'."

Annie shuddered. Crooked! With their violence they were unlikely to straighten things out. To think she'd crossed town on her own at night. Not that a band of thugs could be worse than what she was being subjected to. But if thugs hurt her, it would be for real. At least, she couldn't physically be hurt in the nightmarish scenes. "I think we ought to stay here tonight," Annie said. "Being out alone could be dangerous." Being at home might be dangerous too.

"I was hoping you'd say that," Ayana said, grinning. "I even have a spare nightie that might fit you."

Annie could imagine whose it was. The thought of sleeping with Ayana in her former girlfriend's nightie was troubling. Yet after what she had been forced to do to her friend, she couldn't bear to hurt her any more. "What was her name?" she asked, unable to conceal the edge in her voice.

Ayana looked up, startled. "Who?" she asked, clearly not understanding.

"Your girlfriend. It was her nightie, wasn't it?"

"Ah." A wistful look crossed her face. "Gete." She sighed. "Let's not talk about her." She picked up their empty mugs and, trailing her blanket, headed for the door saying, "We should get the bed ready, if you are okay to go inside now. It's late and cold out here."

Annie wearily got to her feet and, picking up the box, carried it into the kitchen. Together they carried the chairs inside and Ayana went into the bedroom. Annie followed, only to freeze on the doorstep.

"I don't think I can lie down in that bed, let alone sleep in it," Annie said, gripping the doorframe. All the blood-splattered images came rushing back.

"It's Gete, isn't it?" Ayana said, shaking her head. "I'm not trying to replace her with you if that's what you think."

Annie sighed. "No. It has nothing to do with her. It's Kard." It was the only exlanation she could find. She knew it was far-fetched. But how else could she explain her waking-nightmares? It was just the nasty sort of thing he would dream up. "He does things to me…"

"I thought you hadn't seen him again."

"I haven't. But he's got a way of doing things at a distance."

"Like sending you a phone?"

"Worse. I don't know how, but he is able to give me daymares. Worse than nightmares, they feel so real. I am fully awake and terrible things happen that I am powerless to stop. One occurred in this room."

Ayana looked shocked. "Poor thing. No wonder you didn't want to come in." Ayana stared at the bed then back at the kitchen. "I only have the one bed." She scratched her head. "Maybe we could shift the mattress into the kitchen. Would that work?"

Annie nodded.

They pushed aside the kitchen table and piled the chairs in one corner, then Ayana lugged the mattress into the kitchen and together they made the bed.

When it was time to undress, Annie was shy. It wouldn't be the first time her friend had seen her in her undies. But back then it had never crossed her mind that Ayana might desire her. Like a boy would want a girl. She waited till Ayana went to the bathroom before hastily casting off her clothes except her underwear and donning the nightdress. Gete must have been both taller and broader. Annie floated in the nightie.

Annie curled up under the sheets, tense and vigilant, afraid Ayana would jump her and try to kiss her. Or worse. But Ayana lay down on her back and stared up at the ceiling. "You asked about Gete." She paused, then chuckled. "It is odd being in bed with you, even if I've dreamed of it often enough."

To think she'd shared so many things with Ayana without ever realising. Had she been that blind? "It'll probably sound naive, but I never imagined you could be…" She hesitated about the word. "…attracted to me."

"I was careful. I didn't want to scare you and risk losing your friendship. Even now I am being cautious." She ran her fingers through Annie's hair. "Short really suits you."

Annie turned to face her. She saw the same mix of anticipation and doubt in Ayana's eyes. If they kissed now, her life would change forever. "Friends," she said, closing her eyes. Not wanting to witness Ayana's disappointment. "For now."

She felt Ayana's warm breath on her face and couldn't suppress a tingle of anticipation. When her friend planted a kiss on the end of her nose, it was her turn to feel disappointed.

Annie awoke with a start and sat bolt upright. Something was wrong. She turned to see if Ayana was awake, but the girl was not there, only crumpled sheets and blankets. Annie swivelled in search of her friend, but she was nowhere.

The kitchen light was on and silhouetted in the doorway stood a tall girl with long, pitch black hair. The moment she turned and light fell across her face, Annie recognised her immediately. "Gete," she gasped. The girl was majestic. Like a lithe, black goddess.

"How dare you wear my nightie?" the girl said, her accent more cockney than African. She inched closer. "And in my bed." Behind her, leaning on the doorframe, Ayana stood outlined.

"What makes you think you can steal my girlfriend?" Gete asked between clenched teeth, her eyes sharp as daggers. She flexed her muscles then flung herself at Annie, her nails outstretched like claws. Annie rolled over and set the bed between them. Gete hissed, her teeth bared, a shocking white against her dark skin. And all the time, Ayana watched unmoving, unspeaking.

Gete flung herself over the bed and landed on top of Annie. Her nails aimed at Annie's face. Annie gripped the girl's wrists, struggling to push her away, but Gete was much bigger and stronger. Annie felt the sting as the girl's nails dug into her cheek and cried out in pain.

Gete moved to pin her legs to the ground. Catching the girl off balance, Annie pivotes sideways and used the girl's own hands to punch her in the face. Gete wrenched free and lashed out in a wild fit, raining blows wherever she could. Annie struck back, aiming for her face.

They rolled several times, getting entangled in the bedclothes as each strained to get the upper hand. The more they fought, the more the blankets bound them tight.

"Stop struggling," Ayana said. "You're having a nightmare."

Annie's eyes flew open to find she was not in the bedroom fighting Gete, but on the kitchen floor by the mattress, rolled up in a knot of sheets and blankets.

"Not a nightmare," she said. "One of Kard's daymares." Then she felt the smarting on her cheek and her hand came away stained in blood.

13.

"I know you don't want to talk about these 'daymares'. I wouldn't either," Ayana said, clasping Annie's hand between hers, pale against her dark skin. The warmth was welcome. They were seated on the mattress with their backs to the kitchen wall. "But if you keep it all bottled up, you'll burst." She sucked in a deep breath then let it burst between her lips like an explosion.

Annie shook her head. "You have no idea."

"Not even to your best friend?"

"It's not a question of friendship. I just can't." How could she possibly tell Ayana she'd stabbed her in the back? Or that Ayana had just watched on, impassive, as Gete tried to kill her?

"Well, if not me, what about Megan?"

Annie could imagine confiding in Megan. She was the sort of woman who'd make a good mother. Someone who listened. Someone who gave meaningful advice. Someone who made you feel relaxed and reassured. And anyway, Megan already knew something about her daymares. "Maybe," she replied.

"Good." Ayana scrambled to her feet and held out a hand to Annie. "Let's go."

Annie glanced at the clock on the cooker. "Come off it, Ayana. It's five o'clock. We can't go now."

"Sure we can. When she's not in court, Megan's a night bird."

Annie pulled the blanket tight around her and curled up on the mattress. "Later."

"Now! Later may be too late."

Annie shuddered. Surely Ayana hadn't meant what she said.

Yet, for all their bluntness, her words might be prophetic. The daymares were coming more and more frequently. How many would it take to break her? "Okay."

The first rays of dawn were nudging a sleepy East End into wakefulness as the two girls hastened across town. Light streamed from all-night shops. Bottles clinked as late shoppers staggered away to drink. Newsagents were opening. Sunday's headlines were already splashed across shop fronts. Kard Enterprises to invest in police. New law on deviants discussed. Prime Minister refutes claims of abuse. Whiffs of freshly baked bread wafted from bakers' back rooms. But the girls avoided main thoroughfares, relieved that most of the town still slept.

Walking through a housing estate, Ayana motioned to a shortcut between two buildings. The narrow alley looked sinister. The streetlamp hung askew between two windowless brick walls. It had been smashed and the path was deep in shadow. Just the sort of place where Kard would attack. Despite her fears, they made it to the far end and emerged onto a deserted street. If this went on much longer, she wouldn't need Kard to dream up her nightmares. She'd be doing it well enough herself.

They stopped at a baker's, Ayana treating them to chocolate eclairs. "Her favourites," she said. They were joking about having such a good breakfast when a male voice called out, "Give us a mouthful love." They spun round to find three youths slouching against the baker's wall, cigarettes hanging from their lips. The one who'd spoken, a gangly boy with rings in his ears and nose, took a step towards her. It was then she felt the familiar lurching in her stomach. Again! She turned to warn Ayana, but it was too late. "Wow! A darky," one of the boys said and grabbed her, pressing her against the wall, as he forced his knee between her legs.

"How about a lick?" the boy with the rings asked, stepping so close she could make out a hint of stubble on his chin.

"Here." Aiming for the ring in his nose, she rammed what remained of the eclair in his face and drove her knee into his groin. He sank to the ground, one hand clawing at his nose, the other grasping his crotch. Her triumph was short-lived. The third boy grabbed her from behind, pinning her arms against her body and dug his teeth into her neck. Screaming with pain, she drove her elbow in his stomach only to connect with his belt. The shock sent a jolt shooting up her arm and around her neck. He twisted her arms behind her back, almost wrenching them from their sockets, and shoved her towards the boy who was ripping open Ayana's t-shirt.

The boy with the rings struggled to his feet, wiping flecks of chocolate and cream from his face. When he spotted her, he stumbled over and, clenching his fist, punched her in the gut. The blow knocked the wind from her and she doubled over, only to be pulled up by the boy holding her. She steeled herself for a second blow, but instead she saw her assailant shaking his hand, his face twisted in pain. He must have hit Kevin's phone.

With his other hand, he ripped her t-shirt from top to bottom and wrenched at her bra, snapping the clasp, baring her chest and stomach. He yanked aside the waist of her tracksuit and plunged grubby fingers down her underpants. She squirmed trying to stop him reaching any further, but strong arms held her tight. Locating Kevin's phone, his hand withdrew, to her relief, and he took a step back. Barely glancing at the thing, he cursed then flung it with all his might at the baker's wall. It shattered, adding silvery parts and circuit boards to the refuse already littering the ground. The crash was so loud, it should have brought the baker running. But nobody came. If people were about, no one paid them any attention.

Turning back to Annie, he smirked, then, grabbing her by the arm, he dragged her to Ayana. Her friend's lip was split and bleeding, one of her eyes was swollen. Only shreds were left of her t-shirt and her bra was gone. Bloody scratches marred her breasts. Pausing a moment to size up the scene as a film director might, the boy squashed them chest against chest like a human sandwich. "Black against white," he crowed. "Show us how two lezzies make out?"

With the telltale lurch in her stomach, Annie found herself in Ayana's arms, sobbing. To her relief, her clothes were intact and the boys were gone. Instinctively her hand flew to the bite on her neck. It was sore, but there was no mark, no blood.

"What the...?" Ayana began, then her mouth fell open. "Oh no! Not again." She pulled Annie close and cradled her in her arms. As Annie breathing settled, she asked,"Can you walk?"

Annie nodded, although her first steps were unsteady.

Megan opened the door, apparently unperturbed by early morning callers. Over jet-black pyjamas, she was wearing a colourful apron that proclaimed, 'Danger! Women at Work'. "Up early," she said brightly. Then she noticed the look on Annie's face. Rather than launch into questions, she ushered them inside. The kitchen was spacious and well appointed. It was much better equipped and more welcoming than their tiny one at home. "Sit," Megan ordered, gesturing to wicker armchairs in a bay window.

"I couldn't sleep," she said, pouring each a mug of tea. "Milk? Sugar?" Then she pulled open the oven and drew out a tray of croissants. "So I did some baking."

Kevin wandered into the kitchen, bleary-eyed and yawning, her cropped hair a riot, but as striking as ever. She was wearing dark blue satin shorts and a matching top that hugged her body. Evidently she did not keep her breasts bound at night. At the sight of her, Annie's breath caught and she blushed. Kevin nodded to Ayana then gave Annie a broad grin. Annie glanced at Ayana then smiled back.

14.

Annie leaned back, a mug of tea in hand, content and sleepy. On one side, Ayana was chatting with Megan about Kard's Keep London Straight movement. "The crooked crowd they are calling us," she said. "The cheek of it. If anyone is a crook, it's him." On the other, lay Kevin curled up, her head on Annie's shoulder, her eyes closed. Annie threaded her fingers absently through Kevin's hair making the girl purr like a cat.

"So what happened to you?" Megan asked, turning to Annie.

Suddenly self-conscious, Annie stopped stroking Kevin's hair and sat up.

"Don't stop," Kevin murmured.

"Your father must have had cats for ancestors," Megan chuckled. "Let the girl talk."

Annie glanced at Megan, then Kevin. What she had taken for granted suddenly appeared strange. Why was Kevin at Megan's house? Were they lovers? Surely not. Yet Kevin seemed at home there. But then…. "Are you Kevin's mum?" she blurted out.

"None other," Megan replied, making a mock grimace. "This delightful child is my daughter or son or whatever."

"I vote for 'whatever'," Kevin said.

Ayana leaned across Annie and punched Kevin on the shoulder. "We should start a movement called 'London Whatever'," she said. "As a call for tolerance."

"Good idea," Megan said. "We should. But enough distractions. Annie was going to tell us why she looks like she's just stepped out of a horror film?"

"Because I have," Annie began. "Not a horror film." She thought of the boy aping a film director and shook her head in disgust. "A daymare. Like the one I told you about in that warehouse."

"Something happened outside the baker's, didn't it?" Ayana blurted out.

"Let her speak," Megan said. "Her words, her time, her story."

"We were attacked," Annie said.

Ayana began to protest, but Megan silenced her with an imperious look.

"It always begins the same way. There's a lurch in my stomach as if someone were trying to turn my guts inside out. Then everything goes wrong. Ayana and I were attacked by three youths. One tried to undress Ayana, ripping her clothes. Another tried to kiss me but I rammed my chocolate eclair in his face."

"What a waste," Ayana muttered. Kevin, however, burst out laughing and clapped in glee which earned her a stinging look from Megan.

"Unfortunately the third one grabbed me from behind and bit my neck..." She went on to describe how the fight degenerated. "They wanted us to demonstrate how two girls make out. Then abruptly it was over. No torn clothes. No bites or bruises. No boys."

"But that's not possible. I was with you all the time. I saw nothing," Ayana exclaimed.

"It looks like these daymares, as you call them, take place outside our time," Megan said. "That would explain why Ayana saw nothing. Did any damage or injury make its way back with you?"

"Nothing. Except the memories and emotions," Annie said.

"That's bad enough," Megan said. "When did these daymares start and how many have you had?"

"Like I told you yesterday, the first time was that evening when Kevin came to fetch me. That was the only time Kard has been an actor. Two more happened later, one that evening and the other during the night at Ayana's hideout. This morning at the baker's was the fourth time."

"Apart from this lurching feeling, does anything else warn you something is going to happen?"

"Not that I've noticed. At the baker's I wanted to tell Ayana it was starting, but it was too late."

"You were already caught up in it," Megan said.

Annie nodded. "I remember wondering why no one came running from the baker's when the boy smashed Kevin's phone against their wall. I see now that no one was aware what was happening."

"They smashed the phone?" Kevin asked.

"I haven't checked. But I don't think so." Annie undid her tracksuit and unhitched the phone from her pants. "I have no idea how it works, so I can't check if it is OK."

"An interesting hiding place." Kevin laughed, taking the phone from her. "Especially when it rings."

Annie giggled. Megan tut-tutted, but there was a smile on her lips.

"At least it's nice and warm," Kevin said, holding the phone against her cheek. Annie blushed and hastily re-knotted her tracksuit trousers.

"Kevin!" Megan exclaimed. "We are going to have to have a talk about what can and cannot be said and done in front of others."

"Sorry. It's just that blushing makes Annie look so delicious."

Annie turned to glare at Kevin when she felt a churning in her stomach. A fraction of a second later, Ayana arched her back like a wild cat then flung herself across the kitchen table at Kevin. "You bitch," she screeched. "Get your bloody hands off." The two rolled onto the floor, pulling the table cloth with them. Mugs and plates crashed on top of them, cutlery scattering in every direction. Enraged, Ayana tried to pummel Kevin's face, screaming, "Mine! Mine!" Kevin flung up her arms in defence. Not before several blows hit their mark.

The two rolled over sending chairs and the table flying.

Kevin must have got in a hit because Ayana's nose was bleeding.

"Young girls are so immature," Megan said, drawing Annie's attention away from the fight. Both of them were seated in armchairs watching. Megan was sipping a glass of champagne. "What you need is a woman like myself with experience of the world and its pleasures." She leaned closer and caressed Annie's neck. Annie shuddered and jerked away. The battle raged on. Ayana had picked up the bread knife and was slashing at Kevin who defended herself with a leg broken from a chair.

"Don't be so shy," Megan said, reaching out to grip Annie by the neck and pull her close.

Kevin's screamed. Ayana had stabbed her in the arm. Blood was streaming from the wound and dripping onto the floor. Enough! Annie ripped free of Megan and flung herself onto Ayana before she could stab Kevin again. With Kevin's help, they managed to remove the knife from Ayana's clenched fist and pin her arms and legs to the floor.

Ayana lay beneath them limp, all the fight gone from her. She looked beseechingly at Annie then burst into tears. To see her friend ravaged by jealousy wrenched her heart. In took her a moment to realise that the wrenching marked the end of her daymare.

She was kneeling on the floor, the others staring down at her, a look of concern creasing their faces.

"Again?" Megan asked.

Annie could not reply. She was wracked by wave after wave of despair and revulsion. It was hard not to be angry at Megan and Ayana. She had to remind herself that this was all Kard's work. How could anyone do such a thing? He was inhuman.

Ayana helped her to her feet. They stood for a moment at arm's length, then Annie flung her arms around the girl's neck and sobbed. "I'm so sorry," she whispered.

Ayana pulled back, looking at her, perplexed.

"I love Kevin and it's breaking your heart."

Kevin's face lit up, a grin spreading from ear to ear.

Ayana smiled too, although her smile was tense and tinged

with sadness. "Is that what you think?"

Annie nodded, tears streaming down her cheeks.

Ayana ran her hand through the hair on Annie's neck. Annie shuddered. It was the same gesture Megan had used in her daymare. Ayana's face clouded and she withdrew her hand. "Am I so repulsive?"

A new wave of despair broke over Annie. Life was so complicated. How was she to find the words? "It's not your hand, but the memory of another." She glanced at Megan and quickly looked away, embarrassed.

Ayana appeared appeased. "I know you love Kevin."

"I wish she'd told me," Kevin bemoaned.

"Shhh…" Megan said.

"I've known ever since she spoke to you at Marcie's." She took a step back and scrubbed her eyes with her knuckles. "I'm happy for you both."

15.

Annie stepped out of Megan's car and cracked open the garden gate, glancing at the terraced houses across the street as she did. What would the neighbours think seeing such a posh car draw up in front of her house? No good, no doubt. Especially if they'd seen her mum call her a whore on TV. How many of them were already reaching for the phone to call the police?

Megan pushed open the passenger door to let Kevin shift to the front. "We'll wait till you're inside," she called out. Annie nodded then waved Kevin goodbye. They had dropped Ayana at her home. She was to have a traditional Sunday dinner with her family. Ayana's folks might have had their roots sunk deep in Ethiopia with all its customs, but that didn't stop them enthusiastically embracing many English traditions. In comparison, Annie couldn't remember the last time her family had a Sunday roast.

She turned the handle. It wouldn't budge. She tried again, rattling it. Her parents must have gone out locking the door. She fished under the mat. The key was not there, although a telltale mark revealed where it had been. She searched around the dustbin. Maybe it had been displaced by accident. Nothing. She pressed her face to the window. No signs of life.

"Looks like I'm locked out," she told Megan, returning to the car. "I'll just have to climb in my bedroom window. I left it open on purpose."

"Let me give you a hand," Kevin said, clambering out of the car.

They scrambled through the overgrown wasteland that

bordered the house and squeezed between the end of the house and the high brick wall that fenced off the slip road. In the yard, amid discarded boxes and a broken bicycle, she looked up at her window. It stood stubbornly shut.

"Your parents afraid of burglars?" Kevin asked.

"No." She shrugged. "There's nothing worth stealing. More like someone wanted to make sure I couldn't get in."

It was an odd feeling being locked out of her own home. Was this another of Kard's daymares? She couldn't recall having felt a lurch in her stomach and there was none of the foreboding that accompanied such episodes.

"Look," Kevin said, pointing to a small downstairs window. "The bathroom window is open."

"That's too tiny. I'd never get in there."

"No. But I can."

Annie didn't like the idea of Kevin entering her house alone. She was ashamed. She thought of the threadbare carpet on the stairs and the damp patches on the walls in the bathroom, not to mention her clothes hung from hooks from the rafters in her room because there was no wardrobe. What's more, it was just the kind of situation that could spark one of Kard's daymares. Surely some twisted nastiness was long overdue.

"Give us a hand-up," Kevin said, pulling off her jacket.

Annie helped Kevin clamber onto her shoulder from where the girl wriggled into the tiny window. There was a crash and a curse. "Sorry," she heard Kevin call out. "Only tooth brushes and tubes of toothpaste."

Annie went round to the front door and waited for Kevin, trying to appear nonchalant for the watching eyes. There were always long-standing tenants posted at their front windows with nothing better to do than spy on their neighbours. The longer Kevin took, the more worried she became. What if the girl was caught in a vicious trap unable to cry out for help? What if her mother had hidden in the cupboard under the stairs waiting with a rolling pin to brain an intruder? What if…? And the door opened to reveal Kevin grinning at her.

"What took you so long?" she asked, trying hard not to sound peeved.

"Picking up toothbrushes. One rolled under the sink."

Annie scowled. "I was worried."

"Sorry. I was just trying to set things right."

Once inside, she hurried up to her bedroom, trying to ignore the strong smell of sweat and cheap perfume. It must have always been there, but she'd never noticed. The door to her room hung off its hinges. The frame had been smashed. Stepping over the contents of her desk littered on the floor, she halted and gasped at what she saw. Someone, her mother, judging from the spelling, had scrawled, 'my dorter no more' in blue felt pen on the wall. Surely this must be one of Kard's daymares. It was his blue. But there were none of the telltale signs.

Fortunately her other belongings had not been vandalized. She gathered up clothes and books for school on Monday and stuffed them with a change of underwear in a carrier. She went to fetch her pyjamas from under the pillow only to discover an envelope in the folds of her night clothes. One word was written on the outside, 'Annie'. She recognised that handwriting.

Kevin had followed her up the stairs and was looking at the door. "Is it always like this?" Then she saw the writing. "Nice," she exclaimed. "Real welcoming." Kevin got down on her knees and rummaged through the clutter on the floor. She must have found what she was looking for, because she got up. "May I?" she asked, brandishing a marker.

Annie shrugged. Did it matter? As the message said, this was no longer her home.

In neat script, Kevin crossed out the offending word, wrote the correct spelling above and then stepped back to admire her work. Annie was not proud at all. That her mother had not finished school and had never learnt to spell shamed her. She knew Kevin only meant to take a swipe at her mother for being so mean, but as her daughter she'd been slapped too.

"Your mother?" Kevin asked, nodding to the letter.

"No. My dad." She hesitated about opening it. Goodness

knew what he'd written. At least it wouldn't be full of spelling mistakes.

Kevin must have sensed her need for privacy, because she picked up the carrier, saying, "I'll take this out to the car. See you there."

Annie sat down on the edge of her bed, drew in a deep breath, then tore open the envelope, pulled out a single sheet of paper and read.

Dear Annie.

Your mother has gone to a meeting of Keep London Straight.

I'm leaving. I can't stand it any longer. Her nonsense is driving me mad.

I'm so sorry. You deserve better than this.

Come and see me.

Love. Dad.

The letter ended with an address not far from Bow Cemetery, a regular haunt of hers. She folded the paper and stuffed it in her pocket, but she didn't get up. Instead, she stared at the inscription on the wall. Her dad couldn't have seen it, or he would have made a remark. Her mother must have scribbled it after he'd gone. For all his own defection, he still believed she had a place to stay. She felt numbed. She had lost her reputation thanks to her mother. Now she'd lost her family and with it, her home. It was hard not to lash out at the woman. She was incurably insensitive and embarrassingly dim. Yet, for all her anger at her mother, she knew full well the real root of the trouble lurked out of sight and beyond reach.

Getting to her feet with a sigh, she pulled the old suitcase from under her bed, the one she'd used a year earlier for the only school trip she'd even been on, and began packing her belongings.

16.

"No. Here's fine," Annie said, climbing out of the car. "I need to walk a bit."

"We'll take your things to our place," Megan said. Earlier, she had offered Annie a room in her house, the run of the fridge and a shoulder to cry on, should she need it. Annie felt uncomfortable accepting such generous hospitality. Her mother had drummed it into her, self-respecting people didn't accept charity. But Annie was relieved she had somewhere to stay. Maybe later she could find lodgings with her father, if that worked out.

She wanted time alone, to think, to breathe fresh air, to be amongst trees and flowers, outside, where nature was still wild, or at least seemingly so. Megan had dropped her at the main gate to Bow Cemetery, as locals called it, next to the Lodge, a building that actively shied away from repair and renovation. Her father's digs lay on the far side.

The cemetery, which dated from the Victorian era according to her history teacher, had long since ceased to serve as a place of burial. Successive owners had neglected it, but that decline had gifted it with a chaotic, untamed beauty that appealed to Annie. She had spent several free days wandering its alleys and pathways, wishing she had a camera. She liked early morning best when rising mist trailed around toppled tombstones and crept along deserted alleys. As she set forth, all traces of mist were long gone and walkers, out with their dogs, made the most of the late-morning sun before heading home for their Sunday roast.

Rather than take the direct route across the park to Cantrell

Road and the gate by the railway line, she followed a leisurely path that wound from glade to glade. The last of the bluebells were withering, but wild roses were in full bloom, rambling over tombs and bushes alike. Birds were everywhere, chirping and squawking, almost masking the distant drone of traffic.

Some of the tombstones that remained standing were extravagant columns topped with carved urns draped with stony tissue. She imagined Kard insisting on such a tomb, he who was all show and bluster. But no. Of course he wouldn't! Despite a smattering of ostentation, this was more of a commoners' burial ground. Kard would never have stooped to being laid to rest with so many plebs. She shook her head. Blasted man sneaked into her thoughts irrespective of what she was doing.

She halted before a line of ornate memorials, stiff and upright, like noble figures opposing time. The first, an elaborate Celtic cross, festooned with grapes, had a young angel carved at its base. The child, for all its demure pose, would have had both strength and beauty had it not been for its left-wing, which was broken, and its right arm severed at the wrist. Another victim of senseless violence.

Enough. She had wandered the whole length of the cemetery and was farthest from where she needed to be. Turning back, she was suddenly aware of noises that were out of place in the peace of the graveyard. The rumble of electric generators. The squeal of electric feedback. Laughter. And, above all, incessant chatter.

When she reached the only large area in the cemetery that was free of trees and graves, she stepped out into the open to be greeted by an extraordinary sight. Had she stumbled on a film set? That's what it looked like. She checked her feelings to make sure Kard wasn't pulling strings again. He wasn't. Blast! She was loathed to walk back to the lodge and round by the road. It would take ages.

Where grass normally would have been, a large expanse of water had been created, barely inches deep. Perched at one end was a raft made of rough planks lashed together with ropes, the whole structure moored to a mock landing stage. On the raft was a red carpet in the middle of which stood a small round table and two armchairs. Scattered across the grass that sloped away from the water were many round tables each with a bevy of chairs, the likes of which she'd seen in would-be posh bistros selling fake French cuisine. Chatting at the tables was a crowd of people dressed like they'd all hurried straight from church.

A forest of spotlights flooded the scene in dazzling white light, and cables crisscrossed the ground in every direction. Several cameras were trained on the raft, others roamed the crowd. Boom microphones were perched over the man-made island, their holders at the ready. A group of makeup artists were scurrying around one of the two armchairs. Whoever was seated there was getting a VIP makeover. When they scattered like frightened animals and scurried out of sight, the crowd fell silent and began to applaud. The man in the armchair lazily got to his feet, his massive frame impressive in the brilliant light and raised a hand for silence. Kard, of course.

Annie had a very bad feeling. Across the far side, her escape route down the lane by the railway line was blocked by three giant vans sporting the logo BBC Outside Broadcast. She'd have to double back through the wood till she reached the cutting and then sneak behind the vans. She turned to slip away when a lone voice from the audience called out, "Look! There!" All heads swivelled in her direction as did several cameras. "We have an unexpected visitor," Kard's amplified voice said. "It's not every day we get a chance to meet one of the crooked crowd from Marcie's, that den of perversion. Come here child." The way his voice slithered over the word 'child' would have made anyone who had not yet reached adulthood bolt in terror.

Annie turned to run but several bodyguards had come up behind her and blocked the way. One took her by the arm and led here through the audience to the landing stage. People stared at her, intrigued or disgusted, a couple even hissed. As she was walked out towards the raft, a low murmur of whispers or was it snarls rose at her back.

Kard stood to greet her. He was on his best behaviour for television. He bowed and indicated she should use the other armchair. She remained standing, both terrified and defiant. She didn't know how, but he was about to trap her like he had her mother. With his smooth talk he was going to force her to say things she would regret.

"She may not look dangerous, but this young..." He made a point of hesitating over the choice of word. "... person is one of those crooked people that are the gangrene of our society. Behind an innocent face, a twisted mind works to undermine the values that you and I stand for."

In a split second, the crowd morphed from a well-behaved congregation still smelling faintly of incense and quietly respectful of the niceties of life into a surging mass that would have been more at home at a match of catch or a riot in Hell. "Kill the crooked crowd," they yelled. "Keep London Straight."

Once again Kard imperiously raised a hand for silence. "Maybe the young creature can explain why she does such things. Only the other day her mother told us she sold her body for money..."

The mention of her mother and Kard reminding everyone of her accusations made Annie's blood boil. However, when Kard handed her a microphone, despite her anger, she remained silent, at a loss for words.

"No swearing, please. This is family television. We don't want you besmirching the children watching."

Like you have besmirched my life, she thought, with your filthy hands and your vicious daymares. A grim determination seized her as she took the microphone. Ayana's words flashed through her mind and she raised a clenched fist in the air and shouted two words, "London Whatever."

The moment she'd spoken, she tossed away the microphone, hearing it plop into the water. She rammed into Kard, catching him off balance, and pushed him backwards into the man-made lake. She jumped in after him, leaving him to flounder on his back in inches of water, screaming for help, shouting that he was drowning, that he couldn't swim, that he wanted to live, while she waded to the far side and scrambled out.

"Catch her!" several voices shouted, but everyone continued to sprawl at their tables vociferating. No one making the slightest move.

She dived in amongst the bushes, getting scratched as she did, and crouched beside a large gothic tomb dedicated to young Esther, the 'dearly beloved daughter' of her stricken parents who 'will always remember her'. Lucky girl that could count on her parents even after she was dead.

Annie's trousers were sopping and she was shivering as she surveyed the chaos beyond. A few adventurous people were running in every direction, shouting, gesticulating, but no one had come to the rescue of Kard who was unable to right himself and continued to cry for help. It was as if the audience were loathed to soil their Sunday best. Unperturbed, the TV crew gleefully continued to film as if everything had been scripted that way.

In the distance she could hear sirens approaching. The police probably. She had to flee before they sealed off the area. She glanced across the lake. The TV crew filmed as Kard was finally rescued and carried dripping to land. An ambulance pulled up and the sodden, but very vocal politician was manoeuvred inside while well-wishers jostled to get a glimpse of their unfortunate hero.

17.

Annie stood on the doorstep shivering, her sopping trousers clinging to her legs, and rang the doorbell. A plaque next to the bell read, 'Mrs. Reynolds' lodgings for single men'. After a long wait, the front door cracked open and an old woman in a flower print dress peered at her through thick glasses. A powerful smell of cats wafted out.

"Who is it?" Mrs. Reynolds asked.

"I'm here to see my father, Mr. Wight."

"I'll fetch him," the woman said and closed the door.

When next the door opened, her father stood there, his mouth fallen open at the sight of her. "Whatever happened to you?"

"It's a long story."

"Hold on. I'll fetch a towel." The door closed again, leaving her feeling unwelcome. She glanced over her shoulder. This was a slightly better-off neighbourhood that her mother's. There was room for people to park on both sides of the street, the front gardens boasted enough room for two dustbins side by side and there was no flyover with its constant rumble of traffic. But she was sure there were still watchful eyes behind the lace curtains.

The door reopened and her father handed her two tiny towels that were frayed at the edges. He stepped inside and closed the door once again while she dried what she could in full view of the watching eyes. "Here," he said reappearing with a dingy brown blanket and his own cloth cap.

"Let's go somewhere warm and get you a hot drink. I'll just

get my coat." He took the towels and the door closed yet again. Mrs. Reynolds should add an extra line to her plaque, 'Welcome strictly limited. No visitors allowed'.

Wrapped in her blanket, her face half concealed by the cap, they set out at a brisk pace. Her father was about to enter the park when she held him back. "Better not," she said.

He turned around and headed up Bow Common Lane with its row upon row of terraced houses and small blocks of flats but not the slightest café or pub between them.

"So what happened to you?" he asked.

"I fell in a lake."

He chuckled. "A lake? There's no lake near here."

"There is now, in the cemetery."

He shook his head, but didn't pursue the subject. "But why didn't you go home and get changed?"

"Because Mother kicked me out."

He nodded knowingly. "I was afraid of that."

By the time they reached Mile End Park and turned up Burdett Road her trousers were almost dry. Thinking she was too conspicuous with the blanket wrapped around her shoulders, not that anyone paid her any attention, she folded it and held it under her arm while her dad told her about Mrs Reynolds and her cats. At least she understood the buffoonery with the woman's door, to stop the cats straying.

He took them to an Italian cafe with a row of chairs parked in front of the shop window forming a minuscule terrace on the pavement. There was a lot of traffic and the place was noisy, but the view of the park on the other side of the road was better than a dingy interior. She sat in the farthest of the chairs from the door with an empty table next to it while her dad fetched two cups of steaming tea then sat across from her.

She described the writing on the wall.

He shook his head. "She wasn't thinking straight." Annie couldn't help snorting at the use of the word. Straight? Crooked? Whatever! "That Kard guy is like a drug," her father continued. "No wonder crowds go crazy at his meetings. But what happened between you and him?"

"I was just passing by on my way home from school when someone forced me into his campaign bus. He tried to touch me up but I managed to get away and broke his nose in the process."

He chuckled. "So you were the band of thugs."

"Yeah! But I stole neither his whiskey nor his cigars."

"Well, good for you. I'm glad that's over."

Annie groaned. "You must be joking. He hasn't ceased to harass me ever since. He sent me a phone. He transferred money to my account. He set the police on me when I was at Marcie's. He manipulated my mother to call me a street walker on television." She paused to look around and leant closer before continuing. "He's been sending me daymares."

Her father glanced up from his tea, intrigued at the word. "Daymares?"

"I have no idea how he does it, but all of a sudden I'm torn out of this world and plunged into a scene of his making. It is invariably violent and terrifying."

"I don't understand."

"Imagine," she lowered her voice, forcing him to move closer to hear, "I'm sitting here with you. I feel a lurch in my stomach and things change. Maybe you try to kill me with a knife. Or you try to seduce me. Or I see you in the arms of other women than Mum. I can do nothing against it. Then just as abruptly it's over. And you are staring at me wondering why I am panting or shaking with terror. No time has passed for you. You see nothing of what happens."

"That's awful. If it happened to me, I think I'd go bonkers."

"I will go nuts if it goes on much longer." Annie groaned. "How the hell am I supposed to stop it?"

"Has it happened often?"

"Four times so far. But tell me about you and mum."

"That's my own private daymare."

Annie grimaced at the word. He had meant it as a metaphor, but it had her wondering if others might be plagued by Kard's twisted imaginings.

"She's stubbornly set on defending Kard's cause and insisted I do too. I want nothing to do with the bloke. He sucks the life out of those who come in contact with him. They become puppets. Take your mum. I've always found her ideas narrow, but love, then affection, made me overlook a lot. But at least we could talk, a little. Then yesterday evening all I got was 'Kard this' and 'Kard that'. He suggested you were a …" he couldn't say the word. "You know. And she swallowed it, no questions asked."

"He offered you a job…?"

"Yeah. I refused."

"Why?"

"Not sure. Don't trust him. There's sure to be a heavy payback. I don't want to be in his debt." He glanced through the window at the clock over the counter. "Is that the time? I have to go. I'm to visit a room to let."

They rose and were about to leave when, through the open door of the café, she saw the news beginning on a TV suspended in a corner of the room. Centre screen stood Annie, her fist raised then she pushed Kard into the lake and plunged in after. "Turn up the sound," a customer with a strong Italian accent called out.

The presenter was saying, "Nolan Kard was taken to hospital but was quickly discharged. The girl who attacked him has not yet been found. If you have any information about her whereabouts, contact this number or your local police."

Her father gripped her arm and hurried her out of the café and away down a side street till they were hidden from view. "You don't do things by halves," he said, spinning to look at her. It was at that moment her phone rang.

"Kevin," she answered. "Yes. Just now." She turned to her father, "What's the name of this street?" She relayed his answer to Kevin. "Okay. In five minutes."

She pocketed the phone and said, "Friends are coming to fetch me."

18.

Annie climbed onto the back seat of the car next to Kevin, wound down the window and stretched out a hand in her father's direction. "Take care dad. Love you." He nodded and mumbled, "Love you too."

Love? The word struck her as odd. They had never been close and she couldn't recall him ever telling her he loved her, nor her him. What upset her even more was the thought that they might never say the words to each other again. It was as if a tide were pulling them apart and in so doing revealed how little they'd actually been together. She closed the window and Megan sped away.

As they drove up Mile End Road towards Forest Gate, Annie watched the East End rush by. She craned her neck to follow the River Lea as it wound its muddy path through scars of the past and emerging hopes for the future. Rows of run-down terraced houses like the one in which she had lived her formative years might soon become an anomaly.

Megan took a sharp right into a narrow road bordered on both sides by brick walls topped with barbed wire, a disused factory or warehouse dotted in between. Was one of those their destination? Megan seemed to have a predilection for the lefto-vers of another era. They rounded a corner to discover a large brick structure the ground-floor windows of which were boarded up and drove slowly along a hoarding painted black and coiffed with barbed wire that ran the length of the property. Megan halted opposite a giant inscription in rainbow colours: London

Whatever!

"Look at your handiwork." Megan said, nodding at the inscription. "Do you have any idea what you've done?"

Annie was indignant. The tag had nothing to do with her. "That's Ayana's phrase," Annie replied, wondering who could have sprayed such beautiful characters. They were iridescent in the early afternoon sun.

"No. It's your slogan," Megan said. "The one you so triumphantly brandished on national television before you shoved Citizen Kard into the lake."

"Wonderful!" Kevin exclaimed, leaning over Annie to get a better look. "I hadn't seen that one."

"That one?" Annie was beginning to feel alarmed. "How many are there?"

"They are springing up all over the place," was Megan's reply.

"You're a national hero and I'm your number one fan," Kevin gushed. "Can I have your autograph?"

Annie pushed her away. "Stop making fun of me. This is serious. He set the police on me."

"I'm not poking fun," Kevin protested. "You are a TV hero. Everyone has been longing to get one back at Kard, but no one knew how, no one had the courage. It was as if he ran circles round us and had us hypnotized. Then you came along, with a raised fist and a hefty shove, and you broke the spell."

"Kevin's right. Although if I'd had a say, I'd have warned you not to be so rash," Megan said. "Kard is a dangerous player with a lot of influence. Better not attack him head on. I doubt he can be beaten that way. He turns every attack to his advantage. Look at what you did. Now he is the innocent victim of a crazed lesbian, one of the crooked crowd who plan to undermine true British values. You just fuelled his campaign to Keep London Straight."

"Sure," Kevin protested. "But she also fuelled a powerful grassroots opposition."

"True. But enough of that, we need to get you to a safe place before anyone spots you. I wouldn't be surprised if they don't plaster the place with wanted posters and your pretty little face will be on each one of them."

"But I have to go to school tomorrow. I've got a test." Annie was more or less ready, but a few extra hours swotting wouldn't go amiss.

"I very much doubt you'll be attending school for quite a while," Megan said.

Annie was dismayed. She liked school, she appreciated her teachers and got on well with her small class of fellow students, for all their ethnic diversity. This was a key year. She had to take A levels if she was to realise her dream of going to university.

"Lucky you," Kevin muttered.

Annie shook her head. If only pushing Kard into the lake had been one of those daymares and she could awake to the world as she knew it. She'd go up to her room, hearing her mother bumbling about in the kitchen downstairs preparing supper and would finish her homework, then set off to school tomorrow and do her test. She would get good marks, of course, she always did. Then next year she'd study creative writing at university… Basking in such pleasant thoughts, she closed her eyes and dozed off.

When she awoke, they were driving along a narrow, winding lane with the trees arching above as if trying to conceal them from prying eyes. Then they burst from the leafy cover and drove up amongst grass-covered fields. Had she still been in the countryside where she was born, they would have been peopled by grazing sheep, but here the fields were empty. For once Sunday weather was clement and a brilliant sun shone down. Craning her neck, she could just distinguish the outskirts of London, a dirty smudge sprawled across the horizon behind them. To think she hadn't even noticed when they left.

"Annie could disguise as a boy," Kevin said in reply to something Megan must have said. "We could be two boys together."

"I don't think that would work," Megan said. "She looks too much like a boy already. We'd be better off disguising her as a girl."

But I am a girl, Annie wanted to protest. She thought of Ayana. Now there was a girl for you. What with her long straight hair, her perfect chocolate skin and her curves always shroud in dresses and skirts. Crikey! What if Kard knew she was her best friend? "What about Ayana? Won't she be in danger?"

"Kard is an out-and-out racist. I wouldn't put it past him to pick on a girl just because of her colour. And if she happens to be your best friend, well…" Megan sighed. "I'll have someone keep an eye on her."

Annie wasn't reassured. She'd seen how some older white men reacted to Ayana. It was as if her colour was a licence for them to behave like animals.

Megan pulled off the road and halted in front of a gate. It was made of plain wooden bars darkened by time and the weather like so many other farm gates in the area. Kevin jumped out to open it. The gate led to a rough lane that wove its way through the folds of the hills, appearing and disappearing from sight till it came to an abrupt halt in a hallow where an old farmhouse lay, at least, that was where Megan told them they were heading.

Annie had long since ceased to be a country girl. Her parents had moved to London when she was only five. Her father had got a new job. She stared at a knot of trees huddled like gnarled old ladies on a windswept hill top. All this open space made her feel uncomfortable. But maybe there, in the middle of nowhere, she'd be sheltered from Kard and his schemes. Unless, of course, the daymares continued. There'd been a welcome lull. She had no idea why she had been spared so long. Perhaps the shock of plunging in the lake had distracted him. She chuckled at the thought of him floundering in inch-deep water.

The car hit a bump just as they turned a bend and drove into the yard revealing the farmhouse. Annie was flung sideways ramming into Kevin who pushed her roughly away. The reaction was so uncharacteristic she stared at Kevin, but the girl paid her no attention, her eyes riveted on the farm ahead. Annie followed her gaze and saw a familiar figure step out of the farmhouse, Kard.

Panicked, she turned to open the door and run, but Kevin

seized her wrist and held her in a vicelike grip. "You don't think you are going to run away when we went to so much trouble to bring you here," Kevin said, her voice hard and unfamiliar.

"So. Here's our little crooked star. You've kept us all waiting," Kard said, waving Annie over. "Now we can get down to serious business."

19.

Kard gripped Annie so tightly by her arm she yelped. He ignored her protestations, propelling her inside, while Kevin trailed behind. Where Megan had gone she had no idea. The door led into what must once have been the kitchen. Only a small area around a central table and part of the working surface by the cooker were recognisable as such. The rest of the room was more like a TV set, littered with cables and cameras and lighting. Grey technicians scurried everywhere.

"Welcome to my world," Kard said, stressing the word 'my' as he wiped away sweat that pearled on his brow. After the fresh, country air, the sultry, stuffy kitchen was suffocating. With an apparent display of magnanimity, he added, "Let me take you on a guided tour." She was getting to know him. He could only act so loftily when he was sure of being superior.

They crossed the kitchen into the dining area. Here only the table, which had been laid for two, was free of television paraphernalia. The lounge was the same. Two armchairs by the fireside flickered in the artificial glimmer of an electric fire. "I won't take you up to the bedroom yet. Let's keep that pleasure for later," he said, as if delaying the delights was the ultimate generosity. "And here is the toilet," he smirked, "if ever you need it." He opened the door to what had once been a bathroom but the bath had been ripped out and several cameras had taken its place. She made a mental note to drink as little as possible.

He led them back to the kitchen, confidently striding over cables as he did, and sat at the table, inviting her to do the same.

He made a swirling gesture with his hand, which she gathered told the cameramen to film. She glanced at the TV crew who were absorbed in their tasks. They were like shadows, ever present and watchful, yet unobtrusive and almost without substance.

Kevin slid onto Kard's knees, wrapped her arms round his chest, and nuzzled his neck. She might look like Kevin, Annie reminded herself, but this girl was not the person she knew. Kard smiled at Annie over Kevin's head, his expression smug. She wanted to throw the glass of orange juice in his triumphant face.

"May I?" she asked, nodding towards the buttered toast. "Feel free," he said, running a lazy hand over Kevin's breasts. Reaching out, Annie upset the jug of milk which was perched precariously on a mat, sending its contents cascading into Kevin's lap. The girl let out a squeal and jumped to her feet, shooting Annie a poisonous look. "Bitch!" she sputtered as she tripped over a cable in her hurry to leave the room.

Milk must have seeped through onto Kard because he sprang to his feet almost upturning the table. There was a giant wet patch down the front of his otherwise impeccable trousers. Annie wanted to make a snide remark, but played contrite. "I'm so sorry," she said and bit into the toast. Delicious. It was her turn to look smug. The trouble with dreams, she thought, was that they rarely went as the dreamer planned. Daymares seemed to be the same. It might be Kard's world, but he let her into it and she was not without resources.

Left on her own, Annie wandered into the living room, ignoring the television shadows that busied themselves around her. She could hear Kevin and Kard arguing upstairs. As long as they weren't going at it hammer and tongs on the bed, she could ignore them.

There was one room Kard hadn't shown her. The library she guessed. Pushing open the door revealed rack upon rack of monitors each displaying a different part of the house. Grey staff sat at control panels twiddling knobs, but no one paid her any heed. One of the monitors caught her attention. Kevin was sprawled face-down in her underclothes dwarfed by a king-sized bed, while

Kard loomed over her in only his boxers. She had expected to see ripples of fat, but he was surprisingly muscular. Even his fantasies were designed to flatter him.

He unhooked Kevin's bra and sprawled on top of her, his mass almost engulfing her as the girl let out an audible humph. Annie wanted to look away, but there was no escaping. The scene was relayed from various angles by all the monitors. Had Kevin been compliant, Annie could have discounted it as the show it was, but Kevin struggled trying desperately to free herself. Loud-speakers amplified her cries as they did Kard's heavy breathing. He continued to pin her to the bed, his hips gyrating backwards and forwards.

"Annie! Help!" Kevin spluttered.

Helplessness and disgust warred in Annie. It was a trap. She was sure. What she was watching probably wasn't happening, but that thought did little to dispel her discomfort. Her heart wrenched for her friend. It was as if she herself were being abused. The sight and sound of it soiled her, forcing her into un-willing complicity. Yet she couldn't bring herself to go up to that room. Goodness knew what would await her. But standing there and letting it happen was unbearable. She looked around for a way to strike back. Anything to feel less helpless. There were only monitors. Rows upon rows of them. And grey shadows.

Kevin's voice had risen to a scream as she thrashed wildly. Meanwhile Kard continued to grunt like a beast, oblivious to the pain and distress he was inflicting. Annie shoved one of the technicians from his seat sending him flying across the room. He weighed next to nothing. She upended his chair and rammed its metal legs with all her force into a monitor. There was a loud bang as the screen shattered and sparks flew in every direction. She was forced to jump back. Technicians dived out of the way and fled for the door.

She smashed two more monitors and was pleased to see others burst into flames. Enough. At least the disgusting imag-es were gone and the vile sounds with them. Time to get out. She turned to go, only to find the door closed. No amount of hammering or shaking would open it. The technicians had locked her in. She shattered several chairs trying to force a way out, but the door was solidly made. The fires in the monitors had spread till all of them belched smoke and spat sparks. Flames licked the timbers that held up the ceiling and a thick pall of smoke that stank of toasted electrical wares swirled in the air.

In a fire, get on your hands and knees to escape the smoke the teacher had told them during fire drill. She scrabbled around on all fours, her eyes smarting from the smoke, her lungs heaving one cough after another. How did the cables that snaked the floor get in and out? There. A few yards from the door. A narrow hatch through which the cables disappeared. She would never get through. Not even Kevin could manage that. If only she could get rid of the cables, it might be possible.

She tried tugging on them, but they were firmly anchored in the next room. However the fire had freed up many at her end. She stuffed them one by one through the hole, using her jacket wrapped around her hands to protect her from the heat. She hadn't finished, but lumps of flaming timber were falling nearby. It was now or never. She squeezed her head into the breech and wriggled till she managed to get one arm through. If she could get her shoulders through, she'd be saved. She tried breathing out to make herself as small as possible, but she had no leverage.

Then a searing heat bit into her legs. One of the timbers must have fallen on her. Screaming, she shoved with all her force and popped out into the next room, the bottom of her trousers ablaze. She hobbled into the deserted kitchen and scooped water from the sink over the flames.

An ominous crack had her looking up. The ceiling was throbbing red. The fire had spread to the rooms above. She dashed to the kitchen door, praying it would not be locked. It was not. She stumbled out into brilliant sunshine. Glancing back, the whole farmhouse was ablaze, a thick column of smoke rising in the afternoon air. Barely able to walk, she limped across the yard aiming for a deserted copse. Collapsing on a mound of earth, she let her head droop between her scorched knees and cried.

20.

Annie stared out the car window at the charred ruins and screamed and screamed. It had been no daymare. The fire was real. The screaming was so strident it made her ears rattle and she was going hoarse, but she couldn't stop. It was as if she were being ripped apart by her own voice. Neither Kevin nor Megan could console her. Finally, Megan pulled her out of the car and shook her. "Enough. Whatever it is, screaming won't help. Pull yourself together."

Annie gasped for air, it was more of a sob than a breath, and the screaming stopped after a few hiccoughs. She was still trembling but tears ceased to gush from her eyes. She stared at Megan then Kevin, shuddering as she remembered the bed scene.

"I set fire to the farm," she blurted out, tears flowing again.

"No, you didn't," Megan said with such conviction it brought Annie up short. "This place burnt down long before you came. If you don't believe me, go have a look. Plants are already growing in the ruins."

Annie stared, unbelieving, but she had to admit Megan was right. Brightly coloured flowers dotted the charred ruins.

"So what happened this time?" Megan asked, placing her hands on Annie's shoulders and turning her so they were face to face. So close up, Annie could see the tiny wrinkles that spread from the corners of her eyes, the ones said to come from smiling often. The woman's expression was concerned, but not accusatory.

"You two delivered me to Kard." Kevin made a move to

protest, but Annie ploughed on. "He was waiting for me. Every room in the house had been rigged up as a TV studio, even the toilets, each with its own cameras and lighting."

"This obsession with seeing the world through the lens of television is really strange, but not so surprising," Megan said. "He made his name on TV."

Megan was right. Kard was a creature of television. Most people only knew him from the screen. But even on the news he didn't act himself. He behaved as if he were playing a part. The only time she'd met him face to face, he'd been aping a millionaire gangster, lounging in an armchair with his cigars and whiskey, the whole seduction act. At the time it had seemed frighteningly real, but from a distance it appeared laughable. Even there, in his campaign bus, he'd been orchestrating the scene for a surveillance camera.

"Forget the cameras," Kevin said. "How on earth did you get away?"

She told them about the spilt milk.

"Neat," Megan retorted. "Better clumsy than outright defiant."

Kevin was less content. "Why do I get such lousy roles?"

"Not you," Annie said, frustrated. They would get nowhere if they confused her daymares with reality. "Someone looking like you. You would never act like that."

"So how come you set fire to the place?" Megan asked.

Annie was loathed to describe the bedroom scene, but both Megan and Kevin pestered her, so she gave an expurgated version.

"Bloody pervert," Kevin exclaimed, spitting into the long grasses.

"Maybe," Megan said, thoughtful. "But remember it was no more him getting the pleasure than it was you being abused. This whole set up was designed to destabilise Annie. And that's the odd thing. Why ever did he single you out? Surely there must be a host of other people, at whose hands he has suffered much more than you."

"Maybe he fancies her," Kevin said, grinning. "It wouldn't surprise me."

Annie realised Kevin was making a roundabout compliment, but the idea was so grotesque she couldn't muster a thankful smile. How could a successful bloke of his age with his TV programmes and his political career and all his followers have designs on a young girl that looked more like an effeminate boy than a woman? "This is probably not his work anyway. He'd never have the time. He's too busy flirting with actresses and sprawling on TV sets. I imagine he has a hoard of playwrights who work flat out drafting such scenes, made-to-measure for the people he doesn't like," Annie suggested, and shuddered at the thought. "An army of grey people, like those TV technicians."

"You have too much imagination, young lady," Megan said, grimacing. "You could be writing your own nightmarish scenes. Beware he doesn't try to recruit you."

"If I start to turn grey at the edges," Annie said, not at all joking, "promise you'll jolt me back to my senses, till I get my colour back."

"Sure," Megan said, shaking her head as she fixed the girl, a weary look in her eyes.

"I'm serious," Annie insisted.

Megan sighed. "I promise. Now let's go. We still have to reach the house before night falls."

Annie had been so convinced the farm was their destination, she had completely forgotten they were headed for a safe house.

Climbing into the car, she was relieved to leave the charred ruins, although the smell of burning clung on.

The track Megan was following became less and less distinct till it was little more than a grassy surface between hedgerows. After several miles, meadows gave way to woodlands and the track reappeared as it wove between the trees till they reached a clearing. In the middle stood a rambling cottage. If the farm-house had seemed remote, this cottage was lost to the world. She shuddered to think what it would be like in a snow storm.

"However did you know this was here?" Annie asked as they

drew up next to a second car by the front door.

"Because my mother lives here," Megan replied, pulling on the brake and opening her door.

Annie spun round to stare at Megan. It had never crossed her mind that Megan might have a family, apart from the improbable Kevin that was. Maybe she'd even meet Kevin's dad one day.

A tall lady sporting her hair tied up in a bun wearing a pin-striped suit, a pale blue blouse and a flowery silk scarf opened the cottage door and stepped out. She looked more like Megan's elder sister than her mum. She held her back straight and moved with assurance as she came forward to greet them.

"You must be Annie," she said, looking her over as she shook her hand. Her grip was firm, her hands warm. "Hmmm. You need some toughening up. But it shouldn't take long." She turned to Kevin and tousled her hair, saying, "My favourite boy." At which Kevin beamed and hugged her. "Don't be too hard on Annie, she's special, Granny."

"You know I don't like you calling me Granny. Alice is my name. And don't worry about your special friend. I will be as hard on her as she needs and no more."

Megan got a brief hug. "Good to see you," Megan said. Mother and daughter exchanged a meaningful look then Alice turned back to the children.

"Don't you have a case?" she asked. Annie nodded. "Then fetch it and come inside."

Annie opened the boot and lifted out her case and a car-ryall with extra clothes Megan had loaned her. Shouldering the carryall, she was about to pick up the case when she caught sight of movement amongst the trees out of the corner of her eye. Pretending to do up her shoe laces, she kept an eye on the spot. Once again she glimpsed a shadowy form darting behind a tree but when she looked directly, there was nothing to see.

She didn't dare go closer. There might be all manner of wild animals at loose in such a remote place. Grabbing her case, she dashed for the door and quickly shut and latched it behind her.

21.

"She will be safe here," Alice was saying to Megan as Annie crossed a small hall and entered a large common room housing everything from the dining table to the library with a fireside corner in between and a kitchen range along one wall. "There's no one for miles around."

What about the shadowy beings in the forest Annie wanted to ask, shivering at the thought. Instead she said, "Where should I put these?"

"Down there on the right," Alice told her, pointing to a corridor at the back. "That will be your room." She wondered where Kevin and Megan were going to sleep. Maybe there was some sort of annexe out back.

The cottage was built of wood on a single level with the arching beams of the roof forming the ceiling and green tiles with swirling patterns making up the floor. Down the corridor, the walls and ceiling of which were panelled in a light-coloured wood, she discovered two rooms, one that must have been Alice's and the other was hers. It was at least twice as big as her room at home and a side door led off to a bathroom with a shower and a toilet all of her own. What a luxury! No trace of other people's toothpaste stains in the sink or their discarded underclothes on the floor. Everything was neat and clean and surprisingly modern. Not quite the restrained plushness of Megan's house, but discreetly affluent all the same.

Annie dumped her case and the hold-all in a corner and sat on the bed. Comfortable. Not too soft. Not too hard. She ran her fingers over the sheepskin that lay spread across the eiderdown. Letting herself fall backwards as if in slow motion, she lay on the bed, closing her eyes, and let out a deep sigh. Peace at last.

Back in the common room, Alice was heating water for tea in an ancient kettle on the open range as she chatted with her daughter about politics. Spotting Annie arrive, Megan said, "Alice used to be a history professor at Oxford. Don't get her talking about modern politics, she'll drive you mad."

"I'll have you know, young lady," Alice said, rounding on her daughter. "My lectures at Oxford were very well attended." Turning to Annie, she added. "We should talk about this Kard of yours."

"He's not mine," Annie objected.

"No," Alice said, "but he is your adversary. And the more you know about him, the better chance you have of beating him."

She had never thought of Kard as an adversary. It seemed wrong to set herself on the same level. She'd always had the impression he was the master and she was his victim.

"Where's Kevin?" she asked.

"Gone out in search of the cat," Alice replied, pouring water into the teapot.

"Oh no!" Annie dashed to the hall, her heart pounding, and flung open the front door. She promptly tripped on the doorstep, lurching headfirst into a lavender bush. Picking herself up, she ducked low and, bent over double, ran under cover of the fence. Scanning the trees for any sign of the girl, she saw a wood teeming with grey figures encircling the house.

A scream off to her right had all the figures heading in that direction. It had to be Kevin. Annie rose, vaulted the fence and plunged headlong amongst the trees aiming for the seething mass of grey. A muffled scream came from the crush of bodies.

Annie dived into their midst, lashing out with fists and feet. Their bodies were limp and offered little resistance, but they did retaliate with teeth and claws, nipping and tearing at her hands and arms as she dug her way ever deeper into the living mound.

Somewhere in the swirling mass that engulfed her, her friend was being ripped apart. And only she could save her.

"Annie!" a voice called out from afar. "Come back immediately."

The grey figures shied away, scattering in every direction, leaving Annie alone, lying in a heap on the floor, her body twitching, her hands and feet still flailing although no adversary opposed her.

"Annie, snap out of it," Alice ordered, her voice stern. She held out a hand to Annie, helped her to her feet and led her to an armchair.

"Is Kevin alright?" Annie managed amid gasps for breath. Her arms and face stung where she had been clawed and bitten, although no marks showed from the fight.

"Kevin is fine," Alice said. "She's playing with the cat in my room. It's you I'm worried about."

"I'm OK," Annie said, her voice trembling. She rubbed her arms trying to erase the memory of nails and teeth.

"What was it this time?" Megan asked.

Annie shuddered. "The grey people."

"Grey people?" Alice asked.

"They look grey as if they were only half here, half-alive. Their bodies are limp and hardly react if you hit them, but their nails and teeth are needle sharp."

Alice shot a look at her daughter, but said nothing

"They'd got Kevin and I was trying to save her."

"Megan says this happens often," Alice said.

"This is the fifth or sixth time. I'm not sure. Sometimes it lasts longer. Your voice seemed to chase them away."

"Are there always these grey people?

"No. Only just now and at the farmhouse."

"Here," Megan said, handing her a cup of tea. "You can talk about it later." She took Alice aside and the two set about preparing vegetables in the kitchen area. Annie sank back in her armchair and stared unseeingly at the unlit fire.

Kevin arrived cuddling a cat that purred noisily. She looked questioningly at her over the bundle of fur. Annie burst into tears. "Looks like you are the one who needs to be cuddled and stroked." She put the cat on a carpet, much to its annoyance, and perched on the edge of Annie's armchair. Slinging an arm round her shoulders, she nuzzled the top of Annie's head.

"Can you two lay the table?" Megan said. "We need to eat before we head home."

"Home?" Annie asked, alarmed.

"Kevin and I have to be home not too late." Megan replied. "She's got school tomorrow morning."

"Mum," Kevin exclaimed. "Can't I stay a few days to keep Annie company?"

"No. You've got tests coming up soon."

Kevin groaned.

"What about me?" Annie asked, hearing her own desperation. "I've got tests too."

"You are to stay with Alice. I'm sure she'll find ways of testing you, even if it is only your patience she'll be testing."

22.

Annie sat in an armchair by the fireside, a book open in her lap, her finger marking her place. Only the crackling of the fire and the scratching of Alice's pen at the kitchen table could be heard. With Kevin and Megan gone the house felt empty. Even the cat had deserted her.

She read another paragraph and with it finished the first chapter. Alice had suggested the book, saying, "If you want to get the better of Kard, you have to understand what he does." She hadn't realised how complicated the country's governing structures were. Kard had jokingly said he would be the first and last president of Great Britain. The idea was absurd. It would undermine centuries of history and cause long-standing institutions to crumble. Many people would suffer because of it. Yet thousands and thousands took his suggestion at face value. Were they so dissatisfied that they would wreck the system?

"Why does he bother?" Annie asked, thinking out loud. "There's no way he can become president."

"Are you sure he wants to be president?" Alice asked, looking up from her writing.

"He says he does."

Alice got to her feet and came and sat opposite Annie. "But does he?"

Their discussion shuttled backwards and forwards weighing the advantages of claiming to want an impossible post and the disadvantages of actually getting it. After a long while, Alice stood, massaging the small of her back as she straightened up. "Enough. It's time you went to bed. Me too."

"But we've reached no conclusion," Annie protested.

"All the better to keep an open mind," Alice said. "Good night." And she was gone, leaving Annie alone, seated by the fireside staring at the flames.

A slight shift in the air, like a faint draught from an open window elsewhere in the house, had Annie looking up. There in the armchair where Alice had been now sat Kard. She sucked in a sharp breath, horrified. How had he got in?

"You should fit better locks on the doors," he said, leaning forward and lowering his voice as if they were coconspirators. He stretched out an arm, his podgy fingers reaching for her. She cringed, afraid he was going to touch her. Instead, he caught hold of the book and yanked it from her grasp. Letting it fall open at random, he glanced at the page. "Load of rubbish." And tossed it back to her.

"Have you even read it?" she asked, breaking her own newly made vow not to respond.

"You don't need to read that sort of book to know what it's about. Just some dimwit parading as an expert. Stuffing people's heads with misconceptions. I know far more about government in Britain than such self-proclaimed experts will ever know."

"I thought you were a businessman."

He swelled his chest, pulling a cigar from his pocket. "I am. One of the most successful. That's why I know so much about running things. It's my experience in the field that counts. Not some trumped-up theory written behind a desk."

She was going to tell him not to smoke indoors, but it was already too late. He was sucking on the cigar, puffing out dense clouds of pungent smoke into Alice's spotless home. Annie coughed. He grinned, clearly pleased with his efforts and balanced the glowing cigar on the arm of the chair. She got to her feet and gingerly picked up the thing between thumb and forefinger, half expecting him to stop her, and carried it at arm's length to the sink where she doused it with water.

"Is that all you do, start fires?" she asked, turning back to see he had already lit a second one.

"Need I remind you that it was you who started the last fire?"

Hold on a moment. What the hell was she doing chatting with the man that had destroyed her family, her reputation, her future and now was bent on making her go soft in the head? She turned away, walked to the door that opened onto the back corridor and was about to slam it when she remembered Alice and clicked it closed.

Her bedroom door was ajar. Suspecting a trap, she pushed it open a cautious inch at a time, ready to hammer on Alice's door if ever. She needn't have bothered. Kard was reclined in a chair by her bed, his boots perched on the eiderdown.

"Cute room," he said conversationally, nosing around under her pillow. She took a step closer, about to object, but he fished out the pyjamas she had hidden there. "Pink," he said, holding them up to admire as he made appreciative clicking sounds with his tongue. Then he flung them at her. "I'd like to see you in those." As if to underline his interest, he pulled a miniature camera from his pocket and began filming. She turned her back on him, leaving the pyjamas where they'd fallen.

She toyed with the idea of locking herself in the bathroom, but he probably had some way of picking locks or, worse, walking through walls. If she returned to the common room, he would surely follow. She could simply climb into bed, pull the eiderdown over her head and try to drift off, but she doubted she'd be able to sleep with him in the room. Not to mention what he might get up to if she did manage to fall asleep. Then she had a brain wave. At least she hoped it was. She got to her feet and folding her hands behind her back she began a speech.

"There are a good many reasons why Britain has no president and never will..."

He pocketed the camera and looked at her incredulous then started to laugh, only to stop. She imagined she was addressing a giant crowd and enumerated as many reasons as she could remember from her reading. "You're babbling girl," he said, getting to his feet. But she continued to talk, ignoring him. She imagined the crowd cheering her and jeering him. "What rubbish," he spluttered. "A girl like you can't possibly understand such things. You flunked out of school."

That hurt. But it was his fault if she couldn't attend school. She knew he would try to distract her or worse, upset her, but she held on to her speech like a buoy in a storm. "Don't let yourself be deceived by someone who pretends to want to be president when in fact it's the last thing he wants ..."

She didn't have time to explain. Kard grabbed the pillow and bounded across the room, knocking her to the floor. He straddled her, pinning her arms with his knees and placed the pillow over her nose and mouth. She kicked out, trying to roll over. But he was heavy. And the pressure increased. The more she struggled, the more she gasped for breath. Her lungs heaved, desperate for air, and came up short. Fighting was useless. This was it. The end.

Then abruptly she heard a snarl close to her ear, followed by a scream and the weight lifted. The pillow fell to one side and air rushed into her lungs. She almost fainted with relief. Rolling onto her side, she gulped in air, her chest heaving, a roaring sound in her head. When she finally opened her eyes, she saw half-closed, slits looking down at her. The cat. It sat on its haunches, licking its paws which were red with blood.

23.

Annie didn't even try to sleep, she was too on edge, instead she sat on the side of the bed, her feet dangling, trying not to replay the scene that had just happened. Her pyjamas no longer lay in a heap on the floor, but peaked out from under her pillow where she'd left them. Yet the idea of wearing them after Kard had handled them disgusted her. Seeing the cat curled up on her bed was some comfort. She massaged the back of its neck absently. What she needed was someone to talk to. Several times she extracted her phone from its hiding place intending to call Kevin, but then put it away. Pulling it out once more, she glanced at the time displayed on the tiny screen. It was late. Too late. She hit the dial button. To hell with it.

"Kevin?" she whispered.

"I thought you'd never call," the girl replied. "What kept you so long?"

She groaned. "I had a visit."

"More grey people?"

"No. The man himself."

"What did he want?"

Annie sighed. "To chat."

Kevin spluttered. "The cheek. What did you do?"

"Tried not to talk to him. But it's difficult with such an annoying lump and he followed me around. Walls and doors can't keep him out."

"Is he still there?" Kevin sounded alarmed.

"Nope. The cat chased him away." She thought of the blood

on its paws and wondered exactly what the cat had done. However did the cat manage to be in both this world and her daymares? It shouldn't have been possible.

"Wow. Three cheers for Scrubby."

"Is that his name?"

"Her. Yes."

She held out a hand to the cat. "Scrubby," she said and the cat licked her fingers.

"Do you miss me?" Kevin asked.

Annie almost choked on the question. "How can you ask? I'd give anything to have you lying next to me in bed." The thought alone was comforting. At last she'd be able to sleep.

Kevin made a sound like blowing a kiss with a slurping noise at the end.

Annie chuckled. "I said bed, not table. My night visitor would be disappointed if you gobbled me up." Kevin was multiplying the gurgling and lip-smacking concert over the phone. "Enough. You need to sleep. Lucky you. You have school tomorrow."

Kevin groaned. "Wanna take my place?"

"I'd be delighted. But why don't you like school?"

"Cause it sucks."

"That's not a valid reason."

"You are already beginning to sound like my grandmother. I must come and rescue you immediately."

Annie giggled. "I like her. She's good company." She thought of their conversation about governing. The challenge had thrilled her. "In a demanding sort of way."

"Oh no!" Kevin groaned theatrically. "There's no hope for you. Next thing we know, you'll be going round giving speeches for the good of the world."

Annie spluttered. "How did you know?"

"It's the logical next step."

"No. I mean. I did give a speech. To him. To drive him away. I was so convincing he tried to suffocate me with my pillow."

"I think I'd do the same." Kevin chuckled.

"Don't joke about it. He almost killed me." She stared at the pillow and felt her throat tighten. "I thought I was a goner," she whispered, tears welling in her eyes.

"Oh Annie. I'm so sorry. I didn't know."

"How could you?"

"Oh my God!" Kevin exclaimed.

Now Annie was worried. "What's the matter?"

"They've torched Marcie's."

"How do you know?"

"It's on the late night news. They are interviewing Kard."

"Did he do it?"

"Of course not. He wouldn't dirty his hands. No. It was a gang of youths sporting 'Keep London Straight' badges." There was a pause, presumably she was listening. "He's shameless!" Kevin exclaimed.

"Tell me," Annie said, frustrated at not being able to see or hear.

"He says he's against such violence, but it is understandable when places like Marcie's are perverting our youth and undermining our society with their crooked ways."

"What a two-faced bigot."

"Can you kill him next time he drops by?"

Annie was shocked at the suggestion. "I couldn't do that. And anyway, I don't think it would make any difference. Not while it's in my daymares."

"Ah. Your Grey World."

"If it weren't for the vivid colours, that would be a good name for it." Annie shoved the pillow onto the floor and curled up on the bed next to the cat. "Tell me a bedtime story. Maybe that would help me get to sleep."

"Do you know the one about Sleeping Beauty?" Kevin asked.

Annie smiled. "I bet it is about a girl disguised as a boy that kisses the sleeping princess back to life."

"You are too clever for me," Kevin complained.

"Go ahead. Tell me," Annie said, closing her eyes.

"Did no one teach you not to sleep in your clothes," Alice asked as she pulled back the curtains. Judging from the light streaming in the window, she'd slept late.

"It's a long story," Annie replied, embarrassed.

"Good. I like stories. You can tell me over breakfast." Stories. She vaguely remembered the beginning of Kevin's. Her life seemed to be bound tight with stories. Most of them not her own. "And have a shower before you change your clothes."

The smell of freshly baked bread greeted her in the common room. The table was laden with tiny pots of jam and butter in its dish, and a jug of milk alongside another with orange juice, and a basket of dried fruit and nuts and a bowl with a mixture Alice called Muesli. At home everyone ate cereal when there was any, if not toast and marmalade and maybe margarine. Butter would have been a luxury. The idea of having a choice seemed quite foreign. Like a posh hotel she'd only ever seen on TV.

"You wanted to tell me why you slept in your clothes," Alice prompted.

"I had a visit," Annie began.

Alice glanced around, looking worried. "I heard no one."

"You wouldn't have. I was in what Kevin calls my Grey World. That other place ruled by Kard. When I'm there, I'm not here. Time spent in the Grey World takes no time here. Even if you had been sitting by my bed, you wouldn't have noticed anything." Annie shuddered remembering that was exactly where Kard had been.

Alice sat listening as Annie told her tale, at no time interrupting. "I like your speech," she said when Annie fell silent. "I told you knowing more about him would help you win."

Annie screwed up her face. If anything, her knowledge had fuelled Kard's anger and almost got her killed. "Win. Sure. Like being suffocated."

"He got angry. He who loses his temper is always in a weaker position. Intuitively he must have felt his weakness. That's why he resorted to brute force."

Annie thought of the gang that had set fire to Marcie's. They too had used brute force. Did that mean that deep down they felt weaker? "But how do you react to brute force?"

24.

Annie's phone vibrated before Alice, who was looking for a quote, could answer her question. It was Kevin. Wasn't she supposed to be at school?

"What's up?" Annie asked, walking to the kitchen window, not wanting to disturb Alice.

"Got kicked out of school."

"What?" she exclaimed. Several scenarios shot through her mind. All of them had to do with Kard.

Alice was looking at her over a book, her eyebrows raised in question. "It's Kevin," Annie explained. "She got expelled. No idea why." Alice shook her head and went back to her reading.

"Mum said I did it deliberately, to be with you. But I swear I didn't."

"So what happened?"

"There's this clique of girls, the *crème de la crème*, always whispering behind people's backs, or sucking up to teachers. Well, one of them, a poisonous bitch, called you a crooked whore. I said it was all lies. I was no better, according to her. So I bonked her on the nose. That had the whole pack turn on me. They all have bloody noses or black eyes to show for it."

"And you?"

There was a pause. Annie imagined the girl examining herself in the mirror. "A black eye, a split lip and a bruise on my chin, not to mention various teeth marks and scratches on my arms and neck." Judging from her tone, she was inordinately proud of her wounds like a treasure trove brought back from a war. "So what are you going to do now?"

Kevin chuckled. "Come and annoy you."

"Seriously?"

"Mum won't let me come, but I was thinking of sneaking away."

"You must be joking. How would you get here? We are miles from anywhere."

"Maybe you can convince Granny to come and fetch me."

Annie looked at Alice who was scribbling notes in her book. "I doubt it."

"Please."

"Okay. I'll try." She didn't hold out much hope as she hung up.

"Well?" Alice asked, closing her book.

"She got in a fight because a girl called me a whore. The fight turned into a brawl, with a group of girls retaliating."

"And?"

"I am to convince you to fetch her." Annie held up a placating hand. "I know. I know. It's a silly idea."

"On the contrary. I was looking for an excuse to take you on a short visit. We can pick Kevin up on the way back. Ring her back and tell her the good news."

Annie stared at the woman in disbelief. It had not once crossed her mind Alice would accept. "But her mum will never agree."

"Don't worry about that. She may be a lawyer, but I can still run rings round her, when I want."

"I don't understand. I was sure you'd refuse."

"Do you not want her to come?" Alice asked, getting to her feet.

"Of course I do. I couldn't have asked for better. But..."

"My reaction caught you on the wrong foot. When you expect resistance, you act accordingly. But if you misjudge and the person steps aside or moves in your direction, you end up flat on your face."

Annie shook her head. Not out of refusal but disbelief. "I

am constantly on the wrong foot with you."

"Good." Alice grinned. "Let's go."

"But I haven't phoned." She felt stressed by the sudden changes. She had barely settled after breakfast than she was being rushed off.

"You can do so in the car."

"Hold on a moment. You haven't answered my question: How do we react to brute force?"

Alice frowned. Had Annie gone too far with her question? It didn't always do to force the hand of grown-ups. Especially not a university professor. Adults were unpredictable and could get irritated or angry for no apparent reason. Especially those who were convinced they were important. She had some teachers like that. Then the frown gave way to a broad grin. The old woman was playing with her. Not to belittle or poke fun as was the case with many adults, but because she enjoyed surprising the person she was talking to, she enjoyed having fun.

"Okay. You are right," Alice said. "Let's talk while we clear the breakfast things away."

Annie screwed the caps on the little pots of jam and marmalade and looked questionably at Alice, as if to ask, 'where should I put them?'. The woman pointed to a cupboard while she poured the remains of tea on the potted plants. "Kevin reacted with brute force and it got her expelled," Alice said as she put the butter, milk and orange juice in the fridge, chuckling as she did. "Knowing her, it was probably what she wanted. But no doubt she got hurt and others did too."

Annie repeated the list of injuries, saying. "She seemed pleased."

Alice nodded. "The girl who taunted Kevin knew she would retaliate, probably violently. Kevin was trapped. Her situation was intolerable. When people are cornered, they often react by striking out." She ran a cloth under the tap, wrung it out and threw the thing to Annie. "No doubt the headmistress was cornered too. Her hand was forced. She probably didn't want to expel the girl, for all her railing against school, Kevin is a good student, but the head felt compelled to do so. She couldn't allow fighting. If everyone resorted to fists to resolve disputes, school would degenerate into a dangerous jungle."

Rather than answering her question, Annie felt confused at Alice's words. "But I don't see how this answers the question." She immediately regretted her comment. Once again she'd … What had she done? Tried to force the direction of play.

Alice halted stacking the dishes in the sink and turned on Annie, her hands on her hips. She was playing again Annie realised with relief and burst out laughing. Alice smiled too.

"Let me don my professor's gown." She picked up a tea towel and flung it around her shoulders. Annie laughed at her antics. She liked the woman. Being with her was a real pleasure even if she was constantly caught off balance.

"There are several ways to react to brute force. The first is not to react. But brute force doesn't want to be ignored. Doing so may well make the violence worse. Another way involves responding with force. A tooth for a tooth, as they say. Apart from releasing pent up aggression, brute force seeks to awake the brute in others."

Annie had been in several fights at school. Violence quickly became its own master.

"Have you heard of Aikido?"

Annie wasn't sure if it was a Japanese form of combat or a chocolate coated biscuit. She shook her head.

"It's a martial art. When someone attacks you in Aikido, instead of opposing force with force, you step aside and let the unchecked force floor the attacking person. In Aikido, to attack is often synonymous with losing."

"Is that what nonviolence is?" She'd heard about Mahatma Ghandi at school.

Annie pulled the tea cloth from her shoulders with a flourish. "Answering that would take ages and we do have to go. Remind me to loan you a book on the subject when we get back."

25.

The dress, which was a faded blue colour, was more like a long-sleeved artist's smock, reaching to just above her knees. She would have felt cold and exposed wearing it, had she not pulled on dark blue leggings underneath. Her movements were freer than in her usual jeans and t-shirt, but that didn't make her feel any more comfortable. Alice, who had a wardrobe full of what she called 'her disguises', had insisted she be dressed more like a girl. She'd wanted Annie to don a wig. There were several in the wardrobe. But Annie had refused. Instead she wore a matching blue Tammy that covered most of her short hair.

As they drove along the barely marked track through the forest, Annie phoned Kevin to share the good news. The girl squealed with delight and promised to give Annie a kiss for managing it. The prospect of a kiss from Kevin filled her with mixed feelings. She wasn't sure she wanted to go the whole hog. "When you were a girl," Annie asked once she got off the phone, "did you ever kiss another girl?"

Alice burst out laughing and couldn't stop. Annie was worried at first that they might drive into a tree, such was the violence of the fit of laughter. It was just the kind of thing Kard would do in one of his daymares, make them have an accident and blame it on her. Then she began to feel offended. Was she so ridiculous? She had never talked to anyone about liking other girls. To her relief, Alice took a deep breath and grinned. "It's Kevin, isn't it?"

Was it so obvious?

"Don't get your back up," Alice said, stopping at the farm gate. Annie jumped out and held it open while Alice drove past. She was about the secure the gate when the earth trembled beneath her feet. Earthquakes were not common in that area and this was the first she'd ever felt. She looked up, wanting to ask Alice if she'd felt it, only to see the car speeding away down the road.

"Blasted Kard!" she swore.

Startled by a loud snort close by, she spun round to find an immense bull, nostrils flaring, its bloodshot eyes devouring her. She glanced over her shoulder, half-expecting to find a second one on the far side of the gate. But there was none.

The beast raked the ground with its hoof and lowered its horns as if preparing to charge. Annie eased back against the gate and raised a foot onto the first rung. The bull took a step closer then, tensing its muscles, charged. Annie clambered up the gate and crouching on the top rung, readied to jump. To her horror she spotted a knot of snakes writhing on the ground below. The bull rammed into the gate shattering it. She screamed and tumbled backwards into the slithering mass.

A hand snaked down and grabbed her by the arm, pulling her to her feet. "You slipped," Alice said. "Are you alright?"

"Hell no!" She shuddered, still sensing the snakes slither over her arm. "That bloody Kard!" Her back arched forward and her stomach heaved making her terrified it would begin again. Instead she threw up her breakfast onto the lush grass by the gate post.

"Finished?" Alice asked.

Annie nodded and took the hanky she was offered.

Once in the car, she turned to Alice, saying, "Why did you laugh back there?"

"Laugh?"

"When I asked about kissing Kevin?"

"Ah. That. Because Kevin asked me the same the other day..."

"Kevin?" Annie interrupted, finding it hard to believe.

"I know she hangs out at Marcie's and behaves as if she's had loads of girlfriends, but she's really very shy and not as well versed as you might think."

Annie fell silent. Alice's words were completely at odds with her vision of Kevin. She had imagined her having tons of experience messing with girls. Adjusting was going to take a while. So Kevin, for all her show of confidence, might be as hesitant and unsure as she was. That changed a lot.

The drive through the outskirts of London was uneventful, although traffic was busy with motorists avoiding the A1 as they started their working week. Alice was silent, concentrating on the road. Annie stared out the window. Hitchin, Stevenage, Welwyn Garden City, Potter's Bar, Barnet, Cockfosters. A litany of place names that had been part of her life as a Londoner but which she had never visited.

Alice swung round a double roundabout and returned the way they'd come. Had she taken a wrong turning? Or was she lost? She still hadn't said where they were going. Annie's was beginning to suspect they were going nowhere special when Alice eased the car into the only free parking slot across the road from a police station. The sight of several policemen exiting the building had Annie in a panic. What if they spotted her? They would surely recognise her. She breathed a sigh of relief when they peered in the window of the McDonald's next door then entered.

Alice walked Annie a short distance along the pavement only to halt at a pillar box in front of a post office and pull out a wad of envelopes from her bag. Annie imagined she was going to post them, but instead she handed them to her, saying, "Could you get stamps for these and post them for me? I've got to go to Smith's." She pointed off down the road. "They've got a book for me." Alice gave her a couple of bank notes. "This should do for the stamps. Meet you at the car in ten minutes."

The post office was busy for early on a Monday afternoon. It was one of those cram-packed branches that sold everything from stationery to birthday cards to premium bonds to lottery tickets. It even exchanged foreign currency. Annie joined the orderly queue snaking its way back from the two counters channelled by a series of barriers. An old man took a short cut in front of the barriers and pushed between her and the person in front then went and sat on a chair by the wall. He had the sort of face you remembered, powdery skinned, yet all gnarled and gnome-like.

"Have you seen what she's wearing," a girl behind her whispered. "Looks like she pick the stuff up at a jumble sale." Annie heard several girls snigger. They must have been talking about her. She turned to glare at them but all three looked away. Cowards! They were several years younger than her, dressed in navy blazers and skirts that looked crisp and new, not at all like the frayed jacket she wore to school. Their starched pink blouses were open at the neck under a navy V neck trimmed in pink. No socks around their ankles for them. She didn't recognise the school crest. Probably a private one.

The queue moved forward. She was next. The old man got to his feet, sauntered over and, standing in front of her, gave her a malicious smile. "I'm next," she said, suspecting he was going to jump the queue.

"No," the man said with all the conviction of someone sure he was right. "I've been sitting over there waiting."

She recalled him entering after her. "You are mistaken," she insisted. She could feel the eyes of the girls behind her boring into her back. The place was now free at the counter and he moved forward to fill it.

"What a cheek," she exclaimed, suspecting his whole act had been deliberate.

"If you must be so petty," he muttered and stepped aside to let her through.

She refused. She could hear the girls sniggering again. She didn't want to be seen as petty. But she was furious, feeling cheated, and wanted to lash out. "Do you make up such stories every day?"

He spun round and fixed her with his beady eyes. She was sure she detected triumph in them. "You kids." He spat the word at her. "No respect for your elders."

"Not for liars like you. Do you get your kicks from tormenting young people?"

He raised his hand to hit her, but Alice, who had entered unseen by Annie, grabbed his arm and twisted it behind his back. "I saw the whole scene," she said, her voice calm and authoritative. "The girl is right and you should be ashamed of yourself. Now get out before I kick you out."

The man's face twisted with rage, but he did as he was told, muttering "Bitch."

Once out on the pavement, Annie glanced around to check the old man wasn't waiting to ambush them. He wasn't. "Did you really see him come in?"

"Of course not, but when confronted with an inveterate liar, why not beat him at his own game?"

26.

The car swung through the wrought-iron gates into the park, where a large sign announced the name and nature of the institution. The former was concealed by foliage, while the latter was plain to see, Psychiatric Hospital. The words filled Annie with panic. Her doubts and fears came rushing back. So Alice had made up her mind she was crazy and intended to have her locked up. In a horrible way, it all made sense. No wonder she hadn't wanted to say where they were going.

As they wound their way under a dense canopy of trees, Annie could feel mounting resignation numb her whole being. She glanced longingly out the back window at the world beyond the gates. She was partly reassured to see that the gates did not snap shut. Reaching the end of the drive, they emerged from the wood in front of a mansion surrounded by a grassy expanse that extended as far as the eye could see. Alice parked the car at the foot of the steps to the main entrance and turned to face Annie.

"Are you alright?" she asked. "You've gone chalk white."

Annie stared at her horrified. "You wouldn't," she managed to say, her voice shaky.

Alice frowned. "Wouldn't what?"

"Have me locked up."

"Ah," she said, her features drawn as if she were suffering herself. "No. I would never, ever do that. I swear." She stretched out a hand and stroked Annie's cheek with such tenderness tears sprang to Annie's eyes. "So unsure," Alice muttered and lent across to kiss Annie on the forehead, then hugged her. "That

Kard should be severely punished for what he's doing to you. You are such an intelligent, creative person, you deserve so much better."

Alice leant back and stared out the window as if seeing another time, another place. "When I was your age, I was a brilliant pupil but I had a lot of difficulties with my fellows. I would stamp and shout and smash things. My parents were at a loss what to do. A 'friendly' doctor suggested a stay in a clinic much worse than this one. There were high walls and many locked doors and horrendous treatment it wouldn't do to talk about. It was a nightmare. I spent two months shut away till they finally let me go home. So, rest assured, I would never, ever hand you over to a psychiatric clinic."

Annie was touched by Alice's story. She could vividly imagine the anger and frustration not to mention the doubt of someone locked away for being at odds with those around them, all because she was more gifted. To a much lesser degree she had been frustrated by the slowness at school. She was always eager to push on, to learn more, to explore, to rise to challenges but, despite the goodwill of teachers and students alike, everything about school held her back. That she was not just making it up was confirmed by the inspectors' report which said more needed to be done to encourage the brighter pupils in the school.

"So why are we here?" she asked.

"To meet a very good friend of mine. I thought you might appreciate knowing him."

Annie was intrigued, but Alice would say no more. No doubt a fellow professor who had studied psychiatry.

The receptionist greeted Alice like an old acquaintance, calling her 'Professor'. "You know your way," she said, pointing to one of several doors. On the far side, a corridor stretched away into the distance with door-upon-door on both sides. Annie halted, feeling apprehensive again. Being shut up in such a place could so easily become her lot.

Alice held out her hand and Annie took it. She was reassured to have this woman at her side, on her side. They ambled down interminable corridors. Occasionally they met people, some in white coats, others not. They nodded to Alice, smiled at Annie and continued on their way.

Stopping at a door, Alice knocked and, at a muffled call from within, they entered. It didn't look like a professor's office. It was furnished with a single bed, a bare table and a chair. In one corner was a wash basin next to which a towel hung drying. The walls were devoid of paintings or photos or even hard-won diplomas. Standing in one corner by the window staring out was a boy hardly older than herself.

"Don, I have brought someone to meet you," Alice said.

The boy turned to face them and advanced cautiously towards Alice. She opened her arms and hugged him, the two remaining a long moment unspeaking in their embrace. When he stepped back Alice said, "This is Annie."

Don stared at Annie. It was only at that moment she noticed the opalescent colour of his eyes. He was blind. He held out his hand for her to shake. The whole situation was so strange she hesitated a moment, then placing her hand in his, was about to shake it when he spoke. His voice was deep for his age, it seemed to spring from his boots. "You are beset by troubles, Annie."

She stood perplexed at his words, her hand still grasped in his. Surely he must be guessing at her situation. She wondered why he was locked up. Maybe he took himself for some sort of seer. The irony of it pained her.

"I am here, Annie, because the outside world is too cluttered and busy for me." That he answered her unspoken question startled her. Maybe he could read minds. The thought troubled her. "Too many impressions and I get overwhelmed, my brain disconnects and my body goes wild."

He clasped her hand between both of his and stood unmoving for a long time. His touch was not unpleasant. There was no clinging yet his grasp was firm. She looked at his face, feeling embarrassed, knowing he could not see her. It was almost as if she were stealing a peek. She would have liked to say he was handsome, what a tragedy that would have been, but his face was plain and were it not for his eyes, he would never have stood out in a crowd.

"You are brimming over with stories," Don said, after a long silence. "They come tumbling out of you like a bustling crowd, jostling each other, vying for attention. No wonder you fear you might be going mad. You are not mad, Annie. You are special. Like me. But different. You are lucky. You won't have to lock yourself away from the world. There are ways to channel stories and control them before they take over, before others use them against you."

Too late for that. Kard had already taken control of her life.

"You are mistaken if you think others can take over your stories. You are far stronger than them. Their stories are paltry compared to yours. What you see as your weakness is really an immense strength. You must awaken to the riches that reside in you. Your troubles will not fall away when you are aware of that, but you will be more in control of your life."

He let go of her hand, leaving her feeling bereft. She was unsure what to do or say. His words have left her even more perplexed. "Thank you," she said, her voice sinking to a whisper.

He nodded and, turning his back on them, walked to the bed, lay down and curled up. Annie looked to Alice for a clue how to react. Alice just nodded sagely like Don. "Thank you Don," she said. "Sleep well."

Alice opened the door and they both stepped out. Once again Alice offered her hand, it was nothing like Don's seeing hand, but it was warm and reassuring. Annie took it and they walked side by side back down the corridors.

27.

"What kept you so long?" Kevin asked as she opened the door and pulled Annie in a hug that would have done a bear proud. "I love you too," Annie said, gasping for air.

"As do I," Alice said, shooing them inside. "Is Megan here?" Kevin finally let go of Annie and turned to Alice.

"No," Alice said, holding up a placating hand. "You don't need to crush my bones. I am already convinced you love me. Just answer my question."

"She had an urgent call and went out to meet someone."

Alice looked concerned. "Did you tell her we were coming?"

Kevin looked sheepish. "I tried." She threw up her arms. "But whatever happened over the phone had her preoccupied. She hurried out before I could tell her."

Alice pulled off her coat and hung it on the coat stand in the hall. "We'll just have to wait till she gets back. We can't add a missing child to the list of her worries. Be a love, Kevin, make us some tea. I'm parched."

Kevin grabbed Annie by the hand and pulled her along the corridor to the kitchen.

Annie sank into one of the whicker chairs grouped around the low kitchen table while Kevin put the kettle on. Late afternoon light streamed in the bay window behind her, warming everything it touched. Kevin had one glorious black eye and her lower lip was split and swollen. There were several nasty scratches down her neck and on the back of her hands. "So you fought for my honour?"

Kevin grinned then grimaced. She pulled a tissue from a box on the work surface and dabbed her lip. It was bleeding again. "You should have seen me. I was magnificent."

"Did anyone film?" It was meant as a joke, but the moment she asked she shuddered, thinking of Kard. It was the sort of thing he would do. Was she becoming like him?

"Na." Kevin sounded disappointed. The kettle whistled and she poured water on the tea.

"Have you two got lost out there?" Alice called from the front room.

"Coming Granny." A malicious smile formed on her lips. She knew full well Alice hated being called that.

Annie carried the tea through on a tray and Kevin did the honours serving.

Alice examined the girl's lip, her expression grave. "It's probably not a good idea to do too much kissing with a lip like that if you want it to heal."

Annie blushed despite the fact she knew Alice was pulling Kevin's leg. She was getting to know the old woman. Kevin, however, was taken in. "Surely a little kiss would do it good."

"No," Alice insisted, her face deadly serious. "Not for a week at least. Or maybe two."

Kevin suddenly caught on and shook her finger at Alice. "You naughty old lady. Torturing young girls. We'll have to report you." She looked to Annie for support, but all she could do was giggle. "Look at that. One day with you, Alice, and you've already turned her against me."

Annie blew Kevin a kiss which seemed to mollify her.

The phone rang, interrupting their little scenario.

"Kevin Wainsdorf," she answered.

There was a long silence as Kevin listened. The longer the silence lasted, the paler she got. "That's awful," she said, tears welling in her eyes. "Can I come and see her?" The person must have said no because Kevin protested.

Alice took the phone from her. "Professor Wainsdorf here. What happened to my daughter?"

Annie went to Kevin and took her in her arms. "The bastards beat her up," Kevin muttered through her tears. "All she wanted to do was help others."

Alice hung up. "Get your coats. We are going to the hospital."

The entrance to the hospital reminded Annie of a provincial airport. A sort of Dinky Toy Luton. All brick and glass and gay colours and quite soulless. The sliding doors followed by a short corridor lined with notice boards led them to a shining new area generously furnished in pale wood with soft lighting. Behind the chest-high counter was a pastel-coloured mural stretching the length of the wall. The overall effect was calming. Not at all like the incessant buzz of an airport and quite at odds with Alice who was electric, armed and ready to fire.

Alice homed in on the receptionist half-hidden behind the counter. "Where is Mrs. Wainsdorf?" she asked, in no mood to bother with civilities.

Her lips pursed, the young woman squinted at her screen. "Wainsdorf. She's in intensive care. I'm sorry. No visitors are allowed."

"Listen," Alice said, leaning over the counter that smelt of freshly varnished wood, till she was almost nose to nose with the receptionist. "I am one of the board of governors of this hospital. If you don't tell me where my daughter is right away, you won't have a job tomorrow."

The receptionist cowered as far as her chair would let her, a frightened look on her face. "I'm so sorry. I didn't know. Yes. Down the corridor to the right. The name is on the door."

"Thank you," Alice said and marched away, the two girls trotting after.

Megan was the only patient in a small room designed for two with a window overlooking the car park. There was also an emergency exit opening onto a balcony that ran the length of the building with a ramp nearby leading down to a place reserved for ambulances. The equipment looked modern, but the room had clearly not yet been renovated.

When Alice pulled aside the curtain that surrounded the bed by the window, Kevin's mum turned her eyes to see who was there, then they fluttered closed and her head sank deeper into the pillow. A large bandage obscured much of her head. One of her arms and the opposite leg were also bandaged.

"Oh Mum," Kevin said sitting down in the one chair and laying her head on Megan's only free hand. "What have they done to you?"

"Kard's lot?" Alice asked.

Megan remained unresponding.

A doctor hurried in, his white coat fluttering after him. The receptionist trailed behind. "Good afternoon, Professor. I'm sorry, but we do not allow visitors onto intensive care wards, even if they are on the board. This woman has been given sedatives because she was agitated. You won't be able to talk to her anyway."

"Can't I just sit by my mum's bed?" Kevin asked, tears in her eyes.

"That's not possible. What's more we have had strict instructions from the police not to let anyone visit her.

"Why so?" Alice asked.

"I heard she was a suspect in an attack."

Annie was confused. How could Megan be a suspect when she had clearly been attacked? She thought back over the last few minutes, checking if there had been any sign she'd stepped into one of Kard's charming scenarios. She would almost have preferred if she had. No. This was 'real'.

"What attack?" Alice asked.

"A group of young people were attacked with pepper spray."

Alice burst out laughing, startling Annie as much as the doctor. Alice laughed often. But Annie had never heard such a bitter laugh. "Haven't you got your story a bit muddled?" Alice asked. "Judging from the injuries, it seems much more likely the person who was attacked is lying here in this bed."

"I'm sorry, I understand how it must look, but the inspector was insistent. I must ask you to leave. Otherwise I will have to call the police."

"Go ahead," Alice said. "I am intrigued to hear their side to the story."

"I'm afraid it won't do you much good," he said.

"I'm sure you are right," Alice replied. "But I will try my luck."

The doctor shrugged and left with the receptionist, ordering her to call the police.

"Mum always carried pepper spray in her pocket," Kevin said once they were alone. "Just in case. If she had to use the stuff, it was because she was being attacked."

"It's the sedatives that worry me," Alice said, staring at Megan's limp features. "Depending on what you give a person they can be confused and frightened, unable to make sense of questions they are asked. That's how totalitarian governments wring confessions from the opposition."

Kevin turned to Annie and whispered, "You still got that phone?" Annie nodded and handed it to her. Kevin took the phone and withdrew to a corner. Annie heard her talking earnestly but could not make out the words. When Kevin returned the phone, Annie looked at her with raised eyebrows.

"I phoned the network," the girl whispered.

"Network?"

"The Girls' Emergence Network."

28.

"I gave strict instructions that this suspect was to have no visits," the inspector said as he shoved aside the curtain and barged into the cubicle. Dressed in a drab grey suit, he was followed by a policeman and a policewoman in uniform.

Annie recognised the man immediately. He'd taken part in the raid on Marcie's. He'd been at the lake too. She edged behind Kevin, hoping he hadn't spotted her. Kevin must have recognised him because she shielded Annie who turned and found a gap in the curtain.

"Suspect?" Alice said. "The only thing that is suspect in this room is your behaviour."

"Professor Wainsdorf, isn't it?" Annie wondered how he knew Alice's name. Maybe the doctor had told him. Or Kard. "Do not make such wild accusations," he continued. "It belittles you."

"You should know, Inspector. You are adept at belittling people."

"Enough. This policewoman will accompany you to the station for questioning," the man said.

"I am not leaving this room as long as my daughter is here. And certainly not if you are here with her."

The argument gave Annie the distraction she needed. Slipping through the gap, she almost let out a cry as she bumped into the emergency exit which was half open. A nurse stood on the threshold straining to hear what was being said. Rather than shout at her for being so clumsy and reveal her escape, the nurse grinned and raised a finger to her lips.

A second nurse, who was waiting on the balcony with a stretcher on wheels, beckoned her out and, pulling out a nurse's uniform from a bag, held it out to Annie. It was far too big, but pulled over her clothes it fit, more or less. The nurse perched a cap on her head.

"Could you folks please step outside a couple of minutes," she heard an imperious voice say inside the room, "I need to tend to the patient."

After mumbled complaints, the door to the room clicked shut and one of the nurses pulled back the curtain revealing a nurse busy unhooking Megan from the drip feed. The two women Annie was with wheeled the stretcher next to the bed and half slid, half-lifted Megan on to it.

Without a sound, the stretcher was wheeled out the exit onto the balcony. Two nurses strolled away down the ramp, as if they had something important to do, leaving Annie and the third nurse to ease the stretcher down the slope. Annie guessed the nurse was not from that hospital, she might not even be a nurse.

In no time they reached the car park where several ambulances were idling. She hoped the Inspector wouldn't vent his anger on Alice and Kevin. The thought of the look on his face when he discovered Megan had gone had her smiling. Served him right.

One of the earlier nurses was waiting at the back door of an ambulance and helped fold up the stretcher wheels and slide it inside. Annie climbed in next to Megan as did the nurse who had accompanied her. The remaining nurse was seated in the driver's seat. The doors closed, the siren rang out and they sped away from the hospital and the police.

"I'm Leonor," the nurse said, holding out her hand for Annie to shake. The woman had an accent. Mediterranean, Annie guessed. There was something of the sun in her manner. Warm and welcoming. "You must be Annie." When Annie looked surprised at being recognised, Leonor said, "I saw you on the telly." Annie grimaced. "Don't be so hard on yourself. It was great. You inspired many people, including me."

Leonor turned back to Megan and connected up a new drip feed. Annie was fascinated. The woman really was a nurse. That the Network, for that's where she guessed they were from, had such grown-up professionals working for it surprised her. She had imagined it attracting mainly girls of Ayana and Kevin's age. Older people could be gay too she realised. Leonor was checking Megan's blood pressure and noted it on a tablet.

"So you are a nurse," Annie said, voicing her surprise. "I was wondering."

"Sure. I did my training in Lisbon, but there's little work and no money in Portugal. There's not much money here either, but there's plenty of work. I've been in London ever since. Although, the way things are going, I might be forced to leave soon." She screwed up her face in what Annie took to be a comment on those who wanted to cut Britain adrift from the Continent. "Don't think I do this kind of daredevil stuff every day." She chuckled. "This is the first time the Network has been operational."

Annie was amazed they had managed so much in such a short time. But surely they hadn't got their own hospital. "Where are we going?" Annie asked.

"To a private clinic that is more welcoming to people like us."

'Like us'. Annie wondered at the words. She might have pushed Kard into the lake, but was she really part of these - what did he call them? - crooked people? Would they not be angry if they realised she was not gay or whatever?

"I'm not gay," she said, wondering how the woman would react. She could imagine being flung from the ambulance, abandoned in the middle of nowhere. Then she remembered Don. What had he said? 'You are brimming over with stories' and something about them jostling for her attention. He had been so right.

Leonor grinned. "We can't all be gay. Otherwise where would the fun be?" Leonor's face became more thoughtful. "Joking apart, you yourself said, 'London Whatever'. You may not be gay, although that remains to be seen, but you are certainly 'whatever'."

She might have said the words, echoing Ayana's slogan, but Annie was far from understanding what 'whatever' meant.

Megan was showing signs of regaining consciousness. Leonor measured her pulse and checked her blood pressure. "I've no idea what they were giving her in that drip, but it can't have been pleasant," Leonor said.

"I don't understand, " Annie said. She'd always thought of hospitals as places you went to get better, not worse. She'd fractured her arm when she was little. The nurses had been really kind and the doctor had set things right.

"I'm not sure I understand either," Leonor answered. "I imagine the inspector was indirectly in the pay of Kard. He must have spun a tale about Megan being violent and dangerous. It would be easy to convince a gullible doctor or even the head of unit to prescribe sedatives or worse. You can't imagine the drugs they have masquerading as acceptable medicine. It would take very little to transform an intelligent person into a compliant vegetable."

29.

Annie sat at the window staring out at the rolling hills tinged yellowish-red by the evening sky. The lights of an occasional farm house stood out like stars in the shadows queuing up for the night. Lone trees pointed skywards, dark fingers against the fiery glow. In the room behind her Megan slept peacefully, the sound of her soft breathing rippling through the air. The doctor had said she would probably be out several hours because of the drugs. Her state, however, was not critical he had assured Annie.

She had been treated royally by the clinic staff. You'd have thought she was Megan's treasured only daughter rather than a casual acquaintance. Once Kevin's mum was settled, Leonor had offered to drive Annie home, but without Alice she had no home to go to. As no one knew where Alice and Kevin were, she decided to stay by Megan's bedside. It pleased her to imagine she was standing in for Kevin till she returned. She was sure Kevin would have done the same for her.

Leonor had decided to stay rather than return home and had gone in search of food. The young woman was good company. Annie found her easy to talk to. Although a pernicious thought crossed her mind. Could Leonor be acting kind because she sought to get off with her? After all, the girl had admitted she was gay. Annie knew so little about such things, anything was possible. Her ignorance of the correct codes and behaviour left her feeling vulnerable. She might just be decrying genuine generosity. And anyway, she already had Kevin and Ayana to contend with. Two was enough.

When Leonor returned sporting a tray with two plates of steak and kidney pie and peas and chips, Annie tried to act normal. But acting normally was not at all like being normal. Leonor must have noticed because, halfway through the pie she asked, "What's up?"

Annie quickly stuffed several chips in her mouth, making answering impossible. She felt cowardly, but tried to make an apologetic face. Leonor put down her knife and fork and waited, sipping water from her glass as she did. Annie chewed a long time then swallowed with difficulty. "It's not easy," she said and gulped down a mouthful of water, almost choking on it.

Leonor tapped her on the back, saying, "Out with it, before you choke."

Annie blushed. "I am at sea with gay people. I don't know what to think or say." She took a deep breath and blurred out, "I am afraid your kindness might be a ruse to get off with me."

Leonor burst out laughing. Annie sprang to her feet ready to flee. She hated people making fun of her. "Calm your horses," Leonor said. "Let me explain." Annie sank back into her chair, feeling foolish. "For some reason when straight girls learn a girl is gay they imagine she is going to ravish them on the spot." Leonor expression became thoughtful. "Let's imagine you like boys. Do you jump on every boy you see?"

Annie shook her head. To be honest there weren't many boys she fancied. But that was another story.

"Well, neither do lesbians. In fact they are often very cautious about declaring their interest for fear the girl may not like other girls."

The moment she heard Leonor's words she could imagine the scene. How embarrassing and heart-rending if you were to misread the signs. Your loved one turning against you just because you preferred girls.

"Being a lesbian doesn't necessarily mean you are a nymphomaniac. And anyway, I already have a girlfriend."

"What's she like?" The question was out of Annie's mouth before she could stop it. "Sorry. I didn't mean to pry."

"No. That's alright. She's a bit like me, full of life and loves meeting people. When we are together we bubble over with words. Italian, Portuguese, Spanish, English." There was a faint smile at the corners of her mouth as she recalled her friend. "Originally from Italy, she came here to study a number of years before me. She's an assistant at the university and wants to become a professor, if those bloody Leavers let her."

Annie hadn't realised how many ordinary people were threatened by the misinformed desire of a vocal minority to be shot of the European Union. Kard had been one of the loudest and most ill-informed voices of the movement. It gave him and others like him a pretext to openly voice their racism with impunity.

Annie glanced at Leonor. A professor and a nurse? She wondered how that would work out. She would have liked to be a professor. She loved reading and writing and enjoyed explaining things to others. But now she'd been kicked out of school that was unlikely to happen.

"And the love of your life?" Leonor asked.

Annie made a face. "I don't have one. My best friend Ayana wanted more, but I couldn't bring myself to think of her that way. You are right about the caution. She was always very careful. I suppose Kevin is the closest I've come to having someone for whom my heart beats."

"Kevin of Marcie's?" Leonor asked. Annie nodded. "Megan's daughter and Alice's granddaughter? Wow. Good choice."

Annie felt a spike of jealousy. "She fought the other girls at school because they said nasty things about me." As she said it, she realised she was bragging. She was proud Kevin had stood up for her.

Leonor inclined her head and studied Annie. "And you're not sure?"

Annie couldn't decide whether to nod or shake her head. "I really like her. She's fun. I enjoy being with her and when she's not around I feel a bit lost. I know she loves me. But …." Committing would be a big step, she realised.

"But you hesitate, afraid if you go too far you will never be able to get back?"

Annie nodded. "Exactly. It's like there's this line. If I cross it, I'll never be the same again. Was it like that for you?"

"No. I always knew I preferred girls. My mum did too. Dad was just a way to have a baby."

Annie shuddered. Poor man. She imagined having such a subsidiary role in life. No wonder some men drunk themselves silly.

"My mother would disown me if she thought I went with girls," Annie said. Then she remembered the TV broadcast. "Silly me. She already has. On national television. She called me a crooked whore. On the news. And I hadn't done anything."

"I saw. So that was you. You must have felt awful."

"Shrivelled up and died," Annie said. "All my school friends, all my teachers even the neighbours saw that. And my mother came home and boasted about her performance." The anger she felt at her mother's stupidity and the injustice of the situation was murderous. "If I hadn't been so shocked, I could have strangled her."

Leonor shook her head. "I'm glad you didn't. There are some things that really cannot be undone."

30.

There was a second bed in Megan's room that Leonor insisted Annie use. She would make do with the armchair. As a nurse she was used to it. The young woman turned off all the lights but the night light and, settling in the armchair, whispered, "Good night."

"Good night," Annie replied, but she was nowhere near ready to sleep. She lay on her back, staring at the patterns on the ceiling, listening to Leonor shifting from time to time in her armchair. She felt guilty for not sharing the bed, but she couldn't bring herself to offer.

Megan had not yet regained consciousness. There was no risk if she continued to sleep, the doctor had said. She was being fed the minimum via the drip feed. But she was likely to be disoriented when she awoke. Annie hoped someone would be on hand to help. She had no idea how to cope with a lost soul.

A noise awoke her. The faint creaking of her bed. She could see nothing. The room was pitch black. Where was the night light? The bed shifted again. And again. As if someone were clambering onto it. Then a weight settled on top of her. Pressing down. Warm and soft. Covering her from head to foot. A naked body. A woman. She opened her mouth to scream. But a wet form pushed against her lips. A mouth. Lips against her lips. A tongue forcing its way inside. She wanted to clench her teeth. But couldn't. The tongue dug deeper. Her stomach heaved, her throat clenched. Her hands and arms were free. Why not shove the woman away? She tried. But at the touch of the moist skin, hips, buttocks, whatever, her hands recoiled. She lay there. Limp and unresponsive. That it finish. The sooner, the better. The person shifted, the bed creaked and the hips began gyrating. Slowly at first. Then more urgently. Grinding against her. Muscles tense. Skin taut and slick with sweat. And panting. Mouth to mouth. Hot breath filling her lungs. The breath of another. Possessing her. Arching up. Rigid. Then abruptly limp. The breathing calmed. The weight lifted and the bed rocked one last time. Used and abandoned, she lay shell-shocked and shuddering.

Annie cracked open her eyes, terrified of what she might see. The night light was on. Turning her head, she saw Megan lying on her bed, asleep, the drip snaking down from above, wires attached to her body. Beyond, curled up in an armchair in one corner, Leonor slept, snoring softly. It was over. Annie swore silently at Kard between chattering teeth.

Her body was frozen to the core. Her bones were made of ice. She had slept in her clothes. But even with the sheet and blankets pulled tight around her, she could not muster the warmth to fight off the cold. Her whole body was wracked with violent shivers.

She heard Leonor's chair creak. Terror surged through her. It was beginning again. She clenched her eyes, as if that could ward off the coming nightmare. The slap of Leonor's bare feet on the hospital tiles grew closer. Annie tensed to spring away. "Are you all right?" The woman asked, her voice nearby. Annie felt the woman's warm hand on her shoulder and cringed away involuntarily. The hand withdrew.

Opening her eyes, she saw the hurt on Leonor's face. "I'm sorry," Annie said, her jaw still tense with cold. "I had a … nightmare."

Hurt turned to concern on Leonor's face. "Do you have them often?"

"Since I crossed paths with Kard, yes."

"Kard?"

Annie shook her head. The daymares were so hard to explain, especially when floundering in the aftermath of one and confronted by the person who had just been abusing her. At least in Kard's world. "He has some way of sending me nightmares when I'm awake."

"You mean the thought of him?"

"No. He pilots them. I don't know how. One minute I'm here. The next I'm in a horror story he dreamed up. Then I'm out again. Back where I was. Shattered."

"That's not possible. Sounds more like science fiction."

"I know. I wish it wasn't possible."

"Would you like to talk about it?"

Annie shook her heard. "Just the usual. Rape. Violence. Debasement. And me powerless to do anything."

"How horrible! Doesn't surprise me though. He's all about disempowerment. But that he should go so far as to pester people in their private lives, driving them to the brink of madness, is inhuman."

"What I don't understand," Annie said, struggling to give voice to a question that had been tormenting her, "is how he knows what I am doing. Very often his horror story fits what I am up to. As if he were watching me or could read my thoughts." She shuddered. Kard could be spying on her even in her most intimate moments. Did he get a twisted pleasure from denying her the right to privacy? The idea was almost worse than the horror he subjected her to. It struck her as akin to the degradations afflicted on prisoners in the concentration camps. They'd studied the subject in History. Names were replaced by numbers, clothes removed, rights forfeit, bodies used and abused and to end it all, lives were wiped out by the mere turning of a tap.

A groan from the bed had them both turning to look at Megan. She was not yet awake, but she was agitated. Leonor hurried to check the drip feed. Annie took the woman's free hand and holding it in hers, sat next to the bed. "You've been asleep a long time," she said. "This is Annie talking. A good friend of your daughter Kevin. I'm here with a nurse called Leonor. We are both here to see that everything is OK for you."

Annie looked up at Leonor, seeking reassurance. Was she doing it right? The nurse nodded vigorously. So Annie continued, carefully avoiding any subject that might shock. Running out of things they had in common, Annie related school and the teachers, each with their foibles, and the other girls, their loves and hates. The more distant boys she preferred to skip. She toured her neighbours as she took an imaginary stroll down her street, describing the fronts of their houses, their children, the gossip about this affair or that, and the goings-on with the postman,…

"You could wake the dead," a croaky voice said. "If only to avoid the next instalment with the dustmen and the charlady."

Annie grinned at Megan. "Nobody in our street has a charlady. They couldn't afford one."

Megan squeezed her hand. "You did well, girl, very well. Where am I? And how did I get here?"

Leonor stepped forward, presented herself and briefly told Megan what had happened.

"It was a trap," Megan said, once Leonor had shifted her pillow and helped her sit up. "I got a call from a woman supposedly in distress. It was all very confused. But I gathered there was a legal problem with her husband who had beaten her. She gave me an address and I hurried to meet her."

31.

"You should get some sleep," Megan said. Annie didn't feel like sleeping. She wanted to know more about what happened to Megan. "Tomorrow could be another big day and you never know when you might get a chance to rest." Annie made a show of lying down on the other bed. "You can't sleep here. There's too much going on," Megan insisted.

"I'll check with the nurses. Maybe there's a room free nearby," Leonor said and left.

Annie was reluctant to be shut away on her own. Goodness knew what Kard might subject her to if she were alone and being with someone else helped keep her own thoughts in check. Leonor peered round the door saying, "There's a room free just down the corridor. I'll show you where it is."

The room was smaller than Megan's with only one bed and no medical equipment. The view from the window would no doubt have been spectacular, had it not been night. She lowered the blinds, not willing to offer the slightest opening to unwanted eyes. The room was sparsely decorated, but there was a large flat-screen TV.

Annie sat on the edge of the bed and reached for the remote, a sleek curved design that was all black with white buttons. She roamed the channels, not much on at that time of the night, till she found a twenty-four-hour news broadcast and cut the sound. Earthquakes, tsunami, outbreaks of war, hijacks, strikes, police brutality, kidnappings, harassment. The usual joyful stuff.

Then she saw a figure she recognised. Alice. She grabbed

the remote and turned up the sound. It was an interview on the pavement outside a police station that must have been filmed earlier because it was still light. "No," Alice was saying. "How can the police pretend a lone woman in her forties attacked a band of armed youths with pepper spray? It's ridiculous." Annie wanted more, but that was all there was. The camera cut to Kard lounging in an armchair in a TV studio somewhere. "This is a tragic case. Several innocent boys were almost blinded. I'm quite prepared to believe there was a misunderstanding. But this woman is a known activist in a feminist, lesbian organisation. Only the other day one of their demonstrations degenerated into violence. When you put two and two together, you often come up with more than you expect."

"What nonsense," Annie exclaimed.

The image broke up into static then reformed. Kard, comfortably seated in an armchair, was grinning at her. "Hallo Annie. Just thought I'd let you know I was keeping an eye on you. I really like watching you when you least expect it. I particularly enjoy the moments when you are in the bathroom. Maybe you could shower and change more often…"

"You're disgusting," she spluttered and ripped the plug from the wall. The picture flashed out of existence, Kard with it. If only it were so easy to get rid of him.

A pair of pyjamas had been laid out on the bed, but she wasn't going to give Kard the pleasure of watching her change. She grabbed the nightclothes and ran into the tiny bathroom. Closing the door and turning off the light, she quickly undressed in the dark and, feeling around for the pyjamas, slipped them on. They were a tight fit. She transferred Kevin's phone to the pyjamas bottoms, slipping it into a pocket.

Loathed as she was to be in the dark, she climbed into bed and switched off all the lights. She lay on her back staring up the ceiling which was faintly visible in the light filtering under the door. A buzzing against her thigh startled her. It was the phone. She pulled it from her pocket and pressed to receive the call.

"Annie, it's Kevin."

"Hold on a mo." She stumbled into the bathroom, almost tripping over her shoes in the dark, and turned on the shower. When it was running freely, she put the phone back to her ear. "Now we can talk."

"Are you in the shower?"

"No. It's to stop you-know-who listening in. Where are you?"

"The police took ages. Then there was the telly..."

"I know. I saw Alice."

"Then Alice wanted to book into a motel, but the manager told us it was full. I don't believe a word of it."

"So where are you?"

"No idea. Somewhere in the country. It's awfully dark. Alice is driving us to fetch you and see Mum."

Annie was relieved to hear that both Kevin and Alice were OK and to know they would soon arrive.

"See you later," Kevin said and hung up.

Annie turned off the shower and felt her way back to bed. Pulling the covers tight around herself, she closed her eyes and tried to sleep.

Something nudged her from her sleep. She opened her eyes to find the room brightly lit. Wires were attached to her chest and a drip feed had been inserted in her arm.

"There's been a terrible mistake," she said.

The two nurses who were busy around her bed didn't seem to hear.

"Hey!" she shouted, to no avail.

A doctor was talking earnestly to a man in a grey suit who had his back to her. She couldn't hear what was said but the doctor glanced her way from time to time. She was clearly the subject of their conversation. When the grey man turned to look at her, she recognised the police inspector she'd seen in the hospital.

Annie struggled to get up, but her arms and legs were shackled to the bed. She screamed. Nobody paid any attention. In answer to a question from the Inspector, the doctor picked up a syringe and said, "... she will be docile and a little confused, but still capable of answering your questions."

Moving closer, the doctor held up the syringe to examine it, then plunged the needle into the drip feed, releasing the liquid into the tube. A dullness crept over her as if her body were moving away although she stayed in the same place. She tried to focus but her thoughts floated in a rising fog. The growing numbness was both terrifying and reassuring. It would be so easy to let go.

A man loomed over her, his features distorted, his contours blurred. She tried to turn her head away, but her muscles wouldn't respond. She was acutely aware of the smells of him. Cabbage. Garlic. Hair cream. Deodorant. Ink. Cigarette smoke. Leather and wax. It's not important, a distant voice told her. Concentrate. He was talking. A voice that came from afar but roared in her ears.

"So you are the instigator of all this trouble."

How confusing. It was no question. Yet there was a question. No! she wanted to object. Yes! she wanted to answer.

32.

"Annie. Wake up."

The voice was so distant, she couldn't be bothered to respond. And anyway, she was busy. She was trying to see if her thoughts could reach her toes and make them move. Not much success so far. A thick fog somewhere near her stomach kept getting in the way.

"Annie! Come on."

"Leave me alone," she mumbled. She might have explained the difficulty with her toes, but talking required far too much effort. And what was the point? She returned to her toes. She'd already succeeded with her fingers. Surely the toes should be possible. She knew they were down there somewhere. She twitched her fingers to be sure she could still do so.

A hand, warm and soft and not at all unpleasant, folded around her fingers, hampering her movement. Why would anyone seek to make it difficult? She tried to tug her fingers free, but tugging didn't yet work. To think she'd almost managed to reach her toes, and now, thanks to this distraction, she'd have to start all over.

"Blast!" The word popped out of her mouth without her consent. She sucked in a noisy lungful of air. Maybe she could make it come flying back. But the word was gone, lost for ever.

Laughter cascade over her, sending ripples of delight down her spine.

"You silly girl," the voice said. Much closer now. The words curling around her like a soft cloth. "Come out and play."

The voice called to her, tempting her, urging her to make the effort. If only she could. But there were no doors. Were the voice to say more, maybe she could find a way out. The very thought of that voice had her feeling thirsty. She licked her lips. Other lips brushed hers. Soft. Moist. She'd felt this before. But different. Harder. More urgent. Forcing her against her will. She tensed, readying to fight, to get free. But the lips pulled away, leaving her feeling bereft. She wanted them. Oh yes. She stretched upwards, pursing her lips till she reached those other lips. At contact, waves of electric current shot through her, galvanising her entire body and her arms folded of their own accord around the person, crushing those lips against hers, pulling the person in a tight embrace. "Annie," the voice breathed and she sank in a swoon.

When Annie awoke, she was not alone. Curled up next to her lay Kevin, one arm slung around her waist. Annie kept still, not wanting to wake the girl. She was comforted by Kevin's warmth next to her, but wondered at the tender almost bruised feel of her lips. Then she remembered the kiss and beyond the kiss, the drip feed and the inspector plying her tired mind with questions. Her body went rigid with terror. Despite her struggles to stave off the memories, to tell herself it was Kard at work yet again, her body began trembling as she relived the creeping numbness overtaking her.

The movement must have woken Kevin, because she removed her arm, leaving Annie feeling even colder and more abandoned. She flung her arms around the girl and burst into tears. "There, there," Kevin murmured, stroking Annie's hair and planting little kisses on her forehead. "I'm here now. It's all right."

"It was terrible," Annie spluttered between bouts of crying.

"I hope you are not talking about our kiss," Kevin said, sounding uncertain.

Annie shook her head and cried even more, shuddering in Kevin's arms.

She heard the door open followed by footsteps on the bedroom floor. "Good morning," a cheerful woman's voice said.

"You realise it is ten o'clock and breakfast has come and gone." Annie opened her eyes to see Alice standing next to her bed. She wiped the tears from her face with the back of her hand and freeing herself from Kevin, she flung her arms around Alice's neck.

Alice patted her twice on the shoulder then, pulling away, asked, "Difficult night?"

"Kard."

"Him again. You really should choose better company."

Annoyed, Annie looked up to see Alice grinning.

"Come on you two. Get washed and dressed. I may even manage to rustle up a late breakfast, if you hurry."

They found Megan awake, sitting up and chatting with Alice and a doctor. True to her promise, Alice had got them breakfast, two very full trays awaiting them on a table in a corner of the room. They greeted Megan, who introduced the doctor, the head of the clinic. They shook hands and withdraw to a quiet corner to eat.

"I had a phone call from the police," the doctor was saying.

"The same inspector?" Alice asked.

Annie shuddered at the thought of him and his questions.

The doctor nodded. "He seemed to think you were here. No idea why."

"They've got spies," Annie said through a mouthful of bread and ham.

The doctor spun round to stare at her. "Here?" He sounded alarmed. "What makes you think that?"

"He knows every move I make."

"Are you sure you are not overreacting?" His question was polite, but he clearly thought she was fabulating.

"Oh, I'm sure," Annie said, getting to her feet. "He has a quaint way of plunging me into his homemade horror stories."

The doctor looked doubtful. "Like…?"

Reluctantly, Annie described the television scene, the one with the bull and the burning farmhouse TV studio.

The look of alarm on the doctor's face gave way to a condescending expression of comprehension. He didn't believe her. Probably he thought she was nuts. "You think I'm mad, don't you?"

The doctor flinched, but did not reply.

"Well. How do you explain these horror scenes take no time?"

He frowned. "I don't understand."

"Megan and Kevin were with me when the farmhouse scenario happened. Alice was with me when the bull charged. None of them saw anything happen. For them, one minute I was talking to them and the next I had broken down and was crying or terrified or both. For me as much as half an hour had gone by."

The doctor looked to Alice and Megan for confirmation. They both nodded.

"Maybe you dreamt it," the doctor suggested, visibly struggling to find an explanation that did not jar with his take on the world.

"Dreams generally have a particular air to them," Annie said. "These scenes had none of that strangeness. There were no abrupt jumps of time or place. They had all the characteristics of reality, albeit a very horrible one."

The doctor shook his head and sat down by Megan's bed, gripping the arms of his chair. "So you think Kard has developed some way of transporting you into these nightmare scenarios?"

"Yes."

"But why you?"

"Good question. I ask myself the same thing all day long. My only explanation is that he wants to get back at me because I jilted his pride and broke his nose."

"You broke his nose? You mean metaphorically?" The doctor was back to his disbelief.

"No." Annie told him what happened in Kard's campaign bus.

"I saw him on TV just afterwards. It's true his nose was swollen. He blamed it on a band of thugs. What a liar!" The doctor sucked in a deep breath. "If you are right, he's completely mad."

"And very dangerous," Alice added.

Annie nodded. "I doubt I'm the only one who gets such treatment. I'm sure there are loads of people who have annoyed him more than me. I imagine he's got an army of storytellers, busy dreaming up nightmare scenarios for people he doesn't like or wants to get rid of."

"Oh my God!" the doctor exclaimed, the colour draining from his face. "That would explain why the Prime Minister has been acting so strangely. Judging from his symptoms, I supposed he was cracking up under the stress and had been drinking too much. There's been a lot of talk of scandals."

"Many of those rumours came from media controlled by Kard," Alice said.

"You are right," the doctor replied, looking shaken. "I hadn't thought of that." Poor man. His world was being pulled from under his feet.

"If we tried," Alice said, "I'm sure we could draw up a long list of key figures in government and the civil service that have not been themselves these last months."

It was all very well figuring out who the victims might be, but what they really needed was an antidote. Or at least a tonic to diminish the impact. She remembered the nightmare with the syringe and shuddered. "Is there no drug that could limit the effects of Kard's scenarios?" Annie asked.

"Possibly. The sort we use for people with psychiatric problems. But the side effects can be almost as debilitating as these nightmares you describe."

"You should see this," Kevin said, pulling a folded newspaper from her pocket. "It was on the floor outside this room."

Alice unfolded the paper and laid it on the table. The doctor gasped. A half-page photo of the Prime Minister with his head in his hands figured under the headlines, 'PM resigns amid party chaos'.

33.

"Hey! Look at this," Kevin exclaimed. She had been leafing through the paper while the adults argued about how to counter Kard. Annie had tried to follow their conversation, but quickly got lost in the meanders of their strategies and counter-strategies which snaked off in every direction. None of what they suggested had any chance of undoing Kard, but she didn't have the heart to tell them, such was their eagerness to succeed.

Kevin slid the folded paper to Annie. There, on a television page near the back, after all the sports news and the cinema section, was a photo of her, her fist raised, taken no doubt when she'd shoved Kard into the lake. The photo was grainy and she was not sure people would recognise her, but it was her for sure. The tiny headline read, 'London Whatever figurehead to make public appearance'. She scanned the text. *Rumour has it that after her surprise performance near an artificial lake in a well-known London nature reserve she is to reappear at a big London Whatever rally. This time, the journalist quipped, Nolan Kard will not be present.*

"I bet it's a trap," Kevin said, reading the paper over her shoulder. "You go there, the police nab you and you are never seen again."

"Thanks for your positive suggestions," Annie said, prodding Kevin in the ribs.

Alice put out a hand to stop Kevin retaliating, took the paper from Annie and read the piece before handing it to the doctor who passed it on to Megan.

"Kevin's right," Alice said. "Kard's lot are probably behind the rumour."

Annie was perplexed. It was a silly strategy. There was little chance she would rise to the bait. She might not even have seen it. But if she had and did, it might work against him.

"All the same," Kevin said. "It would be great. The movement really needs a figurehead. Someone who's the opposite of Kard."

"No way!" Annie exclaimed, imaging herself a tongue-tied, ham-fisted idiot blushing in front of a jeering crowd, an easy target for Kard's yobs. Being chairperson of the debating society at school didn't qualify her to address such a crowd, even if they were probably supporters. That would be playing in a completely different league.

"I don't know," Alice said, getting to her feet and pacing the room. "It might just work. Nobody dares stand up and oppose Kard."

"Partly because they don't know how to handle his lies," Megan said. "There was a time when expert opinion held sway against loud-mouthed, pathological liars. Nowadays any trumped-up version of the truth goes, the more outrageous and provocative the better. And if you say the opposite tomorrow, who cares."

Annie was certainly not an expert in anything. She hadn't even finished school. But, to her mind, there were other, more likely reasons no one took on the millionaire. "Kard will make anyone's life hell if they do," she muttered. Her fears and reticence were to no avail. The more they talked about it, the more the adults were sold on the idea and began excitedly discussing where best to appear. At no time did they consider what she would do when she did. That she might have nothing to say never crossed their minds. Within a quarter of an hour it was all settled. The Network would organise a series of meetings in different places and Annie would appear in one at random.

"Don't tell me any more," Annie said, making as if to stick fingers in her ears. "Kard has some way of knowing what I am up to."

"Why don't you two go for a walk in the park for half an hour," Alice said. "We've got one or two things to sort out here. Then we'll leave."

Kevin took her by the hand and led her out. It was clear why she should not be there, she had even prompted her own exclusion, but the act still felt symbolic. All that was missing was the blindfold. She hated having others decide for her, especially when it came to such vital questions. Control of her life had been ripped from her. Not that she'd ever had much control, what with her parents and school dictating her life. The thought was ironic though, the way her friends treated her was not that different from Kard. He too subjected her to nightmare situations of his choosing. She was just a pawn.

Half an hour later Annie sat in Alice's car, her goodbyes said to all but Kevin. The girl held Annie's hand and whispered, "I'll come and see you when you appear."

"Don't do that. Kard knows wherever you go I will be there. And anyway, I'll only make a fool of myself."

"No, you won't. You'll be wonderful," Kevin said and bent into the car, planting a kiss firmly on Annie's lips. Annie would have responded with more enthusiasm, but she was acutely conscious of Alice watching. She felt her cheeks glow.

"I love you," Kevin whispered in her ear. "Take care."

"Love you too," Annie whispered back, feeling embarrassed at pronouncing the words out loud. Then she remembered she'd said exactly the same to her father in similar circumstances. Not that there was any comparison. She would never be indifferent to Kevin.

The door closed, waves were exchanged and they sped off down the drive. Just before they left the property, Alice pulled to the side and turned off the engine. Taking a dark silk scarf from her pocket and unfolding it, she said, "Better if we put this over your eyes. Just in case." Annie was to pull her hood around her face to conceal the scarf.

Annie shrugged. "I knew there was a blindfold waiting for me in this story somewhere."

Alice chuckled.

Part of the way Alice drove in silence. Part of the time she went on about the Prime Minister, his cabinet, his studies, his party, his family. Annie was amazed at the extent of Alice's knowledge, but she listened with only one ear, convinced the woman was just trying to distract her so she couldn't guess where they were going. She was pretty sure they would head for Alice's place and kept listening out for the moment they stopped at the farm gate. But instead of driving on deserted roads, there was a constant throb of traffic around them. If anything it got louder, as if they were headed for a large city. Was it possible Alice was driving her back to London? Was she to be sacrificed for the cause? A martyr dragged off by the police in full view of the angry crowds.

"Rumour has it he drinks." Alice was still talking about the Prime Minister. "But I have known him for years and he never touches alcohol."

Annie hadn't realised the professor knew such people. What with her being isolated in a cottage in the woods, she came across more like a hermit. Of course, at some distant time she must have taught at the university.

The car halted and she heard Alice pull on the brake. "We are going to meet someone," Alice said. "Better if you keep the blindfold on for the moment. I will guide you." Alice helped her out of the car and took her firmly by the arm. Wherever they were going, they were expected because the door opened without them having to knock. Inside she could sense a discreet bustle of people, some talking quietly, others sifting papers or typing, but no one addressed her or Alice.

Her feet sank into a thick carpet which masked the sound of their steps as they navigated what seemed like miles of corridors. Whoever they were meeting must be rich. She wished she were better dressed. She must look like a street urchin.

They halted. Someone knocked on a door and a deep voice called out, "Come in." She was surprised to smell flowers. Were they in some kind of atrium or winter-garden? She felt Alice pull back her hood and screwed up her eyes against the light as Alice removed the blindfold.

When she reopened her eyes, she found herself in a large office that looked more like a library. It was lined on three sides by bookshelves. In a bay window was a large desk piled with stacks of paper and an enormous vase of flowers. Seated behind the desk with his back to the window was a stout man with a receding hairline. She could not make out his face, framed as it was by the light from outside.

He stood and came round the desk to greet her, his hand held it. As he did his features were revealed. She recognised him immediately. Who wouldn't? She blushed and her mouth fell open in surprise as she shook hands with the Prime Minister.

34.

"Annie, meet John Underwood, our Prime Minister," Alice said. "John, this is Annie."

He gestured to one of the armchairs grouped round a low table. "Do take a seat," he said. "You must be tired after your journey."

He looked tired himself. His features were drawn, his brow furrowed and dark bags sagged under his eyes. Yet he still struck her as attentive. She was particularly sensitive to his considerateness. Someone in his position didn't need to spend time listening to a young girl.

"I'm sorry to hear you are resigning," Annie said, seeking to return that consideration but not knowing what else to say. She wished she had listened to Alice's description of the man. She couldn't even remember the name of his wife.

He grimaced and she had the impression he sank deeper into his armchair. Poor man. If Kard had been getting at him like he had her, and the man had no inkling what was happening, it must be a nightmare.

"Mr. Underwood, Prime Minister,..." she had no idea how to address him.

"Just call me John."

She shook her head. She could hardly be on such familiar terms, her a mere schoolgirl and him Prime Minister of Great Britain. "Are you having nightmares?" she asked, not knowing how to approach the subject less bluntly. "During the daytime, I mean."

He glanced over his shoulder, his eyes nervously darting round the room.

"Don't worry," she said. "This is not one of them."

He looked at her alarmed. "How do you know about this? I have told no one but my wife and a close councillor."

"I guessed," Annie said. "Or rather Alice guessed. You see, the same thing is happening to me."

He looked at her horror-struck. "You too. Well, at least you don't have a country to run." He made a weak attempt at a smile. "Although you do have a resistance movement to lead."

Annie grimaced. "Only in appearance. I stumbled into that role. It was none of my doing."

He looked surprised. "I thought…"

"A lot of people do."

"Maybe you should tell him about these 'nightmares'," Alice said. "I'm sure John has many important things to do."

Of course. Alice as sensible and to the point as always. Annie briefly described a couple of her horror scenes.

"Not at all unlike what happens to me, although mine are tailored to my situation."

"They always are," Annie said. "I reckon Kard has someone watching us."

"Kard!?" At the mention of the name the Prime Minister turned a pale shade of green. "What's he got to do with all this?"

"He has some way of sending us these horror scenarios. I don't know how."

"But what makes you think he's behind this?"

Annie recounted how she'd bumped into Kard and how his nose got broken. Then about the phone and the money on her account.

"Such behaviour doesn't surprise me at all of him, but it isn't necessarily proof that Kard is doing this to us."

Annie had the impression he desperately hoped he wasn't. She told him about the scene with Kard in the telly talking to her.

The Prime Minister ran a hand across his brow. "If there could be anything worse than these nightmares, it would be knowing Kard is behind them."

"Because he claims he's going to be President?"

Underwood laughed although there was no humour in his voice. "President! He already has more power than a president, more power than the Prime Minister. And anyway he has no desire to be president, not that he ever could be. If he were, he would have to accept the responsibility. That's the last thing he wants. No. Kard is dangerous because he's making a mockery of our whole democratic system. Here I am grappling with serious problems that have to do with the life and livelihood of many, many people and he's making those people laugh at me. I can assure you, having people sniggering behind your back as you try to set things right is the sort of demoralizing experience I wouldn't wish on anyone."

That you could undermine someone by encouraging others not to take him seriously had never occurred to her. "Can't we find a way to get people to laugh at him?" she asked.

"They do. All the time. He's a clown. Not a Prime Minister. What do you think, Professor?"

"Mockery is his arm, not ours. Bad taste too. Not to mention mud-slinging. Most of the underhand tricks used in politics to destroy an opponent won't work on him."

"Surely there must be some despicable act we can accuse him of that nobody would laugh at," Annie said.

"That's a tricky game," Underwood said. "It could easily blow up in our faces. No. This requires more thought. At least I am relieved to know that I am not going mad."

"I am glad we've made you feel better, Prime Minister. Although, if you are anything like me," Annie said, "madness might become an outcome if this continues much longer."

Underwood nodded, his face grim. "Yes. You are right. This cannot go on."

"So will you stay in office?" Annie wasn't sure why, but she liked the man and hoped he would continue as Prime Minister. He inspired confidence.

He smiled, some of the tension draining from his face.

"That's just another of those rumours Kard's bunch put about. My party won the elections and I was chosen as Prime Minister. I wouldn't quit so easily."

Annie nodded. "I'm glad," she said, relieved to hear the rumour wasn't true.

"Thanks for your vote of confidence," Underwood said, smiling, and held out his hand for her to shake. He hugged Alice. And they left.

In the car, Annie huffed out a long breath. Audiences with the Prime Minister were not the most relaxing thing she'd ever done.

"You'll get used to it," Alice said. "Who would you like next? The Queen, the Chancellor of the Exchequer or the head of MI5?"

Annie spun round to stare at her, horrified. Alice grinned back.

"Have you got some sort of wager with Kard to see who can drive me mad first?"

Alice chuckled. "You'll thank me later."

"Like for all the information about the Prime Minister. I knew you were doing it deliberately, but I should have known you were giving me keys. Instead I didn't listen, convinced you were just trying to distract me. To stop me guessing where we were going."

Alice made a noise of disgust. "To think I spent ages figuring out what to tell you about John. I won't make that mistake twice."

"I'm sorry. How foolish of me. I completely misunderstood. I was banking on another story. But I do appreciate your efforts. Next time I'll try to be more attentive."

"Good. Because, as I said before, I think it is time you learned a lot more about Kard."

Annie couldn't help groaning.

35.

Annie sneezed. The air was heavy with dust and the smell of printer's ink.

"Bless you," Alice intoned, not looking up from the pile of newspapers she was leafing through.

They had been allotted a large table in the basement archives of The Daily, a national newspaper, the editor-in-chief of which was a friend of Alice. All around, shelf upon shelf was stacked high with newspapers, many of them turning yellow at the edges, each shelf labelled with a date. The two of them were sifting through articles about Kard that the archivist had selected, before shifting to more recent computer-based archives.

"Look at this," Annie exclaimed, holding up a newspaper. "It says here Kard dabbled in writing scenarios for a TV horror series. Apparently he was not very good so he turned to a ghost writer. What's that?"

"It's someone who writes when, for some reason, you can't write yourself. The person gets paid, a little, but gets no credit for what she writes. The work is signed by the author, even if he didn't write a word of it. In French I think they are called 'negre', 'nigger', no longer a pretty word in polite society. Presumably the French called it that because people slaved away for others without any recompense or recognition."

Black. Annie thought grey would be a better colour. The grey writers in the shadows. She had a horrifying vision of an army of grey shadow writers slaving to draft nightmares for Kard's chosen victims. It suddenly struck her that maybe the man didn't even read what was written. She had often wondered how he found the time for all those he chose to torture. He was so busy haranguing people on television and on the internet or strutting around at galas being photographed with famous actresses or top models. What a life! It had no real substance, yet he seemed bloated by all he did.

"Here's something interesting," Alice said. "Kard messed around with occult sciences during his studies."

Annie shivered. She didn't want to get mixed up in witchcraft or satanic rites. "You mean like black magic or witchcraft?"

"Not only," Alice said. "There are a whole range of phenomena not explained by science. Ghosts, for example."

"Or ghost writers sending people nightmares in their waking life."

"Exactly."

A knock rang at the door. Annie looked up to see the editor-in-chief enter followed by two men, one in his fifties, tall and slim with greying hair and a lined face. The other much younger with slick black hair and a boyish face. He was carrying two cameras slung over his shoulder. "This is John Owen, one of our best journalists. I've asked him to interview you, if you agree. And this," he indicated the second man, "is Brian Hawthorn, our in-house photographer. He'll snap a few pictures if that is OK with you."

Annie looked to Alice, uncertain what to do. She would much rather keep a low profile till they found an antidote to Kard's nightmarish madness. Alice nodded. With a sigh, Annie turned back to the newspapermen and said, "Okay."

The editor-in-chief ran his fingers lingeringly over the newspapers piled on the table and shook his head. "To think that many of these were made in Fleet Street, the one-time heart of the newspaper world. No papers have been written or printed there for quite a while. When Murdoch moved his outfit here to Wapping over thirty years ago, I never dreamed The Daily would end up being produced only a stone's throw from what was once called Murdoch's fortress. We can thank him and your Kard, who also invested heavily in the media,…" He nodded to Annie, who flinched at being associated with the man. "…for putting an end to the Street, although it was probably coming anyway."

"You're giving them too much credit," Alice said. "Changes in technology and ways of working, not to mention increasing pressure on the industry from new channels of information and distribution, were surely the main factors."

"As always, you are right, Alice. But it is easier to get angry at a person than a machine or a technology." At which he took his leave, saying he would see them later.

John Owen pulled up a chair, sitting across the table from Annie. She pushed aside a pile of papers to make room for him. The photographer drew back into the shadows and stood still, watching, his camera at the ready. At first his presence disturbed her. She didn't like being watched letalone being photographed, but as he did nothing, she soon forgot him.

Owen was an easy-going sort of bloke who listened attentively. The two chatted quietly while Alice continued her search. They talked of her school, her parents, her friends, her interests and she began to lower her guard and forget he was a journalist from one of the few major newspapers not in the hands of Kard, till he said. "So why London Whatever?"

The question threw her and she felt rising panic. Here was the very interrogation that had stumped her earlier. Yet she had to reply. "It was the idea of a good friend of mine." She remembered Ayana's excitement at the words and thought of Kevin and their kiss. She wished she were back in her arms. "Rather than pointing an accusing finger at the world, 'Whatever' opens its arms to embrace difference." She chuckled at the image. "'Whatever' is inclusive. It celebrates the richness and diversity of the world. It hugs rather than sniggers. It is open and frank."

"And are you gay?" the journalist asked.

Annie blushed. The question had her feeling like she'd been caught naked stepping out of the shower. "Does it matter?" she asked. "Some of my very best friends are gay. What I am is of little importance."

"Your mother made some damning accusations on television…"

So much had happened, Annie had almost forgotten. Her anger had long subsided but it surged again.

"Yes. She delighted in showing me. It hurt a lot. I was furious. But even the most intelligent people can say stupid things with the arm of a millionaire around their shoulder and a camera crew going to their head. From being no one there is suddenly a promise of becoming someone. That truth gets massacred doesn't seem important at the moment."

"There's a rumour going around that you are to make a guest appearance at a London Whatever rally. Is that true?"

Annie wondered what to reply. Admitting it would be playing into Kard's game, but denial would not help the movement. "I heard it was to be a surprise," Annie said, beaming at the idea. "So if I tell you, it won't be a surprise any more."

Owen smiled and asked a few more mundane questions, like her age and the exact spelling of her name, then thanked her. The photographer gave her a thumbs up, saying, "Good on ya." He had an accent she couldn't quite place. Australian maybe. The two men left and, in the ensuing silence, the room felt very empty.

"Congratulations," Alice said. "You negotiated that rather well."

Annie felt deflated. "I feel terribly empty," she said.

"That's not surprising. It's mid afternoon. You've had nothing to eat since breakfast."

Annie laughed. "True. I'm starving."

"Well, let's go. Fenchaw has invited us to a late lunch."

"Fenchaw?"

"Damian Fenchaw, the editor-in-chief."

36.

"I would have liked to take you round the Tobacco Dock," Fenchaw said, pointing to the building across the street that was dark and trussed up as if it hadn't been used for years. "It was a precursor to Covent Garden Market with cafés, restaurants, posh boutiques and select office space, but it came before its time or maybe Wapping was not the best location for such a venture. The place fell into disuse. Now a company organising events is trying to resurrect the remnants as a venue for concerts and, what do you call them, raves."

As they walked by, a pair of strong-arm guys were standing guard at the gate that functioned as a service entrance. The banality of the forecourt contrasted with the delightful waterway next to it with its ducks and other water fowl as well as a moored three-masted clipper. Annie couldn't help wondering if the captive relic was not a commentary on the demise of the Tobacco Dock and the wasteland beyond that had once been Murdoch's fortress.

"So where are you taking us?" Alice asked.

"A pub that claims to be inspired by the painter, Turner."

"The man who painted all those swirling reds and yellows in seascapes of Venice?" Annie asked.

"That's the one." Fenchaw chuckled. "He was said to have created the original pub for one of his many mistresses."

Alice shot him a dubious look. He shrugged. "A historian friend made a point of warning me to take their claims with a pinch of salt."

The pub lay on the far side of Wapping Green. Fenchaw had reserved a table for three in the beer garden out back with a view over the tiny Green. The pub seemed to be a haunt for Daily staff. Several people she'd spotted at the paper were propping up the bar. There had been a surge of conversation when they entered and she caught several people craning to see her. News about her must have got about.

They paused at the bar to place orders. The person who served them, with his tight trousers, even tighter blouse and short apron, not to mention his sun drenched skin and made-up eyes, was a startling androgynous beauty. He could have been a model. When he caught Annie staring at him, he winked.

"Like your blouse," she said, troubled to discover how much the ambiguity attracted her.

"Thanks," he said, grinning. "It's all the rage in Rio." He clasped his chest as if seizing imaginary breasts and made a coy face. "I'm Luiz." He held out his hand for her to shake. When she took it, he lifted her knuckles to his lips and sketched a fleeting kiss.

Flustered by such a theatrical display, she replied, "I'm Annie."

"I know."

Embarrassed, she turned her attention to the menu, undecided what to take. Her parents never ate out, at least, not with her, so it was a new experience.

"Try the canard à l'orange," Luiz suggested, leaning so close she could smell his soap. "It is 'magnifique'." The accent he mimicked sounded more Spanish than French, but he made her giggle.

Searching for the places reserved for them in the garden, she recognised the photographer at a nearby table and the journalist who'd interviewed her at another.

"So what are you going to do now?" Fenchaw asked, once they were seated.

"I've no idea. I doubt I will be welcome back at school. I wanted to study creative writing at university, but without my A levels that won't be possible."

"Alice tells me your writing is excellent. Why don't you come and work with us? You could train as a journalist and a university sandwich course for those learning a profession is always a possibility."

"I'd like that. If I don't get locked up in the meantime."

More and more people were milling around on the Green. She made nothing of it, thinking it must be a haunt for locals on a sunny day, till someone brandished a poster saying 'London Whatever' and several cheers went up.

Fenchaw, who had his back to the scene, had begun explaining the different jobs in the newspaper business when Annie was distracted by a scuffle on the grass. The crowd scattered as a fight broke out. Two people were trying to restrain a third, but it was hard to make out in the confusion. She shifted to see better and knocked her napkin to the floor. It was as she bent to fetch it that there was a loud detonation. A searing pain shot through her shoulder and she was flung to the floor.

Screams rang out from every corner of the garden and the Green beyond. Cutlery and crockery crashed to the ground. No further shots came, but there were shouts and the distant wail of police sirens or maybe it was an ambulance.

Annie put a cautious hand to her shoulder. It was slick with blood and hurt, but not too much. She had no idea of the extent of the damage. She could feel herself trembling so she checked if it was yet another of Kard's nightmares. It wasn't. What now? Everyone crouched on the ground in shock. Except the photographer who was busy snapping shots. She looked for Alice but the editor was leaning over the old woman, blocking her from view. Annie turned back to see Luiz scampering across the ground on all fours, slaloming between the smashed plates and the splattered food.

"Let me have a look," he whispered. With great care, he removed her jacket and unbuttoned her blouse to get a better look at the damage. He picked up the napkin that had fallen to the floor and dabbed around the wound. She winced. Holding up the bloody napkin he said, "You're lucky. This thing saved your life. I saw you duck to pick it up. If you hadn't, the bullet would have killed you."

"Help me to my feet," she said. Once she was standing, she got some measure of the damage. On the Green, those people who'd scattered were returning, curious but cautious. When they saw her, a cheer went up. "Speak to them," Luiz whispered. "They need you to reassure them."

Who was going to reassure her, she wondered. The broken crockery crunched under her feet as she approached the fence between beer garden and the Green. Raising a clenched fist in salute, she shouted, "They won't get us so easily." A cheer went up from the crowd and they called out her name, "Annie. Annie. Annie." As she turned to go, she realised her blouse was still partly unbuttoned and her wounded shoulder exposed. Covering her shoulder with her hand, she couldn't help blushing. She just hoped the photographer had been distracted at that moment.

It was then she noticed Alice lying unmoving at Fenchaw's feet. She hurried to her side and knelt. The woman's eyes were closed and her face limp. "Did she get hit?" Annie asked.

Fenchaw shook his head. "More like a heart attack."

Annie had no idea what to do. Apparently Fenchaw hadn't either. At least the sirens were close now, bouncing back and forth from the buildings making it sound like a wailing army on its way. She hoped it was an ambulance and not the police. She struggled to her feet and went to fence. "As soon as the ambulance arrives, get them in here. Someone is hurt." Returning to Alice, she placed a hand on her chest. It was rising and falling steadily and Annie could feel the regular beat of her heart. She wondered if there might be another explanation than a heart attack.

Luiz was still hovering nearby as if waiting to catch her should she faint. Annie leaned close and whispered in his ear, "Are you in contact with the Network? We might need their help." He nodded and hurried away.

An ambulance screeched to a halt in the street along side the pub and the siren ceased its blaring. Voices called out, "In there," and two ambulance men struggled through the pub and entered the garden pushing a stretcher between them. On their backs they carried other equipment. Clearing a space around Alice, they forced Fenchaw to get out of the way. They lifted Alice onto the stretcher then one of them pulled a defibrillator from his backpack. Annie recognised it because they had seen one at school. Surely it was only used when the heart stopped or was beating erratically. Yet Alice's heart seemed fine. They hadn't even bothered to take her pulse.

"Get help. Now!" she whispered to Luiz who had reappeared.

She stepped closer to the ambulance men and raising her voice, said, "Stop that immediately." Both looked up at her in surprise. "Listen little girl. Let the experts look after this woman if you want her to live."

Fenchaw shook his head. "Annie. They are only trying do their job."

When Annie refused to budge, the ambulance man moved to shoo her away but she grabbed his arm and dragged him from Alice. "Stop the other one using that machine," Annie shouted. "He'll kill her." She heard Fenchaw remonstrating with her, but she ignored him.

Several big men accompanied by Luiz, stepped between Alice and the ambulance man who got to his feet and backed away. The other ambulance man was struggling to get free. Annie didn't have the strength to hold on. She gave a last tug on his white coat which came away in her hands. As she went to toss it to the floor she noticed a large blue badge hidden behind the lapel. Holding it up she shouted, "Look what we have here."

"Core blimey," Luiz said. "Kard's men."

The two vaulted the fence where they were forced to run the gauntlet of the crowd that hit them with everything they could as the men struggled to reach their ambulance.

Annie knelt beside Alice and held her hand. It was warm and soft.

"How did you know?" Fenchaw asked.

"I was sure you don't give electric shocks to someone whose heart is beating normally. They didn't even bother to check her pulse."

Fenchaw lowered his head. "I'm sorry. I should have trusted you."

"They are here," Luiz said.

"Who?" Fenchaw asked staring around, a worried look on his face.

"It's alright. These are on our side." She recognised Leonor immediately and greeted her with a hug. "Meet some members of the Girls' Emergence Network," Annie said.

37.

Annie sat on the flagstone floor of the beer garden amid the remains of people's meals, her back against the wall, watching Leonor examine Alice, noting the care with which she handled the old lady. The two ambulance men had fled as had the man with the gun. Most of the crowd had drifted away and the clients of the pub, none of whom had been hurt, had finally gone about their business. Soon there would be no witnesses left, but still no police had arrived to investigate. Surely such an incident should have had them running.

"There doesn't seem to be anything wrong with her heart," Leonor said, looking up from her patient. "Pulse, pressure and breathing are all normal. It's almost as if she were asleep." She turned to Fenchaw. "Is there some place nearby where she can lie undisturbed till she wakes?"

"We have a small infirmary on the ground floor of our building. It's only a short walk from here," Fenchaw said. "She could rest there till she recovers. No one will bother her." He pointed to the abandoned stretcher. "We can use that to transport her. I'll get someone to help and show you the way. I have to go. I've got a lot of work to do. We'll be bringing out a special late afternoon edition."

Once Alice had been installed in the infirmary and Leonor had offered to watch over her, Annie accepted an invitation from Brian Hawthorne, the photographer, to take her on a guided tour of the building. They went to the editorial room first where a heated discussion about the headlines was in progress. Fenchaw sat at the centre of it, silent and frowning. She glimpsed several photos of herself on the table. Another caught her attention, it was Leonor squeezing a tube of ointment as she tended the wound on Annie's shoulder.

"Excuse me," she said. All heads turned in her direction and Fenchaw nodded for her to continue. "Please don't use that photo. The nurse is part of an underground movement to help and protect us. If you publish it she'll be in serious trouble, if not danger."

"What about the photos of you?" John Owen asked, as considerate as ever.

She hesitated. Any claim she might have had to anonymity was long gone. "That's alright. I'm in this up to my neck and somebody has to show their face." The muddled image had her smiling despite the gravity of the situation.

Several people clapped and others joined them till the whole group was standing applauding her. She ducked her head in embarrassment. Luckily Brian hurried her away.

"Yeew!" he said, holding up his camera. "That was a cracker."

She hadn't even realised he was snapping her. So he'd caught her in a moment of such discomfort. Not very kind.

He must have noticed her frown, because he held up the back of his camera to show her the screen, saying, "Look." The picture was small, but she could make out the editorial committee on their feet applauding, while she stood, head bowed in front of them. It was a stirring photo that told a story. Not at all unkind, on the contrary, tender and sensitive in a way that was touching.

Much of what they saw as they continued their tour were offices. The whole production process was computerised and individuals often worked alone even if they were linked by the network. Some people were typing copy. Others reworking photos or inserting them into the layout.

"As this is a special edition," Brian said, "logistics are a bit different. We need to get the paper out to newsstands and newsagents before people start to make their way home."

Annie glanced at her watch. Four thirty. They'd need to hurry.

"When the paper is finished, someone will bring us a copy," he said. "How about a drink while we wait?" Annie nodded.

The canteen was a large airy room at the top of the building. Floor to ceiling windows offered a magnificent view over the rooftops of a jungle of new houses and blocks of flats towards Wapping and beyond to the Thames. The river curled lazily off to Greenwich and the sea. Her home, or rather her mother's home she corrected, was lost in the haze over the Docklands.

Chairs were grouped around tables and there was a corner with armchairs.

"What's your poison?" Brian asked.

Annie smiled at the expression. "A tea, please."

He fetched two teas and a large ham sandwich and they sat at one of the free tables. "You got rather short-changed at lunch," he said, pushing the sandwich across the table. She was about to refuse when her stomach growled. Biting into the bread, the taste of the butter and mustard and ham reminded her how famished she was.

Several young people tumbled into the canteen, laughing and joking as they did. The group joined them and Brian introduced each one. Several were learning to be journalists. Another, a girl in overalls and a cloth cap, was a graphic artist. The remainder were office staff.

"So. Are you going to the rally this evening?" one of the trainee journalists asked.

"I hadn't planned to," Annie replied.

"Why ever not?" the young journalist asked.

Annie scrutinised their disappointed faces. "I was afraid it might be a trap. Someone might try to assassinate me."

"They've already tried," the graphic artist said, "and didn't succeed. Anyway, I'm sure we can rustle up a bulletproof vest for you."

The door to the canteen burst open and a boy stepped in. He paused on the threshold, then, seeing Annie, hurried over.

"Mister Fenchaw said I was to give you this." He handed her a folded newspaper and turned and left as fast as he'd come. Even before she opened it, she could smell the distinct presence of printer's ink.

Annie spread the paper on the table and studied the front page. Over three columns was a picture of her framed by a smashed window with her bloody shoulder laid bare and her fist raised. She looked grim and determined. The headline read, 'London Whatever figurehead survives assassination attempt'. She began reading.

A well-known member of a right-wing paramilitary organisation affiliated to Kard's Keep London Straight campaign was photographed earlier today trying to assassinate Annie Wight, emblematic figure of London Whatever movement. Luckily the girl escaped with only superficial wounds. The would-be assassin managed to escape despite the efforts of the crowd to retain him. The police were called to the scene of the crime but refused to comply. Asked for an explanation, a police spokeswoman said that no one was hurt and to the best of their knowledge it had been a publicity stunt for the newspaper …

Turning to the next page, there was a lengthy description of the attack and a startling picture of the would-be killer brandishing his gun as the crowd tried to get hold of him. His face was clearly discernible. Brian must have taken a great risk to get that photo. There was also a picture of Annie lying on the restaurant floor, amid the chaos is smashed plates and splattered food, blood flowing freely from her shoulder.

Page three had the article about her signed by John Owen. Across the top of the page was a photo of her smiling. She hardly recognised herself in the confident young woman that smiled back at her. The graphic girl tapped the photo with a curved finger. "When people see that we'll need to set up a fan club for you."

Annie blushed and was tempted to protest.

"Hey! Listen to this," one of the journalists said, waving a remote at a large flat screen she hadn't noticed. Kard was being interviewed. In a small inset at the top of the screen was the photo of her would-be assassin.

"If you look at the photo close enough, anyone can see it's a fake," Kard said with a dismissive gesture. "What I find despicable is that a supposedly reputable newspaper should resort to such disinformation to shore up its flagging readership."

Several of the young people booed or jeered. "What a ponce," the graphic girl exclaimed. "So are you going to the meeting?"

Annie stared at the figure of Kard lounging in his armchair, smug and self-satisfied. What a liar. A barefaced liar. The worst was that many people gobbing down his rubbish would believe it. The police certainly had. "Yes," she replied. "Let's see if the bullet that gets him is fake or not." The cheers that erupted from the young people rocked the canteen, causing several alarmed passersby to look in, fearful about what was happening.

The graphic girl patted her on her good shoulder by way of congratulation, saying, "Let's go get you that bulletproof vest."

38.

Annie was delighted to find Alice sitting up reading the newspaper. Taking a seat opposite the old woman, who had regained a healthier colour and whose eyes had recovered their familiar twinkle, Annie asked, "Whatever happened to you?"

"It was nothing," she insisted. "Loud noises knock me out."

"I wished I'd known. I was worried."

Alice gave her a friendly pat on the hand, saying, "You needn't have, but I appreciate your concern."

Annie looked around, realising Alice was alone. "Where's Leonor?"

"She had to go. Anther emergency." Alice brandished the newspaper. "This'll stir up some muck. I hope you're ready."

"Don't you think the whole story looks exaggerated? I mean, you can't really blame Kard's lot for calling it a stunt. Imagine the scene. The newspaper has its best photographer on hand when there is an attempted assassination of someone they have just interviewed and who happens to be having lunch with the editor."

"Truth often seems more improbable than lies. The notion of truth has always been tricky. It is not as absolute as some people would have us believe. Very often our take on it depends on our point of view. As for Kard, he is in another league. He's gone way beyond truth. He's even gone beyond bullshit."

"Bullshit?" She'd heard the word but thought it meant 'nonsense'.

"It's a complicated concept. A liar knows he's not telling the truth. Whereas with bullshit, the person tries to create an alternative 'truth', a world where his 'truth' holds sway. Maintaining such a 'truth' can be exhausting, especially when the rest of the world goes a different way. But in both case truth is the reference, one way or another. What Kard does is radically different. He has done away with all reference to truth. In a way, he's cut us loose from truth. He affirms one thing one day and a completely different thing the next. It doesn't matter if others claim it is not true. He said it. That's all that counts. His words are the reference. What's more, Kard denigrates all those experts and scientists who found truth on facts or long experience and could challenge him. He accuses them of ignorance, of lying, of serving vested interests."

"But surely people will spot the difference."

"Apparently not. Leonor told me the police didn't bother to investigate the shooting, pretexting it was a publicity stunt."

"Maybe he's got a lot of influence over the police."

"That may well be. But what about the millions of people who follow him on TV, who read his newspapers, who attend his meetings, who would vote for him if he stood for office? They take what he says at face value. The world he portrays only exists on the surface. No one wants to grub about underneath to see if the foundations are rotten, or if there are any foundations at all."

The door opened and Brian and the graphic girl stepped in. Annie introduced them, hesitating when it came to the girl. "I didn't catch your name."

"Ella."

"Ella's a graphic artist," Annie explained.

"Ready?" Ella asked.

"Where are you lot off to?" Alice asked.

"An encounter with destiny," Ella replied before Annie could say anything.

"I decided to attend the rally," Annie explained.

Alice sighed. "I'm all for heroics, but whatever happened to the timid schoolgirl who weighed up every option before taking a step?"

Annie laughed. "I've been looking for her everywhere, but

she seems to have got lost." It was meant as a joke, but being lost really did describe how she felt. It was as if she were being carried along by a strong current with precious little say about where it went.

Ella held out a heavy-looking jacket. "You might need this."

Alice whistled. "Better prepared than sorry, they say."

Annie gave Alice a long hug. How much their relationship had changed in such a short time. The woman was no longer a distant university professor. She was more of a benevolent grandmother.

"Take care," Alice said, running her fingers through Annie's hair. "I'll get a message to you so you know where I am staying."

The bulletproof vest was heavy and uncomfortable, but she felt reassured wearing it. To some extent at least. She didn't need to remind herself that no amount of bullet proofing could ward off Kard's nightmare attacks. "I wonder what Kard's minions will make of this jacket?"

"They'll never know," Ella said as they reached Brian's car.

"Sure they will," Annie said, with a bitter laugh. "They see everything I see."

"However could they do that?" Ella asked.

Annie climbed into the car, explaining that Kard had a way of tracking her or rather what she could see and hear.

"That's terrible. They'll know where we are going," Ella said.

Annie was loathed to mention it, remembering the misery of being cut off from the world, but she felt obliged to tell them. "Alice had me blindfolded."

"Trust Alice to find such a simple solution," Ella said, chuckling. She pulled a scarf from her bag and, apologizing for having to do so, covered Annie's eyes and bound it behind her head.

She felt alone and abandoned on the back seat, unable to see, while the two chatted up front in whispers too low for her to hear. She wondered what Kevin was doing. Reading about her in the newspaper probably. She would willingly have phoned her friend, but their conversation might give away what was planned.

She was relieved when Ella announced they had arrived

although the two refused to remove the blindfold when they got out of the car. She could hear the roar of a crowd and the amplified voice of an orator, although she couldn't make out the words. Ella helped her along a path then up some steep steps. She stumbled several times but the girl put her weight behind Annie and she didn't fall. Finally, she stepped out onto a platform which trembled when she moved.

When the blindfold was finally removed, Annie was standing behind a group of people who were all looking the other way. As she had guessed, they were on an improvised platform. At first she thought it was playing fields, but then she recognised the flat oval expanse of grass, bordered with trees. They were in Stepney Green Park. Stretching away from the foot of the platform all the way to the path that encircled the park, she could make out an immense crowd, far bigger than the one she's seen at Kard's meeting.

The amplified voice announced, "And now the person you have all been waiting for, survivor of a foul attempt on her life this very afternoon, Annie Wight."

A roar went up from the crowd as the small group parted and Annie stepped forward. Several people patted her causing her to wince when they touched her wounded shoulder. Others shouted words of encouragement. Seeing the size of the crowd from the edge of the platform took her breath away and her head began to spin. She grasped the railing and tried to suck in a deep breath. The crowd roared again like a wild but joyful beast. She raised her fist in salute and the crowd followed suit, a sea of raised fists swaying in front of her. The sight was exhilarating, but also terrifying. There was a power in this situation that she could never have imagined.

What next? The crowd fell silent and someone handed her a microphone. She stared at it, unsure what to do. She had not anticipated this. She had no speech ready. Her mind went blank as she struggled to keep the billowing panic from engulfing her. If only she'd known, she'd have tapped Alice for ideas. The old professor might have been retired, but she would have known what to say. She thought of the Prime Minister, of all his worries and what he'd told her about Kard undermining those who did the work.

She took a shaky breath, raised the mic to her mouth and spoke. "It is so easy to stand on the sidelines and sneer at those who are trying to get the work done." She halted to catch her breath and to look around the crowd, giving the words time to come. A swaying fresco of faces stared up at her, expectant. She gripped the railing even tighter, almost giving in to the vertigo. "It is so easy to mock and poke fun at the institutions on which society is built." She felt her voice grow stronger as if she had unearthed an untapped source of energy. "It is so easy to point a finger at those who are different and say they are to blame." The words flowed more easily now. Goodness knew from where. She didn't dare question their source for fear it dried up.

She lowered her voice almost to a whisper, her lips brushing the mic. "If you are one of those who snigger at these antics, if their bad taste makes you laugh, if you would vote for the buffoon thinking he is different and will set things right, remember one thing." Progressively she raised her voice. "Driving the vision of a straighter, Greater London is the dubious humour of a madman whose sole aim is to build a personal empire over the ruins he leaves behind. There will be nothing great or straight in the nightmare he has in mind. There will be no freedom at the end of the road. A twisted smile may still linger on your lips, but if you do not see him for what he really is, whatever you are, wherever you live, whoever you know, you will stand alone, powerless, a slave to the will of a man who cares nothing about anyone or anything but himself."

"I am reminded of the story of the emperor's new clothes. In this version the Emperor is a would-be President." Laughter rippled through the crowd. "He stands before us in his dirty underwear expecting us to pretend he is richly dressed." The crowd roared with laughter. "He is mistaken. It is us that are richly dressed in all our gay colours and pretty makeup." Some whistled, others called out 'love you', most just returned her smile.

"He would have us all clad in grey, each of us straight-jacketed into uniform thoughts so he can feel special. No way!"

"No way!" cried the crowd.

"This afternoon, a journalist asked me why we call our movement 'London Whatever'. I replied that rather than pointing an accusing finger at the world, 'Whatever' opens its arms to embrace difference. 'Whatever' is inclusive. Why shouldn't girls love girls or boys love boys? Why shouldn't gender be a question of personal choice? 'Whatever' celebrates the richness and diversity of the world. It hugs rather than sniggers. It is open and frank. And as part of that frankness we stand up and laugh at the bully in his dirty underwear who has this crazy notion that we should bow down to him as if he were a richly dressed President."

Enough was enough. She lowered the microphone. The crowd erupted in cheers and stamped their feet. Before the cheers had time to die down, someone pulled out a drum and began hammering out a wild beat. Only to be joined by a pair of bongos. Another person shouldered a fiddle and added a melody to the beat. Several others took out flutes and in no time the crowd was transformed into a colourful, dancing mass.

The people on the platform behind her pressed forward, each eager to congratulate her. She was hugged and kissed by so many people she didn't know, she was beginning to long for a quiet place on her own when Ella rescued her. The girl led her to the back of the platform and down to the ground. "Someone is here to see you," she said with a sly smile. For a moment Annie feared Kard had managed to squeeze his way into their celebrations but then she saw Kevin and in no time they were in each other's arms, their lips pressed together in a passionate kiss.

39.

Annie and Kevin stood, their arms laced round each other, half hidden in the shadow of the makeshift platform. On the far side the crowd danced and sang to wild Celtic music, as if some pagan ritual were taking place.

"You were marvellous. Wherever did you get that speech?" Kevin asked during a lull in the music. "And the pictures in the paper were superb. I've pinned them on my bedroom wall."

Embarrassed, Annie chose to close her eyes and kiss her rather than answer. When Kevin screamed, Annie's eyes flew open. Her friend had been ripped from her and was being dragged off by two thugs. Annie sprang after them, battering the men with her fists trying to free Kevin. One thug brushed Annie aside as if she were an annoying bug, sending her sprawling. He pinned Kevin's arms together, while the other pressed a cloth over her nose and she went limp.

"Help!" Annie screamed, but her screams were drowned by the music. She vaulted the steps to the platform two at a time, only to find it deserted. Her heart sank. Surely this must be one of Kard's nightmares. It couldn't be real. Seeing the microphone, she grabbed it and shouted, "Stop!" Her voice bellowed over the music which abruptly halted. "Thugs have kidnapped my girl-friend," she said her voice breaking on the last word. "They went that way." She pointed behind the platform.

The crowd surged forward, streaming around both sides of the raised structure, sending up blood-curdling cries as they spread out, a dark mass combing the park. She scanned the limits of the park and spotted the red tail lights of a car speeding away. "Too late," she cried in anguish, forgetting she was still holding the microphone. She sank to the floor and buried her head in her hands. If this was one of Kard's nightmares, it was time it stopped.

Feeling a hand on her shoulder, she looked up. Through tear-filled eyes she saw Ella and Brian leaning over her, concern on their faces. Both bent forward and helped her to her feet then Ella pulled her in a tight embrace. When Annie freed herself, Brian offered a handkerchief to wipe the tears from her face.

"Let's get down from here. We're too exposed," Brian said, ushering Annie towards the stairs.

Even inside Brian's car with the heating on, Annie couldn't stop shivering. Ella wrapped a blanket round her and sat next to her in the back of the car. "I will have to blindfold you," she said, "but, if you want, I'll put an arm round your shoulders to keep you company."

Sitting in the dark, feeling miserable, Annie had no desire to chatter. Mercifully, Ella soon gave up trying to engage her in conversation and turned to Brian. Left to her own thoughts, Annie repeatedly ran over the kidnapping. She blamed herself. Without her addressing the rally, Kevin would never have been there. And anyway, Kevin had not been taken because of who she was, but because she was Annie's friend. She was furious at herself. If only she'd known karate or jujitsu. What a stupid idea. She'd have had no chance against those brutes. How on earth were they going to find Kevin and rescue her? She ran through dozens of impossible scenarios.

Only once the blindfold has been removed, did she realise they had taken her to Ella's flat. She shared it with a beautiful Indian girl in a colourful sari who had pitch black hair and an engaging smile.

"Meet Riya," Ella said, giving the girl a kiss. "She's a computer wizard. You can't be a proper Indian without being one."

Riya ignored the jibe and kissed Annie lightly on both cheeks, enveloping her in a cloud of floating silk and incense.

"Whatever happened to you, my dear?" Riya asked in her lilting accent.

Annie sank into an armchair, her blanket pulled tight around her, while Ella and Brian told the story and Riya made tea.

"We should see if there's anything about the rally on the news," Ella said switching on the TV.

Sure enough it was the first subject. It began with a sea of raised fists and Annie on the platform, her fist raised too. Then they cut to Annie giving her speech. She hadn't even noticed there was a television crew at the rally. They chose to air the extract about Kard in his underwear. The idea seemed to amuse the newscaster who struggled to hide her grin.

The woman turned to look at a screen on which Kard could be seen lounging in his familiar armchair. "So are you naked Mister Kard?"

He laughed although it struck Annie as forced. "I might try a rally in my underwear, but I'll wait till the weather is more clement."

"He'll never do that," Ella muttered. "He might play the buffoon, but he doesn't want to be seen as ridiculous."

The camera cut back to the rally with Annie alone on the platform crying out, "They've kidnapped my girlfriend."

"Rumour has it that your men kidnapped her girlfriend just like they tried to shoot her earlier in the afternoon."

"What nonsense," Kard said, dismissing the suggestion with a wave of his hand. "But you've got to hand it to them. They have no lack of imagination. Now they've invented a girlfriend so she can get kidnapped. Whatever will they dream up next?"

"Hail the fountain of truth," Ella said, turning off the telly.

Annie thought of Alice's words about truth. "There is no truth in Kard's world," she said, exhausted at stringing the thoughts together. "There are no lies either. All that counts are Kard's words."

"Wow," Ella said. "I'm beginning to understand where that speech came from."

"Mostly other people," Annie said, her eyes fluttering closed.

Brian had hooked his camera to Ella's portable and was scrolling through photos of the rally. "Stop," Ella said. "That one." Annie opened her eyes to see what the fuss was about. The picture depicted her seen from the side, her fist raised. "Can I use it?" Ella asked.

"Sure," Brian said. "But you'd better ask Annie."

Annie nodded. Photos were the least of her concerns. Constantly worrying about Kevin was exhausting her. She curled up in the armchair and let her eyes drift closed.

A peal of laughter awoke her. Brian, Riya and Ella were grouped around the screen. Annie stretched her legs and shakily got to her feet to see what they were gawking at. It was a coloured drawing. Annie was dressed in brightly coloured clothes, fist raised before a cowering Kard in his underwear, his hands clasped over his private parts.

"He looks too much like a victim," Annie muttered.

"How about this then?" Ella said. She changed Kard to have him holding open a filthy overcoat exposing his underwear.

"Horrible," Brian said.

"Much better," Annie added.

"The rise and fall of an empire," Riya said.

Ella added the caption and posted it on Facebook and Twitter and several other platforms Annie had never heard of. Within minutes people were busy reposting it. The caption often morphed into a less flattering comment about Kard. By the time Rita had cooked them a vegetable curry, the Empire picture was trending on Twitter. Many news sites around the world had picked it up, apparently overjoyed to get in a blow against Kard.

The others congratulated Ella and were delighted at her efforts, but Annie was anxious. Kard had Kevin in his filthy paws and would surely take out his fury on her. She shuddered to think what the monster might do to her gentle friend. "We've got to get Kevin back," she said, tearing off a part of her chapatti and wiping the last of the sauce from her plate. "How do you find someone who's been kidnapped, if the police refuse to help."

"Posters," Ella said.

"Word of mouth," Brian added.

"The Network," Riya said.

"Have you got a picture of her?" Ella asked.

How pathetic. She didn't even have that.

"I might have something," Brian said, sounding embarrassed. "I kind of stole a few pictures."

Annie wondered how on earth he could have laid his hands on photos of Kevin, but if he had some, she'd be grateful to have one.

Brian plugged his camera back into the computer and scrolled to a folder labelled private. At the sight of the name, Annie was afraid of what he might reveal. They were photos of Kevin by the platform waiting for Annie and then of the two embracing. "I'm sorry," he said. "I shouldn't have done that. They just made such good pictures."

"I'll beat you up later," Annie said, deadly serious. "But for now I'll settle for a copy of that photo of Kevin alone."

Brian nodded, visibly relieved.

"I need a copy too," Ella said, enthusiastic.

Riya shot her a reproachful look.

Ella huffed. "For the poster, silly. To help find Annie's friend."

40.

"Megan? Is that you?" Annie asked. She'd got the number from Alice. "How are you?" Megan might be a solid, down-to-earth person, but Annie didn't want to be a bringer-of-bad-news if the woman was still in bad shape.

"Fine. I was about to leave and return home. Is Kevin with you?"

Annie felt her heart pinch. She couldn't keep it a secret. Megan was sure to see Ella's posters soon enough. "Kevin got kidnapped."

"What?" Megan's voice was almost a screech.

Annie had hardly begun telling her about their meeting at the rally when Megan interrupted.

"Why ever did she go? She knew it was dangerous."

"I didn't expect to see her." As if saying so could allay Annie's guilt. When she described the two thugs, she heard Megan groan.

"Sounds like the two that attacked me. My poor baby. She must be terrified. What about you? I heard you got shot."

Annie was relieved at the change in subject. "I'm OK. It was only superficial."

"Did the police nab the person?"

"The police did nothing." Annie couldn't hide her bitterness. "They claimed it was a publicity stunt for the newspaper."

"And Kevin?"

"As far as I know they are doing nothing. Kard went on television to insist we'd invented a girlfriend so we could pretend she was kidnapped."

"What rubbish! You wait till I get my hands on them." Her voice trembled with anger. "They'll move their backsides fast enough."

Annie remembered Brian's photos. "We have photos of Kevin and me at the rally. Maybe Brian also has pictures of the kidnapping."

"Who's Brian?"

"The photographer from the newspaper. It was him that took a picture of the man who tried to kill me."

"Good." There was a short pause and Annie heard a rustle of papers over the phone. "I'm going to get a dossier together against the police. It's about time they were reminded what their job is and who they are supposed to be doing it for. So what is being done to find Kevin?"

"Ella made posters."

"Who's Ella?"

"I'm hiding at her place. She's a graphic artist. The posters are being distributed by the Girls' Emergence Network. There's also a call out online for information. Ella's friend Riya is looking after that."

"If you had a photo of the attackers, we might be able to identify them."

"I'll ask Brian."

"Where are you? I'm coming over straight away. God! I hate to think what must be happening to Kevin. Has there been any contact with the kidnappers?"

"No. None at all. I'll ask Ella to phone you. That would be safer. I have no idea if my phone is being tapped."

As soon as she got off the phone, Annie went in search of Ella. She found her with Riya cuddled up on the sofa exchanging kisses. "You wanna join us?" Ella asked, with a wicked smile. Riya hit her over the head with a cushion. Once Ella had wrestled the cushion from Riya's hands, of course, they had to make up with a fresh wave of kisses.

"When you two have finished," Annie said from the doorway. "Can you call Kevin's mum and give her your address? And where can I contact Brian?"

"I think we'll have to spank her for abusing GPT," Ella said, nodding at Annie.

Riya looked as confused as Annie felt, so she guessed it was some joke of Ella's. "GPT?"

"Gay Private Time," Ella said with a grin and turned back to continue kissing Riya, but the young woman pushed her away and got to her feet, despite Ella's protests. "Seems like you've got things to do," she said to Ella. "And I have to check if there is any news about Kevin's whereabouts."

"You lot are way too serious for me," Ella said, getting to her feet.

Annie wanted to reply that it might be a question of life or death, but she knew Ella was joking. "Here's Megan's number." She had scribbled it on a piece of paper. Ella took the note in return for Brian's number and Annie returned to the spare room that the couple had allotted her, pulling out her phone.

"Brian?" she asked. "It's Annie."

He sounded pleased to hear from her and began telling her all about tomorrow's paper and the photos of her in it.

"Sorry to interrupt, but I have a question."

"Fire away."

"Did you manage to get any photos of the kidnappers?"

There was a pause. "Yes. It's almost as embarrassing as snapping you and your girlfriend kissing. I mean. I could have tried to save her, but I took photos instead."

"I don't know if you noticed the size of those blokes. You would only have got hurt. Taking their pictures might do them much more harm than your fists." She wanted to tell him of Megan's plan to prepare a dossier about police negligence, but thought better of doing so over the phone. "Why don't you come over when you've got a moment?"

He was delighted and promised to drop by as soon as he'd finished at the Daily. Annie returned to the living room to find the two back on the sofa. She wondered if she lived with Kevin whether they would be kissing all the time. Probably not. "Do you two ever get fed up with kissing?"

"You have a false impression. In reality, we only do it when you are around," Ella said. At which Riya shoved her off the sofa causing her to tumble at Annie's feet. Annie held out her hand to help her up, but instead Ella tugged her to the ground creating a muddle of limbs. Annie tried to get free but Ella made a show of holding on to her. Riya flung herself into the mêlée and set about hitting them both with a cushion.

It was then that the doorbell rang. All three scrambled to their feet, breathing hard, their faces flushed. The cushion must have broken open, because feathers floated in the air and stuck to their hair and clothes. Riya, visibly pouting, went to answer the door while Ella and Annie hurried to push the furniture back into place.

Annie recognised Megan's voice immediately and dashed to the hall to greet her. Seeing Kevin's mum standing there solid and dependable, Annie burst into tears and flung her arms around Megan's neck. "There, there," the woman said, patting her gently on the back before extricating herself from Annie's grip. Annie would have felt rejected had not Megan taken her by the hand and followed Riya into the next room.

Blowing her nose and wiping her eyes, Annie introduced her new friends.

Megan looked questioningly at the many feathers strewn around the room. "Isn't it a bit early to be plucking chickens for Christmas?"

Annie and Riya stared at their feet, embarrassed, but Ella laughed. "No, we just had a problem with a leaky cushion." She brushed off one of the armchairs and invited Megan to take a seat. "Would you like a cup of tea?" she asked.

While Ella was in the kitchen and Riya went to help her, or maybe to kill her, Megan pulled a folded paper from her coat pocket. "You've made quite a splash," she said, brandishing the Daily.

Annie shrugged. "Alice took me to meet the Prime Minister

and then we visited Fenchaw. Things snowballed after that."

"Mother has a way of scheming with other people's lives that can be annoying if not dangerous."

The irritation in Megan's voice revealed a side of Kevin's family Annie hadn't noticed before. Megan must also have been a victim of her mother's plans. Ella carried in the tea and Riya brought a plate of biscuits. Once tea had been served, Megan said, "Show me this poster you've made."

Ella fetched a print out and handed it to Megan. Kevin's mother stared at it a long time, visibly moved at the sight of her daughter. "Who took the photo?" she asked, her eyes still fixed on the poster.

"Brian," Annie informed her. "He should be here any moment. It's him that has photos of the kidnappers."

Both Ella and Riya looked at her surprised.

"Good. The more evidence we can get the more chance we have of finding Kevin quickly. And I want to get up a case against the police for gross negligence."

The doorbell rang so loud Annie felt her seat shudder. "That'll be Brian," she said hurrying to open the door before Ella could go. Standing on the doorstep stood Kevin in only her underclothes, every inch of her body peppered with bruises and cuts. "It's your fault," the girl whispered through swollen lips and keeled over backwards down the stairs. Annie screamed and collapsed in a heap, her whole body trembling uncontrollably.

"What's wrong with her?" she heard Ella ask. "Is it an attack?

"No," Megan answered. Annie felt herself being eased back onto the settee. Someone wrapped a blanket round her but the trembling would not stop. "Kard has found some way of plunging people into nightmares. He's been subjecting Annie to this torture for a while."

"Poor thing. That's terrible," Riya said. "Is there no way to stop it?"

"We haven't found one yet," Megan said. "Would you like some hot tea, Annie, with lots of sugar in it? It is supposed to help against shock."

Annie managed to nod, although she kept her eyes clenched for fear of seeing that bloody, beaten body again. Someone, Ella probably, held the cup to her lips and Annie sipped. She was glad of the help. She was shaking so badly, she would never have managed alone. Despite Ella's care, some of the tea dribbled over Annie's chin. Ella wiped the liquid away with a paper hanky. The kindness of it had tears flowing freely from her eyes. When the girl leant closer to kiss her on the forehead, Annie heard the rustle of tissue and smelt the incense that clung to Riya. It had not been Ella after all.

The surprise of it had her cracking open her eyes. Riya held out her index finger and gently touched a spot at the base of her forehead between her eyebrows, making slow circular movements. Annie felt the terror fall away, like a heavy coat cast off, and the trembling abated. She looked Riya in the eyes and whispered, "Thank you."

Turning to see Megan and Ella, she apologized. "Kard will be the death of me."

"Don't ever say that," Megan insisted, her expression grave. "We will get him in the end."

The doorbell rang and Annie began trembling again. Riya took her in her scented arms and hugged her tight. "Don't worry," Ella said. "I'll go. It is probably only Brian."

41.

"The two thugs are clearly recognisable," Annie said. "What do we do now?"

"Surely if we make the photos public, that will discredit Kard and his nonsense about an invented girlfriend," Brian said.

"I doubt it," Annie said. "He'll just brush them aside as fakes, like he did with your photo of the man who shot me." Alice's words about truth and lies sprang to mind. Proof didn't exist in a world without truth. And without proof how could you decide if someone was guilty or not? Anything was possible.

"Unfortunately," Megan said, scrolling through the photos, "Annie is right."

"But surely we can't just keep silent," Ella said. "There must be some way to use these photos to find Kevin and bring those men to justice."

Megan got to her feet and paced the room. "What do we need to do?" She counted the points off on her fingers. "Find Kevin. Catch these men so they can be punished. But for that we need to force the police to act. And finally, discredit Kard. You have already circulated a photo of Kevin. Let's see what happens if we circulate the photos of the kidnappers. Someone must know them. Let's make no counter claims. Just allow people to draw their own conclusions."

Annie doubted Kard would leave people free to make up their minds. He'd weigh in with his media, discrediting the photos and casting ridicule on her and those around her.

"Shouldn't we create a site?" Ella suggested.

"It would be an ideal target for attacks from Kard and his mob," Riya said, shaking her head. "Better to have the message all over the internet. You can't whitewash all the walls sprayed with graffiti."

But you could shoot anyone caught out on the street with a canister of spray. Annie shook her head, alarmed at the sinister ideas her mind dragged up. Was this another fallout of Kard's nightmares? Making her think like him.

A familiar vibrating at her waist had her reaching for her phone. Only Kevin would call her that way. The phone was already at her ear before she remembered where Kevin was.

"Hallo, Annie," Kard said. "Would you like to talk to your little friend?"

Annie must have gone pale, because Riya asked, "Are you alright?"

"Yes," she replied. Half expecting him to hand the phone to Kevin.

"Good," Kard said. "Then these public appearances must stop. Or else…" The click as the line went dead was like an assassination.

"Who was that?" Megan asked, taking the phone from her unresisting fingers.

"Kard," she whispered.

"And what does Nolan Kard want?" Megan asked, her voice steeped in vitriol.

"That I stop appearing in public." Annie shuddered. "He threatened to hurt Kevin."

There was a shocked silence. "The bastard!" Ella exclaimed, punching a cushion. A tiny cloud of feathers rose in the air.

"We need to work faster," Riya said, getting to her feet. "I'll post the photos of the kidnappers and circulate them through GENie."

"I'll have them added to tomorrow's edition," Brian said, glancing at his watch. "Fenchaw won't be happy, but there's just enough time."

"Leave a copy of all your photos here," Megan said. "In

case."

It was Brian's turn to go pale. "Sure." He hurried after Riya to transfer the photos.

"We need to talk about what to do when we get sightings," Megan said, "and I have the very person to help us."

Blindfolded yet again, Annie sat on the back seat next to Ella as Megan drove them to an unknown destination.

"What Riya said about graffiti, I know it was only meant to be a metaphor," Annie said, feeling odd holding a conversation with her eyes blindfolded, "but maybe we could come up with a symbol to paint on walls across the country. A sort of show of force. I'm sure there are many street artists known to GENie."

"Great idea!" Ella was enthusiastic. "I could make two templates using the cartoon of you and Kard. One with Kard exhibiting his underpants and one of you with your fist raised and your shoulder nude and bleeding."

"Is the blood really necessary?" Annie asked.

"A hint of a Jesus figure," Ella said. "The power of pictures has a lot to do with how they relate to iconic images." Annie vaguely wondered what biblical figure Kard corresponded to, but came up with a blank. She could hear Ella rummaging in her bag. She must be looking for her iPad. The girl didn't waste time.

When they arrived, Ella guided her as they followed Megan into a hallway that smelt and felt expensive. The polished wooden furniture, a faint whiff of oils from paintings on the walls, the scent of cut flowers, the rustle of an indoor fountain, the thick carpet under foot, the calm atmosphere sealed off from the noise and bustle outside. A hushed exchange was taking place some distance away. It lasted several minutes, only ending when someone made a phone call.

"Let's go," Megan said, sounding annoyed. Once in the lift Ella removed the blindfold. The lift, which was large enough to take four times their number, was as plush as she had imagined, all gold fittings and marble panels set between full-length mirrors.

When the lift halted and the door slid open, they stepped out into a short corridor lined with a wall of windows on one side.

Annie could make out the Tower of London nestling in its walls and Tower Bridge spanning the river just beyond. Below, a set of railway lines emerged from buildings that must have been Fenchurch Street Station and scurried off eastwards to East Anglia and Essex. In the distance, the Thames curved away to the east into the long shadows cast by the setting sun.

A door at the end of the corridor opened onto a foyer that served as a reception. The girl behind the desk greeted them with a smile and nodded to a door. It led to an immense office. A semicircle of desks filled part of the space, each topped by several computer screens at which people were busy working, the whole arrangement organised in front of a wall covered in screens. Standing on a slightly raised area in front of the screens stood a tall man in jeans, shirt and tie. He was balding, but had a magnificent handlebar moustache. He reminded Annie of a character from a film, but she couldn't remember which.

"Meet Arnold Decker," Megan said. "Arnold, this is Annie and Ella."

"The illustrious young lady with the bloody shoulder," Arnold said, shaking her hand.

Trying to steer attention away from herself, she turned to Ella and said, by way of introduction, "Ella drew the cartoon with Kard in his underwear." Decker shook Ella's hand.

"I'm busy on two stencils from that cartoon," Ella said. "Do you have a corner of a desk where I could finish that?"

He beckoned over one of his staff, saying, "Set this young lady up with a desk, a connection and some refreshments." Then he turned back to Megan and said, "Follow me." He led them to a large desk completely free of papers or screens. He indicated the chairs in front of it and went round to take up his seat behind the desk. "So you have a problem for us."

42.

"You are fortunate," Decker said. "We rarely have so many sources of information, and, as you can imagine, depending purely on electronic sources can be unreliable."

"Maybe we should have brought Riya," Annie said, glancing in Ella's direction. The girl was chatting animatedly with one of the younger women working for Decker. "She does all the computer work."

Decker waved an inclusive arm over the rest of the room. "We have no shortage of computer experts."

His dismissiveness annoyed her. How could he judge Riya's usefulness? He hadn't even met her. She was convinced he was wrong. Riya was just the person they needed, but he didn't understand that yet. "I'm sure. But Riya knows all about GENie. She's the one in contact with everybody."

"GENie?"

"The Girls' Emergence Network. They saved Megan here and gave me shelter when people were trying to assassinate me. They were responsible for the distribution of Kevin's pictures. Riya is responsible for collating all the data about Kevin and her kidnappers."

Decker tugged on his moustache. "Interesting. Can you get her here?"

Annie got to her feet and, excusing herself, went to talk to Ella who was half surrounded by giant screens. On one was the familiar picture of Kard in his underwear, stylised to make him recognisable without too much detail. On the other screen a young woman brandished her fist. "Not quite finished yet," Ella said, sliding a stylus across her iPad. "I wish I had such equipment at home."

"Decker says we need Riya here," Annie said. She felt a little uncomfortable saying so to Ella after the tension between the three of them earlier. "So she can help with the data."

Ella pulled out her phone, then stopped. "How is she to get here? She has no car and it's nearly midnight."

"We can send someone to fetch her," a young woman at a nearby desk said. "Just give us her address and warn her we are coming."

Annie left them to settle the details and returned to Decker and Megan.

"I was telling Arnold about the little trick with the nightmares," Megan said.

Annie wished she hadn't, but then those they worked with had to be told something in case she was attacked again. She nodded.

"Could you describe one of these scenes?"

"They are like fragments of stories that I get sucked into. One second I'm here. The next I'm back. But in between I've been through all hell for any length of time. The last one was short and happened a couple of hours ago." She described answering the doorbell. "It often begins with some sort of vibration or shudder, but it can be so subtle I don't always notice it."

She described finding Kevin at the door, almost naked, her body tortured. She repeated Kevin's accusation and would have broken down again, had Megan not laid a reassuring hand on hers. "When she fell over backwards down the stairs, I collapsed only to find myself on the living room floor, trembling at the horror of what had just happened."

Decker whistled between his teeth. "Has anyone else been a victim of these malignant 'stories'?"

Annie hesitated. She wasn't sure she had the right to reveal what she knew. After all, he was the Prime Minister. She looked to Megan for guidance, but the woman knew nothing about that side of her visit to the PM. "I'm not sure I have the right to say. It's very sensitive information."

Megan looked alarmed, Decker faintly amused. His smile would disappear soon enough if ever she told him. When she still didn't say, Decker got up from his desk and came and sat next to them. "I understand that you want to protect one of your friends, but this may be important."

He had no idea. No wonder he'd found her caution amusing. She huffed out a breath and said, "It's John Underwood."

Both Megan and Decker's heads shot up.

"Underwood, the Prime Minister?" Megan asked, shocked.

"Alice took me to see him this morning. I had an intuition that his sorry state was due to attacks like mine. I asked him and when I described what happened, he admitted he had them too."

"This is far more serious than just a missing person," Decker said, springing to his feet then sitting down again.

"When I told the Prime Minister who was behind these attacks, he didn't want to believe me."

"And who is?" Decker asked.

"Nolan Kard," Annie said.

Decker spluttered. "I understand why the PM wasn't willing to believe you." He ran his fingers through the little remaining hair on his head. "What proof have you got?"

Annie told him of her first encounter with Kard, the 'gifts', the scene in the car with Kard and Kevin and the one with Kard in the telly talking to her.

"I agree," Decker said, "Kard certainly seems involved. But if he is the one behind all this, we have a war on our hands, one for which we are very poorly equipped."

"I suspect you've had a war on your hands for a while," Annie said. Decker looked intrigued. Megan frowned. "Kard has been chipping away at our institutions for ages. He's done away with truth. Fact and proof have been flushed down the drain. And as for expert opinion, it has little validity left. The notion of guilty or not guilty have no meaning. How can you condemn the man who shot me if there is no such thing as proof? How can you bring Kevin's kidnappers to justice if people deny Kevin exists? What proof have we got?"

Megan chuckled. "I know it's not funny. But you should be a lawyer."

"I see your point, Annie," Decker said. "It makes the job of finding Kevin that much more difficult, especially if Kard is behind the kidnapping. Our work here," he waved an arm in the direction of the array of desks, "is based on evidence. If all evidence is suspect or can be invalidated, we can prove nothing."

Annie could feel her brain spinning at top speed. "That doesn't mean we can't do anything? Kard will be felled otherwise. By ridicule rather than evidence. Like the spread of those pictures of him in his underpants. And a girl with her fist raised as a symbol that resistance is possible. As for finding Kevin, we need hard information that leads us to her. Your methods will work fine there, I imagine."

Decker chuckled. "You should work for us."

"That's what Fenchaw said."

Riya arrived at that moment. Decker greeted her and Riya nodded to Annie and Megan. "You already ditched Ella?"

Annie winced. Their form of humour made her want to grind her teeth. They joked with as much gusto as they kissed. She couldn't imagine making fun of Kevin with such crassness. "She's working on an idea of yours," Annie said, pointing towards the desk where Ella was hunched over a computer. The two girls waved briefly to each other, but Decker cut short any further conversation. "Show us what you've got."

"Presumably these computers are hooked up to that display." Riya pointed to the screen wall.

"Yes."

"How do I get access?" she asked, pulling an iPad from her bag.

The woman who had fetched her took her to one of the desks and after a short while a map of Southern England flickered onto the giant screen. With the iPad grasped in one hand, Riya used the other to point to places on the map. "We are right at the beginning, but we already have some information.

She pinched out with her fingers and the map zoomed in on Greater London where several places were flagged to the north of the capital. "A couple people have reported seeing Kevin being carried into a deserted house in a suburb of London. We are watching the place but Kevin has not been seen since. And we've just had a report from someone who recognised one of the kidnappers. He comes from Chelmsford and his name is Phelps." She pulled up an id photo of Phelps and slid Brian's photo of the kidnappers next to it.

While she spoke Decker's whole team had gathered in front of the screen, enthralled. "What's that?" a woman asked, pointing to one of the tiny flags on the map.

"Kevin was sighted slumped in the back of a car in the car park of a motorway cafe on the outskirts to London."

Decker chuckled. "I wonder why you think you need our help. This is excellent."

"I can manage this early phase when there is not too much information, but if we get inundated with sightings, I won't be able to keep up and we might miss something important."

"To be honest, we don't deal much with massive input. But we do have some tools that might help," Decker said. He ordered his team to help Riya and then went back to his desk, followed by Megan and Annie.

43.

"Surely there must be some not on Kard's side," Megan said, as she and Decker discussed how to deal with the police.

Annie should have been listening, but it was past midnight and she was fascinated by the map of England on the screen. One part of it flickered in a way she saw nowhere else. As she focussed in on that part, she could have sworn a hand was beckoning her.

"That's weird," she was tempted to say, but the two were engrossed in their discussion and she didn't want to disturb. She got to her feet and strode, with what she hoped would appear nonchalant, to examine the screen. She ran her fingers over the image of the hand which was very distinct close up and, as she did, the hand reached out and grabbed her, pulling her through the screen.

She would have screamed had she not been so startled by the surface which offered no resistance. It was like being pulled through a wall of light. As soon as she realised what had happened, she sucked in a breath to bellow for help but a hand clamped over her mouth. She was about to dig her teeth into the fleshy part of the hand when a voice whispered near her ear, "Shhh. He'll hear."

Whoever had spoken released her. As she gasped for air, she glanced back at the screen. On the other side everything was grey and insubstantial. People were frozen at their tasks. Megan had her mouth open, about to say something to Decker. Ella was leaning over Riya, on the point of stealing a kiss.

"Hallo Annie," the voice said.

She spun round. Much to her surprise, perched on a bar stool, shifting uncomfortably from side to side, sat a man in baggy trousers and a chequered shirt. If you met him at a meeting or a party, you'd forget his name the moment you turned your back and the next morning you would have a hard time remembering his face if ever you bothered. Just the sort of person who surprised his neighbours by murdering his wife or preying on little children. She shuddered at the thought. Kard must really be getting to her.

"Who are?" she asked, her tone none too friendly.

He flinched. "Greetings to you too," he said. "Rather than asking who I am, you should be asking what l am."

Irritated that he didn't answer his own question, she repeated it.

"I'm a ghost writer."

Where had she heard that expression before? Ah yes. Alice had told her about people who were paid to write for someone else. "What do you write?"

That he fidgeted with a button on his shirt a long moment before replying had her wondering if his writings were somehow reprehensible or disgusting.

"I write your 'daymares' as you call them," he finally admitted, shooting her a fearful glance, no doubt terrified of her reaction.

She stared at him in disbelief. All the horrible scenes she'd been subjected to flashed through her mind. She clenched her teeth and balled her fists. If she strangled him, would the nightmares stop?

"Before you try to kill me," he said, holding up a hand to placate her, "let me explain."

She looked around for something to hit him with, but they were in an empty grey space with no walls and no furniture. A wave of exhaustion swept over her and she sagged. "Is there nowhere to sit?"

"Of course. How thoughtless of me."

She turned to find an armchair behind her. It was worn and there were coffee stains on the arms. That he conjured up such a filthy seat had her convinced he didn't give a damn about her. When a second wave of exhaustion rolled over her, she gripped an arm of the chair and sank into it. To her surprise, it was not as uncomfortable as she'd imagined.

"There are lots of people like me,…" he began.

Sure, she thought, the world's full of men preying on teenage girls, making their life hell with the fantasies they dreamed up.

"…proficient at writing," he went on as if reciting a text, "with a smattering of imagination, but not what it takes to be a successful writer." Judging by the ordeals he'd put her through there was no lack of imagination.

"Some try and fail. Most don't bother. Instead, we write for others, those who can't write. We take their ideas, the few they have. We take their money, the little they are prepared to pay. And we do their dirty work, suffering their abuse when they fail to understand the sense and the beauty of what we have written."

She scoffed at the word 'beauty'. He might be painting a picture of himself and his colleagues as victims, but she had no sympathy. She was the victim, not him. It was his imagination that had transformed Kevin into a battered child.

"I heard Nolan Kard was offering work, so I applied. I had no idea what it entailed. How was I to know I was walking into a trap? I thought I might make some money from a successful business man."

How naive did you have to be? You couldn't make money from someone like Kard. His every move screamed: conman. Only the very rich ever made money with him.

He paused, staring off into the grey distance as if he'd got lost in his own story. Annie wondered if Kard knew she was there. Maybe this was a more sophisticated nightmare that had yet to turn nasty. It certainly was different from the others.

"I didn't have to write straight away. Kard introduced me to a scientist who was experimenting ways of projecting story fragments into people's brains. I was to draft fragments and he would show me how to send them." He shook his head, then brushed aside the mop of unruly hair that had fallen over his eyes. "Have you ever wondered how I knew what nightmares to send?"

"I imagined Kard had some way of spying on me."

"He wanted my stories, and those of others like me, to destabilise his victims. To do so, our stories had to fit their everyday life. At first they were not to notice the transition. But to do that the writers had to be present without being seen. That is the terrible irony of our lot. He turned us into real ghost writers. I am a ghost. Here, in between, you see me as I used to be, but if I were in your bedroom or your living room, you'd see me as a ghostly presence, if you saw me at all. Another irony of my situation is that I no longer need to write. Suffice it to think the story and it pops up in the person's head."

She shook herself, realising she'd become engrossed in his tale, almost sympathising with him, forgetting the monster he was.

"Sounds exciting, powerful even," he said. "Don't be misled. It's not at all. It's an unending burden. What you suffer, so do we, every ounce of your terror, every surge of your anger, every last tear of your sadness. And there's a worse price. We are condemned to be ghosts and can never come back."

She shuddered. His story was horrible. Her nightmares lasted a few moments, his had no end.

"Why are you telling me this? You won't win me over."

He shook his head. "I don't expect to. No. I thought it might help you."

"Help me?" She didn't believe a word of it.

"You probably think I revel in torturing you. I don't. It's sickening. But there is very little I can do. I'm trapped. You can't imagine the terrible risk I'm taking talking to you now."

"Won't he find out?"

He shuddered. "I will do everything I can to stop him knowing." He smiled for the first time. "He is not immune to our stories. Although at the slightest hint of betrayal, he will cut our throats. Metaphorically, I mean."

"But, why me? Why help me?"

"I don't like Kard. I dislike what he does to people. And the more I get to know you, the more I want to help you."

"Well, you could start by not sending me such horrible visions." An image of Kevin's scarred body surged before her eyes.

"I can't do that. And you wouldn't want me to."

"Why ever not?" she asked, indignant.

"Because, if he suspected, he would replace me with someone worse."

How could her nightmares possibly be worse? Each one left her wiped out.

"No. I have to continue as if nothing had happened. The best I can do is give you a warning. But I can't guarantee it will always be possible."

"Then this will go on till I break."

"Not if I can help it."

"But I can't take it much longer." She got to her feet, wanting to escape. She stared at the screen, wondering if she could just walk through?

"You must hold on."

"What for? There's no hope."

"You are the hope."

She stamped her foot. He was exasperating. "Stop beating about the bush."

"You too can tell stories," he said, his expression serious. "You must do to Kard what he does to others."

"But I don't want to be a ghost."

"I don't think you have to. The methods of Kard's scientist are clumsy and irreversible. But I suspect there are other ways to dance a nightmare around Kard. Your idea with the underpants was pretty clever. There must be ways of implanting stories in his head without becoming a ghost."

It all seemed far too easy. She was beginning to suspect it might all be a lie to give her hope before finishing her off. "Does he know I'm here?"

"Not in this in-between space."

"Can't you hide from him here?"

"I'm not very good company. Being stuck here forever, remember no time goes by outside…" He nodded to the screen. "I would drive myself mad."

"So how do I do this story thing?"

"I can't teach you all in one go. You'll need practice. But I can tell you how to get started. Figure out a way to observe him. Find out what he's afraid of. Uncover his weak spots. Look closely at those around him. But never attack directly. He'll guess what's up. He might have a twisted mind, but he's not stupid. Use tiny touches. A glimpse here. A nudge there. A slip of the tongue. A misplaced foot on the stairs. So brief, so close to his everyday life, that he suspects nothing. I know it is hard, but be playful rather than vindictive. He doesn't understand play. Heartfelt humour is beyond him."

The prospect was appealing. But what use inventing stories, if you didn't know how to slip them into the other's head? "You've forgotten the most important point."

He smiled. "No, I haven't. But use it sparingly. No one else must know." He leant close and whispered a long moment in her ear, the softness of his voice almost lulling her to sleep.

She was still smiling when Megan touched her shoulder, startling her. "Time for bed," the woman said. Annie stretched, stifling a yawn, and struggled to her feet. Decker shook her hand, saying, "I trust you sleep well, despite the weight on your shoulders."

She must have fallen asleep and dreamt the whole scene behind the mirror. Yet, unlike a dream, it remained vivid. There was only one way to find out. She'd have to try what she'd learnt.

44.

Ella gave directions as Megan drove at a walking pace along the narrow passage that wound around the new blocks of houses on land reclaimed from the docks. "There," Ella said, pointing. Megan halted at the foot of the steps running up. Megan had offered to lodge Annie, but the idea of sleeping where Kevin should have been was unnerving. Annie was about to follow the others when Megan leaned out the car window and said, "I'm going to be very busy, but I want you to keep me informed. Call me the moment you have news." Annie promised. Of course she would.

Riya and Ella continued excitedly discussing plans for Ella's cartoon figures as they climbed the flight of steps to the front door and Ella let them in. Both girls headed for the kitchen, Ella calling back over her shoulder, "A last cuppa?"

Annie shook her head. "I'm whacked." She climbed the stairs using the banisters to haul herself up, past Ella and Riya's bedroom and on up to the top of the house to the spare room. She collapsed on the bed and stared up at the sloping ceiling, repeating to herself, "Tiny steps. Tiny steps."

She awoke to find daylight streaming in the window and her still fully clothed. Some kind soul had covered her with a blanket. Looking out the window, she was delighted to see the narrow canal that snaked round the block. Coming from the East End, she was no stranger to these remnants of waterways that carved their way through the land. It was like coming home although the battered terraced houses of her parents' street, part of a post-war effort to rebuild blitzed areas with affordable accommodation, couldn't measure up to the luxury constructions springing up everywhere with their underfloor heating and their fitted kitchens. However did the girls afford it?

She had the house to herself. A note from Ella announced she would be back for lunch. Annie went down to the bathroom next to the girls' bedroom and showered, relishing in the unending supply of hot water. Once dried, she regretted not having clean clothes to change into. Money was going to be a problem. She didn't want to use what Kard had sent. Maybe she could get a job. Fenchaw might take pity on her. He had offered her an apprenticeship.

Rummaging through the fridge and cupboards, she found stores enough to lay on a banquet. At home there had been days when the shelves were resolutely bare and mother had given her a few coins to buy something on the way to school. She opted for a brunch, delighting in the unaccustomed freedom of choice. Everything was on the table when Ella turned up.

"Wow! A feast!" Ella exclaimed.

Annie was embarrassed. "I hope you don't mind me helping myself."

"Lord no. I'm starving."

"Is Riya coming?"

"No. She's gone to Decker's. We are starting to get more replies." Ella sat down and broke off a piece of bread and smeared it with soft cheese. "I brought you this." She dropped the day's paper on the table. It fell open at the front page. Ella's cartoon of Annie, fist raised, shoulder bared, filled the whole page, eclipsing most of the name of The Daily.

"Aren't you lot going a bit overboard?"

Ella laughed. "Not at all. Our circulation figures just shot up. We are inundated with readers' emails, not all of them insulting." She bit into her bread. "Look at the back page," she mumbled through a full mouth.

The entire page was taken up by the cartoon of Kard in his underpants. Unfolding the newspaper so she could see both the front and the back, she realised it was Ella's entire cartoon. "People can pin it up wherever they like," Ella said, a wicked grin on her lips.

Annie turned over the front page to discover photos of the three thugs in action, the one that had shot her and the two who kidnapped Kevin. To her surprise under each photo was the name of the person with a call for further information. "Is that legal?" she asked.

"Fenchaw checked with our legal team. They okayed it. We make no accusations. Just show the photos and suggest who the people might be."

That seemed very much like a public denunciation. They might be despicable villains and the police a broken machine, but what about justice? Was this the new face of justice beyond truth? Fenchaw was taking an immense risk.

"I need to spy on Kard," Annie said, once they'd finished eating. Saying 'spying' seemed more acceptable than 'observing'.

Ella's surprise quickly gave way to excitement. "You got some action planned?"

Annie shook her head. "Just getting to know my enemy."

According to the internet, Kard was appearing on a TV talk show at five which was open to the public.

"I can't go like this," Annie said, indicating her filthy clothes.

"You sure can't. Everyone will recognise you. You must be the most well-known public figure in London at the moment."

Annie shook her head. However had her life come to this?

"What you need is my friend Jewel." When quizzed, all Ella would say was that Jewel was some sort of fashion consultant.

They walked at a leisurely pace, winding their way between new brick houses besieged by parked cars and building sites fenced in behind hoardings announcing future flats for sale. The quiet of midday hung precariously over this new beginning. Annie was struck by the absence of shops. Architects and town planners had forgotten residents needs in their rush to make money from their slick new homes.

It was only when they passed under the railway lines and

crossed into a much older part of town that shops sprang up. Jewel's 'shop' was just off a busy street peopled with all manner of retail outlets, convenience stores and mini-markets selling everything and nothing. Outwardly, Jewel's place resembled a shop, although none of the wares on display were for sale, Ella explained.

Having woven their way between racks of clothes and shelves of trinkets and wigs, Annie wondered what Jewel did sell. A space had been cleared in front of a window at the rear looking out over a walled-in wilderness that echoed the chaos within. On a dais, stood a single pink chair, like those found at a hairdresser's. Next to it stood a slender, Asiatic beauty straight out of a fashion magazine.

"So this is Annie Wight," she said, in a high, lilting voice with gravely undertones that did not quite fit the person. "Our hero of the day."

"Annie, meet Jewel, London's best transformation artist."

Transformation? Annie looked more carefully at Jewel's face only to realise that at some time in the distant past Jewel might have looked more like a man than a woman.

"So what do you want to be?"

Annie was embarrassed, imagining the kind of clients Jewel must normally cater for.

"Don't worry honey. Nothing will be pasted on permanently or cut off. I'm not into that kind of transformation."

It was meant as a joke, but it sent cold shivers down Annie's spine. "I just need to go unrecognised." She thought of the ghost writer. "Preferably the sort of person no one notices."

Jewel flung her head back and let out a throaty laugh. "That must be the first time anyone has asked me that. Almost all my customers want to stand out." She twirled gracefully on her high heels, her arms reaching up in a pirouette. "What a delightful challenge." She steadied herself with her slender arms outstretched like a bird settling from flight.

"I can't pay very much," Annie said, worried that Jewel's services were likely to be expensive.

"Don't bother your little head over that, sweetie. This is my contribution to the cause. And someday maybe you can do a photo shoot for me, showing off my latest creations."

Annie was relieved she wouldn't have to pay, but alarmed at the idea of being magicked into a model for transformations.

"Good. Show us what you've got," Jewel said, taking a step back as if to size her up.

Annie was perplexed. She'd brought nothing with her.

"Get underdressed," Jewel explained. "So I can see what I have to work with."

Annie glanced around the 'shop' and out the window at the jungle.

"Don't worry honey. There are no hidden cameras. And I'm used to nudity."

What about her? Annie thought. She certainly was not.

Two hours later, the transformation was complete. Jewel had gone for the urchin look, flattening what little breasts she had and padding out her shoulders. Luckily her hips were not too pronounced. Jewel wanted to use a wig, but Annie was afraid it would be too hot and cumbersome. Finally, Jewel had shaved off her pixie style, leaving her with a crew cut over which she wore a cloth cap. Heavy duty Docks, baggy pants, a plain shirt and jacket and a silk scarf to keep her neck warm completed the disguise. Annie refused the single earring Jewel wanted to add. Earnings made her feel uncomfortable. They reminded her of her mother who always wore them, cheap ones that joggled about the side of her face. Annie had no wish to resemble her.

"That's it, honey. You're done. I really am the best!" Jewel crooned.

Annie stared at herself in a full-length mirror, transfixed by what she saw. So much for remaining incognito. Every eye would be turned on her. She was sure of it. But at least she looked nothing like Annie Wight. Seeing the boyish girl staring back had her wondering who or what she was. The ambiguity was some-how empowering. Was that how Kevin felt?

"You're hot," Ella purred.

Ella's tone set alarm bells jangling in Annie's head. It was no longer only Kard she'd have to worry about, she thought, turning away from the mirror.

"Would you like a mini pepper spray?" Jewel asked, grinning widely as she gave Ella a friendly shove. "If ever you have to calm people's ardour."

45.

Ella insisted they hold hands, part of Annie's disguise she said, as they walked down the side aisle to their seats in the TV studios. Annie's scowl wasn't really part of her role. The way Ella flirted with her was getting awkward. She dreaded the moment she'd have to reject her advances.

The two sat at the end of a row close to the set with its cameramen poised for action. Annie pulled her hand free of Ella's and peered around for ways out. Few people in the audience were their age. Most were middle-aged women in their Sunday best but there were also some older men with stern faces and greying hair. So much for not standing out.

"Maybe we should leave while we can," Annie whispered, increasingly alarmed. She tensed her muscles to stand.

"Of course not, my love," Ella said, placing a firm hand on Annie's thigh more to retain her than to placate her. "This is going to be fun." When Ella didn't remove her hand, Annie whispered, "That's my leg you are making free with. Not Riya's." Ella grinned and, leaning close, whispered in Annie's ear, "All part of the role." She finally did remove her hand, but not before squeezing Annie's thigh.

The house lights dimmed as spotlights flooded the set. Cameras whirred into action and the show's host strode up a small flight of steps onto the set amid polite applause. Remaining standing, he turned to face the audience and said, "Our guest tonight is the one and only Nolan Kard, multimillionaire, media mogul, influent politician and recent top model for men's underwear."

Annie wasn't sure if the host was poking fun or recuperating the underwear campaign to Kard's advantage. The man turned to look towards the stairs and Kard stepped out looking like a bloated pig strutting on its hind legs.

Annie sped through the ghost writer's instructions, worried she'd get it wrong, then flung an instant of doubt at Kard as he put a foot on the first step. It would take only a fraction of a second, but enough to make him miss the next step and fall flat on his face. She was the first of the audience to gasp when Kard faltered mid-step and keeled over. Gasps were followed by roars of laughter. Annie laughed loudly too. Kard scrambled to his feet with the help of the host and brushed himself off as if the spotless studio floor were filthy.

Seated, with a smile plastered across his face, Kard greeted the audience. Several people cheered, others applauded. Annie smiled too, her mind racing, revelling in a feeling of power. How else could she heap ridicule on him? Have him muddle his words, revealing his deeper, nasty thoughts. Make him knock things over in a bout of inexplicable clumsiness. Force him absentmindedly to stick a finger up his nose or scratch his privates. Ugh! The thought disgusted her. Enough! The heady feeling of success was making her punch-drunk.

"So, Mr. Kard," the host said, "how straight is London these days?"

Kard babbled on about the success of his Keep London Straight meetings until the host interrupted him. "Tell us something about your new campaign for men's underwear."

Kard hesitated, a flicker of annoyance crossing his face. "That has nothing to do with me. That's just The Daily trying to drum up an audience for a tired old newspaper."

One or two people close to Annie sniggered. She was unsure if they were laughing at the paper or Kard. She glanced at their blank faces. Maybe they didn't know either.

"You must admit, it's had quite an echo. Drawings of you in your smalls are popping up all over the place alongside that girl with her fist raised. What's her name? Annie Wight."

Hearing her name pronounced so openly, had Annie cringing. It was like having a flashing neon hovering over her head screaming, *look, here she is, Annie Wight*. She sank deeper into her seat and pulled her cap over her eyes.

"Popularity has its price," Kard said, waving away the question with a lazy gesture.

Smug idiot! Annie wished she could make him have a violent attack of diarrhoea, but the ghost writer had said tiny steps only, nothing showy. Anyway, she could not do such things in the real world, only in that in-between space that was the place of dreams and nightmares.

Kard had moved on to another subject. "Take Underwood," he said. " Nobody's talking about his underwear, are they? Although I am sure he has some dirty secrets in his closets. He was once a popular politician. These days he looks as worn out as a discarded dishcloth. Not so surprising with all the problems the country has. I heard he was standing down. Do him good to have a rest. It's time someone more competent took over the reins."

The cheek of it. All John Underwood needed was a break from Kard's nightmares.

"Are you that person?" the host asked.

Kard ignored the question. Instead, he got to his feet and scanned the audience. He couldn't miss Annie and Ella in sea of older faces. "It's good to see the country's future in the audience. They don't get much chance to express themselves these days." Sure, Annie thought, every wall is shrieking their comments. "Maybe that young man over there would like to come up and talk to us." Annie didn't immediately realise the young man was her.

The host frowned at having his show hijacked, but a spotlight tracked across the audience and picked out Annie. Several cameras spun in search of her. She turned to pelt for the exit, but her way was blocked by a production assistant. She looked to Ella for help, but the girl shrank in her seat, terrified, as if she'd seen a ghost, or worse, was the victim of one Kard's daymares.

Kard sauntered over to greet Annie, his filthy paw grasping hers, and slid a possessive arm around her shoulders. She stood rigid, struggling not to throw up.

"So what has our youth to say to our prime time audience?" Kard asked, a massive grin across his face. Conceited swine. Cornering someone weaker boosted his overinflated ego.

Annie kept her mouth stubbornly shut. The slightest word would make her Kard's accomplice, his 'voice of youth'. In one second she would go from the figurehead of opposition to a snivelling acolyte. She was caught in her own trap. So much for anonymity. She seemed to have a gift for blundering into the spotlight at the worst time.

"Don't be shy," Kard said, pinching her cheek as if she were a doll. His other hand had slipped to the small of her back. That he thought he could get away with groping her on television was outrageous.

Annie unleashed a flash of light in his head. It lasted only a fraction of a second, but enough for the memory of it to make Kard stagger and grasp his chest as he sank to the floor. Annie raised her fist in salute knowing every camera was on her and yelled, "Fire!"

The audience erupted from their seats screaming as they fought to get out. In the chaos, Annie vaulted from the set and darted down the side aisle weaving between the panicked people in search of Ella. Incapable of fending for herself, the terrified girl was crushed against the wall by a surging throng. Annie elbowed her way through, not hesitating to shove several fractious men out of the way, and, slinging a protective arm around Ella's shoulders, led her to an emergency exit.

46.

Annie sucked in a deep breath trying to calm her hammering heart and immediately spluttered in disgust. The cafe stank. The Formica tabletops were filthy, the walls streaked with grease and the floor grimy. At least there were plenty of dark corners to hide in and no other customers. The blaring television would drown even the loudest conversation.

Annie struggled to settle Ella in a seat, wrestling to free herself from the girl who clung to her like a lost child. To see her new friend, who was such an enterprising young woman, plunged into utter dependence was shocking. Why on earth had she been so affected? Had she been hit by one of Kard's daymares? That seemed improbable.

They couldn't just sit there. She'd have to order drinks. When she rose, Ella stirred and snatched her sleeve, refusing to let go. "It's alright," Annie said, trying to sound reassuring as she unclasped the girl's fingers. "I'm just going to fetch some tea. I'll be back in a tick."

The man slumped against the counter with his back partly turned was sporting an off-white turban and a contrastingly colourful shirt. The sight of Kard's blue badge pinned to his lapel had her panicking. She tried to reason with herself but her whole body tensed to run. He couldn't possibly know who she was. He wasn't even paying her any attention. His eyes were glued to the screen.

The news channel replayed extracts from Kard's appearance. His trip on the stairs. His reply about underwear. They even cut to a picture of Ella's cartoon. His comment about Underwood. Kard calling Annie onto the stage. Her, fist raised, as Kard crumpled at her feet. Kard being carried off on a stretcher. What a disaster. She'd need a new disguise.

Suddenly realising what that meant, she looked at the man to find him staring pointedly at her, dawning recognition giving way to intense hatred. She took a step back, terrified. "Not so fast," he growled. In a second he was round the counter and grabbed her by the throat. "I know some people who'd be delighted to get their hands on you."

Annie clawed at his fingers, but the more she struggled, the tighter he clenched. She coughed and wheezed, desperately trying to suck in air. She mustered her strength to blast him out of existence. Damn the ghost writer's caution. This was an emergency. She slammed an imaginary knife into the man's side. He screamed, his hands flying to the would-be wound. Free, she shoved him backwards causing him trip over his own feet and stumble. Grabbing a chair, she smashed it over his head. The crunch of wood against bone was sickening. He grunted, his eyes rolled back and he sank to the floor, blood seeping from under his turban.

"That's torn it!" she said, and dropped the chair which clattered to the floor as an ad for skin cream blared on the TV. What a mess. The police had had nothing against her. Now they had assault and possibly murder. They might not give a hoot about a thug that tried to shoot her, but they'd be after her with every tracker dog they had.

"I told you not to overdo it," an insubstantial voice said nearby.

Startled, she spun round. The ghost writer was almost invisible. She could just make out the contours of his face and a hint of his chequered trousers.

"He would have killed me," she pleaded.

"I know. I saw. So what are you going to do?"

"Run. Hide. Give myself up. No idea." She pictured the people at the rally. They had been so eager to cheer her. She had been their glorious figurehead. Confronted with Kard, she had been untainted. What would they say now? Tears welled up in her eyes, more out of anger and frustration than self-pity. She brushed them aside.

"There might be a solution, but you're not going to like it," the ghost writer said.

"What?" she snapped.

"I could take him into the other world. It's not easy, but him being unconscious will help."

The idea was appealing. All of a sudden her problem would disappear. But what would it imply? Was it not murder in another form? "He'd never be able to come back?"

The sadness on his face was clearly visible even if his features were indistinct. He nodded. "He would be stuck there like the rest of us."

She imagined the man rampaging through the other world in search of the one who had dragged him into that nightmare place. She imagined him tracking her, armed with a suitcase crammed full of appalling nightmares. "Would he be a danger to you? Would he be a danger to me?"

"He might be. It's a risk we'd have to take."

She removed the cloth cap and ran her fingers through what remained of her hair. It was like signing a pact with the devil, a convoluted agreement with nightmares concealed in every clause. She glanced at the body, blood slowly pooling on the linoleum around its head. "Okay. Let's buy some time."

"Are you sure?"

She nodded and as she did the form of the Pakistani shimmered and dissolved little by little till nothing was left. The ghost writer had disappeared too. She stood staring at the pool of blood for a long moment, dread lodged like a dead weight in her stomach. It wasn't enough to get rid of the body.

Pulling a paper handkerchief from her pocket, she wiped the sticky red liquid from the floor. She carried it at arm's length to the toilet which was little more than a stinking hole in the ground and pulled the chain to flush the evidence away. Only a trickle of water emerged causing a tell-tale pink ring to spread out around the sodden red paper. What if it would never go away? In a panic, she rummaged behind the counter where she found a crate of empty bottles. Grabbing one, she filled it with water. Back in the toilet, it took several trips till all the blood had been washed down the hole.

With a start, she remembered Ella. The girl was slumped in her seat, staring off into space unaware of the world around her. How much had Ella seen? She didn't want anyone else burdened with keeping the murder secret. But that would have to wait. First they had to slip away. Abandoning Ella to her blank nightmare, Annie went in search of a way out. She was in luck, behind a dusty curtain she uncovered a back exit that led to a narrow alley.

Returning to Ella, she helped the girl to her feet. Holding the curtain to one side, she led her out the door, along the alley, past the crates of empties and across the street that lay beyond. Ella went meekly, grasping Annie's hand, like a toothless zombie, plodding steadfastly forward with no will of her own.

Annie knew little about shock, but surely it shouldn't last that long. She wanted to shake Ella. Bring back her familiar self. A horrible thought struck her. Maybe it was something else. Something worse. She had no idea who to turn to. She couldn't possibly contact Riya, the sight of this brainless Ella would drive her over the brink. She needed someone who knew about medicine. Leonor, of course. The nurse would know what to do.

Annie pulled out her phone and dialled. No one answered. Odd. Surely the Network manned the phone nonstop. She tried a second time. Somebody picked up but no one spoke. Alarmed, Annie hung up. Had the Network been raided by the police? How long would they take to trace her call? She had to move. Fast. But where could she go? She didn't know that part of London so well and she had hardly any money.

She might have gone to Jewel's, but the transformation artist had planned to go out. Then there were Decker's offices. They were near Fenchurch Station, but she'd been blindfolded at the time. She could try The Daily which was somewhere close by, but with the trouble she'd stirred up, the place was probably being watched.

The side street they'd been following ended at a busy main road. Several passers-by stared at them as Ella stumbled and almost fell. They were far too exposed. She steered the young woman into the grounds of a church at the street corner. The large open courtyard flanking the church offered no place to hide so she headed along the building and led Ella through a wrought-iron gate into a garden behind the church.

The trees that lined the garden might offer some cover, but her attention was caught by the brick wall. One after another, riveted to the wall, two layers of headstones, one higher than the other, stretched its whole length. Many of their inscriptions had faded. Time no doubt. Were the people buried under the flag-stones that formed a path along the wall? Her thoughts flew to the Pakistani prostrate on the floor, blood trickling from under his turban. She froze, unable to take a step further.

The ringing of the church bells made her jump. The peal called the faithful to evening service. Several cars turned into the space behind her, forcing her to seek refuge deeper in the garden. Reaching a bench shaded by a clump of trees, she settled Ella and sat down next to her. She closed her eyes and was taking a deep breath when her phone rang.

47.

Annie stared at her ringing phone, her hands trembling as she tried to muffle the sound. It rang and rang. Surely it was the sort of trick the police would play. Call back. Find out who answered. Then nab them. Abruptly the ringing stopped, to Annie's relief. But relief quickly spawned anxiety. What if it had been someone else? Kevin who'd managed to escape. Or Riya in search of Ella. Or Megan seeking news of Kevin. Or simply Leonor calling back.

When the phone rang a second time, Annie glanced around the garden, it was empty, then answered. "Hallo?"

There was a pause and she almost hung up, but a familiar voice asked, "Annie? Is that you?"

"Leonor?" She could hardly believe she had got through. Then her anguish came flooding back and burst through as anger. "Where the hell were you?"

"Hold your horses," Leonor said, sounding more startled than annoyed. "Everyone's got to pee from time to time. I heard the phone ring but I don't like answering in the loo." She chuckled. "So what's your problem?"

"I'm on the run. With Ella. She's shell shocked. Can't get any sense out of her."

"Where are you?"

"In a park behind a church." She described the strange tombstones.

"That's St. George in the East," Leonor said, promising to come and fetch her.

Momentarily distracted, Annie stared into the distance. A shimmering light between the leaves of the trees intrigued her. Shifting to get a better look, she spotted a large greenhouse half-concealed amongst the trees.

"There's a greenhouse," she said, but Leonor had hung up.

Ella was dozing as Annie got to her feet and went to investigate. Not a greenhouse, a hothouse, brimming with tropical plants. There was even a small pond on which water lilies floated, and a bench sheltered from view by the vegetation. Cracking open the door, a welcome rush of warm air greeted her. She shivered. She hadn't realised how cold she felt.

Retracing her steps, she went in search of Ella. The girl moaned about being awoken, but, with some coaxing, followed docilely. Annie helped her sit on the bench, undoing her jacket for fear she'd faint in the heat. Then she sat next to her and pulled off her own cap and jacket. Every now and then an overhead spray clicked on showering them with tiny droplets that settled on her shaved head and made rainbows in the early evening sun.

With a growing feeling of relief, knowing that rescue was on its way, some of the numbness fell from her and she was able to appreciate her surroundings. The glass roof of the hothouse with its wrought iron framework arched above, fiery red in the last rays of the setting sun. The spectacular tableau was mirrored on the glassy surface of the pond amid water lilies tinged pink by the light. The scene was so undeniably real its very existence punched her in the stomach, moving her to tears. Then the image dissolved as a cloud of droplets rained down from the sprinklers.

Ella dozed, slumped on the bench, her head sunk to her chest. From time to time she made little noises, disturbing the regular click and whoosh of the watering system as it sprang to life. Annie moved closer and slung an arm round the girl's shoulders. Ella snuggled up, mumbling, "Riya." Annie sighed. "Things are going to be alright," she whispered.

A creak from the door, concealed behind dense foliage, alerted her that rescue had arrived. She was getting wearily to her feet when two policemen wearing turbans pushed past the foliage. Turbans? Was that possible? Seeing her, they darted forward. One grabbed Ella, dragging her to her feet. The other loomed over Annie saying,"I arrest you for the murder of a Pakistani restaurant owner."

She sank to the bench, her head in her hands. Just when everything was returning to normal. How could they possibly know? Had there been a hidden camera? Surely not in that dump. Had one of those tracker dogs sniffed her out? What a nightmare. This had all the markings of a Kard daymare yet there had been no warning. The ghost writer had said he would. So much for promises.

"Come with us," the policeman said, shaking her violently by the shoulder, the very one that had been wounded. She winced and put up a hand to fend him off. Rather than hold on to her, he shoved her backwards. Her foot caught on the low line of stones that surrounded the pond and, arms flailing wildly, she tumbled backwards head-over-heels into the water. It was tepid and slimy. She kicked at the tendrils that curled around her feet and legs trying to pull her down. Closer to the surface, a long slender form slithered through the water, brushing against her. She screamed, thrashing out.

Despite her agitation, the snake coiled lazily around her chest, then tightened its grip, pinning one of her arms against her body. With her free hand, she grabbed an ornamental light floating in the water and smashed the bulb over the snake's head. It reared up, opening wide its jaws, sharp fangs bared, ready to strike. She rammed the incandescent filament into the gaping hole. A brilliant flash blinded her. Her muscles seized up as she was flung from the water and hurled against the low stone wall on which the glass and metal structure rested.

Her leg cracked on impact, sending a searing pain through her whole body. She sank to the floor, whimpering. Nothing but a charred mass remained of the snake still coiled about her waist. Disgusted, she extricated herself from the smouldering ruins, her wet hands plastered with charred scales.

From the depths of the long, sinister shadows that now shroud the hothouse came the scrape of a heavy weight being dragged across the floor. It filled her with dread. The noise grew louder and closer till two deadly rows of teeth emerged from the gloom. A crocodile. What next?

She clambered to her feet balancing on her good leg and flung herself against the nearest pane of glass only to bounce off, toppling dangerously close to the crocodile. Hopping away just as it snapped, she smashed into the window a second time. It resisted a moment then shattered and she burst through. Large slivers of glass drove down into the advancing beast. Stabbed through and through, it thrashed, showering her in blood and glass before it sank moaning out of sight.

She swore. This was no Kard nightmare. His were just warnings to frighten her. Whoever was behind this horror was out to kill. The Pakistani!

"There you are," the policeman in the turban said with a grin. She tried to hop a step away, but he lashed out with his foot, the hobnailed boot smashing into her broken leg. She screamed and toppled to the ground, only to have him drag her to her feet and shake her.

"Annie!" a voice shouted. "Snap out of it."

A violent tug of war ensued, her bones being wrenched apart, every tendon stretched to screaming point. Stop! she wanted to cry out, you are tearing me in two. Then something gave and the person shaking won. Only just. Annie cracked open her eyes to find Leonor leaning over her, worry etched on her face. Annie flung herself into the woman's arms and broke into sobs.

"Kard?" Leonor asked when Annie had calmed.

"No. Worse."

48.

Annie yawned, her mouth stretching so wide her jaw almost cracked. The nightmarish ordeal had left her every muscle sore. To ease the aches she shifted cautiously, trying not to wake Ella who lay slumped across her lap. Outside dimly lit suburbs sped by, their inhabitants trudging down dismal streets seeking shelter, unaware that a battered and beleaguered hero was in their midst. Annie scoffed at the dramatic turn her tale had taken.

Leonor drove into a deserted factory that looked strikingly similar to the one Ayana used as a secret hideaway. Coming to a halt under a solitary lamp in view of an open doorway, they eased Ella out of the car, guided her across the deserted space to the door, supporting most of her weight as they did, and pushed and shoved her up the steep flight of stairs till they came out on a large platform where they halted to get their breath. It was indeed Ayana's refuge. Annie was sure. How could she forget the scene of such a terrible nightmare?

She was just wondering if her long-time friend had loaned her flat to the Network when the door opened and Ayana stepped out. She greeted Leonor with a broad smile and nodded to Annie. Was the girl giving her the cold shoulder? What had she done to merit such an unfriendly welcome? Then it struck her that maybe Ayana didn't recognise her. Could Jewel have done such a good job on her?

"What's wrong with her?" Ayana asked, pointing to Ella.

"She's had a bad shock," Leonor said. "Give us a hand."

With Ayana's help, the two shouldered Ella inside while Annie hobbled along behind.

Much of the familiar flat had been transformed. Maps of London covered most of the walls. Over the sink a copy of Ella's cartoon was taped to the tiles. A group of women were seated around the kitchen table busy typing on laptops. Through the open bedroom door she spotted someone unpacking medical supplies.

"Still no luck tracing that boy?" one of the women at the table asked.

Leonor chuckled. "Forget that. It's no longer important."

"Why ever not?" The woman asked, spinning round to look at Leonor. It was then she spotted Annie. "Where did you find him?"

"Not him," Leonor said. "Her. Meet Annie Wight."

Several women gasped then all rose as one and hurried to hug or embrace her.

"I heard your speech," one said. "It was marvellous."

"So it was you that knocked Kard out this evening. A daring move."

When the praise and greetings subsided, Annie looked around for Ayana. She stood leaning against the far wall, looking perplexed and unsure. Annie took a step, then a second, in her direction. Last time they had met she was leaving to be with Kevin. Now Kevin was a hostage and she was a hero. So much had happened. She opened her arms and Ayana reluctantly, almost fearfully came towards her.

She halted a foot away studying Annie who lowered her arms, waiting. "You've become such a hero," Ayana whispered. "I didn't even recognise you." She stretched out a tentative hand and ran it over Annie's almost hairless head. Her fingers sent a shiver down Annie's back. "Sexy!" she said, her former self-assurance absent from her voice. Once again Annie opened her arms and this time Ayana accepted her embrace. As Annie folded her arms around her friend and pulled her close, the familiar scent and feel of the girl filled her with nostalgia.

She could hear that the others had returned to their work,

the keys of the laptops clicking softly. The two stood a long moment in each other's arms, unmoving. Finally, Ayana pulled away, looking slightly embarrassed. She nodded to Ella. "Your girlfriend?"

"No. Just a very good friend."

Ayana winced and looked away. A 'good friend'. Exactly what Annie had called her when Ayana had wanted more, so much more.

Annie changed the subject. "Why are you all here?"

"The headquarters of GENie got raided by the police after Kard was attacked on television. He claimed the boy used a taser on him."

"Bloody liar!" Annie burst out.

"So how did you do that?" Ayana asked.

"I think he had a mild stroke," Annie said, lying with such ease. She was getting as proficient as Kard.

"Pretty boys have a powerful impact on him, I've heard," one of the women said, her smile full of malice. Several women sniggered.

"Well, I'm glad he had an attack because he was busy sliding his hand down my back. If he'd reach my bum, I don't know what I'd have done to him."

Everyone laughed. One woman called out, "Good for you."

"But why did the police raid you?" Annie asked.

"Kard found out about GENie," Leonor said, "and he has his cronies accusing us of being a terrorist organisation. That's why the police came."

"Did anyone get hurt?"

"No. We knew they were coming and they found nothing of interest."

Listening to these women describing how they had orchestrated their escape, a plan formed in Annie's head, but first she wanted to get Ella back on her feet. The girl had been laid on Ayana's bed. Turning to Leonor, she asked, "What can we do for Ella?"

"Ella?" one of the women exclaimed. "Not the one who

drew that cartoon?" She pointed to the drawing over the sink.

"That's her," Annie said, moving towards the bedroom. She'd had enough of hero worship. She beckoned for Leonor to follow. Once again Ayana stared at her as if she were a stranger. Yes. She had changed a lot, not all of it the work of Jewel.

"I have various remedies for shock, but maybe good old smelling salts will do the trick." Leonor rummaged through what looked like an old-fashioned doctor's bag and pulled out a small flacon. Written on the side was 'ammonium carbonate'. She waved it under Ella's nose and the girl stirred. When her eyes flickered open, they stared at Annie as if she couldn't believe what she saw. "Oh my God! You're alright. It was terrible."

"A nightmare?" Annie asked.

Ella nodded. "In the TV studio. You were …"

"Better not," Annie said, taking hold of her hands. They were cold and trembling. She rubbed each hand between hers, trying to bring life and warmth back to them. "You've been a victim of one of Kard's daymares. The effect will wear off." Some of it, at least. Until the next time.

"Where are we?" Ella asked, craning her neck to get her bearings.

"In my friend Ayana's hideaway." She beckoned to Ayana who was hovering in the doorway, uncertain what to do. "Ella, meet Ayana." The two shook hands stiffly, warily eyeing each other, as if unsure whether to pounce or to run.

49.

Brilliant sunshine hailed a new day as it streamed in through open windows and arched down from the skylight above. Birds could be heard chirping on the roof and on sagging telephone wires strung nearby. Messages and messengers had gone out early to members and supporters of the Network summoning them to a meeting. Money had been pooled to buy bread and cheese and ham to make sandwiches. Thermoses for tea had appeared. Now it was ten o'clock and everything was ready.

Annie had hoped Megan would be there. She hadn't seen Kevin's mum since the kidnapping and was worried about the whirl of activity the woman had thrown herself into. Was that her way of blotting out the loss of her daughter? Over the phone earlier, Megan had said she was too busy collecting data about police abuse to attend. Apparently she had already questioned members of GENie about the raid.

The room was full to overflowing. Many sat around the table, mugs wedged between laptops, sandwiches in hand. Others stood or leaned against the walls. Women of all ages, a gay assortment. Overcoming a remnant of shyness, Annie had tried to talk to as many as possible. Some had been to university, others worked in factories, some had found no work at all, while yet others were too young to have ever worked. Annie stood facing them, leaning against the sink, her back to Ella's cartoon. Her cap was askew on her head and her hands plunged deep in her pockets. She pushed off from the sink and straighten up, raising a hand for silence.

"I heard Kard was pressing the government to drastically cut back on health care and he's out to set an example in London." The gathered women booed at the mention of Kard. Several shook their fists. "It is his response to the ever-rising costs of the NHS, costs he is largely responsible for. The more he can milk the health system the better, as far as he is concerned. He doesn't care about the poor and marginalised, those who will be most hit by his plan. What does he know about having problems getting health care? He has private insurance and never attended an NHS surgery in his life."

"They were talking about cuts to health services on the radio this morning," Leonor said, disgust written all over her face. "No mention was made of Kard. They were just preparing people for the idea."

"Excuse me if I seem to jump from one subject to another," Annie continued, "but you will soon understand. Today GENie almost got busted. Kard, him again, is orchestrating a campaign against an organisation that helps those gay people in London who have problems, particularly with health. He is labelling them, us, as terrorists, enemies of society. Just like he's trying to get rid of those who are gay. He won't succeed, but he's quite capable of making people's lives a misery."

"That's all he's good at," someone called out. Others nodded. Annie knew well enough. She'd been and still was a victim of Kard's 'talent', although she couldn't tell them that.

"We have always worked in the shadows, fearful of reprisals, especially against the gay community," Annie continued. "Being in the shadows didn't matter as long as our work only addressed a small, local community. We were relatively unknown and passing unnoticed we managed to dodge many a problem. Things are changing, though, and problems have begun seeking us out."

She took a deep breath. This was the difficult part. She had discussed her ideas with Leonor, Ella and Riya but had no inkling how others would react. They might be strongly attached to ' serving only the gay community. They might baulk at the wider challenge, fearing losing contact with the people they knew.

"I think the time has come to step out of the shadows. To

extend our work and our movement to a much wider audience. I'm not suggesting we cease helping the gay community, on the contrary, but there are many so-called minorities, women, for example..." Several people laughed. "... that need help. Nor am I suggesting we abandon the local approach. People need help that is close at hand. Most don't need top-notch experts with expensive equipment in luxurious buildings like those of Kard's companies. In most cases, basic knowledge gleaned and dispensed by the hearth-side is enough. Let's put knowledge of health care back where it belongs, in the hands of women."

A stir of excitement rippled through the room. Several people cheered, others applauded, many grinned.

"But we'll never have enough people," an older woman said.

Annie realised there were so many questions to which she didn't have an answer.

"We train them," Leonor suggested. "Not in a classroom, or an amphitheatre, but on the job. Each person who already has some experience or knowledge takes on an apprentice or two. And apprentices move around as there are different things to learn from different people. We build it up progressively."

"But what about diplomas?" asked a young woman that had told Annie she was out of work. "You can't get a worthwhile job without a diploma."

"No diplomas!" protested a young woman wearing glasses. "Kard makes money by forcing people to subscribe to dubious courses to get diplomas. No. Let's work with reputation and word of mouth."

"By 'job', I suppose you mean earning a living," Annie said. She'd read a lot about women as an unpaid workforce for an essay she'd written at school. Her conclusions had almost sparked an argument with the teacher. "It is true that much of what we as girls or women do for our families or the local community goes unrewarded, financially at least. And in many ways, thank heavens. Money changes things in ways that are not always good. We are probably better off if our activities are not governed by the same logic as the marketplace. But we do need money to live."

"So many people are out of work, especially women," the jobless girl said, "and getting benefit is becoming harder and harder."

The girl's evident anguish made Annie realise how sheltered she'd been with her parents, despite all the discomfort that had entailed. "You are right. We can't work on such a scale on a purely voluntary basis. We'll have to figure out ways to get funding so you are paid for what you do, without people having to fork out a fortune for help and care."

Several people nodded.

"I don't see why Kard should get stinking rich providing posh health care when we help the needy for free," the girl with glasses said.

"Hear, hear," a number of women called out.

"I agree," Annie said. "But dreaming up a solution is going to take some thought."

"We can always change and adapt what we do if something doesn't work out," Leonor said.

Annie leaned against the sink listening to them laying the foundations for a completely new grassroots health system. She was proud of these women and their good sense. She was also pleased to see that, after a good night's sleep, albeit in not so comfortable conditions, Ayana and Ella were talking to each other. Although maybe that was partly due to Riya turning up during the night.

A distant ringing had all conversation halt. In the tense silence that ensued, Annie could hear someone pounding up the stairs. The door burst open and a young girl tumbled in. "Police!" she panted. "They are armed and they're coming here."

"Keep calm," Annie said, catching as many eyes as she could. "We have prepared for this." Turning to Ella she asked, "Is Fenchaw's team in place?"

Ella nodded. "And Brian has photographers posted around the building."

"The internet is up and running," Riya said. "We are broadcasting live to the world."

A loud hammering at the door interrupted their discussion.

"Come in," Annie called out. "The door is open."

Several policemen in combat gear blundered in, machine guns at the ready. The sight of them was terrifying, but Annie took a deep breath. Much depended on her. She was afraid some idiot would shoot one of the women by mistake in the tension of the moment. "Put those guns away,"she said, trying to keep her voice steady. "No one here is armed."

"Hands up!" one of the policemen bawled.

"This is not a film," Annie said. "You are threatening unarmed women and girls. Put your guns away."

"Do as you are told!" the policeman, who was apparently in change, shouted.

"Is that how you treat your mothers and wives and daughters?" one of the women asked. They had agreed that only Annie would talk unless the worst happened, but in such circumstances it was hard not to react.

A second policeman raised the butt of his gun to hit the woman.

"I wouldn't do that if I were you," Annie said. "Everything you say or do is being broadcast live to the internet. The world will know that you hit an unarmed woman."

The man stood with his gun still raised, suspended, undecided, then, to Annie's relief, begrudgingly lowered it.

"Now please put your guns away, before we have an accident," Annie said. "And tell us why you are here."

The leader looked loathed to explain himself but he couldn't just stand there. "You are all charged with holding a clandestine meeting of a terrorist organisation."

"Our meeting can hardly be called clandestine," Annie said. "It's all over the internet. But tell me, what makes us terrorists?"

The policeman huffed, visibly reluctant to have such a conversation. "Enough of your back talk. I want you to file out one at a time and hand over any weapons."

"When has asking a civil question been called back talk?" Annie asked.

Several of the police were edging forward, clearly planning to grab Annie as the ring leader. But the women closed ranks, there were already a great many of them in the room, making it only possible to get her by force.

Cheers went up from outside. "There's a large crowd gathering," Ayana announced, peering out the window. Annie was relieved that so many had already responded to requests Riya was sending out over the internet.

"So what makes a group of women talking about how to improve healthcare terrorists?"

The head of the police clearly didn't have an answer. Exasperated, he waved his gun at her and blurted out, "You are trying to undermine our society with your filthy ways."

"Is caring for people who are ill or in distress filthy?" Annie asked. "Surely it is those that plan to cut back on healthcare and barricade themselves in private clinics reserved for the rich that are undermining our society. By your definition, they are the terrorists. Why don't you arrest them?"

A massive cheer went up that had the windows rattling. It sounded like part of the crowd had entered the warehouse below.

A faint buzz from the policeman's jacket had him listening to something being said in his ear. He lowered his gun, saying, "We'll be back."

"I'm sure you will," Annie said, relieved the confrontation was over. She had been uncertain their bluff would work. "But next time bring your wives and children."

The man didn't bother to reply. He shoved past his colleagues and left, and the others trooped after him, puffing themselves up as they did. Annie could hear booing below as the police ran the gauntlet of the waiting crowd. Worried that the crowd would drive the police to retaliate out of spite, she hurried down the stairs.

"Let them go," she shouted from the warehouse floor. Someone handed her a megaphone. "Let them go."

The crowd began to boo Annie and for a moment she was afraid. Then people recognised her and boos changed to cheers.

It was sobering to see a mass of people swing so easily in its reaction. She saluted the crowd with a raised fist and was about to turn and climb back up the stairs when the people nearest grabbed her and hauled her up onto their shoulders. She knew it was their way of celebrating her, but she couldn't help feeling afraid as she was passed from hand to hand above the crowd. After a moment's resistance, she realised it was easiest to let go and allow herself to be carried.

When the forward swaying of her body ceased and she was lowered to the ground, standing on her own two feet felt strange. A space cleared around her and someone handed her the megaphone which had apparently followed her above the crowd. She took the device, but held it resolutely at her side. She didn't want to make a speech. They'd already heard what she'd said to the police because Riya had rigged up loudspeakers. Instead she walked to the nearest people and began shaking hands, making her way slowly through the crowd back to the stairs and her friends.

50.

Why ever had she chosen to shake hands? There were so many people, her hand was red and sore and her arm ached. Some held on to her hoping to get a chance to talk. Those unable to shake her hand gripped her sleeve, waylaying her with their problems. She wanted to cry out, 'I'm no Messiah' but she plodded forward, putting on a brave face. How did politicians manage?

All of a sudden she shivered as if someone had opened a door letting in a draught. Despite the bright sun, she couldn't shrug off a feeling of bitter cold. People became more insistent. Fingers dug into her wrist, clawing at her skin. She tried to pull away, but a body closed in behind her, blocking any escape. A woman with a twisted nose, broken teeth and hate-filled eyes raised outstretched nails to scratch Annie's face. She dodged just in time, sparing her face, but the nails sank into her wounded shoulder. She cried out, first in pain then in indignation. Stop! she mouthed. Leave me alone!

Boney fingers clawed at her, ripping her clothes, tearing her skin, tugging at her arms and legs, trying to pull her to the ground. She held her hands over her face. Her eyes. Her mouth. Her nose. Please don't, she beseeched. The rest of her body, slick with filth and blood, smarted from cuts and bruises.

One brute upended her with beefy hands, plunging her to the ground, head first. Fingers tore the clothes from her body. Then the pounding began. Hob nailed boots. Pointed stilettos. Muddy wellingtons. Wooden clogs. Brightly coloured plimsoles.

Shiny, black Sunday-school shoes. Girls' court shoes, lace-up ballerinas, lousy loafers, spring-loaded sandals. Prodding. Pounding. Pummelling. Her ribs. Her chest. Her crotch. Her stomach. The small of her back. Her shoulders. The back of her head. Relentless. Unyielding. Her hands clasped over her face, screaming. Blow after blow. And them yelling. Hate fuelling every kick. The murderous glee of it. Let it stop. Let it stop. Let it stop.

She was hauled to her feet, ready for another round. All strength sapped from her. If only it would stop. She'd rather die than go through it again. A hand shook hers. Then another. Something was out of joint. This was not violent, but friendly, encouraging. Relief flood over her. It was over. But the memory of terror and pain raged unabated. She couldn't let on. These people must not know. She clenched her teeth, forcing a smile to her lips. Far away stairs and friends awaited as she staggered through the crowd.

Ayana, Ella and Riya stood at the foot of the stairs, arms outstretched to catch her, worry barely concealed on their faces. Once the door closed on the crowd, Annie sank to the ground and sprawled across the first stairs, her whole body shuddering with shock and pain. "I can't," she moaned over and over.

Ayana called for Leonor who vaulted down the stairs two at a time.

"Kard?" Leonor asked, halting just above her.

Annie had no strength to explain the inexplicable. Her friends carried her up the stairs and a place was cleared for her on the bed, many of the women crowding round, worried, jostling her with questions. Had the police attacked? Had the crowd turned on her? Or were there thugs on the loose, hidden amongst the supporters?

"Please," Annie managed to whisper, wanting but unable to plead for peace. She didn't have the force to form the words. She wanted nobody. Luckily Leonor understood and shooed everybody out, even her closest friends. The click of the door as it shut ushered relief and she sank deeper on the bed. She'd had enough. Maybe dying would be a solution. To slip away, unnoticed, slinking off to the other side, maybe to find warmth in the light. To curl up like a little child in her mother's arms, her real mother, not the monster Kard had turned her into. Safe and sound.

You're delirious. Nobody is going to die. A hand touched hers. She jerked away. Enough. Never would she shake a hand again. Don't be silly. It's only Leonor trying to console you. She cracked open her eyes. Sure enough Leonor was seated beside her on the bed.

"It's not Kard," she said, launching into the unknown, her hands mentally stretched out in front of her feebly fumbling for the way.

Leonor said nothing. Outwardly she looked calm and attentive. Yet her eyes spelt deep concern. How could you be both interested and disinterested in one breath? Did priests look like that during confessionals? You're wandering.

"I killed a man," she said, startling herself by the brutality of her words.

She looked up at Leonor expecting disapproval or worse, condemnation. Leonor stayed Zen.

"He had his hands grasped around my throat trying to strangle me. I had no choice."

Of course you did. You could have let him do it. Anger and indignation surged. That's no choice. No one could stand by and let themselves be strangled.

"I sent him to the other side. Well, I didn't, but I made it happen."

You are making no sense. How do you expect her to grasp your muddled words? You insist on telling disjointed chunks of the story while you skirt the rest.

"He can't come back. But he can try to kill me. Or at least his nightmares can."

You know that's not true. He can't kill you. But he can wear you down. Drive you to the brink. And laugh when you fling yourself over.

"Kard's minion only frightens me. The Pakistani wants me

dead."

For the first time, Leonor reacted, raising an eyebrow. "Pakistani?"

"I was with Ella hiding in his cafe. He recognised me from the TV. He was a Kard supporter. He wore the badge. It was him or me. I had no choice." Something gave way in her mind and at last she was able to tell the story in something resembling an order, although she didn't mention the ghost writer. She had promised.

"Is there no way you can stop this Pakistani?" Leonor asked.

"Maybe I can beat him at his own game."

"Game?"

"Telling horror stories." As she said it, she realised she had ventured too far.

"You can do that?" Leonor abruptly sat up straight, a faint ray of hope crossing her otherwise furrowed brow.

Annie hesitated then nodded. "You must tell nobody. I promised I would never tell."

"Is that how Kard had his attack?"

Annie nodded, guilt clawing at her guts. She didn't trust herself to speak. Unguarded words were saying too much.

To her surprise Leonor smiled. "That's good news. I was wondering how we could outdo Kard when he had such devastating arms in his arsenal."

51.

When Annie awoke the clock by the bed indicated nearly four. She rubbed her eyes and stretched. Her mind still ached, but her body was rested. The bustle so characteristic of the small flat over the last twenty-four hours had subsided. The members of GENie had left to spread the news and prepare the way for their new health network. Riya had gone to see Decker and get the latest on the search for Kevin. She was confident they would locate the girl and her kidnappers very soon. Ella had gone to meet Fenchaw, hoping to convince him to support the Network. She'd been accompanied by the young woman with glasses who'd spoken out against diplomas, just in case Ella was attacked again. Leonor was visiting the staff at the clinic where Megan had been treated, seeking active support for the Network. Only Ayana remained to keep her company and a couple of women manning computers and answering phones.

Rather than get up, she folded her hands behind her head and lay staring at the ceiling. She thought of Don with his unseeing eyes. He had sought refuge in a psychiatric hospital struggling to come to terms with visions he couldn't control. What had he said? Stories were both her weakness and her strength. She would only cease to be plagued by those of others when she finally managed to master her own. He might not have meant mastering literally, but she could at least try.

She knew no one who wrote novels or short stories, apart from the ghost writer. No one who could give her advice. Most people of her age and background never crossed paths with authors. Her English teacher might have known an author or two, but she was so obsessed with grammar and spelling, Annie doubted it. Fenchaw surely knew many. But he had other things to do. Alice! The professor knew everybody that was worth knowing. Had she not introduced her to Underwood and Fenchaw, and Don too?

She fished out her phone from the folds of her trousers.

"It's Annie," she said when Alice answered.

"I've been following your exploits on TV. Exciting times."

Annie groaned. "Don't believe everything you see."

Alice chuckled. "Becoming wise in your old age?"

"Do you know any writers … of short stories?" Annie asked. "Someone who can help me get control of stories."

"'Get control of stories'. Now that's an unusual request. You make stories sound like bucking horses. Most authors are struggling to find their stories, not control them. Those who do stumble on one, pen it in with scenarios and plots and all manner of rules and restrictions till it dies of inanition." There was a long pause. "I might. Are you up for another of my visits?"

"Sure." Annie was both relieved and anxious. Alice would drop by in an hour, time to wash and snatch a bite to eat, if anything was left. A pack of women bent on changing the world could be ravenous and supplies had not been unlimited.

When Ayana learnt where Annie was going, she was eager to tag along, but Annie feared she would be a distraction. She needed to concentrate. Yet she was loathed to say 'no'. Ayana was constantly teetering on the verge of chronic rejection, not to mention dejection. It came as a relief when Leonor called. Ayana was to join her. They had decided Ayana was to be Leonor's apprentice, learning to heal and healing by learning.

Alice arrived late. "Had some difficulty convincing our person to see us," she said as they drove away. "She lives a life of a recluse and only emerges when a new book is to come out."

The idea that their visit might not be welcome had Annie apprehensive. "Tell me something about her."

Alice might have prepared her at length for the visit to the

Prime Minister, but this time all she would say was, "You'll see."

The author's mansion was a fortress parachuted in suburbia. The high wall surrounding the grounds was topped with barbed wire. The gate was manned by a uniformed guard who checked their credentials and phoned to verify they could be let in. The drive up to the house was dotted with surveillance cameras. At the front door a second guard cross-questioned them before showing them into what seemed akin to a dentist's waiting room, except there were no magazines, only the author's books.

Penelope Djaganov. Annie had heard the name, but never read any of her novels. She picked one up, glanced at the title, Nowhere Man, and cracked it open to a page near the middle. She was about to read when the door opened and a portly lady in slippers shuffled in. She was wearing a tattered housecoat bound tight around her considerable waist by a length of rope and had a black beret perched on her silvery hair. To make her look even stranger her lips were painted scarlet and her cheeks excessively tinged with rouge. The writer's mother? An ageing servant no one dared to sack? The caretaker's wife? An eccentric relative on a prolonged stay?

"Come in," the woman said without the slightest formality.

They followed her into what seemed like a junk room littered with heaps of papers and tattered books. Some of the piles towered over Annie.

"Careful not to knock anything over," the woman called back over her shoulder.

For a junk room, the place was enormous. Annie would have got lost in the paths through the maze had she not had the woman to follow. Finally, the path opened onto a clearing around a desk that was also littered with piles of papers, jam jars full of pens and empty bottles of ink and, to top it all, an old-fashioned typewriter.

The woman eased herself into a swivelling chair and studied them. There being no other chairs, Alice and Annie were obliged to stand. The woman, whom Annie guessed must be Penelope, fixed her with an intensity that borderded on menacing. "What do you want?"

Did being a celebrity give you the right to be rude? "I am glad you…" Annie began.

"Cut the small talk. Answer my question."

"To control my stories."

The woman cackled. "That's a good one."

"They are killing me," Annie protested.

"Good."

Annie was furious. She imagined smashing a jar of pens over the woman's head. The thought filled her with inordinate pleasure. "Killing was no metaphor," she said, raising her voice.

Penelope ignored her. "Do they haunt you at night?"

Annie nodded.

"Do they track you like wild animals during the day?"

Annie realised that the woman probably had no idea what was really tracking her. Penelope's wild stories were nothing compared to the Pakistani's murderous nightmares. She nodded all the same.

Penelope beckoned for her to come closer and leaned forward till her mouth almost brushed Annie's ear. "Keep your sentences short," she whispered. "Never waste words. Avoid unneeded trimmings. Let your words kill. Work with scenes. The shorter the better. Short and sharp. Like a blade slicing between the ribs. In and out. Before you get caught. Then strike again. Elsewhere. Hard. Fast. Make each word count. Drive them home. Till the page is red with blood. The characters are yours to use. Have no pity. As for the readers, leave them breathless. Gasping for more."

Penelope sank back in her chair, her face devoid of emotion, and tugged on a bell-pull that hung from the ceiling then turned away and, her head bent over a sheet of paper, began scribbling frantically.

52.

Annie looked back at the mansion. "I wouldn't like to spend a night there," she mused, imagining a bloodthirsty author roaming the darkened halls in search of a story gone wild. "You'd probably get your throat cut."

Alice chuckled. "Penelope always was a little strange, fellow students shunned her, several of her boyfriends are rumoured to have disappeared, but her novels are extremely powerful."

'Strange' was hardly the word. Weird, dangerous, flaming crazy might have been nearer the mark. "You do have some odd acquaintances, Professor."

"I've known her for years, but she never acknowledges the fact. It's as if I were a complete stranger. Yet I still get to see her. Which is more than most can say."

Annie wondered at Penelope's 'advice'. The stories the woman grappled with were in no way akin to those that asailed Annie. Yet the suggestions rang true. The delivery had matched the words. Short. Sharp. And deadly. Like Don's advice before. Not a ready solution, but pointers to puzzle over. How could a sharp sentence ward off the Pakistani? He was just as likely to reply with a knife. And Kard? How could a few words defeat him, he who was all words? You'd probably drown in a flood of his words before your three-word sentence was out of your mouth.

Then again, maybe a well-chosen, hard-hitting word could bring Kard down if you found the right one. It was like dreaming you'd win the national lottery. You could always hope. But you knew you'd never hit the jackpot.

A familiar buzzing in her trousers announced a call. She pulled out her tiny phone and answered. It was Riya.

"They've found Kevin," she told Alice, grinning widely at the news. "Or at least where she's being held." Riya gave her an address which she relayed to Alice. "We are to join them at an abandoned cafe nearby," Annie explained. "No one is to get too close till Decker's surveillance is ready and his strike team in place."

Having hung up, Annie turned the tiny phone over in her fingers. Should she ring Megan? Kevin's mum must be desperately awaiting that call. Yet what if it was a false alert or Kevin got badly hurt. Annie shoved the thought away. Megan was unlikely to get hysterical, but her emotions might distract. No. She'd call later, when things were wrapped up. She stuffed the phone back in her trousers, a manoeuvre which earned raised eyebrows from Alice.

They drove through an open gate into a large area cordoned off and awaiting demolition. As they neared the disused cafe, they were stopped by a woman wearing a yellow armband on which she could read GENie. They were to enter the cafe by the back.

The neighbourhood was grim and joyless. Almost all the houses were boarded up, some with gaping holes in their roofs, others were on the verge of crumbling. The backyard of the cafe was littered with broken bottles and upturned dustbins. A second woman sporting a GENie armband ushered them inside. The place was dark and dingy and smelt of damp and human waste.

They followed a third woman up creaky stairs to a large room on the first floor which had been cleared to make way for several computers and various screens and gadgets on an improvised table. A couple of small windows looked out over the street directly onto the house where Kevin was. Thick lace curtains that hadn't been washed in years prevented anyone seeing in.

Riya was there with Decker in quiet discussion, pointing at the screens. Ella was talking to Brian, who had several cameras slung over his shoulder. Ayana and Leonor were sorting through heavy-duty medical equipment ready for use. Annie hoped none of it would be necessary.

"We planned to broadcast live to the internet," Riya said, keeping her voice low. "Like we did when the police raided our meeting. But that might tip off the thugs, so we will record and post extracts later." She beckoned to Annie and showed her the screens. There were several views, even some inside the house, robots, Riya explained, but there was no sign of Kevin.

One screen was covered with a cloth. "What's that?"

Riya pulled aside the material to reveal a basement room. The lighting was surprisingly bright. Annie could clearly make out Kevin on a narrow bed, her clothes torn and filthy. She didn't seem to be attached, but her face, arms and legs were peppered with cuts and bruises. Annie winced. "You see why we keep it covered," Riya said.

Annie looked again. Next to the bed was a tattered armchair in which a man sprawled, his eyes closed, his arms bare. Tattooed on his right forearm was a magnificent cat licking its paw. The pretty image was at odds with the vicious truncheon that lay across his lap. A second man sat at a table, digging holes in the tabletop with a razor-sharp knife. A hefty gun lay within easy reach. Several bottles of beer stood nearby next to the messy remains of a takeaway meal. Congealed sauce and lumps of meat had spilled onto the table, attracting a swarm of flies.

"We have a problem," Decker said. "I had thought we'd use gas to knock them out. But the one at the table would just have time to shoot Kevin before the gas took effect. And anyway," he pointed to a dark object on the table Annie hadn't noticed. "They have gas masks."

"If only we could warn Kevin so she could roll off the bed," Riya said. "And we had some way to distract them, we might get her out unharmed."

Annie looked at the screen again. There was a narrow space between the bed and the wall. "Supposing you could," she said, "how would you do it?"

"We've got marksmen with stun darts," Decker said. "They'd have to shoot through the window. One could burst through the door. We know it is not locked."

"That's far too risky," Alice said, moving forward to join them. "What if the window is reinforced? Or the door has a special locking mechanism? Your distraction would be wasted. No. You need to lure them out, one at a time."

"How would you do that?" Decker asked.

"I don't know. A noise in the house."

"Can we hear them?" Annie asked.

Riya leaned forward and turned a button. Faint moans came from Kevin and there were the dull thuds of the knife digging into the table.

Annie stared at the tattoo of the cat cleaning its paws. She had an idea.

"Ok. Here's what we do." She explained the details. Both Decker and Riya were dubious and tried to dissuade her till she asked if they had an alternative. Short, sharp attacks, Penelope had said. That was exactly what she would do.

When everyone was in place and Decker gave the go-ahead, Annie sent the faintest sound of a cat miaowing into the cat lover's head. That her ruse had worked was obvious when the man's head jerked in the direction of the door, cocking his ear to hear better, although no one else could hear anything. Several people around her gasped. Annie ignored them. It was no time to let herself be distracted by what people thought of her.

"Did you hear that?" the thug said.

"Nah! Just the kid moaning."

"No. It was a cat. I heard it." He cocked his head again, listening. Annie was excited at how easily it worked and was eager to get it over, but she forced herself to wait.

"Yer going soft in the head. Relax, you raving loony."

Only when he lay back, fingering his truncheon did Annie send a stronger miaow. This time he was on his feet in seconds and headed for the door.

"What yer doing?" the other asked, alarmed and annoyed.

"The cat."

"There ain't no cat. You're hearing things."

Annie sent a third miaow as if it came from just beyond the door. The man grabbed the handle and wrenched aside the door, plunging out into the darkness, leaving the door wide open.

"Come back, you blasted nutter!" his colleague shouted and drove the blade of his knife deep into the table."Why do I have to put up with such idiots?"

Decker, who had earphones perched on his head, was listening to feedback from his team. He nodded to Annie and gave the thumbs up. The first thug was down. Annie struggled to calm her excitement. The trickiest part was yet to come.

"Kevin," she said. She was tempted to shift the girl to a comfortable bed in a room with a blazing fire. But she kept Kevin where she was. The transition would be easier. "It's me, Annie."

"Annie? Am I dreaming? Are you really here?"

"No. You are not dreaming. I'm sending you a message. I'm very close by. We are coming to rescue you. But you must do something very important for me. When I say 'Now', you must roll across the bed and slip between the wall and the bed, out of sight. Can you do that?"

"I'm not sure. I hurt so much. But yes. For you, I will do it."

"I'm going to release you. You will be back in the room with one of those men. Don't move. Don't make a sound. Pretend you are asleep. Are you ready?"

With Kevin's "Yes," Annie let go and turned her attention to the man, sending him sounds of someone rummaging around in the corridor.

"What the hell are you doing out there?" he asked.

No answer could be heard, although Annie knew he heard his colleague say, "You'll never believe what I've found."

"For God's sake, we are not here to rummage through rubbish."

He got to his feet and glanced nervously at Kevin, presumably gauging if she was asleep. He picked up his gun and took a couple of steps towards the door then stopped and turned back to the bed. Turning his gun so the hilt was pointing forwards, he raised it as if her were going to hit Kevin. "Now," shouted Annie in Kevin's head. With a grunt, the girl rolled over and disappeared behind the bed. The thug's blow narrowly missed her and bounced off the mattress. Annie hurled a blinding light into his head as several armed men burst into the room and grabbed the thug.

Annie sank to her knees, exhausted. It was over. Kevin was safe.

53.

An alarming thought tore Annie from her exhaustion. If it got out that she had a secret way of influencing people at a distance everyone would begin to fear her. What's more, she'd become Kard's number one target. "Whatever you do," Annie said to Riya, "do not post this on the Internet. People must never suspect what went on here."

"Why ever not?" Riya asked, helping Annie to a chair. She looked exhausted herself. Decker's people were checking for booby traps and Leonor and Ayana were on hand to look after Kevin as soon as the coast was clear.

"We need to post something," Riya continued. "If only to thank those who phoned in or messaged us with information. I realise we can't broadcast what happened in full, but perhaps we could piece together highlights. So people know Kevin got out all right. We owe them that."

"Maybe we could film you making a statement, Annie," Brian suggested, "saying that Kevin has been rescued. You could be with Kevin as proof it is true."

"Truth doesn't matter much anymore," Alice said from the shadowy corner she'd retreated to. "Kard and his gang flung it out the window."

"Alice is right," Annie mused. "The strongest story wins out." She shuddered at the thought. A raging battle with each side drumming up the hardest-hitting story at the expense of those caught nearby. Ordinary people were just expendable stand-ins in a bigwig's reality show. Penelope's words came back to her. Short, sharp and simple. No unnecessary embellishments. That would distinguish them from Kard and his bloated tele-visual oneupmanship. "I hate the idea, but we must hit home with Kevin's rescue, stressing the violence men do to women and how women defend themselves when they get together. We need to depict Kard not as the negative hero, but as the petty, vindic-tive criminal he is."

"I know Kard's a monster, but go easy on men," Brian said emerging from the shadows. "Not all are like him or these thugs."

"You are right," Alice said. "Not women against men, but everyone against violence, cruelty and oppression."

Riya, who had donned Decker's headphones, was busy talking into the mic. Turning to Annie, she said, "It's all clear. I've warned Decker you are coming."

One of the GENie women led Annie and her friends down to the street and across into the house opposite. The two men were being held in a ground-floor room, but Annie paid them no heed. Instead she hurried to the basement. She was glad of the temporary lighting. The way was littered with rubbish and treach-erous. She found Kevin lying on the now familiar bed, although Leonor had spread a clean sheet over the filthy mattress and the food had been cleared from the table. Maybe they should have left it so the scene appeared authentic. Authentic! She almost sneered at the word. Every TV programme, especially the news, dressed up the world to appear authentic.

"Annie!" Kevin called out at the sight of her, her voice crack-ing.

Annie sat cautiously next to her on the bed, wary of the cuts and bruises. She stroked her fingers through Kevin's hair. "It's growing," she said. "Looks good longer, too."

"Yeah. I completely forgot to go to the barber's." She winced as she tried to smile.

Annie was aware of Brian filming, but as long as he kept to the background she could ignore him. "As soon as Leonor and Ayana get you cleaned up, we'll move to a better hotel."

"Stop making me smile," Kevin complained. "It hurts."

"There's someone who's going to be very relieved you've been rescued," Annie said, pulling out her phone. She dialled Megan's number and handed the phone to Kevin.

"Mum," Kevin said, her voice unsteady as tears welled up in her eyes. "Yes. Annie and her friends came to rescue me." She glanced at Annie as she listened to her mother. "Nothing serious. Just cuts and bruises. Leonor is here to take care of me." Kevin held out a trembling hand to Annie and she took it. "No. No more rallies. Must go. The nurses are getting impatient. See you very soon. Love you." She handed the phone back.

"I've never heard Mum break down and cry like that," Kevin's said, tears flowing down her cheeks. "It's unbearable." She burst into sobs as Annie took her cautiously in her arms. They stayed a long while in that careful embrace, both of them shaken by Kevin's emotions. When Kevin calmed, Annie handed her a handkerchief and the girl wiped her eyes and blew her nose. Annie looked at Kevin, her body battered and beaten, and felt her heart lurch. This violence had to stop.

"I'm going to make a statement for the Internet," Annie said. "To thank all those who helped find you. Would you like to say something?"

"Sure would."

"Fire away," Annie said, stepping from the bed to leave room for Kevin to face the camera on her own. Kevin propped herself up on one elbow and stared for a long moment at the camera.

"I'd like to thank all of you who helped rescue me or who sent information to help locate me," Kevin began. Annie had planned to say the same, but it was better coming from Kevin. No need to play the hero or the figurehead. "You can't imagine how alone you feel in the company of two thugs whose only way of communicating is with fists and truncheons. I've had lots of time to think, lying here on this filthy bed, every part of my body aching from the blows and cuts. I was never hit as a child and I thank my mother and teachers for that. But I know many people, women and children in particular, are beaten every day, for no reason other than they are an easy target for someone's anger or frustration. It has to stop! If they are unable to protect themselves, if the police cannot stop it, then we must gather round to fend off the bullies. I will never forget what happened to me. How could I? The memory has been battered into me." She shuddered. "It's the same for them. The least we can do is welcome them with open arms, offer them love and care and make sure it never, ever happens again."

"Annie?" Brian said, after a pause, inviting her to speak.

Annie shook her head. "Kevin has said it all. Let's just use her short speech. Nothing more. No me. No thugs. No derelict house. No Kard. Just a young woman talking from her heart."

54.

Annie slung an arm around Kevin's waist and helped her up the unsteady stairs from the basement. Behind, Brian and Ella talked quietly about choices of material for the internet. Everyone else had left. Alice had offered to drive them to her house. The idea appealed to Annie, but she refused. Alice's place was too isolated and she needed to be close to the action. She could have sent Kevin with her grandmother, but she was loathed to be parted from her friend. So they were returning to Ella's flat until they found a home of their own.

The ground floor of the abandoned house was in a sorry state. The front door lay smashed in two and many windows had been broken, shards of glass scrunching under their shoes. The only room intact was the one used to hold the two thugs. Annie was surprised to discover a couple of Decker's people standing guard at the door.

"What's going to happen to them?" she asked, nodding towards the room. They surely couldn't spend the night there. Why ever not? A voice chipped in in her head. Hadn't they'd forced Kevin to do so for several days?

"Not sure," the man replied, frowning. He was the tallest of the two guards, both of whom were dressed in combat suits with bullet-proof vests and sported rifles designed to stun. "It's tricky. We can't hand them over to the police. There never was a kidnapping as far as they are concerned. They'd probably let them go."

"They can't stay here for ever." It was evident, of course, but Annie had to say it. Maybe she could threaten to haunt them like

Kard had done to her. She shuddered at the burden that would entail. Anyway, she didn't want to ape Kard's solutions.

All the time they talked, she was aware of Kevin at her side, the one who'd suffered at the hands of the thugs. She wondered what thoughts must be going through the girl's head. Punishment, maybe. Torture, perhaps. Giving them a dose of what she'd been given. Kevin said nothing. Ella and Brian were silent too.

She was about to leave, but halted. She couldn't just turn her back on the problem. The two guards might be hired hands, but they probably had children and would willingly return to the warmth and safety of their home. It would soon be midnight. She was tired. They were all tired.

"Can I talk to them?"

The tall guard looked worried. "That might not be wise. One is very aggressive."

"OK. Let's begin with the other." She imagined it was the cat lover. She looked at Kevin. The girl was exhausted. "You up to this?" Kevin swayed on her feet. No other answer was necessary. She'd had more than enough of thugs,

"I'll take Kevin home while you finish up here," Ella offered. "Brian can drive you to my place later."

Annie looked questioningly at Kevin. The girl leant closer and gave Annie a kiss. "Be careful," she whispered and left with Ella supporting her.

"Got any battery left?" Annie asked Brian.

He nodded. "You wanna film?"

"Maybe." Her idea hadn't quite taken shape that far.

"Where?" the guard asked.

"In the basement. Give us a couple of minutes to set up."

Annie had the thug, whose hands were attached behind his back and whose legs were shackled, sit on the bed where Kevin had been. All sorts of revengeful ideas full of blood and screams surged in her mind, but she slammed the door on them.

"What's your name?" Annie asked.

"Lionel."

"Kevin, the girl you kidnapped and mistreated, is seventeen. What did you do when you were seventeen, Lionel?" she asked. She nodded to Brian to film.

The thug looked at the camera, then back at her, perplexed. No doubt he'd been expecting pain and torture. He hesitated a long moment as if suspecting a trap, his expression tense and wary. Annie waited, watching. Then he spoke.

"I... er... was an apprentice. I wanted to be a vet. But you can't. Not without A levels and a university degree." He shook his head. "And anyway, they don't take the likes of me. Only posh kids go to university."

Posh kids like Kevin, Annie thought. In comparison to him, she herself was well off.

"I had no money, no job, no family to support me."

She knew something about not having a family to support her.

"But I loved animals. So I started an apprenticeship in a pet shop. The owner was a real bastard. Made me do all the dirty work. I rarely got to handle the animals. He would taunt me. One day I snapped. Punched him on the nose. Glad I did. But the police came. The man said I was violent. Said it wasn't the first time. How could I accuse him of lying? Who would believe me?"

She thought of Kard and his accusations. She had been able to do little against his lies.

"They shut me away in a home for problem kids. I rubbed shoulders with some hard nuts. They taught me a thing or two." He winced. "When I was released, buddies of theirs sought me out and found me work. The job was not so difficult. Protecting a bigwig called Kard. Just stand there and frighten people off. In his rallies. On the TV set. In private dinners. When he met his clients. See nothing. Hear nothing. Just play the strong guy. But it paid good. Then Kard sent us to kidnap that girl. I didn't like it. But you can't say no to Kard. Thought the girl was a boy at first. We were to rough her up. But she saw my tattoo and talked about cats. She liked cats. How could I hurt someone who liked cats? Georg, the other guy," he motioned to the floor above with his head, "said I'd gone soft in the head. He hit her. Said he'd show me how to do it. Over and over. I couldn't stand her crying. It cut into me, like a sharp blade. When I stuffed fingers in my ears, Georg jeered at me. Said I was a wet rag. He hit her even more. In the end, I hit her too. Out of self-defence. To get him to stop. To stop her crying. Her moans were like the meowing of a wounded cat...." A sob broke from his mouth and his body shuddered so much it shook the bed.

"Remove the restraints," Annie said.

The guard looked at her, alarmed, and shook his head.

"Remove his restraints," Annie repeated.

The guard reluctantly pulled the keys from his belt and unlocked the restraints, then hastily withdrew, his gun pointed at Lionel. Lionel rubbed his wrists.

"I would willingly set you free," Annie said. The guard muttered under his breath that she was crazy. Lionel looked hopeful. "But that would be no solution. You'd be defenceless against Kard. You'd be picked off by an assassin before you opened your mouth. You know too much. I want you to stay alive. Maybe, one day, you'll become a vet, who knows. I think you'd make a good one." Lionel smiled, weakly. "So we need to hide you in the meantime." She turned to the guard. "Can you manage that?"

He looked dubious. "I'll have to ask." He shifted away into the corner of the room keeping a constant watch on Lionel.

"Did you get all that?" she asked Brian. He nodded.

"Lionel, I want your permission to use what we filmed. You must realise that doing so will put you in more danger. But we will help you change your identity."

"You mean, like evidence against me?" Lionel asked.

"No. You bear witness to a plight that must plague many poor young people. I will have your words posted on the internet, just like Kevin's words were posted. So that people know and understand. That the violence stops. Not only violence against a young girl, but also against a young apprentice."

55.

Annie took a deep breath and immediately wished she hadn't. The stink of the basement had a long and unpleasant history to it. Out of instinct, she must have been breathing shallowly. She glanced around. The sticky ruins of a takeaway might have been removed from the table, but the stains remained and stray lumps of meat and splatterings of sauce littered the floor. She was sick of the sordid hideaway. However had Kevin put up with it so long? Stupid question. She'd had no choice.

"It's OK," the guard said, getting off the phone. "What about the other one?" His disapproval clear on his face. "Is he to go free too?"

The question sapped any of her remaining energy. Caught up in Lionel's story, she'd forgotten the second thug. She glanced at Brian. He didn't look nearly as tired as she felt. "Could you get some printouts showing... What was his name?" She pointed to room above.

"Georg," Brian said.

"... photos showing Georg hurting Kevin? For early tomorrow morning?"

"Sure."

"Good." Turning back to the guard, she said, "Make sure the man is securely restrained and leave him here alone all night. We'll get the photos to Decker. Have them left near the man in the morning and call the police anonymously. Let them deal with it. We'll see what fish that drags up. And thanks for your help."

"Good luck," she said to Lionel and left with Brian.

"Do you want to go straight to Ella's?" Brian asked as they drove along deserted streets. "Or would you like to come with me to the newspaper and choose the photos?"

Annie yawned. She longed to be curled up next to Kevin in the warmth of their bed. "I'm sure you'll choose the best."

"What about Lionel? If we post his story on the internet, everyone will know someone else was involved. Should he be in the photos?"

She had no idea. How could she tell which way her decisions would play out? She closed her eyes and leaned against the head-rest. In the warmth and safety of the car she wondered if she'd got it all wrong. And anyway, who was she to decide? What if Lionel returned to free his colleague? What if the police went on a manhunt for those who'd 'kidnapped' Georg? What if people said the photos were fake? And how would Kard retaliate? So many questions. Turning to Brian, she said, "I suppose so. He was present, wasn't he?"

"So Ella's place here we come."

Brian's phone rang.

"It was Riya. She's got news."

"What?" Annie was unable to stop yawning. Couldn't people just sleep at night? Wasn't that how it was supposed to be?

"She wouldn't say. Not over the phone. Said we should meet her at the club near the newspaper."

Annie sighed. Why wouldn't they let her have a break from the hero business?

The club was members only, but as Brian was a member and, recognizing Annie from the TV, the doorman let her in, congrat-ulating her on how she handled the police. So the broadcast on the internet had already seeped through to the telly. She won-dered what they would make of Kevin and Lionel's testimonies.

The club was surprisingly informal, looking more like an oversized sitting room. Not that she had any experience of clubs. Maybe the impression came from the pastel light cast by small lamps on each low table, lost amongst an array of drinks and plates with half-consumed sandwiches. Groups of armchairs of various sizes and shapes were scattered around the room, many of which were occupied, some by people she recognised from her tour of the newspaper. Several nodded greetings. There was even a fireplace, although if they sat too near Annie was sure she'd be asleep within minutes.

Riya waved from an alcove where she was huddled with Decker and Fenchaw. Annie was about to join them, but thought it better to go to the loo first. She'd needed to go for a while. Derelict houses were a bit short on creature comfort and conveniences. A little embarrassed about having to mention it, she asked Brian for directions, saying she would be with them in a moment. The toilets were at the back of the premises along a dark corridor and down a couple of uneven steps. She almost tripped, misjudging their size in the murky light.

To her surprise the room leading to the cubicles was packed with girls from her school who were playing some sort of game that involved pushing and shoving your neighbour till she was forced out of the square she was standing on. The squares on the floor, from the little she could see of them, were tiny. Squeals and hysterical laughter filled the air. The atmosphere had Annie cringing. It reflected the very worst of girls of her age. She tried to squeeze between them, but was immediately caught up in the action, being shoved sideways and squarewize till she was in the thick of the game. The more she struggled to reach the toilet, the tighter the girls boxed her in.

"Let me through," she shouted, venting her frustration. The girls just cackled and jostled all the more, schoolgirl hysteria morphing into spiteful cruelty. Her situation was untenable. The pressing need was too strong. She could hold on no longer. Despite her desperate struggles, a trickle of liquid escaped. Within seconds it gushed beyond control, soaking her trousers, wetting her socks and shoes and forming a telltale puddle on the floor. She hung her head, her face burning. The shame of it!

The crowd of girls pushed and shoved their way back till a wide circle separated them from her. They stood, noses wrinkled in disgust, fingers pointing. "Oh. She wet herself," one girl said.

"Peed in her pants," said another. "And that's supposed to be a hero!" a third exclaimed. One by one they turned their backs and walked away leaving her, head bowed, standing in a puddle of her own making.

Hearing steps approaching down the corridor, she dashed into a cubicle and fumbled to lock the door.

"Is that you, Annie?" she heard Riya ask.

Annie sat on the toilet, shivering and sniffling, her nose running from the tears. It didn't matter that her trousers were no longer wet. That it had been another of Kard's friendly gifts. The shame lingered.

"Annie, are you alright?"

She pulled up her knees and laid her head on them, tears tumbling onto her trousers.

"Annie. Whatever it is, we'll be stronger together."

Annie unlatched the door, but remained stubbornly perched on the toilet seat. The door cracked open little by little and Riya peered in. "Oh Annie," she said, stepping into the cubicle and taking Annie in her arms. "Daymare?"

Annie nodded. "I can't possibly face Fenchaw and Decker." She felt soiled. Sordid. Debased. Humiliated.

"Sure you can, " Riya said, gently easing Annie towards the exit.

Annie shook her head, resisting Riya's efforts to coax her out.

"I should introduce you to a friend of mine. She's a specialist in herbal remedies. Maybe she has something to ease the aftermath of these daymares."

"Not now," Annie said, her eyes pleading.

Riya chuckled and kissed her on the top of her head. "No. Not now."

56.

Fenchaw leaned forward and whispered, "Kard's pushing for a new bill to be fast-tracked through parliament to outlaw organisations like GENie. He's not alone. He's got the backing of more than half the Conservative MPs and all the right-wing groups, not to mention the pharmaceutical companies, the private clinics, as well as nurses' trade unions and doctors' professional organisations."

"How can he possibly justify that?" Annie asked, appalled. "None of the people we cater for use private clinics, they are too poor, and we are not against doctors or nurses, on the contrary, we'd willingly work with them. All we want is to help those that can't or won't use the existing system. Those that fall between the cracks. How can that be bad? Especially when the government is cutting back on funding, hitting the most vulnerable, and the health service is struggling to meet demand."

"I agree entirely. But many professional bodies insist that using staff who are not properly trained according to standards set by them is dangerous. In some cases that may be true, but they are also defending their turf and the status quo at the expense of those they are supposed to care for. Above all Kard and his supporters claim that an organisation like GENie would be undermining state structures, like health care. The moment he finds out what happened in that derelict house, he'll add policing to the list."

"That's why I'm hesitant about posting those two testimonies on the internet," Decker said. "We might just be handing him stronger arguments against GENie."

"But he's the one undermining the structures the state is built on. Underwood told me himself," Annie said. She was loathed to withhold the testimonies. They were hard-hitting and to the point. It struck her that Kard had always profited from the silence of others. Nobody dared speak out. The story of the emperor's new clothes sprang to mind. Somebody had to dare stand up and point out that the emperor was naked.

"Underwood is more and more isolated amongst the Conservatives," Fenchaw said. "If this bill goes through, despite his opposition, it will be the end of him as Prime Minister. We could well be lumbered with Kard as PM. Imagine what a delight that would be."

"That's exactly what Kard wants," Annie exclaimed. "That's why he's doing this. Not to protect the health service."

Both Fenchaw and Decker nodded.

Annie puffed out a frustrated breath. "Not speaking out is what maintains Kard in power." She glanced at a clock on the wall. One o'clock. "I'm too tired. We all are. We can't figure this out now. And I want to talk to Underwood. And maybe others you might suggest. We can hold off the publication of those testimonies, but not for long. I am determined they be made public before Kard starts spreading his version of the truth."

Listen to you, a voice sneered in her head. You are talking to two of the country's leading figures. How dare you tell them what to do? Are you forgetting who you are, what you are? How can a girl from a lame background like yours possibly imagine changing the world? How can a mere schoolgirl know anything about grown-up issues like politics and healthcare? You haven't even finished school. You have no diplomas. No job. No money. No family. No support.

She slammed a mental door on the voice, but it continued muttering through the keyhole. You know I am right. I'm the voice of reason.

"I am so tired," she said, getting to her feet, "I hear the voices of my parents, my teachers, the vicar and all the reasonable people of this world sermoning me for being so arrogant as to think I can have a say in all this."

Fenchaw patted her on the shoulder, smiling. "You're doing fine. Don't let doubts and disparaging voices get you down. You said it yourself, 'someone has to unmask the imposter'."

"But what if it is me that is mistaken and not emperor Kard? What if I am the one who is the laughing stock of the crowd, the one who stands before them naked?"

"Why do you think we listen to you and act on your words?" Decker asked. "It is not you that is mistaken, although it is reasonable and probably healthy to doubt. What you did with the police was remarkable. And, although I admit it scares me, your decision about that thug, both of them in fact, was audacious and eminently just. I hope you continue collecting testimonies because I sense they are our best weapons to fell Kard, but also to build a better alternative." She saw Riya and Brian nodding in agreement. "No. You are not the imposter, even if the real imposter will use every last ounce of his influence to convince you and everyone else you are."

57.

Annie awoke to Kevin's fingers meandering over her shaved head as if exploring uncharted territory. She lay there, unmoving, savouring the ripples of pleasure the caresses sent through her belly . "Don't stop," she said, when Kevin pulled away.

Opening her eyes she was shocked to see the bruised, swollen face of her friend. The sight sickened and angered her, so much so it was a struggle to conceal her emotions.

"I know," Kevin said, wincing. "You don't need to hide your feelings. I've seen myself in the bathroom mirror. I look a mess."

"You do indeed." She wondered whether she'd done the right thing releasing Lionel. She had to put a dampener on her outrage which clamoured for revenge. Better to tell Kevin and get it over with before someone else told her. "I let one of the two thugs go."

Kevin tensed, her look becoming frightened, then she relaxed, a little. "The cat lover?"

Annie nodded.

"I had the impression he was there by mistake," Kevin said, peering off into the distance. "He tried to protect me, at least in the beginning, but it only made things worse."

A knock came at the door and Ella peered in. "Morning love birds. Or should I say afternoon."

"Come off it," Kevin replied. "It's only ten."

"Leonor is here to dress your wounds," Ella said. "And Riya phoned to say she will be here with Brian and Fenchaw in an hour. Madame is to be received by the Prime Minister." She made an exaggerated bow.

"Don't mock, you grinning loon. You have no idea," Annie said. "You wanna go instead?"

Ella shook her head. "Oh and Jewel is going to drop by with clothes."

"Jewel?" Kevin asked, searching Annie's face for answers.

"A transformation wizard," Annie explained, leaving Kevin looking perplexed. "You'll like her. I'm sure you will. You two have some things in common."

"I'm jealous already."

"There's no reason. Who knows, maybe she has some clothes for you in her wardrobe, young man."

Kevin beamed, then winced when her split lip reopened.

Jewel arrived as they sat down to breakfast. She was dressed in an outrageous pipe dress that hugged her figure in a way most women would have shied away from. It revealed the slightest curve or bump. Annie wondered how she managed it.

"Oh my dear!" Jewel exclaimed, catching sight of Kevin. "Whoever did that to you?"

"Him!" Ella said, turning up the television. The news was on. Georg could be seen wrapped in a blanket, sipping a mug of tea. "After a telephone tip-off, police discovered this man trussed up in the ruins of a house where he'd been forced to spend the night. Nearby was a wad of poorly made fake photos aimed at implicating him in a kidnapping." The camera cut to a bundle of papers, although none of the pictures were shown. "According to a police spokeswoman, the purported kidnapping was a publicity stunt linked to a well-known daily newspaper."

The camera cut back to Georg, who whimpered none too convincingly. "Two thugs in black combat dress jumped me as I was on my way home," he said. "They dumped me in that stinking hole full of rats saying the police would be coming for me in the morning." The presenter went on, "An investigation is under way to find the perpetrators of the crime. The police are looking for this young man…" A picture of Annie dressed as a boy, fist raised in salute flashed onto the screen. "… in connection both with the kidnapping and the attack on London's top celebrity, Nolan Kard. If you have any information, please contact this number."

A phone number flashed across the screen followed by Kard lounging in his armchair, an impressive bandage around his head. Ella hissed at the sight of him. "Self-centred pig," she muttered.

"Enough is enough!" Kard exclaimed, cautiously fingering the bandage. "People are getting hurt. It's time the government put a stop to these antics. Are we going to let underground organisations, acting outside the law, injure and abduct innocent people? If Underwood can't get his act together, maybe we should find a new Prime Minister."

When the camera cut back to the presenter who began talking about rises in food prices, Ella hit the off button.

"I knew we should have released that video of Kevin earlier," Annie said, annoyed at herself for having given in to Decker and Fenchaw. "Now it'll probably be too late."

"Video? I love videos," Jewel exclaimed.

"You might not like this one," Annie said, grimacing. "It's Kevin here talking about being beaten."

"Maybe it's not too late," Ella said. "Many people will not have seen the news."

"I'm sure it will have been on the radio too," Annie said, feeling defeated. She should have insisted. They had lost precious time. "The moment Fenchaw arrives, we'll talk to him."

The door opened and Riya walked in, her laptop under her arm. "The men'll be here in a tick."

"Did you see the news?" Ella asked, giving Riya a hasty kiss. Riya made a disappointed face as if to say, 'Is that all I get?' before replying, "Brian saw it on his iPad. He described it to us. They didn't even show one of the photos."

"Do you have them?" Annie asked.

Riya nodded.

"Let me have a look."

Riya pushed aside the breakfast things and placed her laptop on the table. She pulled up a series of photos. Jewel gasped to see a shot of Kevin on the bed as one of the thugs threatened her with a truncheon. Annie had to close her eyes. Several of the photos were unbearable. The images were deeply sickening. How could the police pretend they were fake? She imagined a beaten woman staggering into a police station only to be told to return home and stop playacting. Who was to protect people if the police didn't?

"We could send them to the press agencies," Riya suggested. "They'll be hot stuff right now. Newspapers will fall over themselves to publish them in their online editions."

"It might be better if someone else publishes those first, rather than the Daily," Ella said.

Annie poured a cup of tea for Jewel and buttered herself a piece of toast, but let it fall back on the plate, unable to eat. She tried to imagine how Kard and the police would react to the release of the photos. Denial probably. Outrage maybe. Most likely they would proclaim the photos fakes. Releasing the videos might help. She imagined it would be more difficult to fake a video. And anyway Kevin's testimony was so striking it didn't matter if it was fake or not.

"Go ahead," she said, coming to a snap decision. "Send the file of photos to the media, anonymously. We'll post both videos shortly after."

58.

"I hope you don't mind," Annie said, handing Fenchaw and Decker a mug of tea. "We thought it better if other papers posted the photos first."

"That makes sense," Fenchaw replied. "If we are constantly seen as instigators of trouble, it will end up working against us. Kard will probably draw up a law to make us illegal."

It was meant as a joke and Annie was tempted to laugh, but it wasn't funny. "What will you do?" she asked.

"I'm not sure. If others talk about the photos, we might not mention them."

"But surely you'd talk about the kidnapping," Ella protested.

"I know it will sound cruel," he nodded to Kevin, "but it's more of a distraction at the moment and that suits Kard fine. We need to concentrate on this bill to outlaw organisations like GENie."

Annie wondered how an attack against any woman could ever be classed as a distraction, but she could see Fenchaw's point. "Let's go see the Prime Minister."

Jewel had brought her a wig. They'd agreed it wouldn't be good if the boy who'd so rudely attacked Kard was seen visiting Underwood. The shoulder-length wig went with a grey skirt to her knees, a tight-fitting blouse and a matching jacket, pulled in at the waist. Tan tights and some of Jewel's make-up wizardry completed the illusion of a smart, young, up-and-coming business woman.

Underwood hung suspended for a second when she entered

his office, no doubt wondering who she was, until Fenchaw said, "I believe you've already met Annie Wight."

The Prime Minister gasped and held out his hand for her to shake. "Extraordinary disguise! The one as a boy was excellent too. You must tell me who does the work for you. I might need a good disguise soon."

Another of those jokes that wasn't funny. Annie laughed all the same.

Taking a seat, she decided it was best to get to the point. "Do you plan to counter this new bill against 'illegal' associations? And if so, how can we help?"

He huffed. "You don't beat about the bush. I would dearly like to stop it. Even I, as a long-standing Conservative, draw the line somewhere. But more than half my cabinet are in favour of it and I suspect it will pass in the House, especially with this new business about that man who was kidnapped."

"Have you seen the photos?" Annie asked.

Underwood shook his head.

Decker laid the portfolio of prints on the desk.

Underwood rubbed his forehead as he flicked through the pictures, halting at one in which Georg was savagely beating Kevin. "I suppose these aren't fake."

"No. Unfortunately they are very real," Decker said.

"What is the world coming to?" Underwood said leaning back in his chair and stared out the window.

"I would like you to do something for me, for Kevin, the girl that was beaten, and for all those people who are the victims of violence," Annie said. "I'd like you to bear witness to having seen these photos and to react to what you see."

The man raised a hand in front of his face as if to ward off a blow. "As much as I like you and appreciate what you've done, I can't do that. I'm the Prime Minister."

"Not for much longer, from what I've heard," Annie said. Underwood winced, but did not deny it. He knew his time was up. "You can do this and I am sure you will. No dancing about the bush. No political talk. Just your reaction as a human being, as a man, faced with the brutal beating of a young girl, and the crass denial it ever existed."

Underwood sighed. He glanced at Decker and Fenchaw. "With you alone," he said to Annie.

"You do realise we will publish what you say on the internet?" Annie pointed out.

Underwood nodded, his features set, his expression resigned.

She was relieved. She had been sure he would refuse. "Me and Brian who films," she replied.

When they were alone and Brian was set up, Underwood looked through the pictures again before talking. The portrait of the Queen behind his desk stared over his shoulder.

"When I was a kid," he began, "I had a neighbour whose son revelled in torturing stray cats. He forced me to watch. I knew what he did was wrong and watching him sickened me, but he threatened to torture me if I told. I am ashamed to admit it, but I have never spoken about that. This is the first time. As I look at this picture." He turned it to face the camera. "I feel that same revulsion and feeling of powerlessness I had as a kid." He halted a moment, wiping a hand across his forehead as if that could erase the memory. "People are shamefacedly denying this photo is real. People are denying they raise their hand against young girls, against women and children in general. Yet they do. This photo is no fake. Neither are the others that go with it." He held up the wad of photos to the camera, his hand visibly trembling. "It has got to stop. These liars, these bullies, these criminals have got to be stopped." He glanced over his shoulder at the portrait of the Queen, and shook his head. "I might be Prime Minister, but you have as much power if not more than me to stop this. How? By speaking out. Don't make the mistake I made all those years ago with that cat. Speak out. And if the police and the media won't listen to you, then speak to your neighbours, to your children's teachers, to people you meet in the street, to the Internet." He paused to glance one last time at the picture of Kevin. "And when they threaten you, like they will me, for speaking out like this, stand up together. Bullies can only handle one at a time.

They work behind the scenes. In dark corners. They are afraid when people join together. So we must stand up together, out in the open, and say, 'We won't let ourselves be bullied any more.'"

59.

"Riya posted those two testimonies to the Internet," Decker told her, grinning, as she closed the door to the Prime Minister's office. The secretary smiled at her and Annie was about to say she was hungry when a solitary explosion behind her put a halt to everything. Frozen in horror she stared at Decker and Fenchaw's faces that must have mirrored hers. She turned, dashed back to the office door and flung it open.

The room looked unchanged. Yet something was not right. Where was Underwood? Fearing the worst, she rounded his desk. The folder of photos lay scattered across the floor with several of Kevin's battered body clearly visible. Taking another step, she saw Underwood's feet sticking out from behind the desk. Blood had sprayed across the wall and dripped slowly to the floor.

Annie sank to her knees, her head clasped in her hands. She had done this. She had pushed him too far. The man was already desperate, but she had shoved him over the brink. 'They will threaten me,' he'd said. But she had finished him off. Kard had been torturing him for months, but in one encounter she had put a fatal end to the foul work. Kard would be proud of her. She could picture the headlines: PM takes his life after interview with rebel leader. People would hate her, even if they didn't appreciate the PM.

She felt her body and brain go numb as someone grasped her arm and helped her to her feet. She was sat on a chair and offered a drink which she did not touch. In her desolation, she could not comprehend what was happening. Underwood had taken his life and it was her fault.

"Annie," Fenchaw said. "Snap out of it."

Why should she bother? Everything she touched ended in disaster. Her father was homeless and without a job, not to mention her mother who'd become one of Kard's groupies. Megan had been attacked by thugs. Kevin had been battered almost to death. And now the Prime Minister was dead.

"Drink this," the secretary said. "It will do you good."

Annie pushed the cup away.

"What's all this commotion about?" a familiar voice said.

She looked up to see Underwood standing in his doorway, concern on his face. How could that be? He was dead. Then she realised. She sprang to her feet, dashed across the office to him and flung her arms around his shoulders, sobbing.

"Kard?" he asked.

She nodded.

Putting an arm around her waist to steady her, he led her back into his office and closed the door. A knock brought the secretary carrying the steaming cup. She said nothing, only handed it to Annie and left.

Sipping the herbal tea, Annie felt better. Of course it helped to have tangible proof Underwood was OK.

"Here. Try this." He upturned a pill into her outstretched hand. "It's the same plant extracts that are in that herbal tea, but more concentrated. My doctor prescribed it to combat the after-effects of nightmares. Of course, I didn't bother him with their origin. I'm sure he can dream up an explanation."

What with all the political difficulties in the news, it was easy enough to imagine.

"We need to put a stop to these nightmares," Underwood said. "But I haven't the slightest inkling how."

"I may have an idea." She told him about her encounter with the ghost writer.

"That's a nightmare in itself," Underwood said, raking a hand through his hair. "An army of ghost writers, writers who are really ghosts, and whose task is to make our life hell, all at Kard's behest. Both of us have first-hand experience of that hell. Surely there must be a way to counterattack."

There were possibilities, but they were far-fetched and she had no idea if they'd work. Ideally she needed to talk to her ghost writer, but he'd made no new attempt to contact her. "Let's hope so."

Underwood scooped up the photos from his desk. "I have to go to the television. An interview for a news programme. To be broadcast live." He glanced at Annie. "Would you like to accompany me?"

Annie stared at him, caught off guard and unsure how to respond. Was this a trap? Would her presence be seen as legitimation for a failing politician? Would being there compromise her cause? Would GENie suffer? Or could she turn this to her advantage, grasping the chance to explain their project?

"I don't want to oblige you. I certainly don't want to embarrass you. If you have the slightest hesitation, say no. I won't be offended."

"I cannot guarantee I will endorse what you say."

"I would not expect it. But I do want to talk about these photos and you will be free to have your say."

Annie wasn't sure the TV would let her. Surely there were ways they could shut her out of the discussion. "If they let me."

"Oh they will." He seemed so sure, she was wary. "You have no idea how much weight your words have at the moment. They will probably be more interested in what you have to say than anything I could tell them."

Shaking her head, she thought of Fenchaw's words. If the kidnapping really was a distraction, she'd do well to talk of more important things. "I realise this kidnapping business is important, and I would welcome a chance to talk about it," Annie said. "But if I have the possibility to speak on national TV, I'd much rather talk about this proposed bill that will make outlaws of me and my friends when all we want to do is help people in need."

Underwood sighed. "That's a tricky subject."

"I do not shy away from difficulty."

Underwood grimaced, shaking his head. "No. I noticed."

She wondered if he would shirk responsibility. "I would like to post your testimony to the Internet before we go on air. Do you agree?"

He made a face, the sort she imagined a chess player would make when he'd walked into a trap knowing full well it was coming. "Well. I did say we needed courage. So go ahead." He glanced around the room as if it were the last time he'd see it and sighed.

"Things'll work out. You'll see," she said.

"For you maybe. But not for me."

"Don't be so pessimistic." She immediately regretted her words. How could she be so disrespectful?

"You see. Even a seventeen year-old schoolgirl has to cheer me up."

She winced.

"I'm sorry. I didn't mean to belittle you. I was trying to poke fun at myself. But we must go or all this discussion will be pointless." He picked up a small bottle from his desk and handed it to her. "That's the remedy if ever Kard's ghost writers try to put you down."

"What about you?"

He smiled and pulled a similar bottle from his jacket pocket.

60.

The receptionist at the TV studios was visibly taken aback at the sight of Annie side by side with Underwood. That she had been recognised was clear from the young woman's worried expression. She picked up the phone, turned her back on them and whispered what sounded like a warning. When they reached the studio it was in a state of panic as people rushed about, no doubt preparing for the unwanted guest.

The presenter came forward to greet them, a broad smile plastered on his lips. "Prime Minister," he said, shaking hands with Underwood. "And who is this charming person accompanying you?"

Annie was sure he knew, but Underwood went through the motions of introducing her.

"Annie Wight!" The presenter said, doing his best to sound surprised. "Every time you pop up on television you look different. Was it really you that attacked Nolan Kard in one of our studios?"

"Only in his imagination," Annie replied. "And he has a lot of that."

The man laughed, making Annie shudder. Everything about him struck her as false. "Would you like to watch the programme from the control room?" he asked. "You will learn something about how a TV programme is made."

It was a game, she realised. He knew full well she hadn't come to stand on the sidelines.

"Annie will be taking part, just like me," Underwood said.

"I'm sure her words will delight your audience. Unless, of course, you have any objections. In which case both of us will not waste your time any longer."

The presenter struggled to swallow as if something had got stuck in his throat. "No. No. We'd be delighted." He led them up onto a slightly raised platform on which three armchairs had been arranged in a semicircle. He plumped himself in the one on the right and indicated Underwood should take the one next to him. Underwood declined, offering the seat to Annie. The presenter scowled.

"Five minutes," a metallic voice called out over a loudspeaker.

A stubbornly silent technician came and fitted two mics to the lapel of her jacket. She might as well have been a dummy for all the attention he paid her. He was followed by a girl in startling pastel green overalls who powdered her nose and forehead. Like the technician, she said nothing, but the exaggerated way she dabbed Annie's skin left her acutely aware of the girl's touch. When she straightened up to leave, the girl squeezed Annie's hand as if to encourage her and in so doing placed a piece of paper in her palm. Annie was reminded of school where girls at the back of the class would share secret notes when the teacher's back was turned. Maybe that was why she felt a mixture of guilt and complicity as she slid the piece of paper into her pocket. With lights flooding the set, it was uncomfortably hot, especially wearing a wig. She got to her feet, to the alarm of the presenter, and moved out of the lights, fanning her face to cool off.

Her every move was being watched as if she had 'dangerous enemy' tattooed in bright colours on her forehead. What did they expect? That she was going to assassinate Underwood or the presenter? Or explode a bomb? Under such surveillance, she didn't dare peek at the paper which stayed clenched in her hand deep in her pocket.

"Two minutes," the voice called out.

She needed a distraction. She looked round the studio. The presenter had got to his feet and was coming to fetch her. The moment he went to step off the raised platform, she shot him a thought of his flies being undone. Just enough for him to miss his step and plunge headlong amongst the cables curled on the studio floor. Several people rushed to his aid. When all heads turned to see what had happened, she unfolded the note and read it before hurrying back to the platform.

"One minute," the voice said.

The presenter hobbled back to his chair scowling and sat down almost knocking over the jug of water at his elbow. When the red light came on, he was all smiles. "With us in the studio today we have Prime Minister Underwood as well as a surprise guest, Annie Wight, a rising political figure who has often been in the news these last couple of days."

The man concentrated his questions on Underwood no doubt partly because he had no idea what to ask her. Each time Underwood tried to involve Annie, the presenter countered, asking him a new question. The note had said: Beware they are going to try to make you look ridiculous. It had said more, but she didn't want to think about that.

Frustrated, Annie interrupted the presenter as he questioned Underwood about foreign policy. "What are you afraid of?" she asked him. He ignored her question. "I am talking to you. Maybe you should have the politeness to listen." He stared at her, his lips pursed, his face red, as if his worst nightmare was about to kick in. "You are consistently deflecting the discussion from the one issue your audience wants to hear."

"You mean that fake attack on a young woman," he sneered.

"That attack was a lot less fake than many of the so-called news programmes on television." She paused to look around the studio, leaving no doubt whom she had in mind. "No, I did not come here to talk about that. Others are talking enough about it elsewhere." The presenter stared at her terrified of what was coming next. "I came here to talk about the government's plan to hurry through a bill to outlaw those well-intentioned individuals who get together to help the ill or the needy." The presenter tried to interrupt her, but it was her turn to ignore him. She turned to face the camera. "A group of businessmen, who get rich on the back of a struggling health system, aided and abetted by their politician buddies, are bent on outlawing grassroots initiatives to help the poor, the needy and the marginalised."

The presenter was red in fury at his programme being hijacked. Better to let him speak before he exploded. "You wanted to say something?" she asked, smiling sweetly.

"Healthcare professionals everywhere are worried about the dangers of untrained amateurs taking over the national health service."

"If that is their worry, then let me reassure them. It has never been a question of anyone taking over the NHS nor of syphoning off its scarce resources for other activities. In the imaginary situation that the keys to the service were laid at our feet, we would never accept them. It has enough problems without that." She heard Underwood chuckle. "Our goal is simple. To set up a grassroots service to help with minor ailments and social problems, there where the State is no longer capable or willing to intervene."

"What do you say to that accusation, Prime Minister?" the presenter asked.

"It is no accusation. It's a fact." The presenter looked taken aback. "In an attempt to reduce government spending we have drastically cut back on social services and community-based healthcare. Mental health has also suffered. We have thrown our efforts into shoring up the NHS instead of asking fundamental questions about its ways of working and its fitness for purpose."

Annie was tempted to applaud him for his courage. If this was the end of his career, at least he wouldn't be forgotten.

"The opposition must be rubbing their hands listening to you," the presenter said.

"This is not about party politics. We are talking about the health and welfare of the nation, not bickering over political territories or spent ideologies."

The presenter glanced at the clock on the wall. "A whole new debate there in perspective. But time is up. I'd like to thank our

278   Alan McCluskey

two guests, Prime Minister Underwood and …" He sat suspend, apparently unable to recall her name,

"Annie Wight," Underwood said. "You really should try to remember her name. You'll be using it a lot in the future."

61.

Standing in the spacious hall of the television station, waiting for the PM's car to arrive, Annie screwed up the piece of paper in the depths of her jacket pocket till it was little more than a tight knot. The first part of the message had proved more or less accurate, but it was the second part that troubled her. Just three words. 'I love you.' Surely the girl wasn't serious. They hadn't even exchanged a word. Out of the corner of her eye she spotted the girl in green watching from the shadow of a doorway. It was touching, but she hoped she wouldn't be beset by drooling fans all eager to declare their love. She'd have to make public appearances with Kevin to curb such fantasies.

One of the PMs assistants strode up to announce that the limousine had arrived. Annie followed Underwood out of the TV station, delighting in the sun and the fresh afternoon air, only to discover a crowd gathered at the foot of the steps. The people erupted in jeers at the sight of them. "Hands off our NHS," they screamed.

Annie took a few steps towards the crowd.

"I wouldn't," Underwood said. "You won't get anywhere. They'll only be hostile. You might even get hurt."

Annie hesitated. He was probably right. Yet her inclination was to reach out to them. She raised a hand for silence but the shouting only increased. She was at a loss. She couldn't outshout them. She'd become so used to getting people's attention. In the front row was an older woman and what might have been her granddaughter. The girl, who couldn't have been more than ten, looked lost and intimated, but the woman was bellowing with confidence.

Annie knelt down in front of the girl who looked at her, terrified. Around her mouth and nostrils nasty red parches had formed. In places they oozed a clear liquid. "Does that hurt?" Annie asked.

The woman snatched the girl away. "Don't touch! I don't want her contaminated by the likes of you."

"Why do you say that?" Annie asked, startled at the woman's vehemence.

"You've probably got that illness. All your sort have."

"What illness?"

Instead of answering, the woman turned her back and, taking the girl in tow, shoved deeper into the crowd.

Annie shook her head and climbed back up to Underwood who had been watching from the top of the steps. He shrugged.

"I don't understand," she said. "These are the very people we could be helping. Why do they refuse to speak to me?"

"Some people are beyond hope," he said, turning to leave. "Lack of education? Miss-informed? Stubbornly fixed ideas? Or pure meanness? Who knows?

"You go," she said. "I'll find my own way home. See you soon." He called after her, but she was already jumping down the steps two at a time. She shouldered her way into the crowd in search of the little girl. To her surprise people ignored her. It was as if they hadn't come to protest against her. No one seemed to recognise her. Maybe they'd just joined in for the excitement, to make a noise or to vent their frustration.

She had waded almost all the way through the crowd before she found what she was looking for. Annie pointed at the girl's mouth. "What do you put on those sores?" she asked, shouting to be heard over the row of the crowd.

"What business is it of yours?"

Annie ignored the question. "Does it hurt?" she asked, kneeling in front of the girl who nodded shyly. "Are you hungry?" The girl nodded again. "Would you like a sandwich?" The girl nodded eagerly.

"We don't need none of your charity," the woman said, shifting to tug the girl away.

"Her face is infected. Look for yourself."

The woman begrudgingly glanced at the girl. "So what?"

"The right cream will stop it from spreading and she will not have a scar on her pretty face." Annie felt her patience fraying at such stubborn stupidity. Surely it was simple enough.

"We can't afford no cream. Anyway how am I to know one cream from another?"

"Don't you have a doctor?"

The woman shook her head. To think she'd been bellowing for the NHS yet she didn't even use it.

Annie fished out her phone. "I'm going to call a friend. She's a nurse and she'll have a remedy for those sores. In the meantime, let's get you something to eat and drink."

"I ain't got no money."

"I don't expect you to pay."

The woman put a protective arm around the child. "None of that funny business. I've met people like you. You pretend to help, then you try to snatch the kid."

Annie huffed in frustration. How difficult it was to help.

"My life is so complicated, you couldn't imagine." Annie began, leading them away from the crowd and its racket. "To be honest, I have no time for this. But I stopped. All I wanted to do was help. I haven't the slightest interest in snatching your girl." She tossed her arms in the air, exasperated. "What the hell would I do with her?"

"And we ain't going to no church. Had enough of them and their promises."

"No churches," Annie said, stressing each word as if addressing a simpleton. "No body snatchers. No child labour. No hidden insurance salesman. No bills at the end of the month. Just a hot tea, a sandwich and, if you are lucky, a tube of cream for the girl's face."

There were no cheap cafes near the TV building. Annie

chose the one that looked the least pretentious. It was nearly empty. She picked a table close to the window from where she could watch for her friends. She'd also asked Brian to come with his smallest, least intimidating camera, just in case. She ordered tea for everyone and a sandwich for the kid and the woman. The server smiled at Annie, but looked down her nose at the other two. It was true, they did look out of place. To be honest, she felt out of place herself, despite Jewel's smart clothing. In the bright lights the shoddiness of the pair's clothes were all the more apparent. They looked like tramps. Who knew if they even had a shelter for the night?

62.

Despite the sores that must have stung when she ate, the little girl devoured her sandwich with gusto and craned her neck to see if there were any more. To all Annie's questions, the girl only replied with nods or shakes of her head. Perplexed, Annie was beginning to wonder if she were dumb. Yet there was a sharpness in her eyes and a keenness in her reactions that ruled out simplemindedness.

"You still hungry?" she asked. The girl nodded.

"What's your name?"

The girl looked at her blankly.

"Surely you have a name. Mine is Annie."

The girl glanced over her shoulder at the few remaining sandwiches on the counter but did not reply.

Annie called the waitress over and had her give the girl another sandwich. She also offered the woman one, suspecting she was as hungry as the girl, but she pursed her lips in refusal.

Annie had so many questions. When did the girl last eat? Could the girl talk? Where was her mother? Did they have any income? Did they have a home to return to? But the last thing she wanted to do was to interrogate the woman. She suspected that most of those who were paid to help the needy first pried the gory details of their misery from them as if exacting a fee for their help. If the woman wanted to talk, that was different. The idea of filming an interview or a testimony was probably impossible.

Leonor and Brian arrived, Annie introduced them to the

woman whose name she still didn't know, and the nurse got to work on the girl's sores. "This will sting," Leonor told the girl as she tended the wounds. "But the cream will make it feel better."

Brian had a tiny camera with him which he pulled from his pocket and placed on the table in front of him. He glanced questioningly at Annie but she shook her head. He pushed his chair back so he was a good distance from the table and quietly watched.

When Leonor had finished, the girl clambered onto her grandmother's knees, curled up like a cat and closed her eyes.

"I'll give you this tube of cream," Leonor said to the woman. "Use it three times a day, but make sure you wash your hands before and after you apply it."

The woman nodded, absently running her filthy fingers through the girl's equally filthy hair.

"What's her name?" Annie asked.

Having the child in her lap seemed to calm the woman and dissipate some of her mistrust. She glanced at Annie. "Petunia. But I call her Pet." The woman, who was probably in her fifties, looked a lot older. The folds of her skin were underscored by the dirt that had accumulated there. Her hair probably hadn't been washed in months. She might not even have the wherewithal to wash her hands as Leonor had instructed.

"How did all this come about?" Annie asked, then held up her hand when the woman frowned. "You don't need to reply. But if you do, I'd like to ask Brian to film. If people hear your story, it might make them try to improve your situation but also that of others like you." When the woman did not refuse, Annie nodded to Brian to begin.

The woman continued to stroke the Pet's head for a long moment, staring at the ground, uttering not a word. Judging from the girl's breathing, she had fallen asleep.

The woman sighed. "It wasn't always like this," she said, looking up at Annie, hesitant, her expression one big question. How hard it must be to trust. Annie nodded, willing her on.

"My daughter had a flat and a job. It wasn't well paid. The

place was a dump. But we got by. The three of us. The father was supposed to pay. But he never did. Then my daughter lost her job. Cutting back on cleaners the supermarket said. We got benefit for a while. Then that ran out. Some hitch in the system. They have no money either. The landlord threatened eviction. My daughter took to the street. She was desperate. The money was good. Sometimes. It paid the rent. And we had something to eat. But one of the blokes got violent. Exploded in a frenzy. Roughed her up. Couldn't stop punching and kicking. The ambulance arrived too late. Pet was there when her mother died. Saw it all. I remember it so well. She sat there like a doll, frozen, her eyes blank, not understanding. How could she? It was too much. She was just five. That's when she stopped talking. Hasn't spoken a word since. The police never caught the guy. If ever they tried. The landlord kicked me and Pet out. Didn't want such sordid people in his house. Folks give us food. From time to time. Or a bit of money. Like this afternoon. I was to get a fiver. For taking part in the demonstration. We muddled by. Then Pet got ill. There was nothing I could do. Doctors don't want to treat homeless beggars. The hospital wouldn't have us. Thank heavens she recovered. On her own. Sometimes I wonder why. But the worst is not having a place to go. When evening comes. People are hurrying home to a good meal. And we have nowhere. And nothing to eat. It kills you in the end. I've seen loads of people give up. They find a quiet corner. So as not to disturb. Then just lie down and never get up."

63.

Kevin sighed. "Very touching," she said cuddling into Annie's arms, nestled on her lap. Next to them Riya was perched on Ella's knees twining her fingers in and out of her friend's hair. All four girls were squeezed in front of the laptop which sat on the kitchen table, the remains of a hasty teatime arrayed like a piece of modern art around it.

"Did you find somewhere for them to stay?" Riya asked, closing the computer.

"Leonor knew of a place. It's only temporary, but at least they have a roof over their heads and food to eat, for the moment," Annie said.

"This whole situation is so much bigger than just healthcare," Ella said.

Annie nodded. "If we were fully aware of the immensity of what we are trying to do, I think we'd throw in the towel."

All agreed the challenge was daunting.

"You did a remarkable job with that woman," Riya said. "I'm surprised she talked at all. We really should set up a web site. These videos are so good."

The idea was appealing, but Annie was hesitant. "I don't want to be cornered into making more," she said. "They are good because the moment was right and people had something to say. But if we feel obliged to continue, we might lose that spontaneity and urgency."

A knock at the door announced the arrival of Brian. He was to bring photos of the TV programme with Underwood. As he hurried into the kitchen and greeted them, he didn't seem his usual carefree self. His face was pinched and he looked worried.

"What's up?" Annie asked.

"This," he said dumping a wad of photos on the table.

The uppermost photo was of Annie talking to Underwood at the TV studios. Not surprisingly they were all photos of her and Underwood, which was what she was expecting. There was even one of the moment she flung her arms around Underwood's neck. She had been so relieved to see him alive.

"I didn't know you took this," she said.

"I didn't. All the photos are part of a file that is circulating on the internet to support a claim that Underwood is having an affaire with you."

"That's preposterous," Ella exclaimed.

"Why ever would they say that?" Annie asked, dumbfounded.

"Because you are not yet eighteen," Brian said, "that would make Underwood a criminal of a kind that really doesn't have good press."

Perplexity gave way to indignation. To think that Kard was surely behind this, the very man who had tried to grope her in his bus. So it was true what she'd heard, people accused others of what they did themselves. But how could you prove this nonsense was pure fabrication?

"If I deny it, people will take that as admission of guilt," Annie said. "Once such a label has been stuck on your back, it's nigh on impossible to shake off."

"Maybe you could use irony," Ella said.

"What do you mean?" Kevin asked, extricating herself from Annie's arms and stretching only to groan when her muscles hurt.

"Poke fun at the person who invented the story, for example, or turn the tables on them with a similar accusation."

"Would that work?" Annie asked. The idea filled her with misgiving. What if people thought she was being flippant? It was a serious matter. Or thought her humour was just a way of condoning illicit behaviour? If they could show a testimony of a girl who had been a victim of someone like Kard that might underscore a condemnation of her own. Especially if Kard were in some way implicated. No. That wouldn't work.

"We can't accuse," Annie said. "That's exactly what people expect. Whatever we do, it's got to be unexpected."

"Maybe there is no solution," Brian said.

Annie shook her head. "There is, but I don't see it for the moment."

Her phone rang. It was Underwood. "I'm so sorry." He sounded exhausted. "I wish you hadn't got muddled up in all this."

"How is your wife taking it?"

"She knows enough of politics to know it is pure fiction, but the news makes her look like a fool if not worse. That hurts."

"Do you think she would agree to meet me?" Annie asked, acting on an impulse. "Away from the cameras." Except Brian's, maybe. This could be the testimony she needed. An unexpected solution to an apparently impossible problem.

"Hold on," Underwood said. "I'll ask. She is right next to me."

Anne cupped her hand over the phone and turned to Brian. "You bring that tiny camera with you?" When he nodded, she asked. "Got a couple of hours to spare?" He shrugged.

"Yes," Underwood answered. "She agrees." He suggested a meeting place and, once Annie had shifted out of earshot of her friends, they discussed at length what was to be done and how they would do it.

Annie was apprehensive about meeting Underwood's wife, as if something of the rumour had rubbed off on her and she felt guilty. No matter how she reasoned, the feeling would not go away. Other people's twisted imaginings had contaminated her. She couldn't help wondering how people would interpret this secret meeting between her and the wife of her supposed lover when it got out. She shuddered at the thought, imagining the headlines.

She chose not to bring Brian and his camera. Although the idea of the PM's wife giving a testimony was appealing. To film would have been intrusive if not voyeuristic, and the presence of a photographer from The Daily would not have fit their plan. She had to face this on her own.

Underwood's wife sat at a table, alone. A security guard stood in the shadows. The cafe was otherwise deserted. Presumably that had been arranged. The woman stood to greet Annie and they shook hands.

"I'm so sorry," Annie began, unable to meet the woman's eyes.

"You need not be," the woman said. "It's not your fault. You are as much an innocent victim of these attacks as I am. They don't care what harm they do. Our feelings, our relationships, our reputations are nothing to them. In the eyes of many men, a woman is always guilty, even if she has done nothing. You won't convince them otherwise. We are just expendable pawns in a game in which men are out to grab as much power as they can. They don't care who gets hurt."

A flash at the window had Annie looking up. To her horror, several cameramen were pressed against the glass trying to photograph them. It was the very outcome she had dreaded. They must have been tipped off.

The security guard barred the entrance, but a growing crowd hammered on the door and on the windows, making any conversation impossible. They were like rabid beasts that had flared their prey and wouldn't stop till they'd tasted blood

"Let them in," Annie said with a sigh. Hiding was pointless.

Journalists tumbled into the cafe along with cameramen and TV crews, jostling each other to get a good place. The cafe quickly filled till the media formed a solid wall in front of the two women, forcing them back into a corner.

"You have come to see us," Annie said, raising her voice to be heard. "We have had the politeness to let you in. Now return the favour and listen to what we have to say."

Several journalists fired questions at them. "What are you

doing here alone?" "Does Underwood know?" "Are you going to fight it out?" "Do you form a threesome with Underwood?"

Their insinuations disgusted Annie. "If you want us to talk you'll have to stop interrupting," she shouted over the din.

Finally, the crowd quietened, although Annie doubted it would last.

Underwood's wife spoke first. "That people could imagine such things about us is their problem, but that they splatter their fantasies across the internet and in the press with us as unwilling actors and blameless victims is absolutely unacceptable. They don't care that their filth and lies hurt us and the ones we love. My children have to hear such stories about their father and run the gauntlet of snide comments and insinuations at school. My husband who has devoted his life to this country and struggled to make all our lives better despite the petty quarrels that are common place in politics, is dragged in the dirt by people who don't even have the courage to step out of the shadows and own up to these rumours. These are their fantasies, not ours. Annie Wight, who has been battling to help the poor and needy, to defend the interests of those who are different and marginalised, is brushed aside by men who care nothing for her or those who are dear to her. Young people, girls in particular, should admire her for her courage and forthrightness. Not doubt her because of smears launched by a power-crazed man."

Annie admired the way the woman held herself upright despite the insulting accusations against her husband that ricocheted onto her. She turned to Annie.

"It is so easy to accuse and so hard to shake off the accusations," Annie said, "no matter how untrue they are. These people think they've got us cornered. That we will bow out heads in shame for things born of their own filthy imagination. That's the way many men treat women. Yet we will not bow our heads." She straightened her back and stood as tall as she could. "We stand united against those who would besmirch our names and those of our loved ones. They have done us great harm. And we say it has to stop."

Underwood's wife offered Annie her hand and Annie took it. Together they raised a symbolic fist and cameras clicked furiously sensing the importance of the moment. They hadn't known it and maybe never would, but this was the moment they had come for.

From a door at the side, Kevin and Underwood stepped out. The crowd fell back to let them through. Underwood took his wife in his arms and kissed her. Kevin hugged Annie and they embraced. Then the two pairs turned to face the wall of cameras. "And now," Underwood said, "it is time you left us in peace."

64.

When several photographers continued to linger outside the cafe, Paula, the woman who owned the place and who was a good friend of the Underwoods, led them through the kitchen and up steep stairs to an apartment on the first floor. The flat had recently been renovated and was smartly furnished in a relaxed, but uncluttered way. The owner invited them to sit in the comfortable armchairs in the living room where they were out of sight of any adventurous photographers. She went to fetch tea and cakes.

"I'm really glad we took the time to run through what was going to happen," Annie said when the four of them were alone, "even if it didn't turn out as we expected."

"That was a really neat idea," Christine, Underwood's wife, said. "I thought we'd never find a way out of that trap."

"I told you she was brilliant," Underwood said, beaming.

"Stop that," his wife said, playfully shoving his shoulder. "You'll be making me jealous again."

Underwood laughed, but Annie was embarrassed. "All I knew," Annie said, "was that doubt would have been the end of us. We had to put a stop to it. Journalists seeded the doubt, so maybe they should be the ones to snuff it out."

The cakes and tea arrived on a tray and when the woman turned to go, Underwood stopped her. "This is your flat, Paula, not your cafe. We are not going to force you to wait in the kitchen while we eat your cakes and sip your tea in your living room without you. Do join us."

Paula sat across from the Underwoods next to Annie and Kevin and poured herself a cup of tea. When a knock came at the door, Annie jumped, afraid the newspaper men had found a way in. To her relief, it was the security guard. "Should I send the others away, Sir?" There had been a number of guards hidden in different places, just in case the news people got out of hand.

"Yes. I reckon so. The media will be busy getting their copy to the newspapers or their footage to the stations. Maybe you should keep one or two, just in case."

The man nodded and slipped away.

"I was terrified of those journalists," Paula said, shaking her head. "I thought they were going to smash their way into my cafe. I'm not sure how I would have explained that to my insurance."

Christine agreed. "I knew what we'd planned, I knew the tip off was deliberate, but that didn't stop me being scared stiff. They behaved like animals. Worse. Like a horde of savages. To think many of them have been to university. I find it hard to understand how they feel justified in behaving that way."

"They feed on stories. The prospect of a juicy story makes them frantic," Annie said. "Stories are odd things. They grow and develop almost on their own. These people nourish them and embellish them and spread them around. It's their livelihood."

"But aren't they supposed to check if they are true?" Kevin asked, devouring a slice of home-baked chocolate cake.

"They used to," Underwood said leaning back on the settee. Annie had never seen him so relaxed. "But those who still take the time and the energy to verify, are bowled aside by wave after wave of rollercoaster news that rides roughshod over everything in its path, including truth."

"To think you were going to learn to be a journalist," Kevin said with naive maliciousness. It was a delight to rediscover the sharp-witted girl she had been before the thugs got at her.

Underwood raised his eyebrows.

"Fenchaw offered me a job," Annie explained. "I've always enjoyed writing and now that I've been kicked out of school and can't go to university, it seems like a good solution."

"After all that has happened," Underwood said, "I'm sure many universities would welcome you with open arms and a generous grant to match."

The prospect appealed to her, although she would have preferred to be accepted on the merit of exam results and not because she was a shooting star in the media fermement.

She looked around the room, seeking to distract her mind from the lure of hopes and dreams. There was a full-length mirror in one corner, partly concealed by a potted plant. It had a pretty, gilt frame. She found herself wondering if the ghost writer was in there when the shadow of a hand beckoned from within the mirror. Getting to her feet, she knew full well no one would be aware of her movements.

As last time, the hand reached out and pulled her through. Although now familiar, the feeling of being dragged through a solid mirror was no less alarming. "I haven't got much time," the man said. His clothes were unchanged since the last time, lest it be they were a little shabbier and he was not so carefully groomed.

"I have been muted. I am no longer responsible for your stories."

"Why? What does that mean?"

"Why? I think they suspect I helped you. And what does it mean? They no longer want to frighten you and wear you down. They plan to kill you."

Annie took a step back. The thought of the Pakistani had her blood go cold. "But they can't, can they?"

"Technically, no. But they can drive you to kill yourself or force you to make a fatal mistake. And in between they will make your life hell."

"Is there no way I can fight back?"

"Maybe you could…" His words were cut off as a raging wind tore him away and shoved her back through the mirror with such brute force her thoughts were a crazy jumble.

"Are you alright?" Christine asked. "You look dreadfully

pale."

Annie couldn't collect her thoughts enough to reply. She stared in horror at a nightmare future about to unfurl. Kevin put an arm around her shoulder, but the world refused to right itself.

"Kard?" Underwood asked, his expression pained but sympathetic.

Annie shook her head. "Worse," she managed to say. "Far worse."

65.

"So the Pakistani tried to kill you?" Underwood said.

"He might not have gone that far," Annie replied, rubbing her neck, "but his fingers were mighty tight. I was suffocating and black blotches swirled in front of my eyes."

"How did you fend him off?" Christine asked.

"I hit him over the head with a chair but it was the ghost writer who pulled him through into that other world. If I understand correctly, being taken there is like a death warrant. You can't come back."

"But you went there," Kevin said. "And came back." She pinched Annie who squealed. "Alive, apparently."

Paula chuckled. "I wish I could joke about this. It scares me silly. To think there's an army of ghost writers lurking to dream up nightmares for us, all at Kard's behest. It's a 'super-concentrated' nightmare."

Kevin was right. It wasn't always one way. She was proof. But if travelling worked both ways, maybe she could drag the Pakistani back. He'd be less of a danger here than there. If he caused trouble, Underwood could have him arrested. If the PM still had any sway over the police. She wished she could ask her ghost writer. But she'd probably never see him again.

"If you've got the address of that cafe, I'll get my people to check it out," Underwood said.

Annie shook her head. "We were on the run. I have no idea where it was."

"It must have been near the TV studios where Kard was appearing," Underwood said. He asked Paula for a map. "Here are the studios," he said spreading the map of London on the carpet. It was odd to see the Prime Minister down on his knees, pawing over a map. They were all down on their knees. That was even odder. "Where are the botanical gardens you took refuge in?"

The question embarrassed her. "Er. I don't think they were real. I mean, it was one of those nightmares. Better to look for a church with a large garden." She scanned the map. The building had been on the corner of a busy street. Leonor had recognised the place. What had she called it? "St George in the East," she blurted out when the name came to her.

"That's here," Underwood said, pointing to the map.

Annie traced several paths between the church and the studio. There were few cafes along the way. She shook her head. "I really can't remember and Ella won't know. She was out."

"Can we borrow this map?" Kevin asked, getting to her feet, not without difficulty.

"Sure," Paula replied. "I have several downstairs. You can keep it."

"Let's walk those routes till we find it," Kevin said. "We still have a couple of hours' daylight."

Annie was eager to act, but was Kevin up to it? "It's too soon for you to wander the streets. You haven't properly recovered from your kidnapping."

Kevin attempted a pirouette, presumably to illustrate how fit she was, and almost fell flat on her face. "Well," she said, recovering with help from Christine, "I won't need to do that anyway."

"It's too dangerous," Annie insisted.

"I agree," Underwood said. For a moment she was afraid he'd say he'd come. Apparently it was not enough to stand up to the press to erase all memory of the slur about him and her. "I'll loan you a bodyguard."

"Only if he keeps out of sight."

The car dropped them off near the TV studio and they had to trace several routes till they found the cafe. At no time did they spot the bodyguard. Either he was doing an excellent job or

Underwood had bluffed. The cafe was closed. Of course it was. Peering through the grimy windows, Annie could just make out the Formica-top tables, the unmatched chairs and the linoleum on the floor. She searched for signs of blood, knowing full well she'd wiped it all away.

Half erased lettering on the door said the owner's name was Gorgage. Or it might have been Gurgaje. In the half light of the narrow street, she wasn't sure. "Maybe there's a letter box," Kevin suggested. A door next to the cafe led to a corridor littered with papers and empty bottles. It smelt of refuse and, sure enough, several overflowing dustbins lurked just beyond a row of shabby letter boxes.

The penultimate box bore the handwritten inscription, Gorgage, 2nd floor. Apparently a family of that name lived there. Maybe the owner. Annie was hesitant. She worried about dragging Kevin up two flights of stairs. But above all, the place made her uneasy. She might have come from a poor neighbourhood, but this was definitely poorer than poor.

The second floor landing was mostly taken up by an old-fashioned pram and an impressive line of shoes many with gaping holes in their soles. There were two doors. One had no name. The other said, Gorgage. She glanced at Kevin, as if to ask, 'Ready?', then peered down the stairs, hoping the bodyguard was there somewhere. Seeing no one, she knocked. There was a crash followed by an unnatural silence. Annie knocked again.

"What d'yer want?" a muffled voice asked from within. The woman didn't sound at all Pakistani.

"I'm looking for Mr. Gorgage, the man who runs the cafe downstairs," Annie said.

"He ain't here?" A baby began crying and the woman cursed. The infant sounded sickly or hungry or both.

"Can we come in?" Annie asked.

"If you've come for money, you can piss off," the woman shouted through the closed door.

"We haven't come for money," Annie said, unsure what to say. "I may have news about your husband."

"You can keep your bloody news. I ain't in no hurry to have him back."

Annie pulled out her purse. She didn't have much money left. Taking out the last five-pound note, she slid it under the door. It was snatched up but the door did not open. She'd probably wasted good money for nothing. She was about to turn and go when the door cracked open and a skinny little woman peered out, looking Annie and Kevin up and down, her eyes beady, her skin taut over protruding bones. She clearly didn't often eat.

"What's he done?" she asked, her tone belligerent. "Knocked you up? Wouldn't be the first. Ain't my fault."

Annie was shocked at the suggestion. It really wasn't her world. "No. Nothing like that." Annie wondered if there was any point trying to get in.

The baby cried again. "Is he ill?" Kevin asked. The woman nodded, the banknote still grasped in her fingers. "May I see?" Kevin asked. "I know some things about babies' illnesses."

To Annie's surprise the woman opened the door just wide enough for them to squeeze inside. The place smelt mouldy and unaired. She caught a glimpse of the kitchen that looked filthy and a living room devoid of furniture. The woman led them down a short corridor to a bedroom with a mattress sprawled on the floor. On it lay the infant wrapped in a blanket.

Its face was blotchy and swollen and sweat pearled on its forehead. "Looks like one of those childhood illnesses," Kevin said. "I have a friend who is a nurse. Would you like me to call her?"

"I ain't got no money," the woman said, stuffing the fiver into her pocket.

"She won't charge you," Kevin said. "How long has he been like that?"

"Couple of days. I'm not sure. I lose track of time being shut up here."

Kevin phoned Leonor.

"Is the Pakistani your husband?" Annie asked.

The woman snorted. "He ain't no more Pakistani than you or

I. It's all disguise. Cause of the police."

"Is that why you can't go out?" Annie asked.

The woman nodded. "He was s'pposed to bring up food. But he never came."

"Have you had nothing since then?" Kevin asked, having finished on the phone.

She shook her head. "Ain't 'ad nothing to eat for days."

The so-called Pakistani had disappeared on Wednesday evening, two days earlier. To think the woman lived cut off from the world without the slightest friend or acquaintance and no money or supplies, completely dependent on a violent man for everything. Annie found the thought of such isolation and help-lessness so miserable it was unbearable. She'd read somewhere that loneliness was a major cause of death worldwide. But this went way beyond loneliness. She glanced at the sickly kid. It was probably starving as well as ill.

Kevin must have reached the same conclusion. She pulled a neatly wrapped packet from her pocket. It had been a present from Paula. Kevin adored her chocolate cake. "It's not much," Kevin said, unfolding the packet, "but it's something." She hand-ed the slice of cake to the woman who stared at it in disbelief.

"Eat," Kevin said. "It's delicious."

The woman bit into the cake and her face lit up as if the sun had suddenly shone on her. "Save a bit for the kid," Kevin said. "I don't have any more."

"What happened to yer face?" the woman asked, licking her lips.

"Thugs had a go at me."

"Men!" the woman muttered as she rolled tiny morsels of cake between her thumb and forefinger and fed them to the child. "Mine was always in trouble for hitting women. Thank heavens he didn't dare touch me and the littlun. I'd have taken a knife to him." Her expression was so determined, it was easy to believe her words were no vain threat.

"You said the police were after him," Annie said, hoping to find out more.

The woman looked at her sharply, then shrugged.

"Dunno. Murder probably. He's tight-lipped. A fancy bloke gave 'im a job. Saw him once. Hands him money. To scare his enemies. Rough 'em up. Get rid of rivals."

"But why the cafe?" Annie asked.

"A front. Never were many customers."

No wonder the place had been so deserted and rundown. What must the man have thought when two underage girls turned up for a drink after dark? Could that be what he meant when he said he knew people who'd be pleased to meet her? Not Kard at all.

"What was his real name?" Annie asked.

The woman who had finished feeding the kid, got to her feet. "You from the police?"

"Do I look like I am?" Annie asked.

"No. But they 'ave some tricky ways."

A knock at the door had the woman jump in alarm.

"It's probably my friend come to help your child," Kevin said. "Can I open the door?"

The woman accompanied Kevin to the door. Annie could hear Leonor talking. On the floor next to the bed was a tattered photo of a man quite unlike the Pakistani. Annie was tempted to bend down and pick it up, but she resisted. She was glad she did. The woman was back and saw her looking at the photo. "You want to know his name?"

Annie nodded.

The woman stared a long moment at Leonor applying ointment to her child's skin then turned to Annie and leaned close. Annie had to struggle not to throw up. The woman was filthy and stank. With her lips close to Annie's ear, she whispered the name.

66.

Annie stood alone in front of the Pakistani's cafe. Where had Kevin and Leonor disappeared to? They'd been following her down the stairs, but now were nowhere to be seen. Surely, if they had gone back to the women's flat they'd have said. Anne was relieved to hear the house door open and see Kevin come out, closely followed by a bodyguard. The man must have gone to fetch her.

"Kevin," she called out, but her friend ignored her. She didn't even look up. Instead, she marched, head bowed, hands behind her back in front of the guard who led her to the cafe door. He opened it and shoved her inside. Annie made a move to follow, but the man shouldered her away and shut the door.

Alone again, she tried the door, but it was locked. Pressing her face against the glass, the scene she saw was incomprehensible. A heavy pall of smoke shroud the tables and chairs only to clear abruptly as if someone had opened a window. To her surprise the cafe was full. Men lounged at every table, their clothes shoddy, most of them older, their hair receding if not balding, smoking, drinking, chatting, playing cards. She searched for Kevin but could see her nowhere. Then she spotted the girl surrounded by a scrum of men. She was naked and struggling to get free of a man who looked very much like Kard.

Peals of throaty laughter reached her as the men pressing around Kevin took it in turns to prod, poke and pinch her. Their faces shone scarlet in the lurid light, their features bloated by their efforts. Laughter gave way to grunts and groans as podgy hand after podgy hand kneaded Kevin's flesh.

Kevin sank to the floor with a moan. The group of men tumbled after her, flinging off their clothes as they did. All Annie could see was a pulsing mass of fat and muscle from which a hand or a foot emerged only to plunge back into the fray. She turned her head aside and threw up, her throat burning at the bitterness of the bile.

A burst of laughter had her turn to see Kevin and Leonor leaving the house. Leonor had apparently told a joke, their faces still lit up by the remnants of a smile. Annie leaned against the cafe window to hide her expression, not wanting them to witness her horror. The moment she glanced through the glass, the nightmare clicked back into life.

No! Not again. In an explosion of rage, Annie thrust out with her mind sending the men scattering, smashing tables and chairs in her wake. Screams mingled with the crunch of flesh and bones against the cafe walls. A taste of sweat and blood filled her mouth and the stench of fear and faeces threatened to suffocate her. Thrusting deeper, she broke through into the grey world with a clap of thunder that rang in her ears momentarily deafening her. Like a fiery angel, she scorched a light-filled path through dead air in search of the source of the ill.

At the sight of her, the Pakistani's expression changed from satisfaction to surprise to fear to horror. He staggered back, but there was no escaping. His body folded and crumpled on impact, his screams scattered at the shock of the blow. Where he had been, a dense cloud of stories swirled up, only to fall back in the familiar mushroom form. Crumpled fragments of paper all scribbled with words floated down like giant snowflakes settling with a soft whoosh. A rare tender moment with his wife. Him hitting his kid when it wouldn't stop crying. The sagging breasts of a woman he'd raped out of revenge. His hands smeared with blood oozing from a throat freshly cut. The rasping of his mother's dying words. The police dogs barking and him cornered in a derelict house. The sound of a gun going off. A searing pain in his chest. A brilliant light, stronger than lightning, brighter than the

Sun, only to be eclipsed by pitch darkness slamming down with a hiss and a thud like a guillotine. And beyond the soft whoosh of paper that continued to fall, a heavy silence settled over all.

67.

Annie struggled out from under a heap of paper scraps and stood up, brushing off those that clung to her. With mounting disgust she shied away, realising she was wallowing in all that remained of the Pakistani.

She turned a full circle, examining her surroundings. Grey hills. Grey sky. Grey path. Grey stream. Grey house. Pink stockings. That didn't make sense. Someone must be stranded. Better investigate. She set off, but it was further than she'd thought. No matter how much she walked, she couldn't get closer.

She wandered along the path intrigued by the scraps of paper that littered the way. They were carried hither and thither by a warm breeze. It was difficult not to get distracted. Each scrap had something scribbled on it. She'd made the mistake of snagging one and reading it. She got stranded in a story about sizzling sausages grilled in a neighbours' garden. Mouth-watering, but frankly not very interesting. Like an uninvited guest, she didn't know how to take her leave. She was relieved when a gust of wind tore the paper from her hand.

After a fun time striding along the path kicking up scraps of paper like autumn leaves, she halted in her tracks, alarmed. She could keep on wandering, getting nowhere, for ever. How was she to get home?

The breeze abruptly strengthened bringing colder air. Above dark grey clouds scurried across the sky. Rain began to fall, lashed by a bitter wind. Her clothes were quickly soaked and the more miserable she felt, the worse the weather got till she was being battered by a gale. Rain turned to sleet then hail and the path froze over, each step threatening to send her slipping and sliding to the ground. When she did fall, it was her backside that took the brunt of the blow. She couldn't be bothered to get up. She sat in the wet feeling utterly cold and miserable as a mound of snow formed around her.

"Stop that immediately," she imagined Kevin saying. "You can't slink off like that. You still owe me a ton of kisses." At the thought of her friend, with her boyish features and her spiky hair, Annie smiled. Her mood brightened, the wind abated and the rain and sleet eased off. The sun burst through a break in the clouds, although there were none of the golden hues you might expect after a storm. The countryside stayed stubbornly grey.

Struggling to her feet she was surprised to find her clothes were almost dry and the soggy remains of stories that clung to the path and grass were airing themselves in the unexpected warmth. The abrupt change of temperature made her feel drowsy, but the last thing she wanted was to fall asleep. Who knew if she'd ever wake again? And if she did, she might have lost all her colours like the rest of that world. She broke into a trot, and when the sky began to darken with clouds, she recalled all the good moments with Kevin. The sun promptly reappeared.

To her surprise, she spied several people strolling along the path towards her. Two men, a woman and a little girl who was holding the woman's hand as she skipped along. The men and woman were dressed in grey, as if their clothes had been bleached of colour. Even their hands and faces were a sickly grey. Had she seen them on a bus or in town, she'd have guessed they were clerks or secretaries. Here they looked more akin to passing ghosts.

In striking contrast, the girl was decked out like a rainbow. Her shoes, her tights, her pretty dress even her overcoat, her hat and shoulder bag were a wild mix of colours as if to mock her fellow travellers. She looked more like an apprentice clown or a seamstress's nightmare. It was as if an artist, in a fit of creative fury, had flung a complete palette of colours at her.

"Pretty," Annie said to the girl as she drew alongside the travellers.

"Don't encourage her," the woman said, snatching the girl away, her features stern, her voice forbidding. "How am I to educate the little freak if people like you condone her anomalies?"

"I like colours," Annie countered.

"It's easy enough for you," the woman complained. "Wait till you start to fade."

"Where do all your colours go?" Annie asked.

The shorter of the two men shrugged. "Wrong question."

Had he lost his words along with his colour? "What question should I ask?"

It was the taller man wearing a bowler hat that replied. "Why have you lost your colours?"

She waited for an answer, but none came. "Well?" she asked, giving in to her irritation.

Both men looked up at the sky where billowing cumulus were forming.

"Sorry," Annie said, conjuring up Kevin's image to calm the weather. "Why have you lost your colours?"

"No idea," the short man said. "Not the slightest," the man with the bowler hat said. The woman just shrugged. What a hopeless trio.

"Because they are slaves to stories," the little girl said. "They pour all their colour into stories."

"And why are you so rich in colours?"

"Because I keep my stories to myself. I don't plague others with them."

Annie was tempted to burst out laughing, had it not been tragic. Most children couldn't stop telling everyone, themselves included, a host of stories. The three adults constantly glanced off down the path, shifting from one foot to another, impatient to get on, but they waited for the girl to finish.

"Why do you stay here?" Annie asked.

"Why not?" the girl retorted, as if it were self-evident. "I've heard of that world where all is colour. Adults don't like to talk

308　Alan McCluskey

about it, but I've heard. Here I'm special. I stand out."

Made sense. But Annie had no such reason to stay. "Do you know the way back?" she asked.

The girl opened her mouth to reply, but the woman grabbed her by the collar and dragged her off down the path. The two men hurried after. Any words the girl might have uttered were transformed into squeals of complaint.

68.

Annie looked down from the brow of the hill at the houses below. What she had at first taken for a town with its many thatched cottages scattered over a wide area was little more than a village.

Since she'd left the colourful child and her guardians she had come across no more people, but that encounter had changed her journey. Her wanderings no longer left her suspended at the same spot and the countryside was more varied.

The deserted streets of the village were free of litter and scraps of paper but also devoid of embellishments or flowers. Each cottage was identical. For a community of authors who depended on the richness of their imagination, the monotony was surprising. Maybe they poured all their creativity into writing.

Shifting curtains and hastily closed doors hinted she was not alone. There was no apparent order to the cottages which were dotted along the many streets that wound their way through the village. Perhaps such a refusal of geometric patterns bore witness to a less flamboyant form of creativeness or simply the absence of any social organisation. There was no centre, no town hall, no church, no village square, no shops even. She had seen no signs of vegetable gardens. Whatever did they eat? How ever could they survive?

Annie had not chosen to go there. It was the path that had led her. But her steps had been driven by an urgent question: how to get home? If she spent too long in that grey world she might begin to fade, just like the woman had said. If that happened, any return home would be impossible. Maybe the mention of returning was taboo. The woman certainly hadn't wanted the little girl to talk about it.

Reaching what she calculated to be the centre of the village, Annie halted and took a deep breath. "How do I get home?" she called out. It took three repetitions, each one louder than the previous, before folk reacted. A couple of doors cracked open and solemn-faced people squeezed out. They walked unhurriedly to the road where they waited till all five were together and then, side by side, marched in her direction.

The delegation halted a few feet away. Three women and two men. All secretaries, clerks, scribes and lesser scholars. Not a businessman or a charwoman among them. All grey faced and expressionless, clad in their everyday clothes devoid of any colour.

"Ghost writers," she began. "I…"

One of the women held up a hand. "We know who we are."

Annie remembered her own ghost writer's words: strike home with few words, hard and fast, direct and to the point. "I have come to free you from Kard." Not at all what she'd planned. But certainly hard hitting. Although she had no idea how. It sounded more like one of those hot-air promises Kard was always spouting.

"We have no interest in freeing ourselves." It was the same portly woman who spoke. "We could never return to your world."

"Are you not sick of doing the dirty work of an evil man like Kard?"

"We invent stories," the woman said, glancing at her colleagues who all nodded. "It is unimportant if they result in good or evil."

Annie was at a loss how to reply. 'Nihilism' her sociology teacher would have called it. How could they pretend they remained on the sidelines? This was a battle between good and evil. "You are wrong," Annie said. "You cannot claim to be neutral. You are accomplices. You are murderers. Your stories are used for evil. They destroy people's lives. Innocent people. Women and children. Do you hate my world so much you would cause its downfall?"

The woman hesitated a moment, looking at her colleagues, as if in search of inspiration. "These things are not our concern. It is no longer our world."

"You lie," Annie said, carried away by her indignation. "Your tales are tailored-made for those you attack. You stalk them. You watch them. Closely. Your task is to do damage. You know full well your impact. What if the tables were turned and we started terrifying you with your worst nightmares? Would you be happy? Would you continue to insist that neither good nor evil are important? Do you hurt us out of spite or to get revenge? Or does Kard have some leverage over you? With all your stories, surely breaking away from him should be easy. Imagine being unfettered, composing stories for yourselves. No longer constrained to interfere in another world, no longer bound to do harm to others, but free to embellish your own life, your own world." She stretched out her arms to encompass the village. "What a colourful place this would be."

The woman shook her head, but looked thoughtful. Beckoning to the others, they turned as one and made their way back to their respective cottages. Annie felt deflated. What a waste. She still had no idea how to get home. Instead of playing Joan of Arc, she ought to have asked the way home. She plodded through the remains of the village, dejected. Would people in another village be more receptive? How many villages were there? What if this was the only one?

She had reached the last cottage which lay some distance from the others. Like an outcast. Beyond she could make out rolling hills as far as the eye could see. No signs of any other habitation.

"Psst!" a voice hissed.

Turning to face the cottage, she saw the door ajar. Furtively glancing left and right, she scurried towards the house.

As the door clicked closed behind her, she was shrouded in

swirling shadows. For a moment she recalled the cloud of smoke in the Pakistani's cafe and was afraid. Then her eyes adjusted and she made out an empty wooden table next to which stood a single wooden chair. Welcoming visitors was not in the ways of this world. Beyond, in an alcove, was a raised bed just big enough for one. Along an entire wall hung a bookshelf, although it was home to no books. Row upon row of cardboard boxes filled every shelf. Several were not properly closed revealing scraps of paper, some of which had worked free and floated to the floor below.

In front of the single window, by the door, stood a figure, silhouetted against the grey light from beyond. "I won't say welcome," a familiar voice said. "You have already gathered you are not." The man shifted so that some of the feeble light fell on his face that of her own ghost writer. Hers? Well, attributed to her. Not any more, she corrected. He was in shirtsleeves, his abandoned jacket slung over the chair back. The table, contrary to her first impression was not empty. On it lay a wad of pale grey paper and a solitary biro. "But you certainly made an impression."

Annie shrugged. "What use?"

"Many people in your world will sleep well tonight thanks to you. You disturbed the concentration of a cohort of ghost writers."

Well, that was something. "Must I go out and bang on pots and pans till they listen?" An image of protests in Latin America crossed her mind. She'd been impressed by the local people's down-to-earth bravery and their stolid insistence on being right.

"Oh, they listened. I'm sure their minds are already spinning tales of a sumptuous future. I told you your stories were strong. You have brought a little colour to their bleached world."

Bleached? She examined her hand, fearful that she might be turning grey. "So what do I do now? I can't stay here."

"No. You can't. But don't return home despondent. You may well have done enough."

69.

"Annie! You're awake!" Kevin squealed.

Annie couldn't help smiling at the sight of Kevin's joyful face. "Give me a kiss, you imp," she said and was rewarded with a kiss that took her breath away. "Don't kiss me to death," she gasped. "I want to know how the hell I got here before I die."

"You collapsed outside that horrible cafe. Nothing Leonor did could bring you round. We brought you here with the help of a bodyguard. Underwood's men have called to enquire on your health. Twice. They left a file about that Pakistani bloke."

"Throw it away," Annie said, feeling lightheaded

"Oups! You suffered more damage in that fall than we thought."

"Throw it all away. It's no use any more."

Kevin raised an eyebrow. "What do you mean?"

"He's nothing but a pile of scrunched up papers."

"Leonor said you might be confused. She didn't say, raving mad." It was meant to be a joke, but the girl couldn't hide her concern.

"He will bother us no more."

Kevin insisted on explanations. Annie skipped the nightmare in the cafe and told her of the Pakistani's spectacular demise.

"You've been reading the bible again, haven't you?" Kevin exclaimed. No doubt thinking of the angel of justice striking home. "But I like the scraps of paper. I wonder what my English teacher would say if I handed in an essay like that."

Annie smiled, imagining the teacher's reaction. She said nothing of the grey village or the words of her ghost writer. She still had to puzzle that out. "So where are Ella and Riya?"

"Am I not enough?" Kevin asked, pulling Annie into a savage kiss that quickly veered to a more tender embrace.

"I will be the first girl to die of an overdose of kisses," Annie gasped when Kevin released her.

"What a lovely way to go!" Kevin said, renewing her efforts.

"Okay. Okay," Annie said extricating herself from Kevin's arms. "Where's breakfast?"

"Breakfast? You missed it. But you can have me for lunch, if you like."

Annie playfully pushed her away. "You've been at those hormones again."

"No. Well, just a little."

They both burst out laughing.

As they prepared brunch, Kevin explained that Riya and Ella had gone to help get ready for a rally that was to take place that afternoon against Kard's law which was being rushed through the Commons. "We weren't sure if you'd recover in time. But you are billed to speak."

"What's Kard doing?" Annie asked, more interested in tossing a wrench in his works.

"I heard he was to appear on TV later today. But you're not going to attack him again."

How wrong she could be? "Only a little," Annie said, grinning.

Kevin threw a croissant at her which Annie caught and ate. "And what about Underwood?" she asked through the remains of the croissant.

"In the Commons I suppose," Kevin said. "I saw him on TV this morning, speaking against the bill. A lot of his colleagues are calling him a traitor. They are pressing him to resign."

"Is it possible to see the parliamentary discussions?" Annie asked.

Kevin tweaked the laptop that had become a permanent fixture on the kitchen table. The familiar upholstered green benches swam into view and a surprisingly full House of Commons. Kevin began a question but Annie interrupted. "I have to concentrate."

Her chin rested on her hands, Annie fixed the screen. Government members in favour of the bill were about to launch it when a wet kiss planted on the back of Annie's neck pulled her from the scene. She turned to Kevin. "I love you. But if you don't leave me in peace, the bill will get through."

Kevin's face was torn between disbelief and a hefty dose of hurt. She turned away and stormed into the bedroom where she noisily made the bed. Annie sighed and returned to the House of Commons.

A man from the government front bench got to his feet. "Mr. Speaker," he said, "I beg to move that the Rogue Health Organisations bill be now read a first time. It is with great satisfaction that I bring this bill to the floor of the House in a concerted effort to put an end to dangerous practices that threaten the health of many vulnerable people in our country."

Annie had heard enough. She wrenched the man from the Commons and plunged him in the stench of the mother's bedroom over the Pakistani cafe with the sick baby lying on the mattress, its face bloated with red patches, sweat glistening on its brow. Then she slammed the man back into the Commons. He swayed and tried to continue his speech but Annie threw him back into the bedside scene. The baby was wailing. The wizened mother sat on the mattress, exhausted, bones protruding through taut skin, her expression blank. When Annie let the man return to the Commons, he sank to his bench, his head in his hands, muttering, "It's all a mistake."

Jeers went up from the opposition benches. "Sure is!" someone shouted.

"I'm sorry, Mr. Speaker," the man said, his voice as pale as he was, "I don't feel well."

"Is there a doctor in house?" someone called out amid laughter.

"Maybe the honourable gentleman, my esteemed colleague,

would like to consult one of those women who heal for free before he makes them illegal," the Prime Minister said, drawing cheers from both sides of the House. Several MPs guffawed. "Perhaps the dinner yesterday evening with that sponsor from private clinics was too much for your liver." The comment brought cheers from Labour who clearly understood who the sponsor was. The MP in question turned a pale shade of green.

Was it normal for the head of a governing party to behave that way? The cheek and the audacity of it had her feeling giddy. Was he not gaily waltzing across long-standing party lines? Underwood would either be a national hero tomorrow or a dead political duck.

A couple of members of the government looked at each other, embarrassed, but none stood to defend the bill. Underwood got to his feet again. "Mr. Speaker, as none of my colleagues is willing to stand up for this bill, let me talk of one thing in its favour."

Annie was horrified. Underwood was to speak against the bill, not in its favour.

"Goodness knows I've racked my brain in search of arguments in its favour," he said to peals of laughter from opposition benches, "but it does have one merit. It shines a stark spotlight on a problem which unfortunately it does nothing to solve. On the contrary, it will make things far worse."

"Here. Here," voices shouted.

"What is that problem?" Underwood continued. "The inability of our current health service to cater for the daily health and social needs of the poor and marginalised alongside all the other things it has to do. Many of those needs do not require highly specialised help or sophisticated technology. They need a dose of common sense, a smattering of knowledge about health and healing and a good deal of patience and good will." His words brought cheers from both sides of the House. "Organizations like GENie offer just such help at no cost to an already financially strangled NHS. Why then, you must be asking, are we trying to outlaw such organisations?"

"Why indeed?" opposition backbenchers chanted.

"The main argument put forward is that such people do not have the high level of professional training that has come to be associated with healthcare. While such training has enabled us to make leaps and bounds in complex interventions rendering many of them routine, it is clearly not necessary in much of the first aid and the social care such organisations provide. No. In this case, the question of training is a red herring. The main motivation for this bill lies elsewhere." Half-hearted jeers went up from some of his own Conservative MPs.

"Beyond the misguided belief that the health service can be improved by strictly limiting those who provide it, the main thrust behind this bill comes from those who have a vested interest. They set out to hinder access of the poor and homeless to cheap or free healthcare provided outside the NHS. That sounds illogical. But it isn't, not from their point of view. By outlawing grassroots initiatives, this bill forces the needy to depend on an overstretched NHS for care that could be provided better and at less expense elsewhere. As a consequence, it drives the more well-off patients out of the NHS and into the welcoming arms of private clinics. This bill is poorly named. It should be called, Protect our Private Profits."

The House exploded. Jeers vied with cheers. Voices were raised. Arguments fused amongst Conservatives. Several people almost came to blows. While Labour MPs cheered and gleefully put bets on opponents. It was like a boxing match gone nuts. The Speaker's calls for order went unheard. His hammering likewise.

"Did you do that?" Kevin asked.

Annie shook her head, saddened at the sight. "I just gave it a little nudge at the beginning."

"I saw. That man feeling ill. That was you, wasn't it?"

When she didn't answer, Kevin flung her arms around Annie and pulled her close, whispering in her ear, "I love you, you naughty girl."

70.

Annie watched as women young and old, many with children, filed into the TV theatre. With their slow, plodding steps, their bent backs and their downcast eyes, they reminded her of prisoners of war being shunted into a concentration camp. She'd seen such people in a film at school and the image had been so sickening it had stuck in her mind.

She was afraid that these shabbily dressed folk, many of whom smelt bad and a lot of whom coughed or sported runny noses, would be turned away, but the GENie Network knew people from the show and they had promised no one would be refused. The whole stunt had been organised at the last moment by Leonor and the women of GENie following a call from Annie.

A place had been reserved for her in the front row next to Leonor with easy access to the stage. Thanks to Jewel she was again disguised as a young man, not unlike the one Kard claimed had attacked him. It had been her own idea to dress in grey. Grey knickerbockers, grey socks, a grey shirt, a grey waistcoat, the kind workers once wore, and, over it all, a heavy grey raincoat that she wore like a cloak, slung over her shoulders, hanging open at the front. Even her short hair was concealed beneath a grey cloth cap, the brim of which was pulled down over her eyes. She had refused to let Jewel paint her face and hands grey. She wanted to remind him of the ghost writers, not claim to be one.

Brian had managed to smuggle in friends with miniature cameras to film and broadcast their own perspective on the event. They'd even planted unmanned cameras looking out over the audience, concerned that the TV would avoid showing such things. Outside, now the doors were closed and the show was about to begin, a large crowd would be gathering. Fenchaw had found them a lorry, the side of which was covered with a display on which the scenes from within could be screened.

The house lights dimmed and the stage was flooded with light. Four empty armchairs faced the audience, waiting. The presenter stepped onto the stage amid polite applause and saluted the audience. It was not the usual celebrity. The poor man had been taken ill at the very last moment only to be replaced by a young woman. She was unknown to the public but strode to her seat and sat down, unflustered by the audience or the cameras. The red light flicked on and, as a camera swung in closer, she spoke.

"Welcome to this special debate to mark the passage of the Rogue Health Organisations bill in the House of Commons. The first reading of the bill took place in tense circumstances earlier this afternoon. Here is a flavour of the debate." A giant screen at the back of the stage flickered into life and they were shown the aborted attempt of the frontbencher to defend the bill, followed by extracts from Underwood's speech.

"Now I'd like you to welcome our first guest to discuss this bill, a well-known figure in the media, especially his own, the Mayor of London, Nolan Kard."

The man stepped onto the stage, no doubt expecting riotous applause, but instead he was met with stony silence. Surprised, he faltered, then continued to his seat, a smile plastered across his face. Leaning back in his armchair, in a way no doubt meant to appear relaxed, he peered out at the audience but the stage lights would have made them hard to see.

"Mr. Kard, you have championed this bill. We know it is designed to outlaw grassroots organisations that offer care to the poor and needy. What is your interest in this bill?"

"I wouldn't put it like that. It's about protecting the vulnerable from being exploited and hurt by untrained people pretending to offer healthcare."

"We all heard what Prime Minister Underwood said. He maintains high-level training is not required to handle many of the basic health and care needs of these people. What do you say?"

"Would you trust your ailing mother or child to someone who has no official training? There are so many quacks around pretending they can work miracles. We need to protect the population from such people."

"Let's hear what our audience has to say." The house lights went up and Kard got his first look at the audience. It took him a moment to conceal his horror at what he saw. "Tell us," the young woman said, addressing the audience, "would you trust a dear one to these people?"

Several hands went up. A microphone was passed round and cameras swung to fix an old woman who got to her feet. "My granddaughter had sores down her arms and legs. I took her to the doctor's surgery. We waited hours, but he was too busy to receive us. I went to A&E. Another long wait. Then they turned us away. Not serious enough to bother with. I would have gone to the chemist, but I don't have any money. A neighbour told me about GENie. I phoned. A woman came within the hour, cleaned up the sores and gave me a cream. She even explained how to use it. She also gave me coupons to get food for the girl and me. What is wrong in that?"

"Well, Mr. Kard, what is wrong with that?"

He shrugged. "It's just one example. Think of all those quacks and crack pots peddling healthcare."

"Let's take another example."

A young girl took the microphone offered her. "I have had terrible pains every time I get my monthlies. It hurt so much, I was bent over double. I couldn't attend school. I spoke to my doctor. He said it was normal. I'd just have to put up with it. He suggested aspirin. What use is that? A girl friend told me GENie held an open clinic for women by women. I went along. At last people who took my problem seriously. The herbal remedies they suggested worked well."

"Quacks? It sounds to me more like the health service was unable to respond," the presenter said.

"These are all insignificant examples," Kard said. The audience responded with jeers.

"It would seem the audience doesn't agree, Mr. Kard. You say 'insignificant'. What do you consider significant?"

"Cancer. People die of cancer every day because tricksters claim to miraculously heal cancer, attracting patients away from valid solutions."

"Let's call on our second guest to respond about cancer."

Leonor got up from her seat next to Annie and climbed onto the stage. The presenter rose and came to shake hands, eclipsing Kard as she did. "Meet Leonor, a former nurse, who is one of the prime movers of GENie." The woman indicated an armchair and returned to her own. "Tell us, Leonor, what do you say about cancer? Can GENie cure people with cancer?"

"We are not here to replace hospitals or specialised clinics, like yours, Mr. Kard. They are equipped to intervene in ways we could never do, even if some of them are far too expensive for the majority of people. No. That is not our role."

"What is your role?" the presenter asked.

"Helping women adapt after they've had their ovaries or a breast removed, for example. Or helping people care for a relative with cancer. Or giving advice about herbal remedies to alleviate the side effects of chemotherapy or radiotherapy."

"It would seem these people that you so ardently want to outlaw are not what you think, Mr. Kard." Kard was about to react, but the woman halted him. "We have one final guest to hear. Someone you've met several times before, Mr. Kard. Let's welcome Annie Wight." The audience burst into applause as Annie climb the steps onto the stage. She turned to face them and raised a clenched fist in salute.

Kard couldn't really go grey at the sight of Annie all dressed in grey, but he did a pretty good imitation. She hugged Leonor, shook hands with the presenter and nodded coldly to Kard before taking her seat.

"The trouble with words," Annie began, turning to face the camera, "is that they don't always say what they mean or mean what they say. This bill uses the word 'rogue'. I looked it up, just to be sure. A rogue is dishonest, the dictionary says. What is dishonest in helping women and men cope with health problems when no one else will? Surely the rogues in this story are those who bring this bill. As the Prime Minister pointed out, they claim to have our well-being at heart, but their motives have more to do with their personal profits. Is that not dishonest?"

She paused to stare at Kard who returned her stare with undisguised hate. "What nonsense," he said with a sneer. "What could a schoolgirl know about such complex issues?"

Typical. Attack the person rather than the ideas. Make them look ridiculous. She ignored him. "Advocates of the bill kick up such a stink we fail to see that organisations like GENie are doing a worthwhile job and are complementary to the NHS. There's a newfangled name for what they do. Astroturfing. What does that mean? We could ask Nolan Kard, he's an expert. But I fear his answer would only confuse us. Astroturfing involves secretly paying people to support a cause with false testimonies, fake scientific reports or simply by posting on Facebook or elsewhere, as if it were a grassroots movement. Why? To make people believe the cause has widespread public support when in fact it is solely geared to the interests of its wealthy backers. They spread a version of the truth that suits them, but which is a patent lie. Above all, they seek to confuse and distract us from the real issues."

Kard got to his feet, his fists clenched, his lips pursed, looking like he was about to explode. A scream went up as a smoke canister was flung in the middle of the audience and people panicked, fleeing the foul-smelling smoke. In the confusion, a shot rang out and Annie was flung backwards across the stage and all went blank.

71.

"Thank heavens she was wearing that bulletproof vest," Annie heard Leonor say. "All the same it's going to hurt. I suspect one of her ribs got broken."

"Is there nothing we can do?" Kevin asked.

"Not much. Osteopathy maybe," Leonor replied.

"What about her head?" Kevin asked.

"Are you afraid she'll lose those crazy ideas of hers?" Leonor sounded amused.

"No!" There was a sound of scuffling and laughter. "You know what I mean. She hit it pretty hard."

"There may be concussion. But I can't tell till she's awake."

Annie couldn't figure out where she was. The TV studio? A hospital? Ella's place? There was nothing for it, she'd have to open her eyes. It was then she realised her eyes were already open, but she could see nothing. A wave of panic gripped her and she almost cried out. She raised a hand to feel her eyes, sending a searing pain through her chest.

"You hit the back of your head so hard we had to improvise an ice pack," Leonor told her, "so I used a bandage and some ice cubes."

Annie let out a deep sigh of relief. "For a moment I thought I'd gone blind."

"Let me un-blind you," Leonor said, a smile in her voice.

Once her eyes had adjusted to the light, she found she was in a tiny infirmary with autographed photos of TV personalities pinned to the walls amongst notices on how to treat electric shocks or how to stop smoking. She must still be at the TV studios.

"Did they shoot Kard as well?" Annie asked.

Leonor chuckled. "Unfortunately not."

"He scarpered," Kevin said, taking hold of Annie's hand, "without even bothering to enquire how you were?"

"Probably afraid he'd be arrested," Leonor said.

"What time is it?" Annie asked.

Kevin glanced at her watch. "Three." Concern was clearly visible on her face. "You weren't out very long."

"When does the rally start?" Annie asked, making a move to get up despite the pain it provoked.

With a firm hand Leonor stopped her shifting more. "You aren't going anywhere for the moment, young lady."

There was a knock at the door and Brian peered in.

"Brian. Come in. How did the filming go?" Annie asked.

"Excellent. As I suspected we caught things the TV cameras couldn't see. Including the two who attacked you."

"Two?"

"One threw the smoke bomb, the other shot you."

"Are they recognisable?" Kevin asked.

Brian grinned and, by way of answer, pulled a couple of photos from his bag.

"Did you send a copy to the police?" Leonor asked.

"Sure."

"And what did they say?"

"Nothing for the moment."

"They haven't even come to question the chief witness," Kevin said, framing Annie's face with her hands.

Brian and Leonor laughed.

A knock sounded at the door. "That'll be them," Kevin said.

It wasn't. It was Alice. "I saw your spectacular performance on TV," she said, pulling off her hat and coat. "You are getting better every time. By the way, I really like your trousers. My grandfather had just such a pair for hiking in the Alps." She sat on a chair in one of the free corners. "So, have they nabbed the villain this time?"

"Villains," Brian said, stressing the 's'.

Annie shook her head and wished she hadn't. Both her neck and her chest hurt.

"Why on earth do we have police?" Alice asked. "What a useless bunch."

A heavy knock resounded at the door and a policeman stepped in.

"Talk of the devil," Kevin muttered under her breath.

"Are you Annie Wight?" he asked, fixing Annie. It was clear he knew who she was.

"Yes."

"You have been involved in several scams recently."

Kevin and Leonor looked at him, incredulous. Brian quietly pulled out his camera which he discreetly held in his lap.

"You realise that such pranks are illegal," the policeman pursued.

"Would you like to feel my broken rib, Officer?" Annie asked.

"Or see the dent in the bulletproof vest?" Leonor added.

The policeman glanced at the photos of the two assassins that lay on the table by the bedside. "I see you are still in the business of faking evidence."

The man was infuriating. Even if the would-be assassins had been present and confessed to their crime, he wouldn't have believed them.

"Can you prove you are a policeman?" Alice asked, her voice as cold as ice.

"Whatever for?" the man replied.

"Because I believe you are a fake," Alice told him. "Anyone can rent a policeman's uniform."

Making a show of irritation, he produced some sort of police ID from an inner pocket.

She glanced at it, scornfully turning the thing over before handing it back. "Smith? You must be joking. It's a forgery," she said. "You realise it is illegal to impersonate a policeman, especially with a view to intimidating innocent people."

"Enough of your game, Lady," he said, puffing himself up to his full height. "This is deadly serious."

"I am serious," Alice said. "I'm going to call the police."

The man smiled, looking relieved.

"Not your colleagues posing as police," Alice said. "The real police."

The man shook his head, exasperated. "Are you sure you don't need psychiatric help?"

Why on earth did people in positions of authority resort to calling others unhinged when they couldn't prevail with their idea?

"I have never been more lucid," Alice insisted. "If we refuse to believe you are a policeman, there is no way you can convince us. We will reject all proof you produce as fake. Just like you do with us. Annie here was shot. Someone tried to kill her. There were over a hundred witnesses, not to mention the thousands of TV viewers. She has the marks to prove it. But you refuse the facts because, for reasons of your own, you are convinced it's all a publicity stunt, a student prank, whatever. That we refuse to believe you are a policeman is of little consequences. But that you refuse to accept a man tried to kill her means that the person is still at large and might try again. That will make you and your disbelieving colleagues accomplices to attempted murder. I thought the police were supposed to protect people."

The man continued to shake his head, clearly unwilling to give up.

"In a way," Annie began, "that does make you and your colleagues fake, because you masquerade as policemen, but you do not do your job. What are we to do with a police force that refuses to do its job?"

"What nonsense!"

"I am as serious as Alice," Annie said. "Kevin here was kidnapped and assaulted, but you did nothing. Her mother was beaten up. You dismissed it as a publicity stunt. Now I have been shot, for the second time, and you refuse to believe. It would be easy to conclude the police, or your part of it, at least, is not fit for purpose. The challenge we face is to replace you with people who really have our well-being at heart."

72.

They were deep in discussion about what might replace the police and how the transition would be possible when the door opened and the girl in green peered in, much to Annie's embarrassment. Their eyes met for a moment, enough to make both of them flush. Annie ducked her head, hoping Kevin hadn't noticed.

"Come!" the girl said, glancing over her shoulder down the corridor. "The police are here to get you."

"He's come and gone," Kevin said, grinning. The man had left, far from content, muttering about reprisals.

"Not him," the girl said, shifting from foot to foot, no doubt impatient at the delay. "A van load of them. Hurry. You don't want to be here when they arrive."

Leonor and Kevin helped Annie to her feet. Commandeering the wheelchair that Brian had been sitting on before he left, they settled her in it and hurried after the girl and Alice. Much of the television building was a jungle of bare concrete, with electric cables snaking in conduits high up on the walls. Chunks of scenery lay abandoned along corridors. Cameras on wheels, broken office chairs, coils of cable, plastic palm trees, even a giant hair dryer, all gathered dust.

The girl led them off down narrower side-passages, past half-open doors affording glimpses of dressing rooms, store cupboards and tiny, windowless offices. Sliding back a partition, they hurried across a TV set with cameras and props frozen in mid-action, awaiting absent actors and technicians. Emerging into another, busier corridor, the girl greeted people, but hurried the four women fugitives forward.

The sound of running feet behind them had the girl change direction and usher them through a tiny door into an immense garage several stories high. Three large outside broadcast vans were lined up, their engines turning over, ready to leave. Annie wondered why they didn't hide in the closest of them, but the girl seemed bent on reaching the farthest. She helped everyone inside, swiftly folded the wheelchair which she handed up, then clambered in herself.

The moment the door was closed, the van pulled out of the garage. Through a tiny window close to her head, Annie caught sight of several policemen dashing across the garage, but the doors swung shut barring their route. Turning to look around she was embarrassed to find the girl in green seated on the floor next to her. Kevin was across the van, wedged between two consoles, looking very unhappy.

Annie didn't want to upset the TV girl who'd saved them, but she couldn't bear to see Kevin so sad. She beckoned and Kevin squeezed across the narrow space between banks of screens and chairs, wending her way on all fours. Reaching Annie there was a moment of hesitation. She guessed Kevin would willingly have sat on her lap but was afraid of hurting her. The girl in green struggled to her feet, saying, "I'll have a word with the driver."

"Thanks," Annie called out after her retreating back and swaying hips.

"Phew!" Kevin said, shaking her head. "She comes on a bit strong." She leaned closer to Annie and planted a proprietary kiss on her nose. To conceal her embarrassment, Annie looked for Alice and found her half-hidden behind a pile of aluminium boxes, she called out, "You OK, Alice?"

"I'm fine," Alice replied. "It's not me that has a broken rib."

Annie hoped she would be so hardy at Alice's age.

"Anybody know where we are going?" Kevin asked.

"To the rally," the girl in green said, stepping out of the front of the vehicle.

"So that was why you aimed for this van," Annie said.

The girl grinned. "Couldn't have you folks missing the rally because a bunch of policemen were annoyed at you."

"Blast!" Annie said, wincing as her sudden movement jarred her broken rib.

"What's up?" Kevin asked.

"I forgot the bulletproof vest at the studios. You don't have a spare one, do you?" she asked the girl who laughed.

"I have something better," the girl said. "I will loan you my clothes. No one will recognise you if you don't go on stage and make a speech."

"That's hardly necessary," Kevin said, an edge to her voice. "Surely they won't try to shoot you twice in one day."

The idea of wearing the other girl's clothes bothered Annie too, but not for the same reasons. Exchanging clothes was such an intimate act. She imagined the warmth of the other girl's clothes against her skin and immediately shoved the idea away in an attempt to put an end to the strange stirring it provoked in her stomach.

"Do you have a change of clothes?" Alice asked.

"Don't worry about me. There'll surely be a pair of old overalls lying around."

Annie was not convinced. She had the uncomfortable feeling the girl was up to something. But she had no idea what.

When the van arrived at the venue, they had to alight. Technicians needed to set up and test cameras, lighting and sound. Everyone filed out, leaving only Annie and the girl in green. Kevin lingered, wanting to stay and stand guard, but Alice led her outside.

"Let me help you out of those clothes," the girl said once they were alone. Annie felt shy, as if on a first date. She couldn't help remembering the girl's declaration of love on that hastily scribbled note. When it came to unbuttoning her shirt, she wished she could have done so herself but doing so hurt so much. The girl cautiously removed the shirt and hung it alongside the waistcoat and coat on the back of a chair.

She pulled back a moment to admire Annie who felt herself

trembling, but not from the cold. She wanted the girl so badly it almost hurt. Never, even with Kevin, had she felt such a surge of desire. She held herself rigid trying to stem the rising flood of emotions. The girl ran a hand around Annie's neck and pulled her into a kiss. Annie leaned in and responded with as much ardour. The girl's other hand fumbled with the zip on Annie's trousers, ripping it open and pushing her trousers to the ground.

She moaned in Annie's ear, nibbling at her ear lobe. When Annie felt the girl's hand snake over her bare stomach, she knew she had reached the point of no return. She shoved the girl away, gasping for breath and said, "I'm sorry. I can't. I won't."

The girl hesitated, her chest heaving, her breathing laboured, then nodded. She stepped back, pulled off her clothes in a fluid movement, revealing a slender, muscular body, and held the green overalls out to Annie without a word. Annie took them. As she had imagined, they were warm and smelt faintly of the girl. Annie shook off her knickerbockers and with the girl's help pulled on the overalls. She felt like an imposter. How could she possibly face Kevin dressed like that? How could she ever kiss Kevin again with that other girl's kisses hot on her lips?

"I wrote I loved you," the girl said, her voice barely a whisper. "And I meant it. I would give everything for you." She leant forward as if to kiss Annie, then drew back, tears in her eyes. "Now go. I'll come later."

73.

Embarrassed. There was no other word for it. It wasn't just the kisses. Annie felt deeply ill at ease. Not quite herself. She took an unsteady step away the television van, the unfamiliar clothes chaffing her skin, and was greeted by a boisterous Kevin, relieved to see her. But that enthusiasm which should have ended with Annie in Kevin's arms faltered and Kevin halted a short distance away, uncertain, staring at her.

"Is that really you?"

Annie could not bring herself to answer. She had not felt so unsure for ages. It was as if she had been blown up to giant proportions these last few days and now she had shrivelled to her original size. This was the real Annie. Not the one who stood up in front of crowds or television cameras. Not the one who made stirring speeches. She burst into tears.

Kevin took her in her arms, but Annie felt a reticence in that hug which made her cry even more.

"It's the aftershock," she heard Leonor say. "Don't forget she was shot only a couple of hours ago. We should never have brought her here."

All around came shouts and laughter as friends met friends and new acquaintances were made. Annie was lost in a surging sea of excited folk, each buoyed up by the presence of others. That she didn't belong, stranded in the middle of them, was so obvious it hurt.

As if sensing her Annie was not available, Kevin was distant, heavy-handed, unsure. Finally, she let her arms fall to her sides, stepped back and handed Annie a handkerchief. The separation made Annie feel worse. Nothing could stem the grief.

Alice linked arms with Annie saying, "I'll look after her for a moment. You two enjoy the rally." As Alice led her away, Annie looked back over her shoulder. The stricken look on Kevin's face standing next to Leonor must have echoed her own.

The cafe was nothing special. Just a brief halt for walkers after a tour of the park. The place was deserted. No doubt the faithful clients scared off by the massing crowd. Alice bought them tea in mismatched mugs that might have been made by the owner's children. Sitting opposite, she held out a hand to Annie who hesitated then took it. Annie stared at the old woman's wrinkled hand which was warm in hers and felt a rising calm win out over despair.

They remained silent and unmoving for a long moment, the only sounds coming from the owner drying mugs and the distant shouts of the crowd. "I kissed her," Annie mumbled, staring at the table top.

"I thought you might," Alice said sipping her tea.

Annie glanced up, unsure if she was being made fun of. All she saw was benevolence. "I couldn't stop myself."

"It might seem like magic at the moment, but it is little more than chemistry," Alice said. "It's intoxicating, but sadly it doesn't last."

Annie smiled, despite herself, then frowned. "I feel dispossessed."

Alice cocked her head to one side, but said nothing.

"As if a part of me has been ripped away and with it all my potential. I am exposed for what I really am, an insignificant schoolgirl."

Annie expected Alice to rush to reassure her, but the old woman just squeezed her hand and listened in silence. "When I was little," Annie shuddered at the memory. "I would go for days feeling like my soul had shrivelled up. I felt empty inside and terribly uncertain on the surface. I would look at myself in the mirror, convinced my essence was trembling like a jelly. If I hadn't been obliged to go to school, I would have curled up in bed, pulled the covers over my head and disappeared."

The thought of it had tears welling in her eyes. She wiped them away. "And then, when I was out on a solitary walk, I would halt at the sight of a flower, or a sunset, or just a crack in the pavement, and my soul would burst into life with a force that rocked me to the core." She smiled through her tears. "It was great to be alive."

"Doubt is a part of greatness," Alice said. "Those who do not doubt, who masquerade behind a facade of certainty, are the sad dwarfs of this world whose inner world is a ruin."

"Do you doubt, Alice?"

"Sure I do. Especially when I ache all over in the morning or when I see my wrinkles in the bathroom mirror. I think, 'Not much time left,' and I wonder if I haven't squandered my life in useless pursuits."

Annie lifted Alice's hand to her lips and kissed her fingers. "You've had a wonderful life and it's not over yet."

"And your life is going to be wonderful too."

Their conversation was interrupted by the owner. "Do you mind if I turn it on?" she asked, pointing to the flat screen mounted over the counter. "If we can't attend the rally, at least we can watch it on television."

Leonor was on the platform explaining the work of GE-Nie. Kevin stood at her side, a distracted look on her face. The crowd jeered when she mentioned the bill. After a while, Leonor brought forward Underwood, leaving people unsure how to react. Some cheered, others booed. But when Underwood announced the bill had been defeated in the Commons, the crowd erupted in cheers and whoops.

To Annie's surprise a familiar figure stepped to the front of the platform and raised her fist in salute. The crowd went wild only to fall deadly silent when Annie's double collapsed to the ground. "Oh my God!" Annie exclaimed, springing to her feet. "The idiot has gone and got herself shot." She hurried to the door, clutching her chest to allay the acute pain, Alice close behind.

In the general panic it was impossible to reach the platform. Many were in shock. Others struggled to flee, afraid the gunman would strike again. Everywhere people were bemoaning the death of Annie Wight. Annie and Alice had to make their way round to the back of the demonstration but even there they could not reach the platform, their passage blocked by security guards.

"Get out of my way, you oaf," Annie said. "I am Annie Wight. Let me through."

Annie wondered if he would pay any heed, but there must have been authority in her voice, because the man stepped aside and let them through. Annie climbed the stairs wincing at the stabbing pains in her chest and found a group of women kneeling around the body. Ignoring their protests, Annie pushed between them and knelt at the girl's side. "You stupid fool!" she said. "Did you need to go to such lengths? Now you will never know how much you were appreciated."

The group around her had finally realised who she was and stopped trying to push her away. The coat that had been Annie's had fallen by the girl's side. Annie picked it up and slung it round her own shoulders. She removed the cloth cap from the dead girl's head and planted it firmly on her own. Then, getting to her feet, she took hold of the microphone and faced the crowd. An eerie silence fell as people turned to see what was happening .

"This brave soul sacrificed her life to save mine," Annie said, her voice breaking, her head bowed.

"Oh no!" a solitary voice exclaimed in the silence.

Anger surged in Annie till she could no longer contain her fury. "This violence must stop. All of you who have witnessed this needless death will stand up and cry out, 'No more!'" She raised her fist in salute and the crowd responded as one, fists raised, each shouting, "No more!"

74.

Annie put down the microphone and stared at the lifeless girl at her feet. By choosing to be someone else, she had died alone, without the slightest friend or relative to mourn her. Annie didn't even know her name. Turning to look at those gathered round, she caught sight of Kevin watching, her face haggard, tears streaming down her cheeks. Stepping past the body, Annie moved to Kevin's side and cautiously took her in her arms. The girl felt so fragile she might fall apart at the slightest jolt.

"I..." Kevin began.

"Shhhh," Annie whispered. "I'm here." She was tempted to say, 'It's alright,' but it wasn't. It might never be. She shoved aside the dark thoughts and kissed Kevin on the crown of her head. The girl sobbed quietly in her arms.

A wail of sirens had Annie looking up. The police had finally come to do their job. She wondered how Underwood would react to the police. She'd seen no sign of him. His security men must have spirited him away the moment the shooting broke out.

Minutes later, pounding could be heard on the steps and three policemen burst into the narrow space. If there hadn't been barriers around the raised area, several people would have been pushed off.

Heading straight for Annie, the first policeman reached out to grab her, saying, "I arrest you under suspicion of attempted murder. Anything you say..."

Frail though she was, Alice shoved the policeman aside. "And I arrest you," she said, speaking into the microphone, "for crass stupidity and perverting the course of justice."

A cheer went up from below.

"Quit the act, lady. This is serious business," the policeman said trying to push past her. Several people stepped forward forming a protective cordon around Annie.

"I am serious, Officer. Annie Wight had nothing to do with the death of this girl."

The crowd below chanted Annie's name.

The policeman noticed the body for the first time. He glared at Annie. "Not her!" His voice dismissive and scornful. "Nolan Kard."

The crowd cheered at the news.

Annie might have hated Kard, she might even have wished him dead, but the idea that he had been killed troubled her.

"You bring good news," Alice said. "So someone has finally put an end to the blighter."

"He's not dead," the policeman said.

"Shame!" several people shouted.

"Then why all the fuss?"

"Because we have reason to believe this girl tried to kill him."

Another of Kard's attempts to hound her. He'd already accused her of attacking him on the TV set. What would it take to make him give up? Did someone really have to kill him before he stopped?

"What makes you think that?" Alice asked.

The policeman stared at the hostile faces. "This is not the place to talk about such matters." He made another move to reach Annie but the cordon around her held good.

"I think there could be no better place," Alice said, brandishing the microphone. "Some forty thousand people are gathered here to listen to you and goodness knows how many on television."

The policeman glanced nervously around. He'd clearly overlooked the presence of the television.

"Here, at least you can't bully Annie Wight into a confession." Alice glanced at Annie. "Not that you'd ever succeed."

"We don't bully people," the policeman protested, sounding like an exasperated parent trying to reason with a stubborn child.

Annie felt sorry for him. He was incapable of pleading such a case in front of so many people. Whoever had sent him had shoved him into the breech knowing full well he was not up to the task. No doubt they had thought intimidation would suffice. They hadn't counted on Alice. She wouldn't let anyone be intimidated.

"So what makes you think Annie tried to kill Kard?"

It was a risky game. Kard was capable of fabricating all manner of proof to support his stories, much of it extremely convincing.

"We have solid evidence she has been dappling in black magic. She is in league with a secret organisation of sorcerers and sorceresses and has been using occult forces against Mr Kard."

As Annie had expected, he brought claims that couldn't be refuted on the spot.

"Kard certainly has no lack of imagination," Alice said, taking it all in her stride. "He who is always accusing others of faking evidence seems to be trying a hand at it himself."

Annie was about to speak when a hand grabbed the tail of her coat and dragged her backwards, through herself as it were. She half expected to be inside out when she landed in the familiar grey kitchen. "Is there no way you can bring me here that is less alarming?"

The ghost writer made a show of being surprised. "I thought that one was rather creative."

Annie's only response was to snort in disbelief.

On the table in the middle of the room sat a giant bouquet of flowers in a vase. They were all the colours of the rainbow. "Hey!" Annie exclaimed, as she realised. "That's beautiful. How did you manage that?"

He grinned. "I told you your words would have an effect."

He had such a round about way of getting to the point that it exasperated her, but she smiled all the same. "So?" she said trying to nudge him forward.

"We decided to break free of Kard."

"Is that why the colour is creeping back?"

He nodded. "It's a three pronged attack. The first just happened."

"Let me guess. You made Kard think he was dying."

"Not exactly. We hit him with a modified version of the nightmares that plagued you. One after another. Like a shower of terrifying fireworks. Magnificent!"

"I bet that shook him. Are you not afraid of reprisals?"

"That's the second prong. You."

"Me!" He had her alarmed. "What am I supposed to do?"

"Let me explain. In the beginning, before all this started,…"

Get on with it she wanted to say. How come she hadn't noticed he was so long-winded? "I won't tell anyone," she said, suspecting he might feel foolish about what he was about to say.

He looked relieved. "He trapped us. Did you know he dappled in black magic?"

She shook her head. "I might have guessed. He just accused me of doing so."

"He had each of us sign a contract, a collective contract. He spun a tale that it would work much better if we left a drop of our blood on the parchment. Each of us was to get all we needed and a roof over our heads. We believed him. How gullible can you get?"

"And that contract binds you?"

"Exactly. And you are going to destroy it."

"How the hell am I to do that?" she burst out.

"I don't know. You are such a resourceful young lady. I'm sure you'll find a way."

If he was trying to win her over with flattery, it was a clumsy attempt. "Where is this contract?"

He shook his head. "No idea."

75.

The return to the scene on the raised platform was a shock,
even if the ghost writer did try to soften the landing. Annie staggered and had to take a deep breath as she sought to remember
what was happening. A body lay sprawled on the floor at her feet,
a red stain on the girl's chest. Somewhere close by Kevin was
suffering because of that girl ... and her. What a muddle. And
all around a massive crowd waited, impatient. On the other side
of the protective cordon about her, an exasperated policeman
was calling on his two colleagues for backup. It looked like they
would try to force their way through.

"Stop!" she said, taking the microphone from Alice. "You
are about to trample the body of an innocent victim. She was
murdered by assassins that mistook her for me. That you pay her
no heed, that you do not hurry to apprehend her killers, does not
speak in your favour. I understand you have orders, that you are
sworn to obey, but orders can be wrong and obedience misguided. Think about it."

There was no simple way out of the confrontation. If she
did not offer them some form of compromise, they would never
leave her be. "I swear," she said, "with all the people gathered
here as witnesses, that in three days time, after the funeral of
this girl, I will hand myself over to the police to help them in
their enquiries. In return, you will undertake not to pester me or
any of us. We are in mourning and we want to bury this young
person with the dignity she deserves."

The policeman hesitated. She was offering him an honourable way out. She hoped he would have the intelligence to see it and grasp the opportunity. "OK," he said. "At this time in three days at the nearest police station."

"And you undertake not to molest any of us in that time," Annie reminded him.

He nodded.

"The crowd cannot see your nod. You will have to speak up so they can hear."

"I do."

Once the three policemen had quit the platform, Annie turned to address the crowd. "A funeral will take place in three days. Both you here in this rally and all of you at home are invited to join us in a solemn march after the funeral to say, 'No more violence!' You will be informed of the time and place."

She put down the microphone and turned away, feeling empty and unsure. Had she been too hasty in calling for a march? And how was she to survive a police interrogation? Not to mention the task she had to undertake for the ghost writers. The immensity of the challenges left her giddy. She was plunged in a world of notoriety and responsibility, of unconditional fans like the green girl, of threats of assassination and TV performances. What had all that got to do with her? Absentmindedly she scanned those around in search of Kevin. She found the girl sobbing in the arms of Leonor, her back turned. Annie shifted, meaning to get closer, to take Kevin in her arms, to make things right, but Leonor shook her head almost imperceptibly. Annie halted, feeling confused and rejected and angry. How was she supposed to sort things out with Kevin if she couldn't get close to her?

Should she ignore Leonor's warning and take Kevin in her arms as intuition suggested? Or should she turn to those other pressing matters that clamoured for her attention? She stood at a crossroads, hesitating, and in her hesitation she glanced at the body lying abandoned on the floor. "Can no one do something about this girl?" she asked, addressing nobody in particular.

Kevin burst from Leonor's arms and, stumbling across the

platform, battered Annie's chest with feeble blows. "Who cares about her?" she screeched. "She's dead. What about me?" Annie stood there, unresponsive even though her broken rib screamed at each blow. Loss? Remorse? Self-pity? She had no idea what she was feeling as tears welled in her eyes. Dead, maybe. Deadened, at least.

Kevin sank to her knees clinging to the green overalls that Annie was still wearing. Then she abruptly let go and shoved Annie away, no doubt realising whose clothes they were. Leonor helped Kevin to her feet and led her away. Annie stood there, watching them go, alone in the middle of a crowd.

"Come on," Alice said, taking hold of her arm. "Time for you to leave too."

"Do you hate me?" Annie asked once they were in Alice's car.

"Hate you? Why ever should I hate you?"

"You are Kevin's grandmother, and I have let her down. She hates me."

"I very much doubt it. She is hurt and angry. In her confusion she doesn't know what to do, so she hits out. And in doing so, she hurts the very one she loves.

Did Kevin really love her, after all that had happened? The only way to know would be to ask her, but that was out of the question. She glanced out the window. They were speeding through the suburbs.

"We can't go to your place," Annie said. It was far too far from the centre and she needed to be in London, if only to get access to Kard and that contract.

"Why ever not?" Annie was about to explain when Alice added, "Don't worry. I have a flat in the centre of London."

Annie imagined a pokey place used only for quick visits to the capital. She steeled herself for an uncomfortable stay. When Alice unlocked the door, Annie was speechless. The penthouse flat ran the length of the building next to the former Covent Garden Market. Part of the ceiling was sloping but many of the walls offered large flat surfaces for the oil paintings of which

Alice was apparently a collector.

"Make yourself at home," Alice said. "The toilet and bathroom are through there. I'm going to rustle up a bite to eat. I don't know about you, but I'm famished."

"You don't happen to have a change of clothes?" She was sure she would feel better if she could get out of the dead girl's clothes.

"Not in a size that would fit you."

Annie reached for her phone only to realise it had remained in her clothes. "Can I borrow your phone?" She called Jewel who promised to drop by.

"Here," Alice said, handing her a kimono which was pitch black with rampant golden dragons crawling over it. "…in the meantime."

When Annie had changed, Alice picked up the discarded overalls. "I suppose you don't want to keep these as a souvenir?"

Annie shook her head, both at the suggestion and Alice's dark humour, then she thought of the corpse. "Maybe we should give them back to their owner."

Alice gave her a very strange look.

"Maybe it would be better if she were buried in her own clothes," Annie hurried to explain, embarrassed at her own suggestion.

"Do you plan to recuperate your clothes?"

Annie shuddered. "No. I could never wear them again."

"Then leave them to her. I'm sure that would have pleased her."

Alice's comment left her thoughtful. Yes. The girl had not so much loved her as wanted to be her. The idea was worrying, but it was also a relief. "I think you are right."

76.

Alice made a mean curry, the smell of which had Annie's mouth watering long before they sat down to eat. Jewel had brought several sets of clothes, but Alice's kimono had her drooling and she suggested Annie wear black leggings under it for the rest of the evening. They had joked about clothes and Annie had admired the outrageously tight sequin dress Jewel was wearing. Alice invited her to stay for the curry, but Jewel declined, hurrying off to her own dinner engagement. During the meal, Alice spoke of her trips to India and the Indian historian who had first taught her to make curry.

Once the feast was over and Annie had done the dishes, Alice retired to one of the two bedrooms, saying she was worn out by running after Annie and wanted to read. Annie was left to roam the rest of the penthouse. She walked from painting to painting, taking time to study each closely. Alice seemed to have a preference for bright colours, broad bush strokes and abstract, but suggestive art. As a result, the flat was a gay symphony of colours that would have lifted even a miserable person's mood.

All the same, in the relative silence of the flat, broken only by the occasional burst of noise rising from the night life in the converted market below, the misery of Kevin's departure crept back and Annie felt less inclined to do anything other than sit on the sofa and stare up at the bland ceiling.

How ever had all this come about? Should she believe Alice and attribute it to chemistry? She was inclined to blame herself for not saying no. But then how was she to know the girl was unhinged? She'd never come across anyone who wanted to be her, let alone die as her. "Just listen to you," she chided herself. "You claim to be worried about Kevin, yet all you think about is that girl."

She got to her feet and paced the flat, but it didn't help, her mind relentlessly circled back to the girl. It was almost as if she were possessed. She shivered. Given all the talk of black magic, happenings which would have been unthinkable became feasible. With the girl dead, it was as if Annie could not reverse what they had done by exchanging clothes. She was stuck with something of the girl in her.

She headed for the kitchen area and rummaged in the dustbin under the sink in search of the overalls. She found them easily enough but they stank of vegetable waste and were splattered with curry sauce. She was astonished to catch herself feeling regret about the stains. The sooner she got rid of the damn thing, the better.

She carried the stinking mass to the fireplace and built a fire using balled up newspaper, wood shavings and a log. When flames licked around the log, she dumped the overalls on the fire which promptly went out giving off a foul smelling smoke.

"You are gonna have to go about that differently," Alice said, startling her. "If the girl worked at the telly, her clothes might have been treated against fire." She went to the sink and pulled out a large bottle of clear liquid. "Make sure the fire is out, then pour some of this over it and throw a lighted match on it." She handed Annie the bottle and turned to leave, but halted. "If you want to exorcise that girl, I advise you avoid breathing in the smoke."

A shiver of fear ran down Annie's back. To think that she might be further possessed by the smoke of the thing! What a nightmare. She opened a window on the far side of the room, in case she needed to dash for fresh air, then did as Alice had said. It might have been her imagination, or the dye in the cloth, but she could have sworn the flames were green. She watched the fire consume the overalls and then prodded them with a poker to be sure all had burnt.

She stared at the charred mass in the grate and wondered if she dared feel relieved. She thought of Kevin, tentatively testing she could. An insidious thought suggested she might undo the spell by wanting to check the exorcism had worked. She thrust aside the idea, reached for the phone and dialled Kevin.

Someone picked up, but no one spoke.

"Kevin? It's Annie."

She heard a sigh.

"I love you Kevin. I'm so sorry for everything that happened. Things got in such a pickle I didn't know how to get out."

Still no answer came.

"Can you forgive me?"

There was sobbing at the other end. "I thought you were dead," Kevin blurted out. "It was awful. I wanted to die." Her voice was drowned in sobs.

"Oh my love," Annie said, crying too. "I miss you."

"Miss you too."

After a long discussion during which many of the sentences hung unfinished, Annie told her she was at Alice's place in Covent Garden and, wishing each other a good night, they promised to be together the next morning.

Annie lay back on the sofa and stared up at the ceiling but, unlike earlier, she felt only relief and happiness. Now that she had sorted things out with Kevin she could turn to other problems. She thought of the ghost writers and their contract. She couldn't believe that it was really black magic. Had she not been terrified by a piece of green cloth? That had been no magic, but the force of her own imagination. She had given the blasted overalls a power over her.

She knew nothing of black magic and didn't want to. She feared that in knowing she might grant it a hold over her. If there really was such a contract, surely she wouldn't need black magic to destroy it. But first she had to find it. That was going to be tricky. Kard would have stashed it in a secure place. If she'd been in his shoes, she'd be worried someone would steal it. She'd often check to see it was in place and intact.

If she could make him fret over it, his checking would reveal where he'd hidden the damn thing. There was only one problem. She could send him a nightmare that would drive him to check, but she wouldn't be there to see. Even if he checked during the nightmare, unlike the ghost people, she could not watch on unseen. At least, she'd never tried.

She couldn't believe she was envisaging spying on Kard. The man disgusted her. What if he were naked? Ugh! She gritted her teeth. For a brief moment she wondered why she should bother. After all, the ghost writer had been spying on her most intimate moments and had subjected her to terrible nightmares. Yet he had also helped her at great risk to his own life.

She sighed. Pushing aside several cushions, she made herself comfortable on the sofa then closed her eyes. She reached out and went in search of him as if she were about to send him a nightmare, but rather than dream up a nasty story for him, she pictured him and the place he was in, hoping her imagination would not play tricks on her.

77.

Annie had no idea where Kard lived. For all she knew, he might be lounging in one of his plush clinics recuperating from the ghost writers' attack. If that were the case, she might never locate the contract. But she had no alternative. She needed to destroy it before the solemn march and the moment she had to hand herself over to the police. That left just three days.

Kard was there all right, but it certainly wasn't a clinic, unless the massive four-poster bed he lounged on was in his own private ward. He looked up when she arrived, as if sensing a presence, but his eyes slid over her, unseeing. She sucked in a cautious breath, afraid he might hear. She needn't have worried. He went back to fingering through a magazine, ogling the pictures.

She looked around the room, memorising what she saw, just in case she ever had to come back to get the parchment. The room was even bigger than Alice's penthouse. The walls were completely covered in frescoes depicting scantily-clothed young girls in suggestive positions. The absence of subtlety in the scenes made them distasteful if not disgusting rather than stimulating. There was no other furniture and only two doors. One was slightly ajar through which she caught a glimpse of a bathroom. The other was shut.

Time to get to work. She instilled a nagging concern in a corner of his mind. He tossed the magazine on the floor and frowned. Turning on his back, he stared up at the painting of two girls intertwined on the upper panel of the bed. She let the worry take shape using only delicate brush strokes. She wanted him to think of the parchment as if doing so were the most natural thing. She then sent images of break-ins, of thefts. He sprang to his feet and paced the room only to fling himself back on the bed, his head buried in the pillows. Then he rolled over, stood up and resumed pacing.

She upped the stakes, making him smell smoke. He sniffed his way round the room in search of its source, but the idiot didn't get the hint. It was just possible he had treated the document against fire like those horrible overalls. Water then. She sent him visions of the bath overflowing. She wanted to have the parchment floating in water, but she didn't know what it looked like. Showing him anything else would surely tip him off that he was being manipulated.

To her horror, the sound of running water had him dashing to the toilet. At least, she guessed that was why he rushed into the bathroom, almost tripping over the magazine he'd abandoned. The thought of him relieving himself in the next room was repulsive. She waited and waited, expecting the sound of the toilet flushing to come, but it never did. Unable to contain her impatience, she hurried into the bathroom, only to find it empty. There was a second door. Stepping through, she found Kard on his knees in an office, feverishly leafing through what looked like a tattered book. Moving closer, she peered over his shoulder. Written on each page was a short text with a signature at the foot of it and a dirty brown smudge.

Blast! She'd missed it. Where had he got the thing? She looked around. There was no open door to a safe or a draw unclosed. No secret trapdoor left undone. Could it have been lying on his desk? She glanced in that direction. Just a large ashtray, an ornamental lighter and a small tray containing a few folders. She'd have to look elsewhere. To her dismay, the walls were covered in shelves crammed with leather-bound volumes. A library, Kard's private library. Could it be his stash of books on black magic? She shivered.

How could she force him to return the book to its hiding place? She thought of making him imagine he was being spied on, but that was too close to the mark. She could have made him hear someone coming, but she had no idea if anyone else visited the library. It was probably a closely guarded secret. If these books were about black magic, he wouldn't want anyone discovering them. Having finished looking through the book, he got to his feet and, rather than put it back where he'd found it, he left it lying on the floor and, turning on the spot, surveyed the room.

"I thought I felt a presence," he said. Judging from the way his eyes roved the walls, he didn't know where she was. "I warned you never to spy on me." His threatening tone frightened her. Had he some means of retaliation? Would he snuff her out like a candle? Shut up, she told her imagination. Wasn't it enough to think herself into his presence, without her fear giving him power over her?

He picked up the tattered book, clutching it in his arms. "Surely you can't believe I am unaware who attacked me earlier. I know full well it wasn't that Wight girl. Your petty attempts to hide behind her were pathetic." He opened the book at random and tore out a page. She had a terrible misgiving. Had he just ripped the life from the chest of one of the ghost writers? He tossed the book back on the floor and, picking up the lighter from his desk, set fire to the page and laid it in the ashtray. It curled up in flames and rose a moment in the air, only to sink back, a charred memory.

He threw back his head and laughed. "Didn't think of that, did you?" He crushed the cinders with the butt of the lighter. "I'll destroy each page, one at a time, till I get to yours. So you'd better leave now and never spy on me again."

Horror seized her. To think the ghost writer had told her to burn the book and now Kard was doing so himself. Would all the ghost writers die? Had they known? Maybe they were sick of their grey existence. Or maybe without Kard they couldn't survive. But she couldn't let her ghost writer die. She thought of the giant bouquet of coloured flowers in his kitchen. Surely there was hope. She had to stop Kard. He had already torn a second page from the book. It burst into flames in the ashtray.

"Still here!" he screeched and ripped a wad of pages from the book, scrunching them up in the ashtray. "Watch while I kill your friends." The flame burst from the lighter and ate its way into the pages, consuming them as it went. Annie imagined the screams.

"Still not enough? Your turn must come soon." He laid the book on the desk and ripped nearly half the remaining pages from their binding. He waved the lighter above his head, dancing from one foot to another. "Who's about to die? You. You. You." He held the lighter to the pages that overflowed the ash tray.

Annie couldn't stand by and watch the madman kill a whole people. She sucked in a deep, imaginary breath and blew at the papers hoping to scatter them about the room and spare them. Instead her breath fanned the flames setting fire to the pages with a roar before sending them aloft. Like tiny incandescent story fragments they spun in the air and settled on the shelves kindling books as they landed. In no time, the entire bookcases were ablaze, crackling spitefully. She stared, fascinated, as one after another, shelves crumbled to the floor sending up showers of sparks that spurted through oily smoke.

The rising heat jolted her from her torpor. Get out of here, she urged herself. In the distance, amid the roar of flames, she heard Kard scream, "No! Not that!"

78.

"You could have slept in a real bed," Alice said, chuckling.

Annie opened her eyes to find herself sprawled on the sofa. Someone had spread a blanket over her and a pillow nestled under her head. "I didn't intend to sleep here. I just lay down."

"Being shot twice in a day must be tiring, I suppose."

Twice? Not exactly. Annie wanted to make a witty remark but remembered why she had lain down. She must have fallen asleep spying on Kard. Had that really happened? Or was it just a dream? The memory seemed so hazy. She reclined, her fingers interlinked behind her head. "How about breakfast in bed?" she asked, grinning. "Surely I've earned it."

"No way. Get up you lazy lump," Alice said, tugging at the blanket. "You may be the favourite hero of half of London, but that doesn't dispense you from kitchen duty."

They had barely finished breakfast than Kevin arrived. The two girls flung their arms around each other and hugged in desperation. You'd have thought one of them was off to the war. The two exchanged a jumble of kisses and words which only made sense to them. Leonor and Alice talked quietly in the background. Annie's mind and body were completely absorbed, so she paid no attention to their discussion till she heard the word 'fire'. It triggered a chain reaction in her mind that culminated in the scene of Kard's library burning.

"Fire?" she asked, extricating herself from Kevin's arms.

"A band of terrorists tried to set fire to Kard," Leonor said. "A good part of his private hotel went up in smoke, but unfortunately the man himself escaped."

"What a bloody liar," Annie exclaimed, furious at the way Kard always shifted blame onto someone else.

"I beg your pardon?" Alice said. "Did the young lady swear?"

"I believe she did," Kevin added, grinning. "She isn't usually so crude. Something must have bitten her."

"The nerve of the guy," Annie ranted. "He set light to the damn building himself."

"You seem rather sure of yourself," Alice said.

"I should know. I was there."

All three looked at her astonished. "Don't say you've taken to making nocturnal visits to Nolan Kard," Alice said.

"You'd have been better off spending your night with me," Kevin complained.

"I wish I had," Annie muttered.

"Explain," Leonor said.

So Annie told the whole story about the ghost writers and what bound them to Kard, about her having to destroy the contracts and Kard tearing them up in a fit of rage and burning them.

"How sad," Kevin said. "So they're all gone and they never did get to launch their second attack."

Annie hadn't thought of that. She had been counting on the ghost writers finishing Kard off before she had to confront the police. Now she'd probably be accused of trying to set fire to him, which, in a way, she had. Although he didn't know.

The doorbell rang and Annie let Ella, Riya and Brian in. "We've come to talk about the funeral and the solemn march," Ella said, looking from Annie to Kevin. "If we are not interrupting."

"We were just about to make voluptuous love on the sofa," Kevin said casually. "But you are welcome to stay and watch if you like."

"Kevin!" Annie exclaimed, blushing.

"Did I mention I was disowning my granddaughter?" Alice asked.

"Positively shocking," Ella said, grinning.

"Just a joke," Kevin muttered, pouting. "You folks have no sense of humour."

"Talking about jokes," Brian said, "have you heard the latest?"

Several people groaned.

"No seriously. It's hilarious."

"If it is anything like Kevin's joke, I'd rather not hear it," Alice said.

Brian looked exasperated. "By 'joke' I meant it was funny, not that it was the sort of 'joke' people tell. Listen. You'll want to hear this. It was on the news. Kard was picked up by the police running naked through a posh part of town screaming that he was being pursued by a gaggle of ghost writers."

Riya and Ella burst out laughing, but Alice, Leonor and Kevin all looked at Annie, not a smile amongst them.

"It would seem your ghost writers did manage to strike one last time," Kevin said.

Brian and the two girls looked from Kevin to Annie. "Me thinks you have some explaining to do," Riya said.

"We'll let Kevin explain," Annie suggested, struggling to hide a grin. "Then I can check how well she listened."

Kevin tossed a cushion at Annie who caught it and hugged it, blowing kisses at Kevin.

"Phew!" Riya said ten minutes later. "So Kard was the one using black magic. I wonder who else was a victim of these ghost writers."

Annie certainly wasn't going to tell her. What's more, she didn't like the ghost writers being blamed. They were as much the victims as the people they were ordered to haunt. "The way you say it, anyone would think the ghost writers were at fault. They just did what Kard forced them to do. There's only one villain in this story."

"Does that mean we no longer need to worry about Kard?" Kevin asked, shifting to sit on Annie's lap and slinging an arm around her neck.

"He's a resilient sort of sod," Alice said. "I wouldn't discount him so easily."

"But surely anything he says now will be discredited," Ella said.

"He's said some outlandish things," Alice said. "And each time he gained more support. It is almost as if the maddest madman wins."

"Well, we are not going to compete with him on those terms," Annie said. "He'd win hands down."

There was a lull in the conversation. Everyone, no doubt, trying to imagine on what grounds Kard could be beaten.

"I thought you might want this," Leonor said, handing Annie the phone Kevin had given her.

Annie hesitated. The sight of it conjured up mixed feelings. True it had been a gift from Kevin. It was a link between them. But it had been next to the dead girl's skin. What if it took possession of her like the overalls? She glanced at Kevin who was frowning.

"I have a feeling it is no longer what it was. As if it had been contaminated. I would prefer not to take it. But thanks, all the same." She glanced at Kevin. The girl looked relieved.

Leonor nodded. "I'll give it to a deserving cause."

"So how are we going to organise this funeral?" Annie asked, glad to change the subject.

79.

It might have been mid morning and the sun was out, but the air in the park was still chilly. Annie was pleased Alice had loaned her a shawl. She and Kevin strolled the paths, hand in hand, heading for Speakers' Corner. She had never been there and was curious what people would have to say. The closer they got, the more people they encountered. Most paid them no attention, but a few stared, others frowned and some even scowled. Never having publicly held hands with a girl, she had no experience of the hostility of the run-of-the-mill person towards a gay couple.

The wide expanses of grass and the flourishing flower beds that characterised most of Hyde Park, apart from the Serpentine, had been done away with at Speakers' Corner, which had been entirely surfaced with tarmac. Here and there men and women had climbed onto boxes or chairs to address passers-by, but few managed to hold their audience for long. Onlookers meandered from one to another before continuing on their way.

One man caught Annie's attention. Perched on a stool, he harangued the crowd, waved his fist, stamped his feet, but not a word of what he said, for all his animation, was comprehensible, at least not to Annie. It was almost as if he'd been pulled into the world backwards and his words had got all muddled up. She wondered if anyone could understand the gibberish. As they moved away, she and Kevin had fun trying to imitate him. It wasn't easy.

Some yards further on a woman sat on an upturned box, crying. "He wasn't very good," she wailed. "But he was all I had."

She tore at her hair. "I tried to tell the police. They wouldn't listen." She began striking her chest with clenched fists. "He just disappeared into thin air. Pouf! Like a candle going out." Annie wondered if that was how the ghost writers had been taken.

"Was he a writer?" she asked. The woman stopped crying, startled at being addressed, and, suspended in her incomprehension, didn't immediately answer.

"Yes. A beautiful writer. Wrote like a dream. But now he's gone." She wrung her hands in distress. "Abandoning me with nothing but the memories."

Annie glanced at Kevin wondering whether she dared follow her hunch. "Would you like a cup of tea?" she asked. Judging from the woman's unbelieving expression, nobody had ever invited her for a drink. How long had she been bemoaning her situation, unheard by those who passed by?

"Somewhere warmer than here, a place where you can tell us all about that man of yours."

Although the woman never said yes, she went meekly as Annie linked arms and led her across the park. The path traced a straight line to the near end of the Serpentine where a café overlooked the water.

It'd soon be time for lunch, but the place was not yet busy with diners, so they picked a table by the floor-to-ceiling windows with a view of the ducks turning circles on the murky water. She even spotted a brightly coloured parrot winging in the wild. The odd assortment of ill matched wooden chairs and tables contrasted with the fake marble floor and the white designer ceiling. At least the air was not heavy with the smell of food and the light flooding through the windows gave the place a cheery feel.

Kevin headed to the counter in search of a pot of tea, while Annie got the woman seated and settled across from her. "Tell me about your man."

"He told the most lovely stories." She seemed to blossom at the memory. "I'd tell you one myself. I remember them all by heart. But it would never be as good as him." She sighed and fiddled with the frayed cuff of her sleeve.

"Did he sell his stories?" Annie asked.

"Nah! Nobody would buy them. But he did earn money writing for other people. Them as couldn't write well themselves. They'd tell him what to say and pouf! he'd write it for them."

"A ghost writer," Annie said, excited that quite by chance she might have bumped into the wife of one of those she'd met.

"That's it."

"He disappeared, you said?"

"Yeah. He got this big job. He was so excited. We were to have a house and a garden. I've never had a garden. We would grow vegetables he said and maybe have some hens and even a goat. We were so happy we waltzed around our tiny kitchen. All he had to do was sign a contract."

"Do you remember who gave him the job?"

The woman shook her head. "He did say, but I was so taken by the garden and the goat, I hardly listened."

Annie hesitated about mentioning the name. She could be completely wrong. Or the woman might just say, 'yes' to please her. "Was it Kard?"

The woman looked up startled. "How do you know? He made me swear never to tell. It was to be a secret. That was part of the deal."

"Kard made similar deals with other ghost writers. It was a trap. They were whisked off to another place and forced to work with no way to return."

Had this man braved Kard's threats to reach out to his wife? "Did he appear to you in dreams?"

The woman's hand flew to her mouth in alarm and she struggled to her feet knocking over her chair. "How can you know all this? I don't trust you. There's something you're not saying."

"Sit down," Annie said. "And I will tell you what I know."

Kevin arrived at that moment balancing a tray with three mugs and a pot of tea on it, a triumphant smile on her lips. "They didn't want to serve me,..." she began, then noticed the woman standing and glanced at Annie as if to ask, what's up.

"It's OK," Annie said, helping the woman to right her chair

and encouraging her to sit down. Returning to her own seat, she took her time serving tea, wondering just how much to tell. "I kept having nightmares and I had good reason to suspect that Kard was behind them. He was angry at me. Anyway, it turned out to be those ghost writers meddling with my dreams under orders from Kard. One of them took pity on me, unbeknown to Kard, and explained what was happening. He took me to their world, to the place where all the ghost writers were trapped."

"Did they have gardens?" the woman asked, leaning forward in her excitement.

"Yes. Each writer had a pretty little cottage and a garden." The woman's attachment to the garden was touching. How could Annie possibly tell her it was all grey and devoid of flowers or vegetables? That the ghost writers were trapped and miserable?

"Oh, lovely. He'd have loved that. Do you think I can go?"

Annie stirred her tea, staring at the liquid swirling round and round. There was so much hope and longing in the woman's eyes. "It's not possible."

"But you went there."

"It's complicated." Annie sighed. She didn't want to have to tell the story. "You mentioned they had to sign a contract. Well, it was no ordinary contract. It was like…" she hesitated to use the word "… magic, bad magic. As long as the document existed, they were held prisoner and had to do Kard's bidding. They begged me to destroy the contract, to set them free. I agreed, but I didn't manage to do so because the bad guy set fire to it himself. None of us knew that the moment the contract was burnt, all the people who signed it…" She was about to say, 'went up in smoke' but that sounded so violent. "…disappeared, never to be seen again."

The woman cupped her hands around her mug and stared wistfully off into the distance, saying nothing for a long time. Annie was worried she'd be so distressed she'd start screaming, or break down and sob in public. Instead, the woman finally looked up and gave her a pale smile. "At least he had his cottage and the garden. That's the important thing."

80.

"That woman was bit simpleminded, if you ask me," Kevin said as they sauntered along Oxford Street, heading for Covent Garden and Alice's home from home.

Annie had been so engrossed in the woman's story she'd hardly noticed. "I'm just glad she wasn't cut up about losing her man. I'm not sure how I'd have handled that. I suppose, as far as she is concerned, she lost him ages ago."

Annie glanced at her reflection in a shop window. Jewel's flower-girl disguise with a blond wig might not suit her, but at least it stopped her being recognised by the many passers-by on the busy street. Kevin, true to style, was dressed as her beau. The young couple held hands as any young couple might out for a stroll window-shopping on a Sunday morning.

They halted in front of a store selling electronic equipment to watch the antics of Kard, multiplied twentyfold by the many TV screens all showing the same picture in various hues. Kard was giving a speech, although none of his words penetrated the thick glass. "That must have been filmed a while ago," Kevin said. "He can't possibly have recuperated so soon."

"Who knows? He does manage some remarkable things." Her reply was meant to be ironic, but, to his credit, Kard did promote his ideas with a determination that invariably got results and made his opponents look wishy-washy. Of course, he was not averse to cutting corners and employing despicable behaviour if not illegal acts to get his way.

"What does he eat for breakfast? Steroids?"

"He probably has clones of himself," Annie joked, then shuddered, fearful it might be true or that by saying it, she might make it come to pass. They hurried on their way, unable to avoid the gesticulating figure staring out of televisions in several window displays. "Underwood doesn't get a fraction of the coverage Kard gets," Annie said in front of yet another TV display.

"That's 'cause he's our President," said a bald-headed man in jeans and a t-shirt standing next to them. He was staring at Kard with admiration.

Annie was tempted to reply 'this country doesn't go in for presidents', but she couldn't help but notice the man's large hands and bare, muscular arms. She ducked her head, swallowed her retort and let the crowd carry them off along the street.

Reaching the major junction where Oxford Street crossed Charing Cross Road, a young boy at a newspaper stand was calling out, "Special Edition. Kard defies government."

Annie paid for a copy and they crossed into the shadow of the long-deserted and increasingly dilapidated Centre Point House. Leaning against a wall, Annie unfolded the newspaper to be greeted by a giant photo of Kard waving his arms in the air like a human windmill. There was even the familiar picture of her with her fist raised, tiny, in the bottom corner of the page. She read.

The Lord Mayor of London has announced that the Greater London Area will apply the legislation recently refused by the House of Commons. In a press conference, Nelson Kard declared, "Someone has to show these weak-willed fools in the government that things have to change. Take the Prime Minister. He's so enamoured of that Wight girl he now supports gay and lesbian movements and their attempts to sink the health service. He even spoke at their rally. Whose side is he on? I can't understand why his fellow conservatives continue to put up with him. We need a strong figure as Prime Minister. Someone who stands up to these perverts. Someone who is dedicated to making Britain straight and great again."

Annie groaned. Had they not dealt with the rumour about her and Underwood? The ordeal she and Christine Underwood had undergone, had it all been in vain? And had not the parliament voted down the bill against GENie? She and her friends had worked hard to make that happen. Would Kard ever take no for an answer? He persisted in ignoring those that didn't think like him, or made a fool of them, and ploughed on with his ideas, delighting in the havoc they wreaked.

In addition, he was trying to isolate and weaken Underwood. He was so stubborn and single-minded, he wouldn't stop till the man was forced to resign. Surely there was no way Kard could become Prime Minister, yet he spoke as if that were his sole goal.

"Is he allowed to do that?" Kevin asked, reading the paper over her shoulder. "I mean, apply a law that has been refused by parliament?"

"Probably not." Annie resolved to ask Alice. She would know. "When has he ever paid any attention to what is allowed and what is not? I've been reading a lot about him. His supporters adore his refusal to comply and his disdain for existing institutions. It amuses and excites them. They see him as an iconoclast. Alice was right about that. His antics have them believing he heralds change. They are fed up with the same governing class, whatever party they come from. Politicians don't listen to them. And people are partly right. They are prepared to smash the whole show to make things change. And there will be change. Lots of it. But nothing in the interests of those who support him. Kard has cleverly led them to believe he is their man, the sole person who can solve their problems. But it's all a lie. He is bent on doing his own thing, to the exclusion of all else. He is incapable of representing the interests of others."

"But surely he won't be able to enforce that law?"

"Well, he has most of the police force in the capital on his side, not to mention the support of much of the judiciary as well as part of the business class. So maybe he could."

"Won't his decision be challenged in court?"

"It's sure to be. But that might take ages. He could do a lot of damage in the mean time, especially to people like us, and other large cities might be tempted to follow suit."

81.

Kevin's phone rang.

"It's Leonor," Kevin said, her voice tense. "The police are trying to force their way into Alice's flat."

"Call Riya," Annie said. "Get her to send out an alert to women via the internet. Have them gather in Covent Garden. Call Brian. Get webcams installed around the place. Oh, and tell him to warn Fenchaw."

"Yes, Sir!" Kevin said, her hand raised in mock military salute.

Kevin's reaction troubled Annie. Had she been too bossy? Maybe. Surely. Oh damn it! This was no time for negotiations. She turned and ran, calling out over her shoulder, "Love you. See you at Alice's."

As she ran, she ripped the wig from her head. She must be recognised for what she had to do. They needed support, fast. She didn't halt at Covent Garden, but continued on to the Royal Opera House. She'd recently visited it with Alice who had introduced her to Gerda, one of the opera singers. Asking for the woman at the lodge, Annie was ushered into the auditorium. She was in luck, the singers had just ended dress rehearsals and the orchestra was filing from the pit. Gerda climbed down from the stage and hurried to greet her.

"The police are trying to arrest Alice," Annie said, struggling to get her breath back. "We need all the help we can get."

Gerda ran back to the stage and, planting herself in the middle, called out, "We have an emergency." The cast, which was mostly women, halted their discussions to listen. Gerda explained what had happened. The cast called out greetings to Annie and agreed to come along. As they prepared to head for Covent Garden in their costumes, a messenger was sent to the Theatre Royal to invite them to come too. Then, arm in arm with Gerda, the two headed for Alice's flat followed by a colourful crowd, shouting and laughing. Each woman they met on the way was invited to join them and the crowd swelled the closer they got to Covent Garden.

A group of angry policeman had gathered at the entrance to the block of flats in which Alice had her lodgings and were hammering on the door. They wore yellow armbands on which were printed the words, London Police. From a window under the gables Leonor was shouting, "Not today thank you."

Annie was unsure how to react, but when a woman from the opera handed her a megaphone, she climbed the steps in front of the former market and took a deep breath. "Policemen of London, you undertook not to harass these women until after the funeral. Why are you here?" To her amusement the women singers grouped on the steps around her took up her question, improvising an aria out of it. Inquisitive passers-by and customers from the shops and restaurants paused to listen. The growing crowd cheered and applauded. The police scowled.

Riya had clearly done a good job because more and more women were pouring into the square around the market. She caught sight of Brian busy talking to a couple of colleagues and Kevin waved from the far side of the square. Next to her stood Fenchaw and several of his staff. Then the people from the Theatre Royal arrived. With them was a girls' choir which was to perform that night. The girls massed on the market steps and sang several Gaelic songs to the delight of the swelling audience. Annie made the most of the distraction to push her way through the crowd and join Kevin and Fenchaw.

"Well done," Fenchaw said, greeting her. "What better way to counter Kard's false police than with music and a joyful crowd."

Annie glanced in the direction of the police. The men would

have slunk away, had the dense crowd not blocked their escape. Some of them must have felt threatened because a scuffle broke out. Afraid that someone would get hurt, Annie wove her way through the crowd till she reached the spot where two policemen were trying to force their way through a reluctant crowd. "Let them through," Annie shouted. "We have no need for them here. If they want to go, then so be it." The crowd parted and the policemen hurried away.

When the last of the songs was over and the applause had died down, Annie raised the megaphone to her mouth. "Thank you all for answering our call for help so promptly." Many people were surprised to find she stood in their midst and turned to face her, drawing back to leave a respectful distance around her.

"We have shown Kard that he cannot bully women with his phantom police." Cheers went up. "We have countered truncheons and threats with music and laughter." The crowd was all smiles. "Kard claims he can be our president. No way! How can a man, whose knowledge of women is limited to groping them in the dark,…" Several people sniggered, others jeered. Annie remembered his attempt to grab her in his bus and let anger fill her voice. "… how can he claim to represent us? The only thing he represents is himself."

She paused and looked at the expectant faces. She felt uplifted by the force of all these women. "People like Kard will never win out against us if we stand together. Don't let his lies, his promises, his threats intimidate you. Don't let yourself be misled by his web of falsehoods. He wants us to doubt. He wants us to feel inferior. He wants us to bow down and let him have his way." She paused, allowing the image sink in. "We are strong. We bow to no one. We are the creative force of this world. We give birth to the future, our future."

She paused, savouring the hush that came over the crowd. "We stand united against those who would plunder society for their own satisfaction. We raise our fists." She raised her fist and the crowd, as one, imitated her. "We say, 'No' to the Kards of this world. We call out with confidence, a mighty 'Yes' to a future we create ourselves."

The crowd roared in approval as fists pumped the air in salute. Annie lowered the megaphone, feeling extenuated, and wished she could be whisked away to a quiet place where she was alone with Kevin, by a blazing fire, just the two of them, curled up together, kissing and caressing.

82.

Fenchaw leaned against the kitchen table surveying those gathered in Alice's penthouse flat, his expression tense and worn. "A group of influential Conservatives have called on Underwood to resign. The opposition has jumped on the opportunity, tabling a motion of no confidence. If the government topples, Underwood will have no choice but to go."

"Could you get me a meeting with this opposition?" Annie asked, the words out of her mouth before she could weigh the consequences. She couldn't shake off a feeling of invincibility, swayed as she was by her speech in the market.

Alice chuckled. "You may have taken on too much there. You are no superwoman. I don't hold out much hope against that band of ideological bigots."

"I wouldn't be so categorical," Fenchaw said, frowning. "Some of them are more open to other opinions."

"Well, if you insist," Alice said, making no attempt to hide her scepticism, "we'd better brief you about those you are going to meet."

Alice was right, but Annie didn't want to meet these people weighed down by the heavy baggage of Alice's prejudices. "If I am to talk to them, I'd rather not do so convinced they are bigots."

Alice scowled. "They are. All their Marxist Leninist gibberish."

Fenchaw smiled. "I may have a solution. There is a Labour MP you should meet. She is probably the most liberal-minded amongst them. I think you'd enjoy a discussion with her. Talk to her and then decide if you want to meet the others."

Annie agreed and Fenchaw made a call. "In an hour," he said. "In the House of Commons."

"You can't go dressed like that," Kevin exclaimed. "They'll arrest you for vagrancy."

Annie resisted the temptation to throw a cushion at Kevin, doing so suddenly seemed childish, and followed her to her bedroom to sort through the clothes Jewel had left. Kevin wanted her to dress in a smart suit, but Annie disagreed. "No offence meant, but I don't have to go dressed as a man so they will listen to me." She expected Kevin to kick up a stink. Instead, the girl ran appreciative fingers down the crease in the trousers and hung the suit back in the wardrobe before pulling out a dress.

"I like you as a girl," Kevin muttered, helping Annie into the dress. "It's not because I need to dress as a boy that I expect you to."

"Need?"

"Maybe not 'need'. But I feel more at home dressed like that. It's more 'me'."

Annie buttoned up the dress down the back and knotted the belt around her waist. Twirling in front of the mirror, she thought the black dress suited her well. It had broad shoulders but was tight at the waist and hugged her legs, although not so outrageously as the dresses Jewel wore.

"Sexy," Kevin said, stealing a kiss.

A knock interrupted them. It was Fenchaw. Through the closed door they heard him say, "We should go."

Fenchaw and Annie were admitted to the Houses of Parliament with no problem. The security guard was expecting them. He rang to announce their arrival and five minutes later, a woman in her forties dressed in a sober skirt and jacket greeted them. The woman seemed so unimposing, Annie wondered if the MP hadn't sent her aide to fetch them.

"You must be the famous Annie Wight," she said, her manner confident and relaxed. "I'm Gabrielle Dillinger, shadow minister for health."

So this was her. In a way, Annie was impressed. She had expected someone who gave herself airs and looked down on her. On the contrary, this woman came across as friendly and accessible.

"Let's find a place to talk where we won't be disturbed. If others see you, you'll be beset by people wanting to talk to you," she chuckled, "or to be seen talking to you." She led them down a side passage and into an empty room.

Closing the door, she turned to face Annie. "Take a seat. Fenchaw here tells me you'd like to talk."

Annie wasn't sure how to begin. She imagined echoing Alice's words, but that wouldn't be polite and might be seen as hostile. She could ask the woman about her work with health, but that seemed like beating about the bush. "What do you think of Nelson Kard?" she asked.

"Straight to the point," the woman remarked. "Kard is a clever madman. I'm not sure which we should fear the most, his cleverness or his madness?"

"You realise, of course, that if you depose Underwood you will have Kard to contend with."

"Wow," she said, glancing at Fenchaw. "Working in this place, I had forgotten what a frank conversation was like. You are right. By voting a motion of no confidence we hand Kard the premiership."

"Do you think that would be better for you and the country?"

Dillinger hesitated. "I'm not sure. Some of our group think we should force Kard to take on the responsibility he is always clamouring for. They are convinced he will botch it and be discredited."

"Do you agree?"

Dillinger hesitated again. "No. Giving him so much power could prove a risky gambit. After each catastrophe he rebounds stronger than ever. But I can't see an alternative. It's the Conservatives themselves that want to get rid of Underwood."

"Excuse the pun, but what if you shuffle the cards."

Dillinger looked at her perplexed.

"At the moment there are two main blocks in parliament, on paper at least. They exist and get their identity because they strive to appear different from each other. By shuffling the cards, I mean, what if you regroup. Those conservatives who support Underwood join those of Labour who can identify with his policies. Having talked to him about a number of issues, I suspect that a lot of your colleagues might have affinities with his ideas."

"But our respective parties have existed for years. What would our electorate say if we suddenly joined the conservatives?"

"You would not be joining the Conservatives. You would be forming a new progressive group, in part to bar the way to Kard, but above all to adopt an approach that is closer to the people. One that reconsiders health and education and social affairs, not to mention justice. People vote for Kard because they mistakenly think he will change things. People are fed up. They see MPs locked in party bickering. No wonder they turn to someone who claims to listen to them, to do things differently. You have to show people you are listening and are prepared to take the risk of changing things, changing even the century-old structures that define you. You need to give them hope and a credible project they can identify with."

Annie turned to Fenchaw. "You were right, I did need to talk to Mrs. Dillinger. But I was wrong about wanting to talk to Labour MPs. What I need to do is address all those who might form a new group in parliament, whether they be Labour or Conservatives."

"But I was elected as a Labour MP," Gabrielle Dillinger protested.

"No, you weren't," Annie said, startling the MP. "You were elected to represent not only those who voted for you but your whole constituency. And if you can do that best by joining a new group, then so be it. Of course, you'll have some hard explaining to do."

83.

"That's ridiculous," one of the MPs exclaimed, waving his arms such was his agitation. "We've been fighting these people for years." He looked with scorn at those gathered on the other side of the room. "There's no way we could possibly come together."

Others were muttering their agreement. Annie looked around the room. With a few exceptions, the assembly had divided up into two groups reflecting their division into parties. If she did not do something radical, they would trudge on as they always had and would never get any closer. So far Annie had said nothing. It was Dillinger who had presented the idea and Underwood had spoken in favour of it. They were all aware she was there. Some had stared at her with curiosity. A few had looked at her with hostility, clearly underlining how much she didn't belong. But most of them deliberately ignored her.

As she listened to them aligning argument after argument why such an idea was preposterous, she began to doubt. Surely these people were too set in their ways. She thought of Alice's word, 'bigots', only to shove it aside. Somebody had to shake them up. There was only one person in the room who could do that. She sighed. Why her? Because she had not spent years playing the political game. Yet the thought of ploughing into those set ways left her intimidated if not exhausted.

"Stop!" Annie said, getting to her feet. When many ignored her and continued talking, she climbed onto a chair, which wasn't so easy in her tight dress, and raised her voice, "Stop!"

And they did stop, surprised that anyone would dare interrupt them and in such an uncouth manner. Many looked at her in astonishment almost as if they were seeing her for the first time. Quite a few were scowling and, amongst those, several were looking around, as if in search of security to throw her out.

"Good," she said. Unsure how to continue. She could try to re-explain the idea, but that would only start them arguing again. "Each of you will team up with someone from a different party. Your task is to find one policy issue you share. Then we will pool those ideas and see what we can make of them."

Several voices went up complaining. It was too much like school or some business training course. Who was she to order them around? She wasn't even elected. "Save all that for later," she said, having to shout to be heard. "Now find someone to talk to."

When small groups stuck together, as if clinging to a raft in a storm, she gently pushed them apart, forcing individuals from the two sides together. She was relieved to see both Underwood and Dillinger doing the same. When they had finally got couples or threesomes formed, she wandered from group to group listening. Many complied with her instructions, but quite a few continued to argue. She was tempted to say, 'You will look very silly when you have no policy ideas to put forward,' but she didn't want to resort to naming and shaming. That really would be too much like school.

"What's the issue you most want to see resolved?" she asked an older MP who was blustering about party values. He halted mid-sentence in surprise, as if caught out of step in a dance. "Well, er... the health service." Too general, she thought. "Any particular aspect of the health service?" she asked. Before he could answer, the old woman he had been arguing with butted in, "The poor treatment of mental health." "Well, yes," the man agreed. "And waiting times in A&E." Annie slipped away and let them get on with it.

Half an hour later when she called for them to stop, most were reluctant to cease. Belligerence had given way to a working atmosphere, with smiles here and there and even laughter. Good. She let Dillinger and Underwood take over, listing common policy issues on flip charts while she retired to a corner.

As she watched, she wondered why people complained politicians didn't listen to them. It was a frustration people like Kard capitalized on. Dillinger had told her she regularly met with people in her constituency. But whom did she meet and how often? The existence of political parties polarized the public into supporters and detractors. Maybe Dillinger only met supporters. Was it possible to create a party that didn't polarize political opinion? Silly question. The moment there was opposition, there was polarization.

She got to her feet and headed for the door, wondering where the toilets were. She didn't get far. A young MP from Dillinger's party ran after her. "You can't wander around here unaccompanied. Did you want to see something in particular?"

Annie smiled. "Yes. The loo."

"Well," the woman said, smiling back, "that's easily done."

Looking round for the young woman who had waited for her outside the toilets, she didn't notice the delegation heading down the corridor and, turning, bumped into one of them. "Sorry," she muttered. To her horror, she looked up to see Kard, surrounded by a bevy of bodyguards each wearing the familiar yellow police armband.

In her confusion, she lashed out before she could consider if it were wise. "I see you've decided to get dressed this time."

Kard frowned then recognised her. "Ah yes. The schoolgirl," he said, his voice full of scorn.

She heard a peal of laughter and turned to see the young woman behind her. "I thought you were barred from hanging around outside women's toilets, Kard," she said, linking arms with Annie and leading her away.

"Look at the lesbians," Kard sneered. "It's a wonder the perverts are not thrown out of Westminster."

Attacking them as lesbians was a bit strong coming from someone whose bedroom walls and ceiling had been plastered with pictures of young girls making out. Not that anyone else was privy to that. The woman accompanying Annie turned to face Kard, motioning towards his bodyguard with her head. "What about you and your boys?"

"Arrest them both," he spluttered.

"You and your boys have no jurisdiction here Kard," a male voice said behind her. She turned to see Underwood surrounded by all the other MPs exiting the meeting room.

"Neither will you, Underwood, soon," Kard said, scornful.

"I wouldn't bank on that if I were you," Dillinger said coming to stand next to the Prime Minister.

Kard glanced from Dillinger to Underwood and frowned. "You two make strange bedfellows."

Looking at Annie, Dillinger ignored his comment. "Still trying to pester young girls, Kard? Be careful. You'll find they are much stronger and more intelligent than you. And they bite. Now run along and play with your boys."

84.

"I wish I'd seen that," Kevin said, chuckling as she removed her apron and made herself comfortable on Alice's sofa. "Kard must have been furious."

"That's what worries me," Annie said, laying the table. The man went beet red and looked like he was going to burst an artery. If half of parliament had not been gathered there, he might have slaughtered someone. "He's such a vengeful specimen. I'm afraid of the reprisals."

"Do you think this new coalition party will work?"

"Well, it got off to a good start. Underwood and Dillinger are determined."

"Let's hope it does," Alice said, looking up from her desk where she was writing. "There are so many ingrained ways of doing things and age-old parliamentary procedures, it could run aground so easily."

Kevin's phone rang. "Hi Mum," she replied. "No. Not at all. We are having a quiet evening at Alice's place." Kevin grinned at Annie, then her face turned serious. "What makes you think that?" There was a long silence. "I hope you are wrong. No. We'll stay well away. Yes. I promise. Gotta go. My beef casserole is ready. Love you. Yes. I'll give your love to Annie. And to Granny." She blew several kisses before hanging up.

"She's worried about Kard's police," she told Annie and Alice. "She got an anonymous tip off that they are going to carry out a series of raids. She wants us to keep well away. Typical..."

Kevin was interrupted by her phone ringing a second time.

"Mum again, probably," she said, answering. "Oh no!" She sat bolt upright. "When?" The moment she hung up, she turned to Annie, a distressed look on her face. "It was a friend who runs a gay bar not far from here. The police raided the place. Several people were hurt."

"Kard won't stop there," Annie said. "He'll go on a rampage. Can you call out GENie and get the whole network on alert?" She picked up Alice's phone. "May I?" she asked. Alice nodded. "I'm gonna call Decker. See if there is not some way to counter these police thugs."

"You'll need a new strategy," Alice said. "Getting a crowd together won't work if he hits in many places."

"We might set up a cordon around places they are likely to hit," Annie said. "But that would take a heck of a lot of people."

"And if the police caught on," Alice added. "They'd just go to another place that was not protected."

"You might make a virtual cordon," Kevin suggested.

"How would that work?" Alice asked.

"Imagine a map of London on the web. The moment a place is attacked, the people type it in on the web and it lights up on the map. All those who are nearby hurry there. People take pictures or write eyewitness reports and add them to the map. They can also tell everyone if medical help is needed."

"It's an appealing idea but I doubt if you could have it working at the snap of your fingers. Why don't you talk to Riya about it?" She wondered if Kard might not catch on and start sending in false alerts. It was the sort of twisted thing he'd do.

When Annie got off the phone, Alice had already dished up Kevin's beef casserole, which lay steaming on the plates, and insisted they eat before they rushed off.

"Did you get everybody?" Annie asked Kevin as the two joined Alice at the table.

"Even got Brian so we have media coverage. Riya and Ella will be here in a short while."

"Good. Riya should go see Decker. He's got work for her."

"I told her about my idea," Kevin said. "She's going to talk to Decker about it."

Alice skewered a lump of meat and pointed meat and fork at Annie and Kevin. "Slow down you two. You'll get indigestion."

"Do you think we could skewer the police like that?" Kevin asked. "Maybe that would give Kard an indigestion."

"Kevin!" Alice exclaimed, frowning. "There's something seriously wrong with you."

Annie burst out laughing. "I suspect it was meant as a joke, a pretty good one at that."

Kevin bowed before attacking her beef and carrots.

"You are a bad influence, Annie. I'll have to talk to Megan about keeping you two apart."

"Won't work," Kevin said, munching an oversized morsel. "We've been glued together."

The doorbell rang. It was Riya and Ella.

"Would you two like some of Kevin's delicious beef casserole?" Alice asked, putting out extra plates and cutlery.

"Just a taste," Ella said, indicating how little by the tiny distance between her thumb and forefinger. "We already ate."

"I spoke to Decker," Annie said, addressing Riya. "He needs your help. Something about slipping unnoticed into a server at Kard's police."

"Thank heavens there are no mics here," Riya said.

"I have a Mike under my bed," Alice said, straight faced. "But he only comes out when I'm alone."

"Granny!" exclaimed Kevin. "You are shocking my friends." Everyone laughed.

"I heard you were at the Houses of Parliament," Ella said. "Did they make you Prime Minister?"

"They wanted to," Annie replied, grinning. "Unfortunately the post was already taken. I bumped into Kard. Literally! He offered me an unpaid job as a house elf, but I declined."

"You should make a caricature of him with his police boys," Kevin suggested.

"No need to be homophobic," Alice said. "Some of my best

friends are gay."

"Talking about gay," Annie said, grimacing at the thought of the hurt and misery Kard's minions were causing. "We should get going."

The police were long gone when they arrived at the bar. Nurses and helpers from GENie were already at work. Several people were laid out on stretchers, arms and head in bandages, but most lounged around in a state of shock or talked in subdued tones about what had happened.

Kevin knew the owner. He was wringing his hands, muttering, "The damage, the damage."

"What happened?" Annie asked. Brian arrived at that moment touting his camera. "Do you mind if we film?" she asked.

"Nah. I always wanted to be a film star." He laughed nervously, pushing back the lock of blond hair that hung over his face. "They burst into the place. No warning. Not a word about why they'd come. Just laid about with their truncheons. It was terrible. The screaming. The smashed glasses. The blood. A nightmare. One of them called us 'gay scum' and shattered the mirror behind the bar. Cost me a fortune. I thought they'd arrest someone. But they just left."

"Thank you," Annie said.

"Are you going to get them?" he asked.

"I very much hope so," Annie said, wondering how the hell they might. "Can we take some pictures inside?"

He nodded.

It took several flying visits before they caught up with the police.

"They picked on the smallest and youngest," a woman said nursing her elbow which was in a sling. "I tried to intervene." She winced as she indicated her arm. "They didn't give a damn who or what they hit."

"Why? Why?" The young girl sat on the pavement rocking the limp form of her friend in her arms. "Is loving so wrong?" She moaned, her face streaked with tears. "Four times they hit her. Four times. On her head."

"Wild animals," the bartender said, wiping the blood that dribbled from his nose. "Bared their teeth and roared. Blindly laying into people." He wiped his blood-stained hand on his apron. One smear more. "Brutes." He broke down and cried.

In the next place, the customers had been forewarned and had barricaded the door. Annie saw three burly policemen using a bench to ram the front door. With a crash the bench drove through but remained stuck at a weird angle. The door held good. Realizing they were still no closer to getting in, one of the policemen turned on the watching crowd. People fled screaming as he raised his truncheon and charged.

Annie hit him with a nightmare flash. His eyes went wide, he screamed and keeled over. Wrenching free the handcuffs that dangled from his belt, she cuffed his hands behind his back and attached him to a metal fence.

"Look out," someone screamed. She rolled sideways, narrowly escaping the truncheon of the second policeman that hit his handcuffed colleague instead. She rammed mentally into him, fury gaining her. As people attached the man, she searched for the third.

"Inside!" someone shouted.

She hesitated. The lights had failed. From the darkness she heard yells and moans and the brittle sound of glass breaking. She leaned against the broken door frame, closed her eyes and sought the mind of the man as if she were a wildcat prowling her territory. He was easy enough to find. He left a trail of pain and misery behind him. She slammed into him, ploughing through his mind with a mental roar that frightened even her. She heard his scream and the thud as he sank to the floor.

She opened her eyes, feeling wild and blood thirsty. She only just managed to restrain her lust to hurt and maim as someone touched her elbow. "Are you okay?" It was Kevin. Annie let out a long, shuddery breath and shook her head.

"I can't do this anymore. I'll go mad."

85.

The three policemen had been chained side by side to the fence, their eyes staring off into nothingness, their expression vacant. Someone had removed their boots and trousers. They looked a lot less intimidating in their boxers and socks. It had taken the concerted efforts of Annie and two nurses from GE-Nie to stop the crowd ripping all the clothes from them. Annie had horrible visions of the men being stoned to death by an angry crowd as scenes from within the bar rose in her throat like heartburn. Anger and hatred bred more anger and hatred in an unending spiral towards death and destruction.

Several more bars and clubs were attacked that night but they were forewarned and barricades and pepper spray kept injuries and damage to a minimum. The teams from GENie continued their work, but Annie didn't go with them. Instead, she returned to Alice's penthouse with her friend, where Kevin's grandmother was anxiously waiting for them.

Kevin began excitedly describing what they'd seen in all its gory detail, but Annie stopped her. "Please don't. One more scene of violence and I may not be able to hold on any longer." Kevin looked hurt and a little scared. Alice took Annie in her arms and rocked her gently, patting her on the shoulder whispering, "There, there." She settled Annie on the sofa and went to make a cup of tea.

Kevin sat next to Annie, looking unsettled and unsure what to do. Alice handed them both a mug of hot tea. Annie curled her fingers around hers as if she were freezing. It did little to thaw the ice that had crept into her heart, but the warmth was comforting.

"Terrifying," she said, shaking her head.

Alice and Kevin looked at her, waiting.

"Those men were worse than animals," she began. "But the most frightening was that I felt myself becoming like them."

Kevin was about to say something, no doubt trying to reassure her, but Annie silenced her with an imperious hand. "How do you think we managed to overcome them? They were bigger and stronger than us." She paused, but did not expect an answer. "I battered their brains out." She burst into tears. For once they let her cry, making no move to console her. They were surely horrified. She was a monster. Worse than those men. "The wounds they inflicted can be patched up. But who can put a plaster or a splint on a damaged mind?"

The silence that followed was long and thoughtful.

She should slip away. Go north maybe. Where nobody would recognise her. Stay in a hostel. Get a job. In a supermarket. Rent a bedsit. On her own. Safer that way. Take some courses. Forget all about Kard, his vicious police and the nightmare power she wielded. She closed her eyes, but the blank stares of the three police thugs followed her, their mouths hanging open, bloodstained drool trickling down their chins. She shuddered. She didn't ever want to use that power again.

"No!" Alice said. "Whatever you are thinking, the answer is no."

The tone of the old woman's voice was caring, not judgemental. "I wish you'd been my mother," Annie said, laying her cheek against the back of Alice's hand.

"You probably wouldn't if you knew me better," Alice replied, stroking Annie's hair with her free hand. "My generation set limits and that can be reassuring when the world threatens to fall apart but, over time, it can be exasperating, especially when you are young."

Kevin continued to look perplexed and hurt. She clearly didn't understand and probably felt excluded. Hugging her would not dissipate the malaise. "I have the ability to destroy people's minds," Annie said, shocked at the brutality of her words. "In a flash. Without apparent effort. It is a terrible and terrifying gift. This evening it probably saved several people's lives, but I sincerely wish I didn't have it. At that bar I came face to face with the devastation I can cause. I felt what it was like to be consumed by anger and hate. I know for certain that sooner or later, if this continues, the fuses will blow and my mind with them. It must stop. I must never ever do that again. That's why I have decided to leave. I will go away. Disappear. Start again…"

Kevin's "No!" was more of a wail than a word. Annie had never witnessed anyone fall apart in such a sudden and heart-rending way. Tears sprang to Kevin's eyes, the life drained from her features, her shoulders slumped and her arms hung uselessly at her sides. Annie was wracked with guilt. Here was another victim to add to the list of those she had destroyed.

"Before the two of you throw yourselves over the edge of the world in desperation," Alice said, "I'd like to point out that the world is not flat and there are other alternatives." She chuckled. It was an odd sound at such a moment, both an annoyance and a relief. "You are right, Annie, you must not use this frightening gift lest it be in extreme circumstances. But that doesn't necessarily imply you have to run away and bury your head in the sand. Unlike ostriches, you can't breathe through your backside."

Annie had to smile. As much as she would have liked to wallow in dramatic desperation, she had to admit that Alice was right. She didn't want to leave Kevin. Or Alice for that matter. And the cause she had championed was both noble and necessary. She still had things to do and to say. People listened to her and appreciated what she did.

"I didn't know ostriches could do that," Annie said. "It is a clever trick. I must practice."

"Better not," Alice replied.

Realizing the danger was over, Kevin flung her arms around Annie's neck and, rather than kiss her, bit her ear.

"Ouch," Annie squealed, pulling away as she wiped the blood

from her ear. "Why did you do that?"

"Never frighten me like that again," Kevin said.

"Being the man in the shadow of a great woman can be a trying experience," Alice said, affecting a sigh.

Both Annie and Kevin flung a cushion at the old woman, who nimbly ducked.

86.

The central table in the newsroom was littered with photos. Annie, Brian, Ella and Fenchaw shuffled around the table shifting and sorting the pictures. Fenchaw had agreed to publish a supplement about police violence in the capital and Kard's decree against gay people and alternative health organisations.

One photo in particular caught Annie's eye. It was a disturbing image, even for someone who didn't know the story behind it. Chained to railings with their hands behind their backs, three policemen sat side-by-side on the pavement in their underpants. The photo was shot from some point low near the ground in front of them accentuating the nakedness of their legs and their grotesquely oversized stockinged feet. Judging from their expressions, they looked more like escapees from a mental hospital than working policemen. It was frankly degrading. The horror of it shook her to the core.

"That's really hard-hitting," Brian said, looking over her shoulder. "I thought of it for the cover."

"That's the last thing I'd use," Annie said.

"Why not?" Fenchaw asked. "It had my vote too."

"Look at their faces," Annie said, unable to keep the revulsion from her voice. "How do you explain they got in that state? They look like they've been drugged or, worse, lobotomised. Our opponents will be quick to point it out. They will try to distract attention from police violence by accusing us of mishandling those poor men."

Fenchaw nodded. "Now you mention it, how did they get in

that state?"

It was the question Annie had been fearing. "Their minds got blasted," she said, knowing full well her explanation would not suffice.

Fenchaw shook his head. "Did Decker loan you a new weapon?"

"No," Annie replied. "Someone else did. We'd do well to avoid the subject."

Fenchaw looked intrigued, but didn't pursue, to Annie's relief.

"I like the idea of short eyewitness reports," he said. "At a time when truth is being challenged, the use of multiple perspectives from people who were at the scene gives solidity to the acts portrayed and enriches the narration without being difficult to read."

"We have a number of shots of the police at their work," Brian said. The euphemism had Annie shuddering, but she said nothing. "And plenty of material showing the results. I wonder if we shouldn't concentrate on that as part of the supplement."

The door opened and Riya entered, followed by Decker. The latter glanced at the table and raised his eyebrows. "Powerful stuff. We might have additional information for you." He nodded to Riya.

"We got access to data about Kard's police force, including the personal files of each officer," Riya said with a tired grin. Annie wasn't surprised she looked exhausted. According to Ella she'd been working all night. Riya laid a file on the table. Each page contained the age, address and training of a policeman as well as other details like promotion, family and personal difficulties.

Annie wondered if Kard had blood signatures from his policemen like he'd had from the ghost writers. That would explain their willingness to undertake activities that any normal policeman would shy away from. But then surely the fire would have destroyed them.

"Can we include some of this in the supplement?" Ella

asked, leafing through the file.

"It means we can identify those who are beating people up," Fenchaw said. "I'd have to ask our legal team but we could probably write the name and age of the policeman under each photo."

"What about Kard and his decree?" Annie asked. It was important to implicate Kard in what had happened. In the end, he was to blame and he was their number one target.

"The situation is changing fast," Fenchaw said. "There's to be an emergency meeting in the Commons today to debate Kard's decree and I heard that Underwood and Dillinger are planning to use their new coalition to announce action against Kard."

"Wouldn't it be better to get the supplement out before that meeting?" Annie asked. "Surely it gives weight to the arguments against Kard."

"In which case we would concentrate on the violence and would be less able to connect it to Kard's decree," Fenchaw said.

"What if we got an interview with a Kard?" Annie asked.

"I doubt he'd grant us one. He's big in the media he controls but he has more or less boycotted our paper, especially since we published that caricature of him in his underwear."

Several people chuckled at the memory of Ella's drawing.

It was agreed that Annie would try to organise then carry out an interview and Brian would film, although everyone tried to dissuade her saying it was far too dangerous. Both would be disguised with Jewel's help. Ella would take photos. They were to claim they were an independent team under contract from a major magazine. They couldn't agree where the interview should take place. Certainly not at Kard's place. The Houses of Parliament were suggested, as was in front of one of the gay bars. Annie had her own idea but she kept it to herself. Imagine the shock if people saw Kard in his lewd bedroom, decorated exclusively with nude young girls. It was a shame the fire had gutted it.

The tearoom was empty when they arrived. Brian concealed several extra cameras while the server was out back fetching sandwiches. Kard had chosen the place and, as it had no obvious connection to him, they had accepted. Given the dominance of pink and the lacy curtains, it hardly seemed the kind of place Kard would frequent. Could he be playing a trick on them?

Annie glanced at herself in the mirror behind the counter. Jewel had given her what she called the 'serious journalist look', grey knee-length skirt, white blouse, blue kerchief and jacket to match the skirt. What surprised Annie most was the way Jewel had been able to add years to her appearance with a few touches of makeup and a wig.

Kard arrived ten minutes late, escorted by an assistant and two of his policemen. He clearly thought the interview was not important because he had not even bothered to comb his hair and his jacket was crumpled as if he'd slept in it. He slumped into a chair without bothering to greet anyone and pulled out a cigar.

"Please do not smoke," Annie said. "It is bad for our equipment." And us, she added to herself. He didn't seem to care that it was illegal to smoke in public places. The policemen didn't either.

He stuffed the cigar back into his pocket and snapped, "Get on with it. I haven't got all day."

"As you are in a hurry, let's get straight to the point, Mr. Kard."

87.

"So you are convinced that attacking gay bars and clubs will drive these people out of the city?" Annie asked.

"Yes," Kard said. "But we don't 'attack', as you so crudely put it. We deliver a warning."

His word games annoyed her. She wanted to provoke him to see what other stupidity he was capable of, aware that each time he revealed himself she, and the cause she defended, gained a point. But she was afraid if she overstepped the mark he'd run and she'd get no interview. "A rather severe 'warning', don't you think? A good many people ended up in hospital, the majority of them women."

"It's important they get the message. Some of them are so stubborn, so convinced they are right, only hitting them over the head will have them see reason. As for people getting hurt, the police only responded to the violence of those they sought to warn."

"What impact could unarmed, defenceless women have on your men who were in full riot gear with bullet-proof vests, guns and truncheons?"

He shrugged. "Change inevitably hurts. It's a price we have to pay. This nonsense has gone on too long. I have decided to put an end to it."

"So you eliminate these people?"

"You say 'eliminate'. Not me. We've got nothing against them. We just don't want them infesting our city."

"Infesting? Like vermin you mean? What frightens you so

much about gay people?"

"They contaminate society with their twisted ways." He curled his lips in disgust. "With them peddling their wares, there's a serious risk more and more people will end up like them. In particular we have to protect the young. They are the most vulnerable."

"Are you afraid they will contaminate you, Mr. Kard?"

"Of course not. What nonsense. I didn't come here to be insulted by you." He got to his feet as if about to leave. "You journalists are all the same. Agitators and liars. Goodness knows how you will twist my words against me. We'd be better off without you."

"Before you leave Mr. Kard, tell me, is your disgust sufficient justification? What legal grounds do you have for inflicting such mayhem?"

"Mayhem?" He shook his head. "Order, I say." He turned to face her, trying to intimidate her with his penetrating gaze. "In my position as Lord Mayor, responsible for the welfare of the people of London, I have issued a decree."

"Are not these people you want to drive out also citizens of your city? What about their welfare?"

"Their presence jeopardizes the welfare of everyone else. They must go. If necessary, we will drive them out one by one."

What he was advocating was ethic cleansing, but she couldn't call him out on that. Not if she wanted to keep him talking. Alice had called Kard's approach elimination politics, the crazy belief that you could eliminate problems by eliminating the people you blamed for them. Kard's behaviour was so infuriating it was tempting to want to eliminate him. But that was no solution. "But how do you know who is gay and who isn't?" she asked.

"Start with those who congregate in gay clubs, then have neighbours denounce those they suspect of being gay..." The prospect seemed to excite him and he was willing to say more, but she interrupted.

"I'm intrigued. If someone denounced you as gay, how would you prove you weren't?"

He halted, perplexed. "What a lame question. It's obvious, isn't it?"

"What is obvious to you may not be to others."

"Well, if you can't tell the difference, there must be something wrong with you."

"So you decide. As Lord Mayor, you get to condemn, without trial or jury."

He shrugged, not even bothering to reply.

"What do you think of the fact that elected representatives from across the country refused to endorse the legislation you are enacting."

"They are all weak and corrupt. Just look at that Underwood. He's messing around with that gay girl. How can we trust someone like that?"

Annie was annoyed that he kept harping back to the same accusations. "You should be careful with your accusations, Mr. Kard. People might think you are jealous."

He tried to laugh, but his laughter sounded more like he was choking on the idea. "What nonsense," he said wiping spittle from his lips with the back of his hand. "No one could be jealous of that nonentity."

"So you feel compelled to act against the will of parliament?"

"I don't know why I bother talking to you. You are not listening. I said it was for the welfare of the people of London. It has nothing to do with Parliament."

"I heard," she said, standing to face him. She'd had enough of humouring him. It was time for the show down. "You said gay people would contaminate them." She took off her glasses and pulled the wig from her head. "I'm gay, Mr. Kard. Does that mean you are contaminated? Maybe someone will denounce you. Then you too will be driven out. How would that feel? You should have thought of that when your staff forced me into your bus two weeks ago and you tried to grab my breasts and my crotch. I imagine your nose still hurts where I hit it."

His hand instinctively flew to his nose, fingering the tip of it. "You!" he exploded, spittle collecting in the corners of his mouth, his face twisted in hate. He took a step towards her, a fist raised and roared in anger. "I wondered where you'd got to."

"I would be careful what you say or do Nolan Kard," Annie said, struggling not to flinch. He was one big, angry man who believed he had a god-given right to do as he pleased. "The whole world is watching you," she said. "This interview is going out live over the Internet."

Kard looked around, as if expecting to see crowds watching, then stormed out of the cafe with his assistant trotting after him and the two policemen bringing up the rear.

"Am I relieved that is over," Brian said. "I thought he was going to kill you."

"Is the broadcast over?" Annie asked. She didn't want what they now said to be splayed across the entire Internet.

Brian nodded.

"Please check the other cameras."

When he had done so, she sat down at the table and ordered a hot chocolate. "You want one?" she asked Ella who had spent the whole interview in the shadows taking pictures. The girl was pale with worry.

No one spoke as they sat hugging the three steaming mugs, trying to recuperate from the ordeal. Annie had managed to remain calm throughout, but now it was over her hands were trembling. It was as if she'd just walked a tightrope in danger of plunging to her death at every moment.

The waitress placed a plate of cakes on the table, saying, "If you have an appetite after all that, it's on the house." She turned to go, then looked back. Addressing Annie, she said, "You must be an angel. How else could you have put up with such a monster?"

"I don't feel like an angel. If I had angelic powers, I would have blasted him into a pile of smoking ash with one almighty thunderbolt."

The woman laughed, but Annie could only make a face.

88.

"Here," Fenchaw said with a smile, leaning across his desk as he handed her the printed version of the supplement. It had just been brought up from the presses and smelt strongly of ink.

She didn't look at it immediately. Instead she stared out the top-floor window of his office over the chimney pots and roof gardens of London. The city was her home, a stimulating place with excitement and a hectic life guaranteed. But for all its attraction, she longed for calm, time to think, to be, not always having to react to save her life and that of others. A wave of tiredness rolled over her.

She glanced down at the cover photo under the headline, 'Violence in the City'. Kard towered over her, his faced red and distorted by rage, a fist raised to strike. The light caught the spittle on his lips making him look like he was foaming at the mouth. And her, apparently calm, standing up to him, only a foot away, dwarfed, her arms folded, a look of pity on her face. She couldn't help thinking the picture was a lie. Kard didn't have the strength it credited him with, on the contrary, his problem was his weakness, and she was far from the calm it depicted. She had been terrified.

"The interview was excellent. The video too. I particularly liked the pink decor," Fenchaw continued, chuckling. "You've earned yourself a job as a journalist if ever that option appeals to you."

Annie shook her head and turned the page. The interview ran on to pages two and three with one or two other, smaller photos of Kard and her. On pages four to seven was a series of photos of police violence, with short extracts from the words of victims. The back cover contained a joint statement from Underwood and Dillinger, photographed side by side in Parliament, condemning the violence. And there was a link to the video on line.

The whole publication was well done and struck her as convincing, but she couldn't shake off the lassitude she felt at the sight of it. The supplement gave added substance to a nightmare. She didn't want to have to fight Kard. His violence sickened her. His self-centred way of treating everyone was unbearable. She wished she had nothing to do with him. She'd much rather live with Kevin, write her own stories, maybe publish a book and have long philosophical chats with Alice.

"You don't look as delighted as I would have expected," Fenchaw said, sounding a little disappointed. "Is there something wrong with the publication?"

"No. It's not the supplement. It's excellent. Rather, this whole business weighs me down and I don't know how much longer I can keep up this act."

"Act?"

"I feel like a fake," she said, feeling herself deflate even further as she voiced the words. "You praised me for the interview. I was terrified. I could never do that again. Ever. And the speeches. I have no idea where they came from. It's as if someone else spoke through me. I could never speak like that." She had been staring at the cover of the supplement. Now she looked up, hoping not to find pity on his face. Instead he was smiling.

"Some of the greatest artists and writers admit they have no idea where their inspiration came from," he said. "I interviewed one famous writer who told me she felt like a medium as she wrote her novels. But that didn't make her a fake. And neither are you. You are an exceptionally gifted young lady. Understandably you find it difficult to accept. Unlike that writer, who did her writing alone behind a desk in a secluded suburban mansion, you are out there in the thick of the crowd or in front of the TV cameras. It must be nerve-racking. I could never do it. But you do."

"Nerve-racking. You are right there. Especially when people are trying to shoot you." Annie managed a hint of a smile.

"Are you up to meeting some people?"

Annie groaned. "Not heads of state, I hope. Or escaped convicts all armed with rifles."

He chuckled, "No. Just some of the staff. They wanted to celebrate this special supplement with an improvised meal."

Annie got to her feet, reluctantly. She did feel hungry. She'd had no appetite for the cakes in the cafe. A glance at the clock on the wall told her she'd missed lunch and would soon miss tea as well. "OK. Let's meet one more crowd."

Fenchaw tapped on his phone and simply said, "She's coming."

The corridors on the lower floors were surprisingly silent. Maybe everyone was taking a well-earned break before plunging into tomorrow's edition. Fenchaw led her down a corridor she'd never taken before and halted in front of the door. "Ready?" he asked. The tone of his voice warned her something was going on, but it was too late. She nodded. He opened the door and she stepped into what must have been the former canteen where she was met by a salve of applause and some cheers.

The staff pressed forward to greet her and congratulate her. Hung from the walls were blow-ups of the photos from the supplement with a giant copy of her confrontation with Kard covering one wall. She almost turned and ran. Fenchaw must have sensed her malaise because he shooed people away, saying, "You can speak to her later." He led her to a table where Brian, Ella and Riya were already seated and she collapsed next to Riya who handed her a glass of wine. Annie refused, preferring orange juice.

On the menu was a mixed salad, spaghetti bolognese and ice cream. All prepared by the staff themselves. Nothing fancy. She was glad of that. She ate and talked quietly to her three friends. Fenchaw had to leave to solve a problem with the next edition.

When the bolognese had been finished and the last drop of ice cream scraped from the bowls, Annie realised she was going to have to make yet another speech, if only to say thank you.

She got to her feet and silence fell in the room. She chose to stand with her back to the giant photo of her and Kard, surveying the room and the expectant faces. "Thank you," she said, wondering if she sat down straight away there would be an uproar. "I get the impression you expect me to say more." Several people chuckled. Some called out, "Sure do."

"Would it surprise you to know I don't like giving speeches? Worse. They terrify me."

A number of people shook their heads but she got the impression every single person leaned forward a little as if to get closer.

"Because I have given a couple of rousing speeches you might imagine I enjoy doing so. You'd be wrong." She shook her head. "It is difficult to know what people really think, isn't it? Let me give you an example. You have displayed the photos from the supplement on the walls. Proud of them, no doubt, or proud at least of fighting back against violence. You are celebrating a success. And rightly so. As for me, they are a nightmare. I have seen each of these injured people. I have held hands with some of them while they waited for medical help. I can still feel their fingers trembling in mine. I can still hear the sobbing. The people asking, 'Why me?'" She paused to wipe the tears from her eyes. "As for him," she jerked a thumb over her shoulder at Kard. "I would much rather let one of you have the glory of revealing what a rabid clown he is. The man is sick in the head. I should have pity on him. But I want only one thing, to never see him again."

She paused, wondering whether to go on. Maybe she'd said enough. "I realise this supplement is absolutely necessary in the battle against violence, for the protection of gay people, but excuse me if I wish it weren't." Tears ran down her cheeks. "It gives a tangible form to something I sincerely wish did not exist. Give me a special edition about the arts or minority cultures any day. I'm sorry," she said, faltering. "I have ruined your party."

There was an uncomfortable silence. Fenchaw, who must have returned while she was speaking, got to his feet to join her. "No, you haven't," he said, putting an arm around her shoulders. "True to yourself, you have spoken out when something disturbs you. That is your strength. People admire and appreciate you for it. Just like you, as the press, we too have to raise our voices when something disturbs us. That is why we have championed your cause and that of gay people. That is why we publish this supplement and are proud to do so. That is why we are grateful to you for all the knocks and shocks and risks you have taken to make it possible."

He clapped and one by one the people stood till everyone was on their feet, applauding her.

89.

Somewhere across the rooftops of London a distant church bell struck seven. Through an open window, laughter could be heard over the faint buzz of conversation in Covent Garden below. People were making the most of a mild late summer's evening. The click of knives and forks on plates and the clink of glasses announced it was time to eat. But Annie was not hungry, even if her stomach did gurgle. She sat alone at the kitchen table, her head pressed in her hands, her heart heavy in her chest. Megan had phoned to invite Kevin and Alice had driven her to her mother's place.

Annie could have gone. Kevin had wanted her to. She would have liked to. But she didn't want to come between mother and daughter. She knew exactly how it would be. A rowdy tug of war. When Kevin jokingly said they were glued together, it was unwittingly close to the truth. Kevin had been apprehensive about returning to her mother, if only for a short visit. Afraid maybe that freedoms gained might be frittered away by motherly concern. All the more so as the near future was fraught with dangers. And Megan knew it.

Kevin was to stay overnight, returning early Tuesday with her mother. As for Alice, she was to come home that evening, though not in time to eat. Annie would not be alone for long. Ella and Riya had promised to drop by. They planned a sort of wake. For tomorrow. The big day. The funeral. The march. And then, Annie shuddered at the thought, the police.

Annie was not entirely alone. Both Fenchaw and Decker

insisted she have a bodyguard. She wasn't sure she felt any safer knowing a hulk of a man stood outside the door. He would have been of no use against the daymares that could slip past even the strongest guard. Luckily they had ceased with the fire at Kard's place. Underwood had told her he too was no longer troubled by them.

She ran her fingers through what remained of her hair. She couldn't spend all evening with her head in her hands. Shoving the remains of Kevin's beef casserole in the oven, she laid two places and went to invite the bodyguard. There wasn't really enough for two, but she wasn't hungry. He refused. She insisted. He gave way, influenced no doubt by the smell of food wafting from the flat.

Seated at the kitchen table, he didn't look as burly as she remembered. Dressed all in black, even his boots, with his cropped hair and his unwillingness to talk, he was the very picture of a guard. She glanced at his face as she served the beef. He had none of the wrinkles of age, but he was not young either.

"Do you have children?" she asked, sitting across from him.

He shook his head and chewed on a lump of beef.

"Sorry. It's only leftovers. My friend made it yesterday evening."

He nodded and forked another piece of beef into his mouth.

A little peeved at his stubborn silence she asked, "Are you going to force me to talk alone?"

He shrugged, tearing off a hunk of bread and dipping it in the sauce.

"There was me thinking you were bored and you would appreciate some company. Maybe you would have preferred the quiet."

"Nah," he said, pushing away his empty plate before wiping his lips with the back of his hand. "Don't like talking when I eat."

She was impressed. She snatched a quick glance. He looked as relaxed as a man in an armchair in the safety of his home after a good dinner, not at all like a bodyguard on duty. "Do you ever get frightened? In your job, I mean."

He looked up at her, startled.

"I've often been frightened," she told him. "That's why I ask."

"Mostly nothing happens. You stand for hours in front of a door. Then you go home."

"To think I imagined being a bodyguard was exciting work."

He shook his head then frowned. "The danger is in your mind."

"What do you mean?" she asked, gathering up the plates and putting them in the sink.

"If you start thinking there'll be trouble, you can be sure there will be."

A loud rapping rang out at the door. "You see," he said, getting to his feet. He glanced around the flat, looking unsettled by the impact of his prediction. There was no other way out. Not even a fire escape. "Better lock yourself in the bedroom till I tell you it's OK."

"Police! Open up!" a muffled voice came from beyond the door.

"Wait a moment," Annie said, picking up the iPad Riya had left. She typed in a message. "There. I've warned my friends and the Network there's a police raid."

The knocking began again. The guard pointed to the bedroom.

Inside, the door locked, Annie strained to hear what was happening. The knocking continued for a while. Then ceased. The guard must have opened the door. She could hear raised voices. Glancing at the iPad, she read, 'On our way. Riya'. She needed to gain time. She hurried to the window and peered out. A sheer drop with no access to the roof. There was a cupboard but too small to hide in and under the bed was out of the question.

Raised voices continued to argue outside. No shots, thank heavens. Then a gentle tap came at the door and she heard the guard say, "It's OK."

She hesitated. What if he betrayed her? What if the police forced him to call her out? She unlocked the door to find her guard and two policewomen. So betrayal it was.

"I see you've come to a gentleman's agreement," she said. She was being sarcastic, but the bodyguard nodded. The policewomen too. Odd.

"They have sworn not to harm you," the guard said, positioning himself between her and the police. "They just want to ask some questions."

"I'm Inspector Tratting," the older woman said, holding out her hand for Annie to shake. She was chubby and had rounded cheeks. She looked like she enjoyed life and appeared friendly enough. "And this is Sergeant Brant." The sergeant was clearly younger, but her gaunt face and her stern expression made her look hostile and unapproachable.

"Shall we sit?" Tratting asked, pointing to the table.

Annie sat across from the two policewomen. The bodyguard remained standing. Brant pulled out a notebook and laid it open on the table, a pencil in hand.

"The police in the capital are in turmoil," Tratting said. "There's a great deal of tension. Even open hostility. Not all agree with Kard's orders. We," she glanced at her colleague, "believe that something is seriously wrong and have come to hear your side of the story."

Annie could hardly believe this turn of events. Instead of arresting her, they came with doubts and questions. What a relief. What a godsend. But what was her story? What part had the police played?

"So much has happened. Maybe the most striking thing was the way the police so readily accepted Kard's explanations without the slightest question. The attack on my friend's mother by a group of thugs. The kidnapping of my friend and her subsequent torture. An attempt on my life in front of a television audience. The murder of a young girl mistaken for me at a public rally. As far as I am concerned, there is no doubt Kard was behind each of these crimes. But even if he weren't, how can the police deny they never happened without the slightest investigation? At the same time, they accept Kard's absurd claims that I tried to kill him or hurt him and hurry to arrest me without any other evidence."

The more she thought about it, the clearer things became. "Considered dispassionately, the influence of Kard far outweighs any willingness to seek evidence. People talk a lot about going beyond truth. If you think that's nonsense, just look at the way the police reacted to the photos and the video of my friend being beaten up by two thugs. They discarded them as fake without bothering to check their authenticity. When truth ceases to exist, there can be no justice. How can the police work properly under the influence of a man who systematically refuses all but his own personal take on reality?"

Brant scribbled frantically in her notebook. Tratting's brow creased in concern and she opened her mouth to speak when there was a knock at the door. All heads turned in that direction. Both women turned pale, as if they imagined hostile colleagues about to catch them fraternising with the enemy. The guard spun round, bracing himself for a fight. Only Annie remained calm. The knock had nothing of the vengeful fist of an angry policeman. It must be her friends coming to the rescue. "Come in," she called out.

The door opened and Riya then Ella peered round. Annie smiled at them and beckoned. They traipsed in followed by a crowd of women some of whom were armed with cameras.

Seeing the cameras. Tratting whispered to Annie, "I hope they don't publish those photos. We need some time to figure out what is happening before our colleagues discover what we are up to."

Annie got to her feet. "Welcome," she said. "Please put your cameras away. For reasons I will explain it is better if photos taken here are not shown elsewhere."

She embraced Riya and Ella, then turned back to crowd which was still spilling into the flat. "I am really glad you responded so quickly to my call for help. I thank you all. It turns out it was a false alert. These two police officers came not to arrest me, as I feared, but to talk to me about police behaviour. It would seem that not all the London police are under Kard's control. For the moment their visit must remain a secret."

90.

"Thank you," Tratting said. "It may sound odd to say it, but I am glad there was a misunderstanding. Meeting all these women has been most instructive."

"What will you do now?" Annie asked.

"I'm not sure. The situation is complicated. We can't just arrest half the police of London. And there's Kard to contend with. We have to be careful how and when we act."

"You realise that tomorrow evening I am supposed to give myself up to the police."

Tratting frowned. "I cannot guarantee we will get this sorted out by then. But I do promise we will make sure you are not harmed in any way."

Annie opened the door, shook hands with the two police-women and stepped aside to let them out. She nodded to the bodyguard who had gone back to blending into the shadows. Then she closed the door, but, rather than returning to her two friends in the kitchen area, she leaned her head against the door-frame, closed her eyes and took a deep breath. Like the shifting tectonic plates that disrupted life on the earth's surface often with devastating results, enormous forces were at play and she was stuck in the middle expecting to be crushed at any moment. Dodging was out of the question. Insignificant though she was, she couldn't help feeling that without her intervention the situa-tion would be far worse. She sighed.

Returning to the table, she sat down with Ella and Riya, asking, "Anyone for food?" She'd let the bodyguard have most of Kevin's beef casserole. She hadn't been so hungry at the time, but now her stomach growled.

"Have you got a food taster?" Ella asked, her face deadly serious.

Annie shot her a questioning look, then searched for something to throw at her. There was nothing within reach. She thought about sticking her tongue out, but decided against it. "Yes. You." Short, sharp words, Penelope had said. A quick kill. Did all stories have to be a slaughter house?

Ella was taken aback, clearly unsure if she'd just been stabbed or playfully poked in the ribs.

"When you two have finished," Riya said, giving Ella a shove. "How about Chinese? There's a good one nearby."

They found a table next to the fish tank. Annie would have preferred elsewhere. The desperate gasps of the fish as they tried to breathe, at least that's what it looked like, and the idea that they would soon be on somebody's plate disturbed her. But the small restaurant was full and it was the only table available. A tiny Chinaman who looked like he hadn't eaten in weeks came to take their order. As he spoke very little English, they had to resort to pointing to the numbers of the dishes.

In the short time they had to wait for their food, Ella and Riya filled her in on preparations for both the funeral and the march. They had managed to locate the girl's family. She hadn't been as alone and isolated as Annie had feared. The close of kin had got it into their heads that Annie and her friends were to blame for the tragic loss of their daughter, sister, cousin, whatever. They were adamant that they wanted a private ceremony. The women's movement had decided to drop the idea of a mass celebration. Centring their protest around an individual who had deliberately got in harms way however tragic her death missed the point. Other issues were more important. They needed to find a better activity to commemorate ordinary women who had been the victims of violence.

As for the march, the police had refused permission, but the women planned to go ahead despite the ban. The idea was to converge on the Houses of Parliament by a series of different itineraries. Various groups were to be allotted routes and it was expected others would join them. The hope being to both surprise and flood the police making halting the march impossible.

"I'm not sure Parliament is the best venue," Annie said. "If the police are going to protect any place, it will be that. And if they feel 'flooded' as you put it, they are likely to respond with violence." Everyone would expect a demonstration to result in a mass march as a display of force. Like in war. But did it have to be that way? How would adepts of guerrilla warfare go about a peaceful march? She smiled at the absurdity of her question. Well, such fighters would try to hide, but the women had to do the opposite. Be seen. Some distinctive mark. Armbands? Badges? Striking colours?

The guerrillas would strike in many different strategic places in a way that was unexpected. Although the women wanted to make an impact, they did not want to destroy. Ultimately they wanted to help other women and the needy. So why not do that? In schools, in hospitals, in playgrounds, in supermarkets,... No. None of those would work. They were all places where access and activities were strictly controlled.

GENie's work was not in hospitals. It was mobile. Wherever people needed it. For the march, such a flexible, independent solution would be better. Like gypsy caravans for first aid and horse-drawn carts carrying food and drink. Surrounded by women helping, engaging people. Each group making its way slowly through the city to a central meeting point.

A delicious smell of food jolted her from her reverie. A bowl of sweet and sour pork sat in front of her untouched. Ella and Riya had already eaten half their meal. She picked up her chopsticks and balanced a ball of meat, bringing it to her mouth.

"Is it too late to change things for tomorrow's march?" she asked, laying her chopsticks down on the paper napkin.

Both Ella and Riya looked at her, alarmed. "You can't imagine how difficult it was to bring this together at such short notice," Ella said, puffing up her cheeks and blowing out a deep breath.

"Tell us what you have in mind," Riya said, one hand laid on Ella's arm to placate or maybe restrain her. "Who knows? Some things may still be possible."

At first, the two listened in silence as Annie let her ideas take form. Then they chipped in with questions and suggestions. The discussion grew animated. A girl that they knew from a neighbouring table joined in and by the time they left for Alice's place there were seven or eight of them giving shape to the plan.

Alice had returned in the meantime, and, as everyone settled around the kitchen table, Annie gave her the potted version of their plan. The old woman was delighted and came up with a whole series of people who might help. When the improvised meeting broke up, each left with a list of people to contact. Annie slumped in an armchair, her head spinning at the thought of what they were trying to organise in such a short time.

When her new phone rang, it took her a moment to realise what it was. Kevin.

"I'm going nuts," Kevin exploded before Annie could say a word. "I just had a screaming match with Mum. She refuses to let me go to the march tomorrow."

"Is Megan there?"

"She's fuming in her office."

"Put her on."

"Not that it will do any good." There was a long pause.

"Hallo, Annie," Megan said, her voice tense.

"Kevin says you are worried about her taking part in the march. I just want to let you know there will be no march. We have planned something completely different, a decentralised event followed by a large gathering."

"I hope you're not spinning a tale to get my daughter off the hook."

"Why would I do that? I want her to stay alive as much as you, Megan." Talking to Kevin's mother that way felt odd. What she said was true, but the way she said it gave it more weight. Conviction? More like she was solidly behind the words. She was sure Megan would give in.

"Kevin is already fed up with my company." Megan sounded bitter. "I will drive her over to Alice's place as soon as she's ready. I want you to tell me more of your plans for tomorrow before I decide to let her attend. And I need to talk to Alice about my dossier on the police. It is almost ready."

"Good. Then I must tell you about my discussion this evening with two policewomen who want to put an end to this abuse."

"Was one of them Inspector Tratting?"

"Yes. How did you know?"

"I've spoken to her but I wasn't sure she would move against the others. Good. See you in a short while." She handed the phone back to Kevin who squealed when she realised she was to be with Annie.

"Behave," Annie said. "There's a limit to what I can do."

91.

Annie gasped as Kevin flung her arms around her neck nearly knocking her over in her enthusiasm. Megan stood in the doorway looking on, shaking her head. "Maybe I should have held firm and kept them apart," she said to Alice.

Alice chuckled. "Hard call. I heard they were glued together."

Kevin grabbed Annie's hand and started tugging her in the direction of the bedroom. Annie resisted.

"No you don't," Megan said, raising her voice. "I have words to say to you Annie."

Freeing herself from Kevin who stamped her foot and pouted, Annie said, "And I have important things to discuss with you, Megan."

Kevin's mum eyed her appraisingly then nodded. Annie sat down at the kitchen table and Kevin, sulking, sat next to her.

"You wanted to know how we plan to organise the event tomorrow," Annie began. Megan sat across from the two girls while Alice busied herself making a pot of tea. Annie described their plans and as she did, little by little, Kevin thawed and joined the discussion, making several suggestions.

"I like it," Megan said once the discussion was over and sipped her tea which had long remained untouched.

Kevin shifted impatiently at Annie's side, no doubt eager to ask if she could take part. Judging it might be better not to press Megan, Annie pushed on with the other subject she needed to discuss, the police, which earned her a pinch under the table from Kevin. "So you spoke to Tratting?" she asked, rubbing her thigh.

"Yes. She was my main source of insider information and she opened the way to a couple of others."

Tratting had talked of half the police force being hostile, but that might just have been a figure of speech. "Have you got any idea how many of the London force would side with her?"

"I'm not sure. She's not from here. She moved from the Home Counties quite recently. She might not have much support from those who have always worked in London."

Kevin must have got fed up because she slouched off to the bedroom where Annie could hear her watching TV.

"I got the impression," Annie said, "that she thought setting things right was feasible in the not-so-distant future. What are you going to do with your report?"

"I had thought I would take them to court, but that would last far too long and would be costly without any guarantee of success. In the end I decided to give the report to the Home Affairs Committee. It's a parliamentary body that looks into policing amongst other things. I know several of the members and I gave them a draft copy. I have been invited to an urgent meeting tomorrow morning."

Annie wanted to ask what outcome they could expect from the committee but Kevin called them. "Come and have a look at this."

She was sprawled on the bed with a laptop propped up in front of her. On the screen Kard was talking.

"I am determined to stop these trouble makers."

And how would he do that, the interviewer asked.

"Simple. Set up blocks along their route. "

Annie burst out laughing. "Road blocks will get motorists' backs up much more than they will hinder us."

"We should scout around and find out where these blocks are," Kevin said. "Maybe they could be included in the plan."

Megan shook her head. She seemed set on reining in any attempt of her daughter to act on her own. What a shame. Kevin's mum had been much more easy-going when Annie had first met her.

"I think it is a good idea," Annie said causing Kevin to brighten up. "We should ask the Network to reconnoitre."

Once Megan had left, saying she would see them the next day before the parliamentary hearing, and Alice had retired to her bedroom, Kevin and Annie were finally alone in Annie's bedroom. At last they could indulge in the hugs and kisses Annie had been looking forward to.

"What's wrong with you?" Kevin asked, turning on her. "I haven't been away more than a couple of hours and you, my best friend, side with my mother."

Taken aback by Kevin's sudden attack, Annie sank to the bed and sat on its edge staring up at the girl. How unfair. If Kevin had had her way, she would certainly have been barred from attending the march. She had no wish to get into a fight. If nothing else, she was too tired for it. "There was me looking forward to a kiss and instead I get accusations. I'd much prefer a kiss."

Kevin frowned. She had wanted to pick a fight, but Annie had sidestepped, catching her on the wrong foot. "You're infuriating!"

"If you want to see someone who is really infuriating, just hold back a bit longer on those kisses."

Kevin roared and flung herself at Annie knocking her backwards onto the bed with a resounding crash. It was a wonder Alice didn't come running. Kevin straddled Annie and, pinning her arms on the bed, made every effort to suffocate her with a barrage of savage kisses. Annie struggled but her efforts only made Kevin wilder. It was not love she was being subjected to, but anger.

When Kevin's fury showed no signs of abating, Annie, whose lips hurt from the onslaught, ceased struggling and let herself go limp and unresponsive. Without any opposition, the girl's anger was short-lived. Instead, she burst into tears and clung to Annie, her sobs shaking both her and the bed. She lay there subjected to Kevin's furious sadness as she had been to her anger. She felt oddly detached. Did she no longer care for Kevin?

The thought made her sad.

Extricating herself from Kevin's arms, she shifted to sit at the top of the bed with her back to the wall. Running her fingers over her swollen lips, she said, "That hurt. Those were not the kisses I was looking forward to." Kevin had stopped crying and looked tense and ready for a fight. "I am not your mother," Annie continued. "You might want to kill her, but I won't let you kill me."

"You act like her."

She had acted differently. It was true. But not like Megan. Not like an overprotective mother. "Megan was angry with you. She was exasperated. As you were with her."

"You see. You take her side."

Annie ignored the comment. "I was neither angry nor exasperated. I was happy to see you."

"But several times you spoke out against me."

"You were eager to ask Megan to let you go, but I felt she was not ready. I did not speak against you, I spoke to Megan about things that are important." Kevin had acted like a spoilt child. She had been so set on getting her way she did everything wrong. Had Annie ever been like that with her parents? Probably. Although the situation had been different. Her parents didn't give a sod as long as she pretended to go along.

"You see. Your plans and your march and your bloody Network are all more important than me."

"GENie was your idea, if I remember rightly." Annie could understand how Megan found Kevin infuriating. The world revolved around her and her desires. "But that is not important. When she left, I had the impression Megan agreed to let you go. So why are you still angry?"

Kevin hovered between anger and appeasement. A fresh tear trickled down her blotchy face. "I'm sorry."

92.

Annie, Kevin and Alice were huddled around the laptop on the kitchen table watching the news, amid breakfast plates and cups and the remains of bread and croissants.

"During the night, artists have been at work in the capital ensuring we don't forget who is responsible for the road blocks," the commentator said, chuckling. The camera cut to a graffiti of Ella's drawing of Kard with his trousers down splayed across a road block. Both Kevin and Annie roared with laughter. Alice frowned.

On the TV, Kard was seated in his usual armchair, scowling. He spent so much time in that chair people must be wondering if he ever left it. "This is totally unacceptable. These terrorists are stopping the police doing their work," he raged.

"How do these artworks stop the police doing their work?" the presenter asked, having a hard time concealing a smile.

"The police have to be taken seriously. Those ludicrous drawings undermine their work."

The camera cut to people admiring the graffiti. "What do you think?" a journalist in the street asked.

"It's a good likeness," a man said.

Kevin and Annie roared with laughter again.

The journalist approached a young woman who was grinning. "It livens up our day," she said. "I wish there were more like this. But not always the same subject. We see enough of him already."

The camera cut back to Kard.

"You who talk of defending the interests of Londoners, what do you think of that?" the presenter asked.

"They are probably not from London. True Londoners couldn't possibly condone such acts."

The camera switched to the presenter. "There you have it folks. According to Nolan Kard the definition of a 'true' Londoner is someone who agrees with him. What others see as art, he calls terrorism because it pokes fun at him and his police." The camera changed again and the presenter turned to face it. "Which brings us to our next subject. Trouble with the police in London. An urgent meeting of the Home Affairs Committee has been called to discuss the violent behaviour of the police in London..."

Kevin turned the sound down. "That was great! They made him look ridiculous."

"Leave the sound," Annie said. "I want to hear this."

"... according to a secret report on police abuse in the capital. And now the sports news."

Kevin turned off the news just as Annie's phone rang. It was Riya.

"Excellent," Annie said. "We'll be there in half an hour." Returning her new phone to her pocket, Annie said, "That was Riya. All is ready for the march. She wants us to see something in a former milk factory."

Riya was waiting on the pavement when Alice dropped them in front of a run-down factory in the suburbs. She had exchanged her usual sari for pale blue overalls and looked tired, but happy. A weather-worn sign above the vehicle entrance read Cavendish Milk. Greetings over, Riya pushed open the gate that barred access to the building and they stepped into a large courtyard full of old-fashioned milk floats. In place of the ad that generally covered the back of the vehicle, each sported a stylised painting of Annie, her first raised. It had become the symbol of their movement.

"We have installed a cover on each float to conceal the graffiti until the march begins," Riya said. "We don't want the police catching on too quickly."

Annie surveyed the yard and all the floats aligned. There must have been at least thirty of them. "Will this be enough?"

"No. But there are four more such factories around London. This is the smallest. Together that should be more than enough."

Impressed, Annie whistled between her teeth. "How come we get to use them?"

"The owner is a good friend of Fenchaw's. I suspect the newspaper has promised to run an article on her. And anyway they are no longer in use."

"Do they all work?"

"Most of them. A team of mechanics have checked."

"What are we putting in them?" Kevin asked.

"Come and have a look," Riya said, striding towards the floats.

Where the milk bottles should have been there were small bottles of fruit juice. "The producer of the juices gave them free. He sees it as a publicity stunt," Riya explained. On the shelves above were piles of the newspaper supplement about violence and the two-page poster, Ella's cartoon of Kard and Annie facing off. Riya picked up a handful of leaflets and handed one to Annie and Kevin. "It explains the work of GENie and how to get in contact," she said.

"And that?" Annie asked, pointing to a pile of grey papers.

"The executive summary of Megan's report about police abuse." Riya grinned, handing one to Annie. "There is one more thing." She stepped back from the float and opened a compartment along the side under the rows of bottles. "First-aid equipment. Each float will have a couple of nurses and their aides. So we can deal with any little hurts and scratches we come across along the way."

Annie hoped it wasn't their own wounds at the hands of the police they'd be tending. As she glanced around the yard, impressed at the organisation, she noticed a number of small trucks, more like tractors. "Do they have anything to do with the march?" she asked.

"To limit drain on batteries, we are going to tow the floats to their different starting points around London. We'll also use them to carry spare batteries or to tow floats, should any get stuck."

"Mornin'!" The call came from the gateway. Several women peered in. Riya waved them in and greeted them. The women were excited to meet Annie and when Kevin was introduced, one exclaimed, "You're the girl who got kidnapped." Kevin made a rather stiff bow.

By the time Annie and Kevin left to meet Alice, there were over a hundred women milling around the floats of which several had already been towed away to their starting blocks.

93.

The four floats came to a halt at Speakers' Corner where they were greeted by cheers from a considerable crowd that had already congregated. The tractors were uncoupled and left immediately to fetch floats for other routes. The way from Hyde Park through Mayfair, where they'd meet up with another group and then on to Green Park and St. James's Park en route for the Houses of Parliament was one of the longest so they had to get underway.

The organising group led by Riya and Leonor had appointed several women responsible for each route. Annie had already met those for the Hyde Park route at the milk factory. They had been issued with walkie-talkies so they could communicate with Riya's team, based at Decker's offices.

Recognising Annie, the crowd clustered around, many wanting to shake her hand or hug her. She presented Kevin, eager to share the glory of handshaking. Kevin joined in with enthusiasm. Annie presented Petra to the crowd, one of the people responsible. "She and her colleagues know which route to follow and what is planned. If you have any questions, I suggest you ask them. They also know what to do if there are any problems. Follow their advice. It's important. Kevin and I have to leave to see other groups, but we'll see you all at the end."

As the two left hand in hand to meet Alice, the crowd had swelled to several hundred people and women were still pouring in from all sides. And this was only one of the groups. "If there are too many," she told Kevin, "they'll split into smaller groups and take different routes. That's why they have four floats."

Alice was waiting for them at the appointed place behind the wheel of her car, reading a newspaper. They set out across London to the Houses of Parliament where Annie was to attend the Home Affairs committee hearing on police violence. Her invitation had been a last-minute affair organised by Dillinger who was chair of the committee.

"Kard has been talking to the media," Alice said as they drove down Park Lane. "Making noises about the nuisance the march is going to cause."

"Well, it will certainly do that," Kevin said. "Far worse than he imagines."

"I wish there was some way we could avoid blocking traffic," Annie said. "Angry motorists are not going to make good supporters."

"Weren't there routes that avoided main arteries?" Alice asked.

"It's difficult," Annie replied. "There will be so many people, they can only walk on the wider roads. Even split up into smaller groups."

"I'm concerned about all those people crammed in around the Houses of Parliament," Alice said. "It's not such a large place."

"A siege," Kevin said gleefully.

"Yes. But who is laying the siege and who will be beseiged?" Annie asked. "There's a serious risk violence will flare up. I was wondering if we shouldn't walk right past and congregate in St. James's Park." She pulled out the walkie-talkie Riya had given her. "Riya?"

"No. It's Ella. Riya is busy."

Annie shared her concerns.

"I'll tell Riya. No time to discuss. Bye." The communication was cut.

Ella was normally so easy-going, it was startling not to get the slightest crack or joke from her. "Wow!" Annie said, shaking her head as she put the device away. "I'm glad I'm not stuck with them. It must be hectic."

They drove past Westminster Abbey and entered Parliament Square where they saw the first signs of massive police presence. The end of Whitehall was completely blocked by police barriers each daubed with Kard in his underpants. Policemen with the familiar armband of Kard's force were milling around looking anxious.

Annie extracted her phone from her pocket and snapped a few shots of the road blocks and the police which she shared with Riya. Traffic was crawling around the square, bumper to bumper under the disapproving eye of the statue of Churchill.

"We're going to be late," Alice muttered. All along the pavement outside the Houses of Parliament police stood erect, eyeing passing cars. One of them, a brute of a fellow, blocking the gateway to the car park, held up his hand. Alice stopped the car and wound down her window.

"We are to attend a meeting of Home Affairs Committee," she told him. "Here's our invitation." She pulled a letter from her pocket and handed it to the policeman. He squinted at it, peered in the car and glared at Annie and Kevin. "It says here two people. There are three of you," he said.

"My granddaughter is accompanying us," Alice said.

"It says two, and two is two," the policeman insisted.

"Listen, officer, we're already late for an important meeting."

It was clear he was never going to let them through, so Annie opened the car door and stepped out amid protests from both Alice and Kevin. "There you go officer. Only two now." He looked at her, his nostrils flaring. He clearly didn't like being outmanoeuvred, but he waved the car inside. "Move along," he said to Annie who had pulled out her phone.

She had planned to phone Dillinger and ask the woman to send someone to fetch her, but the policeman was so stubborn and annoying she did something she had sworn never to do again. She slipped him a sliver of a nightmare, just enough to have him run across the street, dodging between the cars that hooted furiously at him, and plunged his head in the fountain.

What an odd man. All she'd done was suggest his mind was over-heating and he needed a rest.

She sauntered through the gate he'd so jealously been guarding and joined Alice by her car where she was in deep discussion with Dillinger. "What happened there?" Dillinger asked, shaking hands with Annie.

"No idea," Annie replied, frowning. "He suddenly dashed across the road and flung himself into the fountain. Maybe he was too hot."

"Come on then," Dillinger said. "Time to sort out these rogue policemen."

94.

Annie entered the meeting hall with Dillinger, leaving Kevin and Alice to wait in an antechamber. Kevin was annoyed at being left behind, but Alice explained that not even her, great professor that she was, was allowed to attend.

A series of pale oak tables formed a tight U around which some ten people were seated, flicking through what must have been Megan's report. She recognised several from the joint meeting between the two parties. She wondered how their presence would influence the outcome of the hearing. At the open end of the U a longer table was presumably for witnesses. It was there that Megan stood talking to Tratting. Seeing Annie arrive, she beckoned her over. Annie shook hands with the Inspector and all three took their seats facing the committee with Megan in the middle.

The door flew open and in strode Kard followed by two police officers. They could have been his bodyguard the stiff way they flanked him, but they were probably just witnesses, intimidated by the setting. He glanced at Megan then Tratting, nodding a begrudged greeting. When he spotted Annie, he sneered. "You not out walking the streets causing trouble?"

"I thought that was your role," she replied and looked away hearing Megan chuckle at her side. Kard sat as far from Annie as he could. She smiled. His behaviour was more like that of a schoolboy than the Lord Mayor of London.

Dillinger opened the meeting and Megan replied to a series of complex questions about the content of her report.

"So," one MP asked, shaking her head in disbelief, "the metropolitan police did not respond despite clear evidence of a kidnapping?"

Kard bounced up and down in his seat, eager to respond, but Dillinger gave him a disapproving look. He calmed down, but couldn't help muttering, "Load of rubbish."

"No," Megan replied. "They claimed it was a hoax and refused to investigate."

Dillinger addressed Tratting. "What reasons were given, Inspector?"

"I can't see why you ask her," Kard burst out, springing to his feet. "She knows nothing about nothing." His scorn for Tratting shocked more than one in the room.

"I asked the Inspector, Mr. Kard. Not you," Dillinger replied. "If you can't behave in a reasonable manner, I will have to ask you to leave."

Tratting stared at Kard, embarrassed. "I'm not sure. There was a consensus that it was a hoax."

"And did you think it was a hoax?" Dillinger asked.

"No." She glanced at Kard. "The decision was too hasty. The case needed to be investigated, especially as there were several signs the kidnapping really took place. Of course, I was fairly new to London but I could see there were forces at work that were not readily understandable."

She could well have said 'occult' forces, Annie thought. But then Tratting didn't know the truth.

"Why did your officers not follow up on the case?" Dillinger asked Kard.

"There was no point. It was obvious it was a hoax." He cast a withering glance at Tratting. "It wouldn't be the first time Fenchaw's gang tried the trick."

"Did you order the police not to intervene?"

"I didn't need to. They figured it out for themselves."

"What do you say?" Dillinger asked the two policemen.

"It seemed clear to us it was a hoax," one replied.

"On what evidence did you base your decision?" one of the

MPs asked.

The first police officer shifted uncomfortably in his seat. "Everyone said so," the second officer replied.

"And who was everyone?" the MP pursued.

Both officers glanced at Kard, but did not reply. He looked away as if trying to deflect their attention. Annie had to pinch her thigh under the table to prevent herself from laughing.

"So," the MP continued like a dog worrying a bone, "if 'everyone' said a man was guilty of murder, you would arrest him, without investigation?"

"Of course not!" the first officer protested.

"But how is this case different? Did you investigate?"

The officer shook his head. You would have said a little boy caught doing something he shouldn't. He looked to Kard for support, but the man just folded his arms and glared at the member of parliament.

Dillinger addressed Annie. "You were involved in a similar so-called hoax, I gather?"

Annie got to her feet. She felt more comfortable standing to talk. "Yes. I was shot in the shoulder." She rolled down the shoulder of her blouse to display the ugly red mark. Several people gasped. "Luckily I was wearing a bullet-proof vest."

"Why were you wearing such protection?" Dillinger asked. "Is that normal?"

"A gunman tried to shoot me when I was in a restaurant. Luckily he missed. Since then I have been more careful."

Several members of the Commission looked at her with a mixture of shock and admiration.

"Were the police called to either of these shootings?" Dillinger asked.

"Both times. But they refused to come. They claimed it was a hoax."

"Did you think it was a hoax Inspector Tratting?"

"Definitely not. I examined the footage of the second shooting which took place in a television studio in the presence of Mr Kard. Judging from the trajectory and the bullet I found on the set, had the young lady not been wearing that vest she would have been gravely injured. That can be no hoax."

"Whoever gave you orders to investigate that?" Kard exploded. "You're fired."

Tratting eyed Kard who had gone red in the face, veins swelling on his forehead. "I saw a video on the internet when this girl courageously faced down three policemen acting as thugs at your orders. She said to them, 'I understand you have orders, that you are sworn to obey, but orders can be wrong and obedience misguided.' In this case I judged that doing my job as I was sworn to do as a policewoman was far more important than obeying your orders."

"Thank you Inspector. A rather unfortunate pattern is emerging," Dillinger said, her voice cold and hard, "in which you, Mr Kard, have encouraged the members of the police force under your control to deliberately ignore grave events and not investigate serious crimes. The Commission will deliberate in private on what course of action to advise the Prime Minister and the government. In the meantime, I seriously warn you against engaging in any act of revenge either against Inspector Tratting or the women represented here today. I am thinking in particular of the women's march that is currently getting under way. I think you would be well advised to withdraw your men. I very much doubt they will be of any use faced with what is about to unfurl. They are more likely to cause trouble."

95.

"So he'll leave us alone?" Kevin asked when Annie and Megan had finished describing the hearing.

"I very much doubt it," Megan replied. "He's sure to find some nasty, underhand way of getting back at us."

"Our main safeguard," Annie said, "is the unexpected. If we keep changing tactics, he will find it difficult to respond."

"How can he possibly stop us?" Kevin asked. "This whole march is gigantic and so complicated."

Size wouldn't impress Kard like it did Kevin. Annie was sure of it. "You can be certain he'll have spies out watching our every move. He'll be looking for weak points, dark corners where he can get in a hit without the authorities noticing. That's why each float has been equipped with several webcams so we can keep an eye what is going on."

"How on earth did you manage that?" Megan asked. "You've had so little time."

"A couple of sponsors with deep pockets and a lot of devoted, skilful people," Annie said, getting to her feet. There was no denying it, the women's achievements were remarkable. She felt herself glowing with pride. "I need to go to Decker's place to talk to the others about the way forward. Could you drive me there, Alice?"

"What about me?" Kevin asked, an edge to her voice.

"Aren't you and Megan supposed to go to St. Paul's for the beginning of the official march? Even if Kard withdraws his men, that will still be the place where the most action takes place."

"Can't I come with you?" Kevin's tone was almost pleading.

"Surely you don't want to sit in on all those boring discussions," Annie replied. To be honest, she preferred having Kevin out of the way when it came to serious decision-making. Her demands for attention could be distracting. She'd much rather be distracted by Kevin when they were alone lying on a bed.

"Come on," Megan said, taking Kevin by the arm and leading the reluctant girl away. "We have some demonstrating to do."

"Careful," Alice said, once they were alone. "She's more fragile than she looks."

Annie shook her head. "I just wish she knew when to be loving and affectionate and when to leave me some space."

"She loves you all the time. What do you expect?"

"Sure. But when I'm engrossed in something other than her, she niggles me till I am forced to stop and pay attention to her. I can't get anything done."

Alice chuckled. "You're exaggerating a bit. But I'm sure you'll figure it out."

Decker had loaned them a large hall near his offices which was now laid out with row upon row of tables, each with several computer screens and a huddle of chairs. Women and men were grouped around each table examining what they saw on the screens. Several windows had been flung open and a welcome breeze brought the sounds and scents of a nearby park.

Riya greeted them. "I'm glad you came."

"Someone should film this. It's impressive," Annie said, feeling a renewed surge of pride. "Show how serious and professional we are."

Riya chuckled. "You haven't seen us when there's a panic on. But yes. Brian and his team have already been here filming." Riya took them to a table, where a group was busy studying the screens. "These are live feeds from one of the floats travelling from the Elephant and Castle," Riya said in low voice. "They are headed for Westminster Bridge."

"Is there any way they can be diverted to cross Lambeth Bridge instead? There could be trouble at the far side of Westminster Bridge. Kard's men were out in force when we drove by earlier."

"Yes. I saw your photos," Riya replied. "But according to our spies most of the police have gone now."

"All the same, it's a sensitive spot."

Riya pulled up a map on the screen. "There's a GPS tracking device on each float so we know exactly where it is. We could send them down Lambeth Road, the head of the procession will be there in a few minutes." Riya spoke to a young woman with bright red hair, sporting headphones and a mic. "Emily will redirect them. Are there any other changes you think we should make?"

Annie looked around the room. She had imagined holding a discussion with the leaders of all the groups, but each person was tied up in one or other of the groups. "Judging from what happened at the hearing, I expect Kard will try to strike back and get revenge. But I doubt he'll dare do so openly. If we are unpredictable, he will have a hard time coordinating an attack."

"That makes sense. We are quite capable of doing so."

"Do we have any idea how many people we've got?"

"A lot. Close on a hundred and twenty thousand at the last count. Most of the groups have split up with each of the three or four floats taking a separate route, often down side streets. That means there are about five thousand people accompanying each float. The largest group is progressing slowly along the official route. They must be around forty thousand. Those people who hadn't heard our messages about the different groups all turned up there."

"So many." That was where Kevin and Leonor were, at the head of the procession. She felt a twinge of worry having them so exposed, but brushed it aside. "What about the police and the road blocks?"

"Kard ordered his men to withdraw. I heard him say on TV that if there was any trouble it would be our fault and that of

Dillinger from forbidding him to intervene."

"How are motorists reacting?"

"Some shout at us and try to force their way through, then give up. Normally the police would stop them, but they've abandoned the streets to us. Otherwise people are friendly enough and accept a bottle of fruit juice and a chat as compensation."

"And our own security people?"

"They have orders to keep a low profile unless there is serious trouble. Up to now they have not had to intervene."

"How many do we have?"

"About forty or fifty with each group, many of them experts in unarmed combat. We'll need all of them when the groups converge at the end."

"I'm also worried about everyone being squashed together in front of the Houses of Parliament."

Riya halted to reply to a question from one of the group coordinators. Turning back, she went on, "Yes. Ella gave me your message. I agree. What do you suggest?"

"St. James's Park."

"Provided they don't freak out thinking we are going to abduct the Queen, the Palace being so close."

Annie grinned. "Maybe we should invite her." She turned to Alice who had followed her into the room. "Do you know the Queen, Alice?"

"I met her once at a reception in Buckingham Palace, but I can't say I know her. It's a shame Diana is no longer around, she would have loved to join in, even if it caused a stink with the royals."

"We've got a problem," someone called out. Riya hurried over to a table marked Battersea 3 with Annie trotting after. "There. Look," an older woman said, pointing to the screen. Sure enough. A group of thugs armed with clubs and cudgels were lounging against a couple of telephone booths in a passage between two blocks of flats, just round the corner from a fish and chips shop. The procession was only a leisurely minute away. "Being on top of the float," Riya said, "the cameras catch things people on the ground might not see. Where are they?" she asked the women.

"Along Lupus Street heading through Pimlico. Bar turning back, they will have to march past that passage."

"OK. Let's use the security group," Riya said to a younger woman busy talking into her microphone. The woman, who was dressed in overalls and a cloth cap, nodded and relayed the information. "Yes," she said. "Just after the chemists and before the fish 'n chips shop."

All those in the control centre not involved in following a group gathered round to watch with bated breath. The head of the procession had reached a pedestrian crossing right in front of the thugs who pushed off their perches and moved out onto the pavement as if they were going to cross. A solid wall of some twenty men and women shifted to block their passage as the procession continued on its way.

One of the thugs raised his cudgel to strike but got a hefty dose of pepper spray in his eyes that had him tumbling to the ground clawing his face. The others were hardened specimens. None broke rank when their leader fell. Instead several raised their clubs. Annie tensed to intervene but the security group fought off the attack with evident skill. Only one remained wielding a cudgel. Seeing he had no chance, he turned to run down the passage only to come face to face with a little girl who had been watching the fight. He raised his club to knock her out of his way, but Annie hit him with a lightning nightmare blow that sent him reeling down the steps between the two buildings, narrowly missing the girl who clapped as if it were a performance just for her. Several people in the control centre applauded too, although none of them had the slightest idea what they were witnessing.

"What should we do with them?" the young woman with the headphones asked.

"Handcuff them to the railings by the steps so they can't escape," Riya said. "We'll send a van to fetch them."

Annie moved away, wanting to let them get on with their

work but also needing some distance to take in the implications of what was happening. Hopefully Tratting would find a solution. It wouldn't be possible to stand in for the police for long. And she'd promised herself never to intervene like that again.

"Nice one," someone said close by. She glanced round to find Alice standing next to her. When she raised her eyebrows in question, Alice replied, "Saving that little girl."

Annie's only reply was to sigh. All of a sudden she felt empty. "I'm hungry," she said, striding back to Riya. "Have you planned a pause for them to rest and eat? Isn't there a park off Lupus Street?

"Yes. St. George's Square Gardens. It's just behind the church and there are lots of trees, so they'll have plenty of shade." She turned to issue instructions but paused to look at Annie over her shoulder. "That's a good idea. It'll allow the traffic to get by. We have sufficient time. I'll see if I can't organise something similar for the other groups."

"Not too similar," Annie said. "We don't want to be predictable."

96.

Annie sat in Decker's office. Compared with the control room next door, it was a peaceful haven. Apart from Decker, Alice and herself only a few staff were working. Most had gone for lunch. She was glad Decker had sent out for sandwiches because she was famished. Bacon and egg and mayonnaise. She took another bite, suppressing a groan of pleasure, and relaxed back in her chair savouring the snack.

"You need to be more careful," Decker said, addressing Annie as he moved from behind his desk and took a chair next to them. "You have become a walking target. If you take part in the march, you need to be better protected."

"If?" Annie said, swallowing the last mouthful of sandwich, irritated at the suggestion. "There's never been any question I wouldn't."

Alice chuckled. "You'd have to chain her to a giant tree to stop her," she said. "Even then she'd probably talk the tree into letting her go."

Decker did not smile. "That's why I've found new bodyguards for you."

"Bodyguards?" She emphasized the 's'. "Wasn't the one I already had enough?"

"He would look out of place at your side in the march." Decker picked up a sandwich and eyed it suspiciously. It crossed her mind he might be worried about poison. He put it back on the plate with a sigh. "My doctor ordered me to be more cautious. No bacon or eggs for me. No mayonnaise either." He munched on a lettuce leaf and a cherry tomato and they all ate in silence. Outside, in the park, someone was singing, a sweet soprano. 'Take me in your arms and love me tight…"

Pushing aside his plate, the sandwich untouched, Decker said, " I want you to wear a bulletproof vest."

Annie pulled aside her jacket to reveal the one she was already wearing. She was far too warm wearing it inside, but Kevin and Alice had convinced her to keep it on all day.

"Good. What about radio contact?"

Annie pointed to her ear piece. It looked like a typical hands-free add-on people had with their smart phones. "A direct line to Riya."

Decker beckoned to three of the women working quietly at nearby desks. "Meet, Cathy, Lisa and Xenia." The three nodded greetings. "They are to be your bodyguards."

Well, they would fit in alright. They were dressed casually like many of those around Annie. But how could young women who manned computers possibly be any use as bodyguards? "Can you spare three of your staff?" she asked.

Decker chuckled. "They are not part of my staff."

"But…?"

"They were just giving a demonstration of how well they blend in."

Annie stared at them wide-eyed. "Impressive. I hope I can find you when I need you."

The three women smiled. The tallest of them stepped forward, her movements fluid, her eyes alert. The sort of no-nonsense person that you wouldn't mess with. She shook Annie's hand, her grip firm and strong. "I'm Xenia. I'll be accompanying you," she said, her voice deep and melodious. Turning to indicate the others who were already heading for the door, she added, "Cathy and Lisa will join us later."

"Ready?" Alice asked, glancing at her watch. She was to take Annie and Xenia to the march but wouldn't stay herself. Too old, she'd said.

Annie nodded. "Why am I so apprehensive? I've been

through all this before."

"Maybe you're dreading the peace and quiet once it's all over," Alice quipped.

Annie laughed. Alice was not far from the truth. She preferred not to think about afterwards and her rendez-vous with the police. Thanks heavens there was so much going on to occupy her mind.

Riya joined them. "You should be going. They've just left Ludgate Hill and are moving down Fleet Street. Crossing Farringdon Street was a bit of a problem. Some irate drivers didn't want to stop. But a little friendly persuasion convinced them." She shot them a twisted smile. "You could wait for the march to arrive at the end of Fetter Lane. Then Alice you can drive along Fleet Street and back up Chancery Lane."

Alice dropped Annie and Xenia at the corner of Fetter Lane and drove down a deserted Fleet Street away from the approaching procession. Annie leaned against some traffic lights staring off down the road in the direction of St. Paul's. Xenia stayed at her side. A van halted a bit further down the street and Cathy and Lisa stepped out followed by two large dogs. The two ignored Annie and Xenia and wandered off.

Three businessmen in grey suits walked out of offices across the street, halted to see what was causing the racket, then scurried away in the opposite direction, clasping their portable computers to their chests as if to shield them. Laughter burst from the open door of the patisserie across Fleet Street and two schoolgirls about Annie's age stepped out devouring chocolate eclairs. They too glanced down the road, hesitating whether to investigate.

"You might as well stay here," Annie called out. "They'll be here in a short while. We are waiting for them too."

The girls sauntered across the street licking their fingers. "What's it all about?" the taller of the two girls asked.

"It's part of a march to put an end to violence especially against women and children. There are over twenty groups marching through London by different routes at the same time.

This is the biggest. Have you heard of GENie?"

The taller girl shook her head her expression blank, but the other one cocked her head to one side, staring at Annie. "I knew I recognised you," the girl said, grinning. "You're that Annie Wright. The leader of all this. The one that did battle with Kard."

Annie shook her head. Was she the leader? Her picture was on each float and her image had been sprayed over many a free wall of London. Everyone knew her from her appearances on television and at meetings. Had she not told Riya what to do with the march? There were over 120'000 people marching around London causing delight and havoc. All of a sudden she was aware of the responsibility and shoved the thought aside trying not to let it crush her.

"Pleased to meet you," Annie said shaking hands with the two girls. "This is Xenia my... a colleague." Xenia shook hands too.

It was the turn of the taller schoolgirl to look strangely at Xenia. "I know you. You are the all-London champion in un-armed combat. I saw you fight. Wonderful. Could you teach me some moves? I'm learning, you know."

"Maybe not now," Annie said, having to raise her voice to be heard over the music of the approaching crowd. A group of street musicians had formed around the float and the marchers were singing along with them.

Annie pushed away from the pavement and walked out into the middle of the street. The music ceased abruptly and an immense cheer went up when people recognised who was standing there. Annie raised her clenched right fist in salute and a wave of such salutes rippled down the procession and as it did she felt a delicious ripple of pleasure run down her spine. She could get to like being a leader.

97.

Up ahead Annie could just make out the spire of St Clement Danes peeking out white in the sunlight above the trees in the middle of the Strand. They still had quite a way to go along the Strand till they reached Trafalgar Square but from there it was only a short walk to St James's Park.

"I'm going to call Riya," she said both to Kevin who was holding her hand on her right and Xenia who was shadowing her on her left. She tapped on the earpiece and spoke. "Riya?"

"Yes, Annie."

"How are things going?"

"We are up to a hundred and fifty thousand and most of the groups have paused for lunch."

"That's what I'm calling about. Is there some place nearby where we can halt with so many people?"

"Lincoln's Inn Fields. Around Aldwych and up Kingsway. Then off to the right. It's not so far. With so many it'll be a tight fit. But I can't see anywhere else near enough."

"OK. We'll go for it."

Annie let go of Kevin's hand who complained bitterly, saying she was being abandoned. At which Xenia gave the girl a sharp look then returned to surveying the crowd. Annie wove her way between the people at the head of the procession till she spotted Gertie, the group coordinator. Before Annie could say anything, Gertie said, "Yeah I know. Riya just told me. Lincoln Inn Fields. That won't work. Too much traffic in the wrong direction."

Gertie held up her hand for the marchers to halt. She

climbed up the side of the float to get a better view of the masses behind them. "We should have gone up Chancery Lane. But we can't turn back now. It's right at this end of Fleet Street."

"Drop the idea," Annie said. "We'll continue up the Strand, keeping to the left so we don't have to bother should there be oncoming traffic."

"Good. There is an island in the centre of the road. That will help." Gertie raised her arm and waved the marchers on.

The river of people skirted south of St Clement Danes and flowed between St. Mary-le-Strand and King's College. There was a rough patch as they negotiated the crossing between the road to Waterloo Bridge and Aldwych. Then they moved steadily forward despite the car horns and catcalls of motorists travelling in the opposite direction.

"We're getting close to Covent Garden," Annie said to Kevin. "I wonder what your grandmother is doing?"

"Making us sandwiches, I hope," Kevin said.

"You forgot the sandwiches?" Annie said, pretending to be dismayed.

Kevin stared shamefaced at the ground. "So much was going on."

"Don't worry," Xenia said. "I have extra sandwiches, but only enough for you Annie."

Kevin pouted and tears sprang to her eyes.

Annie flung her arms around Kevin and hugged her, which earned them a chorus of whistles from passing drivers. "Silly Billy. She's winding you up," Annie said. "And even if it were true, I'd share my sandwiches with you."

Kevin took a swipe at Xenia and ended up in an arm-lock, begging to be set free.

"I forgot to tell you. She's the all-London champion at unarmed combat," Annie said grinning. When Kevin looked doubtful, Annie added, "No kidding."

Xenia hugged a surprised Kevin and whispered, loud enough for both Kevin and Annie to hear and most of the others around, "I'm not going to take her away from you, pet. I've already got my own princess."

Xenia abruptly stepped back, her finger pressed on her ear. Annie hadn't noticed that she too wore a transmitter in her ear. "Stop the procession!" Xenia called out. "Come with me," she said grabbing Annie's hand. They pushed their way through the halted marchers till they reached Bertie with Kevin trailing behind.

When they found Bertie, Xenia turned to Kevin. "Go find Megan. This is too dangerous." Kevin's face crumpled as if she had been slapped. Something deep inside Annie hurt at the sight of Kevin turn obediently and squeeze her way back through the crowd.

Xenia led them out of the ranks of marchers and headed down an unusually deserted Strand. After some ten yards, she had them enter Savoy Court with the famous hotel at its end. After a quick, sharp exchange with a security guard from the hotel, she pulled the two under the gilded roof that jutted out over the pavement and beyond the sight of the crowd.

"Lisa's dog has sniffed out a bomb. It's in a waste bin near the Adelphi Theatre. It doesn't seem to be very big, but it could cause a lot of damage if it went off."

"So what do we do now?" Annie asked.

"Lisa has called in some colleagues from the military. She often works with them. They are already examining the device and traffic has been stopped near Charing Cross Station. Do you think some of our security force would volunteer to make sure no pedestrians go near?"

"I'll ask them," Bertie said. "Anything else I need to know?"

"Only to keep the news to themselves. We don't want a panicked crowd on our hands," Xenia replied and Bertie hurried away. Annie wondered how much she should tell the marchers. She had to tell them something.

"Sorry about that?" Xenia said.

"You couldn't know there would be a bomb," Annie replied, wondering why Xenia should apologize.

"No. I meant sending your friend back to her mother. She's

very upset. But in such circumstances it is better to have only the essential people in on discussions. Your friend doesn't quite get the whole picture."

Annie sighed. "Let's not spend any longer here. People will be wondering if we stopped the march for the two of us to have a tea at the Savoy while they wait."

Xenia chuckled. "I don't drink tea."

"Try telling them that."

Bertie met them as they stepped out onto the Strand. Ten people accompanied her. "Just tell people there's a danger," Xenia said to security team. "They need to keep away for the moment. The military has put up barriers but some people need persuading."

Once they'd left, Bertie said, "I've spoken to Riya. We'll have people rest here as best they can."

"I thought I'd make an announcement, unless you want to do it," Annie said. "Although I'm not sure what I will say."

"I'll leave that to you," Bertie said, her eyes wide. "Coordinating a group this size is one thing, addressing them is another kettle of fish."

"Tell them we have to sort out a security problem," Xenia suggested. Then turning to Bertie she added, "You'd better have the rest of the security team patrol the march to make sure no other nastiness is awaiting us."

Back at the head of the march, Annie clambered onto Xenia's shoulders with the help of Bertie and Kevin and took the megaphone they handed her. "We would have preferred to make a halt in a park, under the shade of trees but you'll have to imagine those. We have stopped here because there is a security alert further down the Strand. It may be nothing, but better to be sure. Make yourselves as comfortable as possible. I hope we won't have to wait too long."

Kevin called up to her, "Alice is trying to organise food and drink at reasonable prices."

"For those of you who are short on provisions we are trying to organise supplies at cheaper rates," Annie added. "As soon as we have more news, I'll let you know."

The moment Annie got down, a string of explosions rang out, followed by screams. She looked up the empty Strand. Nothing. The noise had come from the other direction, in the heart of the crowd.

"Fireworks!" Xenia shouted. "Cathy has caught the culprit."

"It was fireworks," Annie announced to the crowd. "No need to panic. We've caught the person. If anybody is hurt near you, please raise a hand so the healers can see you."

Already the medical team were pulling out stretchers and bags of medicine from under the float. Annie went with them, closely followed by Xenia and Kevin. Several people had burns and a couple had gone deaf from the blast. Many were in shock. "Why us?" one asked through her tears. "There could have been children here," another said. Annie and Kevin comforted them as best they could.

When Annie returned to the head of the march, she found someone had dug out a large plastic crate for her to stand on. The message was clear enough. She climbed onto the crate and stared out over the crowd that stretched away down the Strand. From her vantage point she could see Cathy holding on to a miserable looking creature in dirty overalls in the entrance to one of the side streets. "Get Cathy to bring that man here," she said to Xenia.

She turned back to the crowd, many of whom were looking at her. "I am shocked," she said, preferring to give voice to her emotions. "I am sickened to the heart. My humanity is hurt. What human being could possibly throw an explosive device into the middle of a packed crowd of unarmed, harmless individuals?" She paused a long moment, letting the tears of shock and anger well up in her eyes. The crowd waited in silence, communing with her suffering and that of the wounded.

"It would be so easy to let anger break through," she went on, raising her voice. "To reply to violence with violence. To dispel our hurt, to drown our fear, to disguise our helplessness, with angry words and fisticuffs. Violence breeds violence. If we want to put an end to violence, we cannot respond in kind. I have no recipe. All I know is that, however unbearable the violence is, whether it be abuse or rape or blind destruction as here, we cannot respond with violence. That only makes things worse."

98.

At her feet, Annie spotted Cathy and her dog with the man. He looked even more pitiful close up. His clothes were torn and filthy. His hair was dishevelled and unwashed. His nose was bleeding, his lip cut and swollen. No doubt Cathy's work in apprehending him. Annie was unsure what to do. He could well be the same one who planted the bomb, although she doubted it.

"I need some way to amplify his voice," she said to Gertie. "And a crate for him to stand on."

Gertie had a gift for organising. In no time a crate was found and a microphone fixed to the collar of the man's coat and another to hers, both connected to a loudspeaker on top of the float. Cathy shoved the man, none too kindly, up onto the crate and kept a tight hold on his hands behind his back.

"Leave his hands free," Annie said. "He's not going anywhere."

The man rubbed his chafed wrists, scowling at Cathy, then he turned to Annie, looking warily from under windswept eyebrows as if she might be his executioner.

"What was your favourite game as a child?" she asked.

He looked at her uncomprehending. She wondered if he understood English.

"Do you not understand?" she asked.

"Sure," he said. "I understand alright. But I ain't 'ad no childhood."

"No childhood? Explain."

"Me dad beat me and kicked me out when I woz seven. Said

I woz good for nothink."

"So what did you do?"

"Begged. Stole. Made meself useful. Mostly ran from the police 'nd social services."

"So you never went to school?"

"Na. Wot use? Blinkin' teachers don't know nothink. Learn more on the street."

"And where did you sleep?"

"In parks, under bridges, in doorways. Loads o' folk do. The dirty unseen. London's secret. Never stray in them centres. Once they get their claws in yer, you've 'ad it. Better to be 'omeless and free than shackled to them good-doers."

"Why did you throw those fireworks into the crowd?"

"A geezer gave 'em to me and told me he'd slip me a tenner if I did."

"And what about the people you hurt?"

"Ain't my problem. Nobody never did anythink for me." A murmur of anger and indignation rippled through the crowd. She wasn't going to get far with guilt.

"If you had a wish, what would you do?"

"Blasted do-gooders." He spat on the ground. "Wishes ain't no flippin' use. Look at me. Even God can't be bothered. Who'd do a bloody miracle for me?"

"But just this once, maybe someone might."

He stood there sullen, his shoulders drooped, picking at a sore at the corner of his mouth as he stared at the ground. The people around Annie began muttering under their breath in their impatience. After a long silence, the man shook his head. "Fireman," he muttered.

"Why fireman?" Annie asked, surprised. In his place she'd have asked for a bath or a good meal or a bed to sleep in.

"Cause they 'elp people 'nd its exciting."

Hope. Not food or a wash. That was what he craved. "And you'd like to help people?"

He glanced at her, wary, as if checking she wasn't poking fun. "Yeah. S'ppose I would." He paused a long moment, wiping the blood from his nose with the back of his hand. "I'm sorry about them people wot got hurt. Seein' such a crowd singin' 'nd 'appy made me angry. I never thought. Like there were so many, the odd one here or there didn't count no more. Just a load o' numbers…" His voice trailed off.

"Do we have any firemen here?" Annie asked the crowd.

A hesitant hand went up not far away. She recognised a member of the security team.

"Would you agree to take this man to visit your fire station later?"

"Sure," the man called out.

"Good," she said, beckoning for the fireman to come forward. "In the meantime, we need to get you cleaned up and fed if you are going to march with us."

Out of the corner of her eye, Annie spotted Alice leading a group of people all carrying wicker baskets or wheeling trolleys. "Looks like food has arrived," she told the crowd.

Annie munched on a sandwich Alice had given her. Ham and lettuce. She was listening to Riya in her ear bringing news of the other marches. None had had serious problems. Several had already reached St. James's Park and were readying the place for the others. A number of TV companies were busy setting up cameras in the park. It hadn't taken them long to figure out where the final gathering would be. At Riya's question, she replied, "We must be about an hour away. But I have no idea how much longer the bomb squad will need." She told Riya about the fireworks and the fireman. "You took a big risk," was Riya's only comment.

Xenia tapped Annie on the shoulder and she turned to see Lisa striding down the empty Strand towards them, her dog trotting at her side. "They've removed the bomb," Lisa said, "and the military will continue diverting the traffic at Charing Cross so we will be able to use the whole width of the Strand."

Annie wanted to thank her, but the young woman had already turned away and was wandering back down the street, as if on a Sunday stroll. Annie shook her head. You'd never guess that she and her dog had just saved the lives of tens if not hundreds of people.

Flags fluttered in the breeze over the hotel entrance as they reached Charing Cross Station. People were leaning out the many windows to catch a first glimpse of the march, whistling and cheering as the head of the cortege swept into view. The station forecourt was packed with people none of whom seemed in any hurry to catch a train. They erupted in cheers and clapping as the first of the marchers drew level with the station.

Annie halted the march and grasped the microphone Bertie handed her. She took several steps beyond the column of people, Xenia at her side. Kevin on the other. The crowd hushed. "Thank you," she said, her amplified voice echoing back from the façade of the station and away down the Strand over the heads of the marchers. "Thank you all for such a warm welcome. It touches us deeply. We, the women, men and children of London, march to put an end to violence. The violence of words, of acts, of fists, of firearms and bombs. We oppose violence not with ever more violence, but with everyday acts of kindness, with concern for those who are poor, rejected and in ill health. It is not easy. But that is our goal. If that goal appeals to you, join us. We are on our way to St. James's Park where there will be speeches, but also music and dancing. You are all welcome."

She paused a moment, the clenched fist of her right hand ready at her side. "We raise our fists in salute, not in threat but as a sign of solidarity. In those fingers held tight we embrace everyone however different they may be. Gay. Trans. Straight. Black. Brown. Yellow. White. All colours of the rainbow. All are welcome in our London." She raised her fist in the air. Behind her, the marchers as one saluted in their turn and with it a roar went up that rippled back down The Strand. Then hesitatingly people in the station forecourt and at the windows above, raised their fists, till a sea of raised fists greeted her.

Annie nodded as a token of recognition and returned to the march, an arm slung around Kevin's shoulders, her heart beating fast with the emotion of the moment. Penelope Djaganov had been wrong. At least in part. Writing good stories wasn't all about splattering the blood of the characters across the pages. Sure, there were necessarily upsets and things didn't always go as planned, but what readers really wanted was a story that made sense of the world around them and gave hope. Bertie raised a hand and signalled for them to set off towards Trafalgar Square.

99.

They left Charing Cross Station as clocks chimed three. From the head of the procession, Annie glimpsed Nelson perched atop his column and, as more of Trafalgar Square came into view, an amazing sight greeted them. The square was packed with people. Some had even climbed into the fountains. Others had clambered on top of the lions or hung precariously from lamp posts. The esplanade in front of the National Gallery was just as crowded. People waved and cheered as the marchers came into view. A second march with its painted float driving proudly at its head was making its way slowly down Charing Cross Road having set out from Euston Station. It passed St. Martins in the Field, and finding no room in the square continued on down as if on a collision course with Annie's marchers. A similar torrent of individuals, no doubt seeking to join them, was flowing round the other side of the square, coming down Cockspur Street from the Haymarket and Pall Mall.

Instead of merging, which Annie feared might be chaotic, if not dangerous, Gertie led her marchers round the south of a large island in the middle of the road while the other group kept to its north, absorbing all the newcomers from Cockspur Street and from the square as it slowly emptied. Then both groups walked side by side, but separately, along the Mall and under Admiralty Arch, shouting greetings to each other across the space that separated them, until they finally joined and the two floats came together as they marched on down The Mall. A distant roar from the park greeted them. The awaiting crowd had spotted them coming.

"Riya says we should turn into the park about half way down," Gertie told Annie.

Annie trotted a few steps ahead of the procession to get a better look. Sure enough, the flag was flying over the Palace. "No," she said, returning to Gertie. "Let's go say hallo to our Queen."

Gertie shot her a worried look. "Riya says there are loads of police patrolling down there."

"Don't worry. It will only be a short visit." Annie looked around in search of some of the musicians who had been accompanying them. She saw one and beckon her over, asking her to get the musicians up front as quickly as possible.

They halted before the Victoria Memorial planted at the end of the Mall and on Gertie's instructions the musicians came to the front while the marchers fanned out on either side facing the Palace. Around the base of the Memorial, a wall of policemen stood in full riot gear, eagerly eyeing the immense crowd like a band of trigger hungry monkeys who'd discovered a stash of guns. Annie wondered if she hadn't been impulsive, putting all these people in danger. A delegation of policemen broke away from the others and was about to cross the road when the musicians struck up the first strains of the national anthem and the marchers began to sing God save the Queen.

The policemen were at a loss what to do. Several halted and saluted. Others looked around for a hint at how to behave. But the marchers sang on. The sheer mass of voices singing together was moving and Annie sang wholeheartedly with them. When the anthem was over a respectful silence fell until Kevin pointed to the palace and called out, "Look!" In the distance, on a balcony a window was open and several people stood there waving. The crowd cheered back, waving too. Then Gertie gave the signal and the marchers flowed off to the left and into the Park to join all the other groups that were already there.

Bordered on one side by The Mall and the other by the Lake, an improvised stage had been set up with its back to the

Palace on the largest open area amongst the trees. With over two hundred thousand people attending, the place was far too small. Annie took Bertie with her to visit the more far-flung groups. She'd come to appreciate the level-headed way the young woman got things to work. Her reaction to the bomb alert had been exemplary. Kevin came too, as did Xenia. Apparently Cathy and Lisa were walking their dogs around the site. Megan had left them following an urgent phone call, saying she had business to sort out.

Annie shook hands, chatted, embraced, placated and commiserated till she felt like a plant in need of water. She would willingly have slipped away, to steal a moment of peace and quiet, but she was too well-known and could not imagine explaining why she was sneaking off.

Back near the stage, she accepted a folding chair Bertie offered and sipped hot tea from someone's thermos. She was parched. As she drank, a worrying but also hilarious thought crossed her mind. How do you cater for a quarter of a million people who need to pee when there are no toilets? She would certainly need to find a solution of her own before she gave herself up to the police.

It was close on four o'clock and they had to get the speeches over so those who wanted to sing and dance or simply make their way home before nightfall could do so. Riya arrived with Ella, who said, "There is someone here to see you."

For one terrifying moment Annie had visions of the girl in green being resurrected, only to dismiss the thought as a child of fatigue and stress. Her mind continually returned to what the police might do to her. When she didn't respond to Ella's words, the young woman took her by the arm and led her behind the stage. There stood Jewel, outrageously dressed in the tightest fitting skirt and blouse Annie had ever seen.

"Look at you!" Jewel exclaimed. "You can't possibly go on stage like that."

"Why ever not?" Annie imagined trying to climb on stage dressed like Jewel, and fell flat on her imaginary face.

Jewel unzipped a large case and pulled out pale blue overalls.

"I don't need to dress as a man to hold a speech," she said, wondering if her words slighted Kevin, dressed as always in boy's clothes.

"You wait and see," Jewel said.

Under the overalls she wore a white blouse with a dark blue kerchief around her neck. Then Jewel produced a calf-length skirt that she was to wear over the overalls. Its colour matched the scarf. The whole outfit was completed with a beret and ankle boots.

Seeing Dillinger, Underwood and Alice, Annie greeted them.

"Do you come from the Palace?" Alice asked, eyeing her costume.

Annie shrugged. "Jewel's work." Turning to Dillinger and Underwood she asked, "You two game to talk to the crowd?"

"That's why we came," Dillinger replied. Underwood just nodded.

"OK. Let's do this," Annie taking a portable mic from Bertie. "I'll call you up when it is time."

She climbed the steps and walked out into the middle of the stage only to be greeted by cheers and a lot of whistles. She spun round several times to show off her clothes then raised a hand for silence.

"I take no credit for my clothes. That's all the work of Jewel. Come on up here Jewel and take a bow."

Jewel hiked up her skirt to be able to climb the steps, then smoothing it into place, strode over to join Annie and kissed her on the cheek. The crowd applauded and didn't stop until Jewel had left the stage.

"There is one very important person we all need to thank for the success of today's march, someone you will not have seen because she was in our control centre piloting all the groups marching today with the help of a dedicated staff who are still busy at their posts even now. "Get up here, Riya, people want to see you."

Not to be outdone, Riya had donned a brightly coloured sari

that looked really sexy on her. The crowd roared their approval.

"Many people need to be thanked," Annie said, once she was alone again on stage. She mentioned the sponsors including Decker and his friend with the milk floats as well as Apple which had supplied much of the computer equipment and iPads. She told the crowd of those who had worked all night to prepare the floats for the march. She thanked the coordinators of each march asking them to come on stage and take a bow. "Finally, I want to make a special mention of three courageous young women without whom some of us might not have been here to take part this evening. It was their vigilance that averted several major catastrophes. I cannot name them, but they know who I mean, and I ask you all to applaud them."

When the applause died down, it was time to get serious. "Our march halted briefly to acknowledge the crowd of well-wishers and supporters gathered outside Charing Cross Station. I spoke to them of everyday acts of kindness as an antidote to violence. That kindness and consideration can take many forms, but one springs to mind, the care we can provide for those that have been cast out, who have been misunderstood, who are ill or distressed, who suffer, who are rejected because of their colour or their sexual or gender orientation. Whether these people need a helping hand or medical care or just a friendly word or smile, we can be there for them. Let's not waste our energy endlessly complaining about those who do us wrong. They do not deserve it. Rather use that energy to build a more tolerant, open, caring society by our everyday behaviour."

She paused a moment as applause rippled through the crowd, punctuated, here and there, by individuals shouting their appreciation. "There's another reason why grassroots movements like GENie are so important. Too many institutions in our world strip us of the power we have over our lives, ourselves, our bodies. That is where GENie is different, giving women - and men - a say in their own health and well-being. Those individuals and groups that thrive and get rich by stripping us of that power tried to ram through legislation outlawing groups like GENie." The crowd hissed. Many people booed or stamped their feet. Annie raised her fist in salute, calling out, "But we won through." A massive roar went up, shaking the stage under Annie's feet, and a sea of clenched fists pumped the air.

She spread her feet to steady herself and lowered her fist as the crowd quietened. Turning to Underwood and Dillinger, who were waiting in the shadows at the edge of the stage, she beckoned. "Two people in Parliament stood up for us and our work, but above all our drive to take back control over our lives. I'd like you to give them a warm welcome. Prime Minister Underwood and the new Deputy Prime Minister Dillinger."

Annie gave each of them a hug then left them to speak. The moment she stepped off the stage, Kevin flung her arms around her and several people wanted urgently to talk to her. She shook everyone off, saying, "It is nothing against any of you, but I need to be alone for a moment." Kevin in particular looked crushed, but there was nothing she could do about it. She went round the back of the stage and headed for the shade of some trees, with Xenia following her at a respectful distance.

She sat with her back to a tree, laid her head in her hands and closed her eyes. The prospect of giving herself up to the police was terrifying. She toyed with the idea of not going. The crowd would protect her. She even dreamt of running away, knowing full well she wouldn't. She had given her word.

"Annie," Xenia called out. "You need to go back. The two are winding up their speech."

She scrambled to her feet and wiped the tears from her eyes with a handkerchief Xenia offered her. "You called us brave," Xenia said as they walked back. "But you are the bravest person I know."

Annie shook her head. "All I want to do is run away."

"But you don't."

100.

Annie climbed onto the stage, her heart heavy as she walked to the middle. The crowd took up her name, chanting, "Annie, Annie, Annie,…" then abruptly fell silent. For a brief moment she thought the police must have come to fetch her early. How typical. Her heart clamoured in her chest. Then she spotted the figure striding across the stage towards her, flanked by two men in dark suits. At first she didn't recognise the tall, ruddy-faced gentleman dressed in an elegant grey suit. It was his smile and his prominent ears that gave him away. The Prince.

"Should I bow or curtesy, your Highness?" she asked when he reached her.

"Neither," the Prince said, holding out his hand for her to shake. She was tempted to hug him but something in the stiffness of his bearing warned her against it, so she shook his hand instead. Then she handed him the microphone.

"My mother has asked me to tell you how much she appreciated your singing for her in front of the Palace. She wishes you well in your endeavours."

The crowd roared their own appreciation. The Queen had heard them, better, she had thanked them. He waited patiently for them to quieten, his expression thoughtful.

"I, for my part, strongly encourage you in your quest against violence. The idea that everyday kindness can counter violence appeals to me greatly and I will do everything I can to further that cause. Thank you." He waved to the crowd as they applauded, then he quit the stage closely followed by his bodyguards, leaving Annie alone once again.

"Time for music and dance," she called out, "but don't go on too late. There's an old lady who lives quite near here and we don't want to interfere with her beauty sleep." The crowd roared with laughter. "We won't," some shouted. Annie left as musicians replaced her centre stage and struck up the first chords of a Celtic melody. Despite its evident joyfulness, Celtic music had an innate sadness that fitted the moment well. For the crowd it was a joyful celebration of their empowerment. For her it was probably the end, a dismal thought indeed.

She smiled weakly when she found Megan waiting for her at the foot of the steps, flanked by Kevin, Riya, Ella and the inevitable Xenia. Alice was also there, speaking quietly to Gertie. Even Brian was there, camera in hand.

"Where do I have to go?" Annie asked no one in particular.

"New Scotland Yard," Megan said, her tone grave. "It's not far from here, but we'll drive."

Annie turned to say goodbye to each of her friends, beginning with Riya. "You don't think we are going to let you go there on your own?" Riya said, hugging her. Tears welled up in Annie's eyes. So she wasn't to confront the police alone after all. At least not at first.

New Scotland Yard was a characterless building backing onto Victoria Street. The public access was in a narrow street at the back. Megan parked the minibus on a double yellow line in front of a chemist's right across from the bunker-like entrance that gave the impression the police were barricaded inside. A policeman stepped out to order them to move along but when he saw who climbed out, he hurried back inside.

Flanked by her friends, hand in hand with Kevin, Annie crossed the road as a number of policemen sporting Kard's armband stepped out of the door from the low outbuilding that served as guards' post and reception. They formed a line on either side of the entrance, a sort of muscular guard of honour with their truncheons at the ready. Kard was the last to swagger out, his hands in his pockets looking, as ever, like a bloated pig poorly disguised as a man.

"So," he said, "you've come. I wondered if you would."

"I keep my word, Mr. Kard," Annie replied, taking a step in his direction.

"Seize her!" Kard ordered.

Several policemen jumped forward but Xenia was there immediately, planted in front of her, as calm and cool as ever.

"It's alright," Annie told her, placing a hand on Xenia's shoulder. "They are just obeying orders."

"It's not alright at all," another voice said and Tratting pushed her way between the ranks of policemen. Annie had never seen the woman in uniform. It was decorated with twisted silver braid and shining buttons and insignias, much smarter than she would have expected of a mere inspector. She looked the picture of authority. As Tratting closed the distance on Kard, a series of policemen and policewomen followed her out, none of whom were wearing Kard's armband.

"Go away," Kard said, with a dismissive gesture. "Nobody asked you to stick your nose in affairs that don't concern you."

"As the new Commissioner of Police of the Metropolis, nominated by the Home Secretary and approved by Parliament this morning and appointed by Her Majesty this afternoon, I arrest you Nolan Kard on several counts of attempted murder and a host of other grave charges too countless to list here now."

Kard burst out laughing, although his laughter sounded hysterical. "You can't arrest me. I'm your boss. I would never have appointed a weakling like you."

"Save your breath for the judges, Kard."

Kard was escorted inside the building, spouting abuse and shouting his objections all the way. To Annie's surprise none of the remaining police were wearing the telltale armbands. No doubt Kard's supporters realised the balance had tipped and there was a new safety in anonymity.

Xenia stepped aside as Tratting turned to greet Annie. "Please allow me to offer sincere apologies on behalf of the Metropolitan Police for the treatment you and your colleagues have received at the hands of some of our officers. Their behaviour was totally unacceptable. An enquiry will be held and disciplinary measures will be taken wherever necessary."

"Thank you," Annie said, struggling to adjust to the change in circumstances. She felt completely out of step. "But what about me?"

"I believe you have a party to attend," Tratting replied with a knowing smile. "Your friends and supporters are waiting for you. And after that, who knows what you will do? Something great, I imagine. But that's a story still to be told."

456   Alan McCluskey

Annexes

458   Alan McCluskey

Thanks and more

Stories People Tell was begun early December 2016 and the first draft was completed mid-March 2017. Althought I quickly began a new novel, I continued to re-work the book throughout 2017 anchoring the story solidly in London. I very much enjoyed walking the streets of the East End letting imagination and reality draw closer together. It may seem odd to say it, but I'd like to thank all my characters, especially Annie and Alice for guiding me through this story of stories. I invariably have no idea where my writing is going when I embark on a new book. It is the characters that take me by the hand and show me the way. As I look back on Stories People Tell, I am amazed at what my characters are capable of and find it hard to believe I penned all that. Additional thanks go to Veronique for accepting to pose for the cover in such strange circumstances. All photos in this book, including the cover, were taken by myself, except that of me which was taken by my son, Iannis. If you'd like to read more about some of the social and political aspects touched on in this novel, two recent books spring to mind. Naomi Klein's *No is not enough. Defeating the new shock politics*, published by Allen Lane in 2017. And George Monbiot's *Out of the wreckage. A new politics for an age of crisis*, published by Verso in 2017. For an excellent online source of information that goes beyond the boundaries of much main-stream media, see Democracy Now! at democracynow.org. And there is the Guardian newspaper at theguardian.com, a reliable and always thought-provoking read.

460　Alan McCluskey

The author
Alan McCluskey

One of his pupils once confessed, with typical candour and ambiguity, that Alan McCluskey had taught her the creative value of madness. His work, whether as a teacher or a video artist or a company director or a scientist or a novel writer, has always been marked by a need to question the obvious, adopting what he calls the Martian perspective in which the self-evident is not taken for granted. He has brought that questioning perspective, along with a passion for images and what they can reveal, to novel writing, together with a long-standing fascination for the dream world and the magic of fantasy.

For information about Alan McCluskey, his books and artwork, see:
Secret Paths: http://secret-paths.com
Facebook: http://www.facebook.com/Secret.Paths

The Storyteller's Quest ~ Book One

The Reaches

Alan McCluskey

The Reaches
The Storyteller's Quest Book One

by Alan McCluskey

The quiet town of Avan with its port, its provincial university
and its conservative seafaring folk would hardly be the place
you'd expect to run into an adventure and frankly neither Brent
nor Sally nor Keira were going out of their way to have one.
At least nothing more than the occasional torrid love affair and
the awkward self-questioning typical of many young adults like
themselves. Sally was finishing her studies in the Theosophy
Department of the University hoping to become Professor
Rafter's assistant, Keira, Sally's best friend and lover, was a young
librarian who occasionally sang in a popular folk group and Brent
was a would-be writer who couldn't quite get his act together and
who spent hours wandering the streets and lanes of the town
in search of inspiration. Yet unbeknown to them forces had
long been at work that would throw them together in a series of
adventures that were going to tax them to the extreme forcing
them to develop abilities that went way beyond what would seem
possible during a voyage from the real world to the realm of
dreams and on into another world called the Reaches that at first
sight looked deceptively like their own.

The Storyteller's Quest ~ Book Two

The Keeper's Daughter

Alan McCluskey

The Keeper's Daughter
The Storyteller's Quest Book Two

by Alan McCluskey

It wasn't Brent's fault if he was stuck in the form of Jake the Owl, at least he didn't think it was as he sat on a branch preening despondently. The threads of all his stories had become inextricably muddled in his owlish head. To think that he'd once prided himself on being a storyteller. His stories had become adventures and some of those adventures had become nightmares, and now he was stuck with them. He'd flown in search of his friend and lover, Mia. She'd been dragged off by a band of thugs just when it was time for them all to return to their world. Only Sally, their mutual friend and lover, had made it back from the world of the Reaches to their hometown of Avan. Hearing her story, despite the dangers she'd had to face, her friends suggested Sally teach them to travel to the Dream Realm and beyond to the Reaches. The idea appealed to everybody. Not that Sally knew how to get back to the Reaches, but the idea of a 'dream class' as they called it pleased her and, above all, she wanted to return to the world where her newly-found half-sister lived and where her two friends had so abruptly disappeared.

The Storyteller's Quest ~ Book Three

The Starless Square

Alan McCluskey

The Starless Square
The Storyteller's Quest Book Three
by Alan McCluskey

A weekend of joyous festivities! Such was the Theosophy department's response to a group of fanatics bent on destroying their
reputation and having them shut down. Theosophy? Professor
Rafter, head of the department, called it "the study of our direct
relationship with that which is beyond and above the normal
range of human experience". He could just as well have been
describing the adventures of a group of young friends who had
been called back from their travels in another world to defend
their department with their new-found abilities. But how could
entrancing singing or breath-taking storytelling or exquisite cook-
ing possibly stand a chance when pitted against the evil black
cloud that threatened to obscure the Starless Square?

Boy & Girl
Revised edition

Alan McCluskey

Boy & Girl

by Alan McCluskey

When Peter awakes in the head of a girl, he is both delighted and alarmed that his secret yearnings have become reality. Very quickly, however, his error is apparent; this girl is not him. Kaitling – that's her name– is twelve years old, like Peter. She's the daughter of a magician, a prominent figure in another world. Boy and girl travel back and forth from each other's minds, but have little time to get acquainted before Kaitling's island is overrun by warrior priests and she has to flee. At home, a conflict erupts in Peter's family forcing him to take refuge at a friend's place. Meanwhile at school, a haughty new girl goads him about his girlishness and, spitting in his face, vows to rid the earth of people like him. The stage seems set for a desperate struggle to survive, but will ingenuity and youthful fervour be enough against folly and fanaticism?

A sequel to Boy & Girl

In Search of Lost Girls

Alan McCluskey

In Search of Lost Girls
by Alan McCluskey

If you listen carefully you can just hear the mournful tolling of a convent bell over the shuffle of girls' feet as they traipse to Mass, nursing bruises and a numbing despair. No one cares. No one is there to stem the torrent of injustice and abuse. They are lost and forgotten. In another world, the walls of the cathedral still reverberate to the sound of angelic singing as the mourners make their way to the exit, heads bowed, voices hushed. If only they knew that those girls who delighted them with their music were really boys in disguise, sanctity would would flee in the face of raging indignation. The scene is set. The author picks up his pen with trembling fingers and begins to write. Time to tear Kate and Peter apart. The thought of making her life hell has him dribbling in anticipation. He ought to know better. Things rarely turn out as an author expects.

www.ingramcontent.com/pod-product-compliance
Lightning Source LLC
Chambersburg PA
CBHW051939020726
47501CB00001B/193